PRAISE FOR
SUSAN JOHNSON

"Her romances have strong, intelligent heroines, hard, iron-willed men, plenty of sexual tension and sensuality and lots of accurate history. Anyone who can put all that in a book is one of the best!"
—*Romantic Times*

"No one . . . can write such rousing love stories while bringing in so much accurate historical detail. Of course, no one can write such rousing love stories, period."—*Rendezvous*

"Susan Johnson writes an extremely gripping story. . . . With her knowledge of the period and her exquisite sensual scenes, she is an exceptional writer."—*Affaire de Coeur*

"Susan Johnson's descriptive talents are legendary and well-deserved."—*Heartland Critiques*

"Fascinating. . . . The author's style is a pleasure to read."—*Los Angeles Herald Examiner*

TABOO

Susan Johnson

BANTAM BOOKS
New York Toronto London Sydney Auckland

Taboo
A Bantam Book / December 1997

Maps by Jeff Ward

ISBN 0-553-57215-6

Published simultaneously in the United States and Canada

Bantam Books are published by Bantam Books, a division of Random House,
Inc. Its trademark, consisting of the words "Bantam Books" and the portrayal
of a rooster, is Registered in U.S. Patent and Trademark Office and in other
countries. Marca Registrada. Random House, Inc., New York, New York.

PRINTED IN THE UNITED STATES OF AMERICA

OPM   10   9   8   7   6   5   4

Dear Reader,

As some of you may know, during the research for my previous book, *Wicked*, I became infatuated with General Andre Massena. I knew I wanted to write a story based on some of the events in his life and in *Taboo*, the hero Andre Duras is my interpretation of Andre Massena. I changed his name in order to give myself a bit more literary license since a strict adherence to historical fact limits the imagination.

So it may be confusing to see Andre Massena in *Wicked* become Andre Duras in *Taboo*. But I hope you can make the adjustment in your mind.

I walked over the battlefields and the streets of the towns and villages where Massena lived and fought those months during the campaign in Switzerland and tried to see it all through his eyes. I traveled to Nice, his birthplace, where a small museum has a very few artifacts from his life. But what astonished me was my discovery that a Niçois face exists. It was extraordinary to see people on the streets of Nice with faces similar to that of Massena. Two men passing by in the lobby of our hotel could have been him—the same build, height, face, hair color. I almost stopped them and hugged them.

Massena's tomb in Père Lachaise in Paris is impressive in its simplicity, the white marble obelisk marked only with his name and his four most important victories—Rivoli, Zurich, Genoa, Essling. At each of those battles his courage, boldness, and determination saved France.

I hope you enjoy this glimpse of the man as well as the woman who introduced him to the wonders of love.

Best wishes,

INTRODUCTION

In 1789, directly after the French Revolution, the great powers, despite their hostility toward the new republican government, were too involved elsewhere to intervene. Austria and Russia were at war with the Ottoman Empire in a grandiose effort to partition the Turkish state. Prussia and England opposed this expansion and encouraged Sweden to attack Russia. War seemed imminent when the Prussian emperor signed a treaty with the sultan calling for the liberation of all Turkish territory.

But England refused to support Prussia since the British themselves were on the verge of war with Spain over the control of Nootka Sound on the Pacific coast.

Fortunately all this bickering allowed France a measure of respite.

By the spring of 1791, the eastern crisis had been settled

by diplomatic means and Austria was prepared to intervene in France. However, another year passed before all the powers interested in invading France could agree on strategy, vital interests, and the division of spoils.

The French Assembly was equally divisive and self-serving. Most French leaders regarded war primarily as a means of attaining political power at home. Strategic and diplomatic considerations played a secondary role. To compound French problems, the nation's armed forces were in such disarray that it was doubtful if the army could carry out the task of defending the state from invasion. Overlooking such critical issues, the Assembly voted overwhelmingly for war on April 20, 1792.

The allied army's main invasion force against France consisted of a huge, slow-moving supply train, obsolete artillery, and many Prussian officers who hadn't experienced serious combat for thirty years. Regardless of their deficiencies, including their cautious, methodical tactical system, the allies won battle after battle, advancing inexorably toward Paris. The French army, comprised essentially of inexperienced, untrained volunteers, proved unreliable in battle. Until the morning of September 20 at Valmy, when the French lines and field guns repulsed two waves of Prussian attack.

Valmy was a watershed, a momentous victory for the new French nation. The first effort of the European powers to crush the Revolution had been defeated.

Over the course of the next twenty-three years, until Napoleon's final defeat at Waterloo, various combinations of nations made war against the French Republic. England was the driving force behind the First Coalition, organized in early 1793 with Austria, Prussia, and Spain. Other powers eager for spoils hastened to enter the alliance: the Papal States, Naples, Tuscany, Parma, Modena, Sardinia, Portugal. But mutual suspicions, differing ambitions, and deepening rivalries plagued the participants. By mid 1795, only Austria and England continued to fight, and in October 1797, Austria signed a peace treaty with France. France was now the dominant power in western Europe.

But Napoleon's disastrous Egyptian expedition in 1798 changed the balance of power and gave new hope to France's enemies. Russia and Turkey temporarily ended their age-old rivalry and together went to war against France. Austria saw the French defeats as an opportunity to reenter the war on advantageous terms. And England found itself in an excellent position to devise a new coalition. By the end of 1798, Austria, Russia, and England had agreed on a set of common war aims.

And in Paris dawned the realization that hostilities would begin as soon as the Russian corps reached Austria.

This is the precipitating factor for the events in the novel you are about to read. As the story opens, a French army division has been headquartered in Sargans, Switzerland, and General Andre Duras is preparing for the renewal of war.

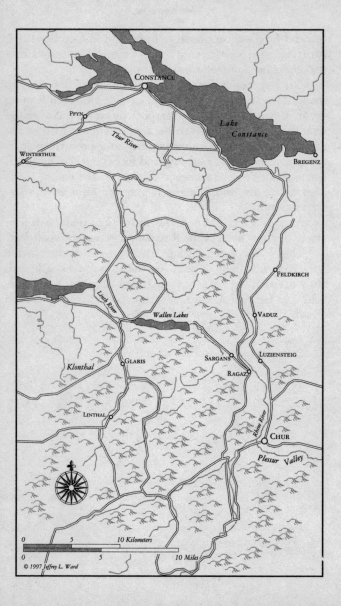

CONSTANCE

Lake
Constance

PFYN

Thur River

WINTERTHUR

BREGENZ

FELDKIRCH

Limth River

Wallen Lakes

VADUZ

LUZIENSTEIG

Klonthal

GLARIS

SARGANS

RAGAZ

LINTHAL

Rhine River

CHUR

Plessur Valley

0   5   10 Kilometers
0   5   10 Miles

© 1997 Jeffrey L. Ward

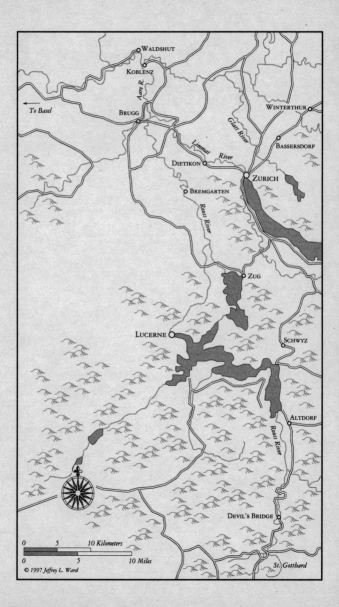

WALDSHUT

KOBLENZ

To Basel

BRUGG

WINTERTHUR

Aare R.

Glatt River

Limmat River

BASSERSDORF

DIETIKON

ZURICH

BREMGARTEN

Reuss River

ZUG

LUCERNE

SCHWYZ

ALTDORF

Reuss River

DEVIL'S BRIDGE

0   5   10 Kilometers
0   5   10 Miles

© 1997 Jeffrey L. Ward

St. Gotthard

TABOO

1

"Beauve-Simone brought in Korsakov's wife."

General Duras looked up from the maps spread over his desktop, his dark gaze piercing. "Korsakov's *wife*?"

"In all her glory," his aide-de-camp said, grinning. "She's in your parlor. Beauve-Simone couldn't think of another room in camp suitable for a Russian countess wrapped in sables."

"How the hell did she turn up fifty miles behind enemy lines?"

"Her Cossacks apparently took the wrong turn at Bregenz. Her carriage is elaborate—a bed, food, a maid . . . very self-sufficient. They had no need to stop anywhere so weren't aware of their error. Beauve-Simone's troop intercepted them at the bridgehead north of town."

Duras leaned back in his chair and sighed. "Her timing

1

could have been better. We're attacking along the whole front in three days. Jesus, I can't send her back *now*."

"Maybe Korsakov's corps will be in retreat by next week."

"And?"

"I thought—I mean . . ." Colonel Bonnay's voice trailed off under the general's sharp scrutiny.

"I could send her back through the chaos of a retreating Russian army?" Duras coolly inquired, his brows raised in cynical speculation. "Even her Cossacks couldn't protect her in that anarchy. How many does she have with her?"

"Four."

"Four fucking men between her and the rabble. Perfect," Andre Duras disgustedly muttered.

"Could the Countess Gonchanka look after her?"

"I don't think so," he sardonically replied. "Natalie isn't known for her kindness to women. In fact," he went on, quickly glancing at the clock on the wall, "you'll have to divert Natalie posthaste. She's planning on having dinner with me very shortly."

"She doesn't listen to mere colonels."

"Relay a note from me," the general said, reaching for paper and pen. "I'll postpone dinner tonight . . . and don't mention Korsakov's wife is here."

"She may have heard already. News like that travels swiftly."

"Which means the Austrian spies will soon have the information. *Merde,*" General Duras swore, swiftly scrawling his regrets to his current mistress. "I don't need this added problem right now. All the men and supplies have to be in place by the morning of the fifth," he declared, waving the sheet of paper briskly for a moment to dry the ink before folding it and handing it to Bonnay. "Will the trestle bridge at Trubbach be finished in time?"

"The engineers promised to have it ready by midnight of the fifth."

"Good. Give Natalie my note and offer her my sincere regrets. How strong do you think the fort's northern defenses will be at St. Luzisteig?" he went on, his mistress dismissed from his mind, his gaze once again on the maps before him. His energies the past two months had been consumed with planning the offensive.

"The spies say it's impregnable."

The general studied the topographical drawings for a moment more, and then his head lifted and he smiled at his young subaltern. "Then I'll have to lead the attack myself."

"The fort is as good as ours then, sir." Henri Bonnay's smile flashed in the room shadowed by the winter twilight closing in.

"It better be. We need that river crossing. Now off with you. I don't want the countess descending on my household with Korsakov's wife there."

"Perhaps they're acquaintances."

"Let's hope not. One temperamental Russian countess is enough to handle."

"You *should* go and see the woman, sir."

"You handle it, Bonnay." Duras turned back to his maps.

"There's nowhere else to put her, sir."

"I'll sleep in your lodgings, then. How would that be?"

"She seemed frightened, sir." His aide-de-camp's voice held the merest remonstrance.

"Well, console her, then. She has her attendants, doesn't she? I'm not playing nursemaid to Korsakov's wife, Bonnay, no matter how woebegone a look you cast my way."

"How could it hurt to offer her your assistance? Tell her she'll be returned once the offensive is past. Korsakov would do the same for your wife."

"My wife doesn't journey beyond Paris, my dear Henri. So unless the Russians march into the city, Korsakov won't be required to play courtier to her. Not that she wouldn't be accommodating should he prove the victor in this contest," the general softly murmured. His marriage had been bereft long ago of all but chill politesse; his wife's indiscretions were legion. But one did not divorce the niece of Talleyrand, political adviser to the Bourbons and the Directory alike, without jeopardizing a hard-won career. And his wife gloated on the position of consort to France's most victorious general.

"Five minutes, sir. I'll tell her you'll stop by."

Duras's mouth twitched into a half smile. "Still trying to make me a gentleman, Henri?"

"You're more of a gentleman than the Bourbons, sir. The young lady seemed anxious, that's all."

"With good reason, I suppose. Very well, Henri, tell her I'll offer her my compliments."

"In five minutes."

Duras grinned, his handsome face taking on a boyish cast, the weight of his command disappearing for a moment. "*Ten* minutes, Henri, because I'm still in command here, but don't ask me to bow to the lady," he added, his dark eyes full of amusement. "My corsair father would never approve."

"No, sir, very good, sir, I'll tell the lady, sir."

It took more than ten minutes, though. In fact Colonel Bonnay had to remind Duras twice more before he set his maps aside and left his makeshift office. Dark had descended by the time he crossed the frozen mud that passed for a street in the small border town on the upper Rhine, the night air damp, chill. His thoughts were on his engineers working around the clock in the icy waters of the Rhine. Two days of warm sunshine had melted enough snow so the river was in flood, the fords impassable. He desperately needed that bridge to move his men and matériel across the river to attack General Korsakov's Russian corps, Austria's newest allies.

What exactly did one say to the wife of the man one hoped to destroy in three days? Not the truth certainly.

There were guards at the front entrance of the burgo-master's house he used as quarters. Bonnay was always thorough—a prime requisite in an ADC. Duras chatted with the men briefly, his easy rapport with his troops the reason they'd follow him anywhere. And they had since he'd first earned his general's stars at twenty-nine and in the years before as well, his success due in part to their devotion. Although those who knew him well understood he had certain natural gifts of leadership separate from the loyalty of his troops—the power of quick decision, faultless judgment, boldness, dynamic tactical skill, and an indefatigable determination.

All of which fueled jealousies not only in Napoleon but in the War Ministry where political intrigues motivated promotions and assignments more often than ability. But they needed him here in Switzerland. He knew it and they knew it. He'd been given command of the single outflanking position between France and its enemies; the possession of Switzerland was of vital strategic importance.

And in three days he began his offensive.

He knocked once on the parlor door before opening it and stepping into a blaze of candlelight. He didn't realize he had so many candles. And on second glance he saw he didn't; the scented tapers were all set in heavy silver Russian candelabra.

A servant watched him from the fireside with wary, timorous eyes, her features Asiatic, her costume Russian. There was no sign of the countess.

"Where's your mistress?"

"In here, General," a clear, direct voice replied in French. "Have you eaten? Do you play chess?"

And when he crossed the carpeted floor and stood in the open doorway to the small dining room, he saw the countess for the first time, seated before a small chess table, apparently playing both sides in the game.

Her dark brows arched delicately against her pale skin as she gazed at him. "Your engravings don't do you justice, General Duras. You're much younger."

"Good evening, Countess Korsakova. And you don't appear to be frightened. Bonnay led me to believe my presence was required here to allay your fears." If she thought him young, she was younger still, he reflected, and exotic-looking. With Korsakov's family well connected at the Russian court, Andre didn't doubt that Korsakov had his pick of women.

"The young colonel mistook my reticence for fear," the countess replied, a luscious small smile lighting up her brilliant green eyes.

"You're not afraid, then."

She made a small moue of negation. "Certainly, General, we both understand the rules. You'll exchange me for one of your officers now languishing in Austrian hands—when the opportunity arises. He'll be glad to come home and I"—her dark lashes lowered marginally—"will return to my husband's household. Do you play chess?"

"Yes."

Her mouth curved upward in amusement. "*Will* you play chess?"

"I'm sorry. Perhaps some other time."

"Have you eaten?"

He hesitated, debating the lie.

"You haven't, have you? You must eat sometime tonight, General. Why not now?"

He was a gentleman despite his disclaimer to Bonnay and it would have been rude to refuse when they both knew he'd have to have dinner at some point that evening. "Something quick perhaps," he agreed.

Clapping her hands, she called for her maid, giving her directions for serving the general. "I'll join you at the table," she graciously said, rising from her chair in a shimmer of absinthe velvet.

She waved away his offer to help seat her across from him and sat instead to his left. "I recommend the ragout and the wines of course are wonderful here. My husband is quite sure of his victory, you know. So sure, he ordered me here to keep him company," she went on, leaning casually on the tabletop, meeting his swift, searching glance with a smile. "I'm just making conversation. He doesn't confide in me but my maids know everything."

Lifting a spoonful of ragout to his mouth, he said, "How old are you?"

She spoke with a girlish candor that he couldn't decide was coquettish or artless. "I'm twenty-eight."

"You look younger." He dipped his spoon back into the savory dish. Her porcelain skin and black hair, her wide, ingenuous gaze and lithe slenderness evoked a youthful delicacy.

"He likes that."

Was her tone *jeunesse dorée* or just cynical? "Do you miss your husband?" he bluntly asked, tipping a tender piece of meat from his spoon into his mouth.

"Do you miss your wife?"

He gazed at her for a telling minute while he chewed and then swallowed. "Will your husband want you back?" he softly inquired, ignoring her question.

"Yes, definitely." She sat back, a new coolness in her tone. "I'm too valuable to misplace. My husband has his own selfish reasons for—"

"Let's just leave it at that," Duras interjected. "I'm not interested in family controversy."

"Forgive me, General. I lack reserve, I've been told."

He ate for a few moments without replying, not inclined to discuss a relative stranger's reserve or its lack and when he spoke, his voice was impersonal. "I can't exchange you now with the state of the war, but we'll endeavor to make you comfortable."

"How long will I be here?"

"Two weeks to a month, perhaps. We'll keep you safe." He put his spoon aside, the campaign once again intruding into his thoughts. He'd moved his troops up to Sargans only two days ago and there was immense work to be done before the offensive began.

"Thank you. You didn't eat much."

He shrugged and pushed his chair away from the table. "I'll eat later. If you require anything, ask for Bonnay," he added, rising to his feet. "Good night, Countess. It was a pleasure meeting you." And with a nod of his head he turned and left. That should satisfy Bonnay, he thought, striding back to his office.

It was well after midnight. Only Duras and Bonnay were left at headquarters when a guard rushed into the maproom, apologizing and stammering, obviously agitated, his broken phrases finally merging into a decipherable account.

The Countess Gonchanka, it seemed, was in Duras's bedroom accosting General Korsakov's wife.

Swearing, Duras decided Natalie must be his penance for his multitudinous sins and then, breaking into the guard's disordered recital, briskly said, "Thank you, Corporal. Bonnay and I will take care of it."

"Why me?" Bonnay instantly protested.

"Because I'm ordering you to," Duras said with mock severity, "and I can't handle two women at once."

"Rumor suggests otherwise," his subordinate ironically murmured.

"Not, however, tonight," Duras crisply retorted. "Now move."

The noise emanating from the burgomaster's second-floor rooms facing the street had drawn a crowd and ribald comments greeted Duras and Bonnay as they approached at a run.

"The show's over," Duras said, sprinting through the parting throng.

"Or just beginning, General," a cheerful voice retorted.

"Everyone back to quarters," Bonnay shouted.

"He wants them all to himself," another voice called out and the crowd roared with laughter.

"That's an order, men." Andre Duras spoke in a normal tone from the porch rail. "Back to quarters."

The laughter instantly died away and the troopers began dispersing.

"I hope the ladies obey as easily," Bonnay drolly said, motioning Duras before him into the house.

"Wishful thinking with Natalie," Duras replied.

Moments later at the sound of the men entering the bedroom, Countess Gonchanka turned from her prey. "Damn you, Andre!" she screamed, hurling the bronze statuette intended for Korsakov's wife at him. "Damn your blackguard soul!"

Swiftly ducking, Duras avoided being impaled by the upraised arms of a Grecian Victory and lunged for Natalie's hands before she could gather fresh ammunition. He caught her wrists in a steely grip. "Behave yourself, Natalie," he brusquely ordered.

"So you can't have dinner with me tonight," she shrieked, fighting his grasp. "And now I know why, you bastard, you deceiving, libertine knave! You've someone new in your bed!"

"Christ, Natalie, calm down. She's a guest," he asserted, trying to retain his hold as she struggled in his hands.

"I know all about your guests," she hissed, twisting and turning, attempting to knee him in the groin. "There're always new ones in your bed, aren't there?"

"That's enough, Natalie," he snapped, forcing her toward the door. "Bonnay will see you home." The Countess Gonchanka had overstepped even his lax sense of propriety tonight. He abhorred scenes.

"So you can sleep with Korsakov's wife undisturbed!" she screeched.

"No, so everyone can get a night's rest," he answered with great restraint, his temper barely in check. And transferring his charge to Bonnay's hands, he watched the Russian countess who'd entertained him so pleasantly the last few months escorted out of his life. He'd see that she was on the road back to Paris in the morning.

"Did she hurt you?" he inquired, turning back to Korsakov's wife, who'd found shelter behind a semainier.

"Does this happen often to you?" she pleasantly said, emerging from her burled-walnut barricade.

"No, never," he acerbically retorted. "You're fine, I see." Immediately after he uttered the words, he realized he shouldn't have verbalized his thoughts. But her slender form couldn't be ignored; it was blatantly visible through the sheer batiste of her gown.

"Yes, I am." Her voice was amiable, not seductive, and the odd disparity between her sensuous appeal and her frank response suddenly intrigued him.

"What's your name?" he said when he shouldn't.

"Teo."

Her voice was genial and melodious although the contrast to Natalie's termagant shrieks may have enhanced its sweetness. "What's your real name?"

"Theodora Ostyuk."

"Not Korsakova?"

"No, never." She smiled as she repeated the words he'd so recently spoken.

"Would you like a robe?" he abruptly said, because he unexpectedly found her smile fascinating.

"Do I need one?" And then she laughed—a refreshing, light sound. "Do you scowl like that often?"

"Natalie's too fresh a memory."

"I understand. Have you ever been just friends with a woman?"

It took him so long to answer, she teasingly said, "You must be ignoring me, General, although your reputation precedes you. But I'm not like Natalie," she lightly went on. "I'm actually faithful to my husband so I'm not going to seduce you. Do you mind?"

"No, not at all."

"How ungracious," she mocked.

"I meant, no, not with Natalie's screams still echoing in my ears. Why are you faithful to your husband?" It was a novel attitude in the current flux and upheavals of society.

"Will you play a game of chess with me?"

"Now?"

Evasive but not a no, she decided, and she found she didn't want to be alone in the middle of the night with her husband's image freshly brought to mind, so she cajoled. "I could tell you about faithfulness while we play and Natalie *has* rather disrupted my sleep," she reminded him.

"A short game, then, while you define a faithful wife. A rarity in my world," he softly declared.

"And in mine as well. Men of course aren't required to be faithful."

"So I understand."

"A realistic appraisal. Should I put on a robe?"

"I think it might be wise."

He played chess the way he approached warfare, moving quickly, decisively, always on the attack. But she held her own, although her style was less aggressive, and when he took her first knight after long contention for its position, he said, "If your husband's half as good as you, he'll be a formidable opponent."

"I'm not sure you fight the same way."

"You've seen him in battle?"

"On a small scale. Against my grandfather in Siberia."

"And yet you married him?"

"Not by choice. The Russians traditionally take hostages from their conquered tribes. I'm the Siberian version. My clan sends my husband tribute in gold each year. So you see why I'm valuable to him."

"Not for gold alone, I'm sure," he said, beginning to move his rook.

"How gallant, Andre," she playfully declared.

His gaze came up at the sound of his name, his rook poised over the board, and their glances held for a moment. The fire crackled noisily in the hearth, the ticking of the clock sounded loud in the stillness, the air suddenly took on a charged hush, and then the general smiled—a smooth, charming smile. "You're going to lose your bishop, Teo."

She couldn't answer as suavely because her breath was caught in her throat and it took her a second to overcome the strange, heated feeling inundating her senses.

His gaze slid down her blushing cheeks and throat to rest briefly on her taut nipples visible through her white cashmere robe and he wondered what was happening to him that so demure a sight had such a staggering effect on his libido. He dropped his rook precipitously into place, inhaled, and leaned back in his chair as if putting distance between himself and such tremulous innocence would suffice to restore his reason.

"Your move," he gruffly said.

"Maybe we shouldn't play anymore."

"Your move." It was his soft voice of command.

"I don't take orders."

"I'd appreciate it if you'd move."

"I'm not sure I know what I'm doing anymore." He lounged across from her, tall, lean, powerful, with predatory eyes, the softest of voices, and the capacity to make her tremble.

"It's only a game."

"This, you mean."

"Of course. What else would I mean?"

"I was married when I was fifteen, after two years of refinement at the Smolny Institute for Noble Girls," she pertinently said, wanting him to know.

"And you're very refined," he urbanely replied, wondering how much she knew of love after thirteen faithful years in a forced marriage. His eyes drifted downward again, his thoughts no longer of chess.

"My husband's not refined at all."

"Many Russians aren't." He could feel his erection begin to rise, the thought of showing her another side of passionate desire ruinous to his self-restraint.

"It's getting late," she murmured, her voice quavering slightly.

"I'll see you upstairs," he softly said.

When he stood, his desire was obvious: the formfitting regimentals molded his body like a second skin.

Gripping the chair arms, she said, "No," her voice no more than a whisper.

He moved around the small table and touched her then because he couldn't help himself, because she was quivering with desire like some virginal young girl and the intoxicating image of such tremulous need was more carnal than anything he'd ever experienced. His hand fell lightly on her shoulder, its heat tantalizing, tempting.

She looked up at him and, lifting her mouth to his, heard herself say, "Kiss me."

"Take my hand," he murmured And when she did, he pulled her to her feet and drew her close so the scent of her was in his nostrils and the warmth of her body touched his.

"Give me a child." Some inner voice prompted the words she'd only dreamed for years.

"No," he calmly said, as if she hadn't asked the unthinkable from a stranger, and then his mouth covered hers and she sighed against his lips. And as their kiss deepened and heated their blood and drove away reason, they both felt an indefinable bliss—torrid and languorous, heartfelt and, most strangely—hopeful in two people who had long ago become disenchanted with hope.

And then her maid's voice drifted down the stairway, the intonation of her native tongue without inflection. "He'll kill you," she declared.

Duras's mouth lifted and his head turned to the sound. "What did she say?"

"She reminded me of the consequences."

"Which are?"

"My husband's wrath."

He was a hairsbreadth from selfishly saying, *Don't worry*, but her body had gone rigid in his arms at her maid's pointed admonition and at base he knew better. He knew he wouldn't be there to protect her from her husband's anger and he knew too that she was much too innocent for a casual night of love.

"Tamyr is my voice of reason."

He released her and took a step away, as if he couldn't trust himself to so benignly relinquish such powerful feeling. "We all need a voice of reason," he neutrally said. "Thank you for the game of chess."

"I'm sorry."

"Not more sorry than I," Duras said with a brief smile.

"Will I see you again?" She couldn't help herself from asking.

"Certainly." He took another step back, his need for her almost overwhelming. "And if you wish for anything during your stay with us, feel free to call on Bonnay."

"Can't I call on you?"

"My schedule's frenzied and, more precisely, your maid's voice may not be able to curtail me a second time."

"I see."

"Forgive my bluntness."

"Forgiven," she gently said.

"Good night, Madame Countess." He bowed with grace.

"Good night, Andre."

"Under other circumstances . . ." he began, and then shrugged away useless explanation.

"I know," she softly said. "Thank you."

He left precipitously, retreat uncommon for France's bravest general, but he wasn't sure he could trust himself to act the gentleman if he stayed.

2

As the general walked back to Bonnay's lodgings, he forcibly suppressed the seductive images of Teo—lush and willing, trembling like a young girl on the brink. How odd that she could still evoke such winsome youthfulness after years as Korsakov's wife.

Her husband's reputation for brutality was well known. Duras had personally witnessed an episode years ago when France had been wooing Catherine the Great's enormous supplies of gold. He'd been sent to the provinces east of the Urals in General Guibert's entourage, their mission to negotiate a useful method of exchanging gold for French cannon. Was it in '83 or '84? The exact date escaped him but he'd never forget his first sight of Korsakov. The scene was etched on his memory, not for its uniqueness—flogging took place in the French Royal Army as well—but for the obscene pleasure evident on Korsakov's face. Korsakov had personally administered the flogging, putting the full weight of his powerful physique behind every blow, taking delight in the man's torture.

The soldier had died under the savage punishment, at which point Korsakov had simply handed over the whip to his aide, wiped the sweat and spattered blood from his face with his embroidered handkerchief, and strolled off to breakfast.

That distant memory hadn't surfaced with his libido at peak levels in Teo's bedroom, but now Duras recognized that Teo Ostyuk was hardly suitable for a casual liaison. With a husband like hers, faithfulness was a prudent choice.

A shame, though, he reflected, his exhalation of regret crystallizing in the cold night air. She was damned desirable. On the other hand, with the Second Coalition forces staging 220,000 men on France's borders, he didn't have time for women.

Taking the few steps fronting Bonnay's lodgings in a nimble leap, he pushed open the door and entered his new quarters.

Unlike the general, who immediately fell into a deep sleep, Teo found her repose elusive. Restless, absorbed with her agitated emotions, she sat before the banked fire in the burgomaster's parlor, trying to resolve the tumult of her feelings.

She wasn't unaware of worldly temptations. The Russian aristocracy was rife with vice and scandal; dalliance and flirtation posed a means of mitigating the ennui of life. And her beauty had always attracted men bent on seduction. But until tonight, her feelings had never been touched. A small jolt strummed through her senses in heated memory, the concept of flirtation too tame for the breathless desire she'd experienced in Duras's arms. And she wanted him still . . .

despite all rationale—with a quivering desperation that was both intoxicating and terrifying in its physicality.

She was trembling.

The memory of him filled her consciousness. His dark eyes, more black than blue, intense with an inner fire; his tall, virile body, whipcord lean, muscled, so different from Korsakov's brute bullish strength, the feel of his hands on her, gentle, offering temptation with an angel's touch, the feel of *him*—hard against her body, the rigid length of his arousal pressed into her belly. She inadvertently whimpered as desire flared inside her, no longer able to repress her vaulting need, wanting him so fiercely it felt as though she were caught in some sorcerer's spell. Abruptly rising from her chair, she paced like a caged tigress, her senses on fire, wondering how she could find him, where he slept tonight, realizing even as the thoughts raced through her brain, how rash was such speculation.

But irrepressible emotion wouldn't be gainsaid, and headstrong, she decided to go out and find him herself. Moving toward the door, she smiled in whimsical elation at the novel sensation of wanting someone with such unbridled passion. It was a rare pleasure, she thought, exiting the room in search of her cloak.

Short moments later Tamyr stopped her from leaving the dressing room, her small solid body blocking the portal, her feet in their red felt boots squarely planted. "You can't go," she challenged.

Teo looked at the woman who'd been her body servant since childhood, her gaze studiously blank. "I'm just going for a walk."

Undeceived, Tamyr bluntly said, "Korsakov takes pleasure in killing. Now take off your cloak and come to bed. Your grandpapa expects me to keep you safe and Duras will soon be gone."

"I don't want your advice." Teo clutched the sable wrap

more tightly around her as if she could protect herself from her husband's malevolence.

"Your mama didn't either and in the end your father could only love her, he couldn't save their lives."

"Maybe I understand for the first time how she felt," Teo whispered, a rare humility in her voice.

"Don't give Korsakov reason to kill you."

"But he's not here . . . and am I not a prisoner?"

"That won't be excuse enough when he finds out. His spies are everywhere."

Teo's chin came up and her voice took on a faint edge. "Maybe I no longer wish to be his hostage."

"Because of Duras."

"Because I feel as though I've risen from the grave after thirteen years, as though I were liberated, babushka," she said very, very quietly.

Tamyr stood silent for a moment and then she softly said to the child she'd helped raise after her parents were killed, "Korsakov won't live forever."

"It just seems like forever," Teo said, unrepentant.

"Don't be hasty, little bird."

"But I feel a kind of urgency . . . like time is running out." She swung away, the soft sable rippling in a tawny, fluid sheen as she swept toward the windows.

"You don't even know where Duras is." Tamyr's voice was deliberately calm. "Every spy in camp will hear of your late-night search."

Stopping mid-stride, Teo abruptly turned back and said with a curt authority that sounded very like her grandfather's autocratic tone, "You find him, then."

"I will . . . in the morning when no unusual reports will go back to Korsakov."

"I'm going to see him whether you like it or not." Each brisk word conveyed determination. "I won't be stopped."

"Write him a note," Tamyr suggested. "I'll find him in the morning."

Teo hesitated, took notice of the brief hours until dawn, and then, sighing in assent, said, "I don't suppose he'd thank me for waking him."

She sat down then and wrote to the man who'd awakened such jubilation in her soul, asking him to come to her, pouring out her heart as if she'd known him a lifetime. She wondered briefly as the words flowed across the page with such abandon if she were feverish, so giddy was her sense of pleasure. But seconds later, as she was lost once again in blissful feeling, the rushing tumult of her words obliterated all considerations of motive or cause.

Tamyr never delivered the note that morning nor the second one Teo wrote the following day, because she wanted to save her mistress from cataclysmic disaster. And in the intervening time, she cajoled and reasoned as Teo became increasingly distraught, citing all the justifications for Duras not replying—his duties as commander on the eve of a campaign, Teo's delicate position as wife to his enemy, other reasons too—ones Teo didn't want to hear—undeniable reports of his brief and casual liaisons.

"I don't care," Teo impatiently declared when she tired of hearing all the expedient cautions, the salacious rumor and gossip. "I don't care what Duras did last week or last month or yesterday because none of that matters when the next thirteen years frighten me beyond bearing. I've been offered a gift of happiness and I'm taking it, because I may never be given another chance."

But as the hours lengthened and gave way to days, Teo could no longer pretend he might answer her letters and she fell into a heartsick gloom, the misery of her life suddenly too burdensome. Was her only hope that of outliving her husband? Could she only look forward to that meager reward for the martyrdom of her life? *Why me?* she cried, overcome with self-pity at the cruel fate that had caused

Korsakov's covetous glance to fall on her. And as each lonely hour passed, her melancholy deepened, her sense of deprivation intensified. How ironic to have been touched by passion at last . . . uselessly.

For Duras the intervening days were a sleepless blur of meetings and campaign planning. His presence and command were required for a multiplicity of tasks, the need imperative to bring every unit of the army to readiness by the morning of the fifth. Although he'd criticized the Directory's offensive plan for its diversity of objectives and lack of clear goals, in accordance with his sense of duty, he directed all his energies to implementing the attack. North of Sargans, Archduke Charles was advancing against Jourdan with 85,000 men. Duras's orders, received on the second, were to protect Jourdan's right flank and move against von Hotze's 20,000 corps in the Grisons. With his 26,000 men split into two forces, there was the added danger of being left in an exposed position if Jourdan's advance failed.

He talked himself hoarse, making sure each regimental commander understood his mission—explaining, detailing, discussing in the open style of command he preferred, until each man was fully aware of his function, of the requirements necessary to meet the large Austrian force. His army was spread too thin, their front miles too long, the possibility of being overrun by superior forces a stark reality. He'd personally reconnoitered the west bank of the river, riding from Ragaz to Vaduz, familiarizing himself with the country, tireless in matters of detail; he'd seen too many commanders draw up plans at headquarters that didn't take into account swamps or mountains or impregnable defenses. The construction of the trestle bridge advanced under his personal supervision as well, his sappers working under the most adverse conditions in the icy waters. Snow was falling again when he'd ridden out earlier that evening to view the

nearly completed bridge, and the sentries posted to guard
the crossing were barely visible through the whiteness.

After Duras dictated final orders at ten, the last dispatches were relayed to his commanders and then Bonnay
sent everyone away and insisted the general lie down for a
few hours.

It seemed only seconds later when Bonnay shook him
awake and thrust a note into his hand. The flowing script
swam before his eyes until the word *desperate* came into
focus.

Please, I'm desperate to see you, she'd written, the plain
words searing his brain.

No, he instantly thought, the boundaries clear-cut and
unassailable, making love to the beautiful Teo was out of
the question. But then he found himself glancing at the
clock, gauging the hours before morning.

"Her maid delivered this a few hours ago. She said the
lady's been in tears for two days."

"But you didn't give it to me?"

"You seemed preoccupied," his aide ambivalently replied.

Duras's brows arched marginally. "What made you
change your mind?"

"At this time of night . . . with the attack imminent . . ."
Bonnay shrugged, not sure himself why he'd wakened the
general.

"I may not come back, you mean."

"None of us might, sir. St. Luzisteig's defenses are
formidable."

"Did you read this?"

"Yes, sir."

"Damned impertinent, Henri." But Duras's mouth
quirked faintly.

"I debated waking you, sir. You've slept so little."

"Neither has the lady, it seems."

"Yes, sir. Perhaps you could spare her a few minutes."

"To comfort her."

"That's up to you, sir. I'll come to fetch you in time."

Glancing at the clock again, Duras frowned and a hyper-sensitive air of expectancy inundated his senses. He swore softly and then, taking a deep breath, tossed the covers aside and sat up, balancing on the edge of the narrow campaign bed, restless, indecisive, staring with an unfocused gaze at Bonnay's finely polished boots. "Jesus, Bonnay," he muttered, his voice tight with constraint, "she's like a damned virgin."

"She's been crying for two days."

"Which doesn't encourage me overmuch. *Merde.* Lord knows I shouldn't."

"Consider it an act of kindness," Bonnay gently said.

Duras gazed cynically at his subordinate. "I don't need encouragement, Henri. I need restraint."

"And she needs *you*."

The silence was palpable, stretched taut like his nerves, and then he abruptly stood, motioned for his boots, reached for his tunic jacket. "Come for me at three-thirty," he curtly said.

Tamyr opened the door with a scowl and a muttered deprecation, her disapproval obvious.

"I know," Duras placated. "I shouldn't be here. But I couldn't help myself."

Her gaze raked him as if vetting his sincerity.

"I won't hurt her," the general quietly said, not sure she understood.

But she nodded in response, uttered a few brief words in her native tongue—cautionary directives, that was clear even to his untutored ear—and stepped aside, motioning him toward the stairway.

He felt her eyes on him as he took the stairs at a run, grateful for her loyalty to Teo. She looked as though she knew how to use the small knife sheathed in her felt boots.

He neither hesitated nor knocked at Teo's door but let

himself in as if he had a right to be there, impatient, prey to a quickening excitement.

She was standing facing the door, her back to the window, her arms rigidly at her sides, forcing herself to calmness when the sight of him sent an uncontrollable tremor through her body. "I was watching the street; it's been busy all day. Thank you for coming."

"I shouldn't be here," he bluntly said, shutting the door behind him, standing motionless only inches into the room, suddenly aware of what he might do, racked with indecision.

"Thank you then even more."

"We leave at dawn."

"I know. Tamyr has been trying to keep me under control the last few days, waiting for you to leave."

"Apparently Bonnay was serving as duenna to me as well. I just received your note a few minutes ago or I probably would have been here sooner."

"I sent you three rather pleading messages. I have no pride, you see." Her brows arched delicately and a small touch of whimsy lightened her voice.

"Only the last one got through." A fleeting smile graced his handsome face. "We have a staff protecting us from our own indiscretions. And I was trying to be honorable," he added with a transient openhanded gesture. "Tamyr doesn't look very pleased, by the way."

"She's against this."

"Strangely," he said with a rueful smile, "I am too . . . and I never am."

Was he hoping such unvarnished truth would deter her? "You needn't bear any responsibility, General Duras."

"Of course I will." He hadn't moved from the door, but it was only because of sheer will, knowing he was putting her in jeopardy. She looked more beautiful than he remembered—barely clothed in a nightgown that clung to her lithe, slender body, like Venus on display, tempting, the luscious apple of paradise; his libido was on full alert. "I know your husband," he said, as if in warning. "We've met several times."

"My servants are loyal only to me."

"I know that, but rumors spread in other ways."

"I don't care."

"One of us should."

"Please no. Don't give me book and verse on the proprieties. I've never done anything like this before, I didn't send for you lightly."

"I'm not sure I want to take on such a damning obligation."

"Your reputation suggests you've overlooked such obligations before. Don't they call you Duras of the Serai? Consider me in that light—another of your transient harem."

He didn't argue the veracity of the sobriquet given him; he only said, "I wish I could." His voice was low, almost threatening. His odd new feelings disturbed him; his entire concentration should be on the coming battle. Where they always had been in the past.

"Then I'll make it easy for you," she gently said, untying the bow at the throat of her gown. "Surely you can indulge me for a few minutes," she added, sliding one shoulder free of the fine linen. "You'll still have time to sleep afterward," she murmured, slipping her arm from the sleeve, exposing one plump breast, the nipple taut with arousal. "I understand you're very good at this." Her cheeks were flushed, the pink glow sliding down her throat, warming the paleness of her skin. The other sleeve puddled at her wrist for a second before she pulled it free and a moment later her nightgown lay in a pool at her feet.

She stepped over it and began moving toward him and he waited, trembling like a callow youth when he'd never trembled even then. He first touched her with his fingertips when she came within range, the hardened pads of his fingers tracing the slope of her shoulders with exquisite gentleness before he pulled her close and said, "We should have met thirteen years ago."

"But we have now," she whispered, feeling the same rare sense of rapport. Of desire. All impediments brushed aside. "Stay with me till morning."

"I'd like to keep you with me for a thousand years." His mouth touched hers with consummate tenderness, a lover's kiss offering love, and she kissed him with a young girl's artlessness and a rush of feeling that brought tears to her eyes.

"Will I frighten you with my love?" She couldn't help herself; there was so little time.

"No," he said, when the thousand times he'd heard that in the past had only brought flight to mind. And then he added very low, so his voice vibrated against her mouth. "So this is love?"

"I think so."

"Perhaps," he said, half under his breath because it was so different. And then he swore in a quiet exhalation of dismay at the irony of such a staggering concept—now, with time so short, with life so short.

"I don't want to wait," she whispered, a sense of urgency underlying every thought and breath. "Must I rip your clothes off?"

He laughed and the odd spell was over. "Let me rip them off. I've had more practice."

And he did so with astonishing speed, taking her by the hand and leading her to the bed with an unhesitating confidence she found charming. He was so assured of his abilities to please. "I thought of this moment," he said, turning back to her with a smile, "a dozen times since I left you—while Foy was informing me of the artillery positions, several times during the discussion of the bridge construction at Trubbach, twice when dictating to Bonnay, and unfortunately at the moment Cambacérès was defining the exact locations of his tirilliers—which meant I had to ask him to repeat the dispositions. So I warn you, madame, I'm not likely to stop once this begins. I've been waiting for days."

"Please don't," she said, overcome with happiness, "when I've been waiting for you all my life."

3

His skin was dark, brown like a Moor's. "You've been in the sun," she murmured, as he pulled her down on the bed beside him, the feel of his body hot too like the sun.

"While you never have, it seems," he gently replied, propped on one elbow, tracing his finger down the paleness of her arm.

"The sun is weaker in Siberia." Stretching upward, she brushed a kiss down his jaw, her sense of having reached safe harbor profound.

"I was there . . . the summer of eighty-three." He remembered the date suddenly; he'd been godfather to his sister's first child when he'd returned that fall.

"Where?" Playfully launching herself at him, she tumbled him on his back, and lying across his chest, she kissed his broad smile. "Tell me where," she murmured, "because I want to know you were close to me."

"At Samorov and Troickoe and you were twelve," he whispered with a grin, "and much too young . . ."

"We were fifty versts away at the summer hunt. Darling, think how near we were." Her kiss was heated this time, lingering.

Moments later her mouth lifted from his.

"Say it again."

Her downy brows rose in query.

"Say *darling*." His palms drifted down her spine.

"Surely you've heard that before, *darling*." A teasing gleam shone in her eyes.

"But not from you," he murmured, his palms warm on her bottom. "It affects me deeply."

She could feel his erection lengthen, feel the pressure of his hands as they tightened on her bottom. "How deeply?" she whispered.

"I could show you."

"I was hoping you would," she softly said, her heart beating against her ribs.

"Are you sure now?"

She nodded, tears welling in her eyes, unsure suddenly of her capacity to handle the inevitable bereavement.

"You can stay with me," he gently said, as if reading her mind. "You don't have to go back to him." A monumental statement, he realized, even as he uttered it.

"I have to," she quietly replied, "or my tribe will suffer."

I'll kill him, he thought. Just like that. How strange everything was . . . unprecedented, without yardstick or clue in his previous life.

"But keep me for now," she said, her gaze intense with longing.

"For as long as you want," he promised. Direct, accomplished, he wondered how well protected Korsakov would be. And then his need for her urgent, he gathered her in his arms, rolled over her and entered her welcoming body.

The feel of him deep inside her melted her bones, the sensation so exquisite, so perfect, she hadn't realized such luxurious rapture existed this side of heaven. She kept murmuring *thank you* against his heated kisses until the leisurely rhythm of his lower body brought her past that languorous, blissful enchantment to a frenzied delirium that ate at her brain, ravished her nerve endings, brought her by excruciatingly slow degrees to a screaming climax.

And when her eyes opened again after a very long time and her overwrought breathing was partially restored, she gazed up into his smiling eyes and faintly said, "It's been a privilege to meet you."

His laughter exploded in the small bedchamber. "The privilege has been entirely mine, Countess," he genially asserted, kissing her with an easy charm, all courtesy and well-bred manners. "Would you like a moment to rest?"

"There's more?" she flirtatiously inquired, delighting in her newly discovered sexuality, in the opulent passions he evoked.

"If you don't mind." Politesse for a man of his repute.

"Can you do that for me again?"

"With pleasure."

"So this is why all the women pursue you."

"I'm sure any man could do the same."

He immediately realized his error. "Forgive me." The delight had vanished from her eyes, a bleak emptiness in its place. Shifting his weight, he gently stroked her silken cheek. "Tell me about your people," he said, trying to distract her. "Take me back to your country before we met all the other people in our lives. So long ago there's—"

"Just you and me."

He nodded, brushing a kiss over her mouth. "Only us," he whispered. "It's summer and the larches are newly leafed, the sky's immense and always blue."

Her mouth curved into a tentative smile at the memory of her youthful summers. "Grand-père says the sky belongs to our people alone."

"Take me walking in the forest under your sky."

Her small hands came up, framing the ascetic beauty of his face, a militant saint's face. "I'll lure you away and keep you for myself."

"Deep in the forest . . . on the banks of a silvery pond where fish talk and fairies dwell. Do you swim?" he asked, his voice deep and low, intimate.

"Foreigners can't tolerate the cold waters."

"You'll keep me warm."

His whisper shivered up her spine.

"I'm on fire for you," he breathed, "so burning hot I'm not sure this is happening to me after all this time. You have to stay with me."

"All summer?" The joy was back in her eyes.

"All summer," he said, although snow was falling outside and his entire army was ready to march at dawn.

The rare circumstances set an unusual tone to his love-making; his affections had never been involved before, nor had he ever wished to kill a man over a woman. Although Korsakov might kill *him*, he realized. So when Teo said, "Wait," as he readjusted himself between her thighs, he almost said, "I don't have time," and it took a moment to steady himself. Taking a deep breath, he said, "For how long?"

"Let me come with you."

"Now?" He wasn't certain he was capable of further foreplay, the pressure of orgasmic impulses intense.

"Take me with you to the fort," she clarified.

Incredulous, he tried to absorb the shock.

"I won't be in the way. I've hunted all my life—at home and in Russia."

"God, no," Duras growled, rolling away, his libido overwhelmed by a flaring anger. Bartering sex for favors was odiously reminiscent of his wife's style. Swiftly rising from the bed, he moved to collect his clothes.

"Andre, please," Teo cried, scrambling from the bed to follow him.

"I knew I shouldn't have come," he bitterly declared, lifting his trousers from a nearby chair.

"I'm sorry," she pleaded. "Please . . ." Grasping his wrist, she tried to stop him. "I didn't mean it like that."

He shook off her hand, his eyes dark with resentment. "You meant it *another* way? You want something more?"

"I just can't bear to see you go," she said so softly he had to strain to hear the words. "I don't want you to leave."

Her black hair fell in a river of silk, tumbling over her shoulders, pouring down her back. Her pale skin was still delicately flushed from their lovemaking, her lush nudity only inches away. And he felt a terrible, uncontrollable desire—animalistic, primal, oblivious to anger, to the most rudimentary morality.

"I *have* to go," he quietly said.

She heard the small nuance, the regret. "Please, not just yet," she impetuously said, impassioned, reckless. "I apologize for everything . . . for anything I might have said." The troops had been moving out all day; she was without pride. "Stay a short time more . . . please. Talk to me." She took a small breath and touched his arm, her gaze on him, watching for his reaction. "Hold me," she said very low, her fingers trailing fire down his arm.

"You can't come with me," he said, not moving, constraint in every stilled muscle of his powerful body. "You have to understand." His voice was grave. "It's too dangerous."

"I'm so frightened for you," she whispered, anguished at the thought of the coming battle, of losing him. With a stifled sob she jettisoned all dignity and threw her arms around his waist, clinging to him.

The fragrance of her hair invaded his nostrils, the compelling warmth of her body assailed his senses, and blind instinct triumphed over reason. His arms closed around her, enveloped her, his strength like a bulwark against the world. "You don't have to worry," he murmured, his response instinctive after years of soldiering. "I lead a charmed life."

"Good," she whispered, gazing up at him, tears glistening in her eyes. "You have to promise to come back to me," she insisted, not even questioning her right to make that demand of him, "and I promise not to be weepy like this again." Gulping back her tears, she tried to smile. "And try to be more sophisticated like—"

"Hush," he interposed, gently brushing his thumb across her quivering mouth. "You don't have to be sophisticated."

"Will you give me a baby?"

"On the other hand," he murmured with a small smile, "I'm not sure I'm prepared for such naïveté."

"You don't *have* children," she said, hushed and low as if that were reason enough to grant her wish.

"You know that, do you?" A teasing note warmed his voice.

"Please, Andre." Her gaze held his. "Don't toy with me when I love you so."

"How can you know it's love," he gently chided, "when you've never been in love before? You might forget me by next week."

"Don't be cruel. I won't—*ever*."

She spoke with such unequivocal purpose, it staggered him. His whole life was equivocal, he sorted through a hundred cynical options every day. He gazed at her, his expression unreadable, a dozen—a thousand—reasons for refusing her prominent in his thoughts. "Even if I were to agree," he heard himself say—a shocking experience as if someone outside himself spoke—"you may not become pregnant tonight."

"I would, I will, I *know* it," Teo breathlessly replied, her warm body pressed tightly against his, the shimmering heat of her skin palpable under his hands.

"If it *were* to happen," he slowly went on, his tone skeptical, his gaze closed, "how could I raise my child? You'd take it from me."

"No. I'd find a way to stay. I would."

"What of your tribe, the consequences to them?" He'd spent years gauging the risks of action and reaction, of victory and defeat.

"Is Korsakov across the Rhine?" It was the first time she'd uttered her husband's name.

"Rumor has it he is." His spies were certain.

"Will you be opposing him tomorrow?"

"Perhaps."

"Do you think he might die?"

"Do you want him to?"

"With all my heart," she whispered.

He should ask why; he should require reasons for such conspicuous hatred. If he didn't want her so, he might. And if he didn't know Korsakov so well, he would. "I'll see what I can do," he calmly said.

"You won't love me when I'm so terrible."

He thought of her life with the man they called the Butcher. "You're not terrible."

"I had to stay."

"I know." He'd stayed in his marriage for less honorable reasons. Out of apathy and indolence or more ignominiously because of expediency. "When the war's over, we'll make the necessary changes in our lives."

"Are you asking me to marry you?" A new cheer infused her voice.

He didn't answer at first and then he said with male caution, "I'm not sure."

"When *will* you know?" she teased, suddenly bursting with happiness, the newfound possibility of a *future* dizzying.

"Keep in mind this is only the second time I've seen you," he carefully said, a problematic undertone to his words. He didn't make a practice of offering marriage.

"The third," she cheerfully corrected, and as incautious as he was not, she added with a smile, "You know you love me."

A small startle reflex flickered across his face.

Laughing, she stood on tiptoe and kissed him lightly. "Tell me later," she murmured. "Give me a baby now."

This time *he* laughed—at her single-minded purpose and enchanting gaiety. "So assured, my lady," he said, his dark eyes amused.

"When do you have to leave?"

"At three-thirty."

She glanced at the clock on the mantel.

"There should be time enough," he softly said.

4

Lifting her into his arms, he carried her to the bed, realizing what he was about to do was an act of madness, but one he could no more stop than he could restrain the events that would begin at dawn. And disregarding practicalities, the imminent campaign, and the very real possibility that his life could be over in a few hours, he quietly said, "What do you want—a boy or girl?"

"You decide," she said, prescient and in love, feeling blessed that she'd not lived her life without knowing this unalloyed rapture.

"Why not both," he said, heated and low. "Or a dozen," he added half under his breath, "so you can never leave me."

The dazzling wish and heartfelt hope, the urgency and prodigal excess flared through her senses, and pulling his face down, she kissed him so violently he stopped mid-stride to absorb her bruising ardor. When her mouth finally relinquished his, he said, captivated by her ingenuous passions, "I'm very glad you took the wrong turn at Bregenz."

"And I'm very glad to be alive," she jubilantly replied, "and in your arms—"

"And under me," he huskily intoned, moving the short distance to the bed, placing her on the green velvet comforter, following her down in an easy, graceful descent. "Where I intend to see that you stay," he whispered, licking a warm path across her mouth, expertly sliding between her thighs, "for a very long time."

"For a dozen children," she softly answered, wrapping her arms around his neck, raising slightly to meet him.

"At least a dozen," he murmured, the vibration of his words fluttering across her mouth. "Because I'm *keeping* you . . ."

Her orgasm began before he'd finished speaking, before he'd fully entered her, her lust inflamed by the notion of being kept, possessed by such a man, and she came in a wild, frenzied convulsion that tore through her with such violence she was left wide-eyed, breathless. "I must want you too much," she said moments later, startled, still trembling from the aftermath pulsing through her body.

"It's never too much," he gently replied, sliding deeper, stretching her, dipping his head to catch her small moan of pleasure. "There now," he whispered, his breath warm on her half-parted lips. "How does that feel?"

"Perfect . . . unbelievable . . . as if—" Her words mutated into a soft, high wail, her nails penetrated the brown skin, and a millisecond later he was sunk hilt-deep inside her. And she was rippling inside, her womb clamoring for him, wild desire filling her consciousness as though she didn't have a life beyond sensation, as if she'd been born to lie with him.

She was liquid beneath him and a dual need possessed

him—to delay, hold off as long as possible, to savor; the
other to rush to a blinding, red-hot orgasm.

She came again right away and he smiled faintly in
the midst of his own passion. The decision made for him, he
slowed his rhythm, the muscles swelling in his upper arms
as he held himself gently against her womb, plumbing deep
into her dazed, simmering afterglow.

Clinging to him, she mewed inarticulate purring sounds,
awed by the naked pleasure, by the rich revelation of carnal
longing.

She was all sweet and good, he thought, intoxicated by
the perfume of her desire, her innocence, and the urge to father a child was suddenly more than a flirtatious nicety to
please her. He closed his eyes for a moment and wondered
what had overcome him that he found himself actually plotting the fate of a child.

It was lunacy when no future existed beyond the few
moments they had tonight—when he might be dead in a
few brief hours. *And you always have choices,* he reminded
himself.

But she whispered, "I adore you . . ." with surrender in
her eyes and voice, in her hot, orgasmic body, and he knew
he had to fill her and fill her again, spill over and fill her
once more. And if fate decreed or the stars in heaven allowed, he would sire a child on her tonight.

Swelling larger at such self-indulgent vanity, he glided
deeper, his callused, muscular hands holding her firmly under him, the delicate swish of skin on skin a whisper between them like her welcoming sigh, her thighs opening
wider as he drove forward. And he perversely thought, I in-
sert myself exactly here and drive faster and then slower,
heat what is hot and open what is already wide open and de-
posit my semen into the very center of her glorious body.

He arched his strong back and she lifted her hips to his
and breathed, "I love you . . ." with such tenderness, her
words almost stopped him. His new inclination for father-

hood was so tenuous, his familiar habits so rooted, there was a brief moment when he found himself still capable of debate.

But the moment swiftly passed, deluged by predaceous lust and unfathomable feelings of possession, and he found he could no more let her go than he could suppress his cresting orgasmic frenzy. "Hold on," he murmured, as though they were about to fall off a mountain or the edge of the world, and she seemed to understand because she twined her arms more tightly around his neck and whispered, "Take me anywhere."

He took her in the next few moments to a place where stars danced and raw need was like a blue fire and they didn't need another chance to get it right.

And he held her afterward in silence and she him and felt a power and glory on earth. They didn't talk then beyond their whispered love words, nor later when they made love again—when he ran his hands up and down her thighs, when his mouth was a dream between her legs, his tongue sliding and darting inside her, nibbling, nipping, bringing her a bouquet of orgasms—because there was nothing to say that wouldn't ultimately touch on his leaving and neither could bear to think of it with paradise in their grasp.

He said, "Thank you," finally when he rose from the bed, coming back twice to kiss her, leaning over her for lingering moments half-dressed, his mouth drifting over hers.

"The pleasure was mine," she murmured with a smile the first time. The second and third time, her words were variations on a theme, graceful, charming words that wouldn't alarm him or disconcert the man who was taking on the persona of commander-in-chief before her eyes.

When Bonnay came to fetch him, Duras was dressed and ready. And Teo knew better than to shed any tears; the daughter and granddaughter of tribesmen who'd waged war against Russia for decades, she understood protocol on the eve of battle.

"Come back to me," she quietly said.

"I intend to." They were standing very close, their fingers twined, her white cashmere robe delicate against his dark tunic and leather riding breeches.

"When?"

"Hopefully in a few days." He shrugged. "It depends."

"Don't be reckless."

He smiled faintly. "But that's how I win."

"Don't be overly reckless."

"I never am." His grip loosened on her fingers; Bonnay was waiting outside the door.

"Thank you for the baby."

This time his smile was genuine. "You have enormous faith."

"Yes," she simply said as his hands slipped away. "Come home to us."

5

"A courier from Paris arrived while you were gone," Bonnay immediately said as Duras stepped into the corridor.

"More operational orders from the War Ministry telling me how to fight this campaign from the comfort of their Parisian offices no doubt," Duras sardonically replied, striding down the hall. "Is there anything in the reports worth reading?"

Keeping pace beside him, Bonnay smiled. "Of course not. With the exception," he blandly added, "of your wife's note of instructions."

Duras's gaze turned briefly to his aide. "More advice from her uncle, Talleyrand?"

"That and she'd like some Russian sables if there's any to be confiscated after your expected rout of the Russian corps."

"No concern for my health, I presume." Duras slid his fingers into a riding glove.

"I didn't notice any."

"I suppose if I were to die, you could see that her Russian sables are sent to her along with my body," he casually remarked, carefully smoothing the leather down each finger, a snug fit essential for saber work.

"In the coffin, sir?"

Duras's grin flashed white against his dark skin. "That would be a nice touch. Tell me, Henri, how you managed to find such a suitable wife when mine is interested only in my name and rank." He adjusted his second glove with the same meticulous care.

"Amalie and I grew up together, sir. She was a ward of my aunt."

"Ah." Duras's soft exhalation drifted behind as the two men swiftly descended the carpeted stairs. "I met *my* wife at what were euphemistically referred to as receptions at Barras's Luxembourg Palace." The more conservative in Parisian society called them orgies, with all the women scantily clad in the new Grecian fashions. The high-stakes gambling and shocking new dances further condemned the entertainments.

"And she was very beautiful," Bonnay leniently noted.

"Yes." No one could deny Claudine's exquisite blond prettiness. "And I was more intrigued with politics at the time." At Barras's and Talleyrand's instigation, Duras had been nominated for a place on the Directory in the spring elections of 1797.

"We're beyond the politicians out here." Bonnay held the outside door open for Duras.

"Thankfully." Although several high-ranking politicians, Napoleon included, had never forgiven him for taking the spotlight away from them that spring. "And we're beyond the orders from the War Ministry as well," Duras went on, drawing in a refreshing breath of cold air. "You signed off on the reports?"

"Your name and mine."

"Well done as usual. And if we're victorious today, the War Ministry will take credit with my blessing as long as they stay in Paris where they can't do any harm."

"All those reports they keep sending out should keep them busy." The lights of their offices were visible down the street.

"While we have an offensive to begin—in what! Ten minutes?"

"Five minutes, sir. I gave you an extra five minutes."

Duras laughed. "You're a true romantic, Bonnay."

A short time later, when Tamyr entered the bedroom suite, Teo was stepping into her fur-lined trousers, her winter hunting clothes piled on the bed. "I'm following him as far as the river. And don't give me any arguments because I'm having his baby."

No visible surprise showed on Tamyr's plump round face. "I'd suggest you have an escape plan ready when the baby begins to show and Korsakov sees you."

"You forget I endured my husband's filthy embraces at Salzburg," Teo calmly replied, reaching for her reindeer-skin boots. "Would he kill his own child?" She cast a speculative glance at her companion.

"The child won't be fair-haired."

"Nor am I. And Korsakov needs an heir, doesn't he?" Teo added, stepping into her boots.

"Are you planning on staying with him?"

"Not for a minute more than necessary." Teo picked up her parka. "But the fiction of his child will protect me."

"You can't be certain about this babe, however much you may wish for it."

"But I am," Teo declared, slipping the fur jacket over her head. "Absolutely certain."

Argument was useless, Tamyr decided. She'd never seen Teo so transported, almost rash. "What of Duras? Does he want a child?"

Teo smiled. "I talked him into it."

"I see. Are we staying, then?"

"If he kills Korsakov today, we could with certainty."

"So the Evil One is across the river?"

"Duras thought so. Now are you coming with me or not?" Teo didn't like to think of her husband or hear his name or be reminded that he still had authority over her life.

Tamyr pursed her thin lips. "Have I ever left you unprotected?"

"I'm sorry, babushka," Teo apologized. "Of course you haven't."

"Your grandfather charged me with your safety," she quietly declared.

"We might have our freedom by tomorrow, Tam, darling," Teo said with relish, "and then I won't need your protection."

"The spirits willing."

"And then we'll no longer live in fear."

"I'll burn some sweet moss tonight and talk to the spirits."

"Ask them to let me keep this happiness, Tam."

"Don't be too trusting, child. Duras may not be interested in love."

"You're wrong. He's wonderful, warm and kind, and he may have asked me to marry him," she lightly went on, smiling at the warm memory. "So you're not allowed to be negative," she blithely added as if the world for a moment bent to her will. "And if you knew him, you'd *understand*." She pronounced the last word without equivocation.

"Hmpf," Tamyr muttered. "As if you know him after a few hours."

"But I'm truly happy, Tam, really and truly. Don't begrudge me this."

"I'm afraid he'll hurt you, child, that's all," her companion gently said. "Women don't stay long in his life."

Oblivious to all but her intense joy, Teo smiled. "I'm happier than I've ever been in my life and I'm going to have the child I've always wanted—*his* child. So you needn't worry," she went on, cavalierly dismissing her maidservant's warnings. "And if you're coming with me you'd better hurry," she briskly added, picking up her gloves, "or we'll miss the river crossing."

A quarter-moon and occasional stars gleamed through the cloud cover, and the possibility of more snow hung damply in the air as Teo and Tamyr arrived at a vantage point on the river bluff. The light infantry units were crossing the trestle bridge in the darkness, spreading out along the east bank, setting up a protective line of defense for the march into Austrian territory. Cavalry companies clattered across next to screen the deployment—dragoons, hussars, cuirassiers—followed by the horse artillery. A dozen horses were needed to move each twelve-pound cannon, and the caisson wheels had been muffled with cloth to stifle the noise. Then the infantry of the line passed over the Rhine, the stream of troops undiminished for almost two hours.

Duras and his staff, mounted, muffled in greatcoats, their weapons gleaming dully in the subdued light, watched the procession cross the river. Partially detached from the group, Duras rarely spoke, observing the passage of troops without expression. Occasionally a soldier would greet him, and Duras would reply with a comment that brought a flash of a smile to the infantryman's face.

Duras believed in the republican principles of equality, his friendliness toward the common soldier unconstrained, natural—a rare quality even in the postrevolutionary army.

How different he was, Teo thought, from the man who'd forced her into marriage. Korsakov's family wealth had gained him his rank, minions did his bidding, and he arrogantly considered no man his equal. But she hoped as she stood with Tamyr behind a shield of dark pines watching the French army move into Austria that the coming battle would put an end to her husband's despicable life and neither conscience nor pity altered her resolute hatred.

She had more reason than most to wish him dead.

Just prior to the advance of the rear-guard detachments, Duras moved onto the bridge at the head of his staff, his bay charger restive on the unsteady trestle footing. The rushing water was visible between the planks, unnerving the high-spirited animal, and it tossed its head, caracoled. Keeping a firm hand on the reins, Duras leaned forward and murmured near its ear, stroked its powerful neck, and the horse instantly calmed.

Touched by such gentle humanity, Teo felt tears well in her eyes. And she thought of her own favorite mare killed by her husband last year for the most minor infraction.

"He'll be back," Tamyr soothed, misinterpreting Teo's tears. "They say no enemy fire can touch him."

"Pray they're right," Teo softly murmured, as the shadowy pines on the opposite shore swallowed up the last glimpse of the man who'd introduced her to the miracle of love.

The snow that had fallen most of the night lent a magical illusion to the dark forest, the tall pines with their powdery mantle gleaming pale against the gray sky. And the narrow path climbing by a shallow gradient lay untouched, pristine before the advance units. It hardly seemed possible enclosed within the still, frosty whiteness that the carnage of battle waited at the end of their march.

Scudding clouds overlay St. Luzisteig, only a few drowsy guards patrolled its walls. Even the smoke from the chimneys rose in slow lazy trails into the dusky sky. The fort sat atop a steep col, its huge mass blocking the main road from Feldkirch to Chur. To its left the Falknis mountain soared steeply to 8,416 feet, forming a natural barrier, while the lesser Fläscherberr on its right dropped sharply to the Rhine.

It was still dark when the French Army of Switzerland arrived at the rim of the forest bordering the snow-covered slope fronting the fort's north façade. Silently, the artillery set their muffled twelve-pounders and howitzers just inside the tree line, out of range of any St. Luzisteig artillery piece.[1] Sharpshooters and skirmishers were sent to scale the heights east and west of the fort, and once everyone was in place, Duras gave the signal for the bombardment to begin.

The predawn stillness was shattered by the deafening thunder of exploding shells, as the well-trained gunnery crews fired in swift, synchronized order. Cannonballs hammered the walls of the fort, leaving great gaping holes where shot struck a weakened portion of masonry, smashing through the east guard post in a bloody slaughter, discharging a murderous barrage the entire length of the north exposure.

The garrison came awake in shock, the attack completely unexpected. The Aulic Council in Vienna had just recalled several regiments from the fort yesterday in anticipation of the French march into the Grisons. Duras had been expected to attack Chur, the capital, thirty miles south.

Scrambling to reach their posts, the Austrian artillery crews sprinted to their cannons and ran them out, the flare of fuses illuminating the gun portals. Running soldiers became visible on the ramparts, silhouetted like figures on a stage against the fiery blaze of shellfire.

With his army safely out of range of the smaller guns of St. Luzisteig, Duras rested in the saddle, surveying the frantic call to arms and the ensuing melee in the Austrian fort, knowing it was a waiting game now. His artillery would take time to soften up the strongly entrenched position.

Duras was approaching the fort in a standard attack, the artillery first opening long-range fire, the bombardment meant to disorganize; even veteran soldiers found artillery fire the hardest to bear. The great iron balls fell thickly, each carving an instant bloody channel through any ranks of men, smashing them to pieces.

The deadly cannonade persisted, leaving death in its wake, imposing heavy casualties on the Austrians in their confined position and with their opposing fire falling far short of the French positions. All the while Duras's men waited for the order to attack.

After a time Duras motioned for Bonnay. "See that the gunners adjust the position of guns four and seven," he directed. "They're missing the target by a dozen feet." The powder magazines his spies had reported on were still intact. Sliding his field glass into its saddle holster, he added, "And move another cannon in front of the gate. I want those doors blown away."

After another fifteen minutes, Duras was visibly restless, his gloved fingers tapping rhythmically on his saddle pommel. He'd discarded his greatcoat and rolled it away on his saddle pack; he'd tested the slide of his saber in his scabbard a dozen times, his pistols were primed.

The munition stores were still untouched.

"Bonnay!" He shouted so loudly his voice was heard above the tumult, his irritation evident. And then as if on cue, one gunpowder store took a direct hit and blew up in a blaze of fire that illuminated the dawn sky halfway to Chur.

Spurring his horse, Duras immediately launched the attack, his huge charger hurtling forward, the whole north rise suddenly black with men as his army followed him. The *pas de charge* of the drums beat their distinctive rhythm, a sound few men however brave could listen to without a moment of fear—the rum dum, rum dum, rummadum dum, dum a reminder to all of the precariousness of life.

An immense solid block of men carried forward by an irresistible wave of momentum surged up the snowy slope into the belt of smoke, poured over the moat ridge, rolled down into the snow-filled crevasse, accompanied by the shouts, the beat of the drums, the blast of trumpets savage, fierce, rising into the morning sky like the roar of the apocalypse. In what seemed mere seconds to the horrified defenders, the engineers had struggled through the deep snow and were throwing up their scaling ladders against the twelve-foot earthen walls with the precision of a well-choreographed dance and the churning mass of men rolled up the slope and up the ladders in a wave of terror.

Riding across the front lines, Duras urged his men on, a rare bloodlust surging through his veins. And his men answered with a shout and rushed on.

When the first companies reached the walls of the fort, Duras wheeled his bay and forced him up the embankment bordering the main gate. The massive doors had been shattered by his twelve-pounders. His cavalry units waiting stirrup to stirrup for the order to attack, Duras unsheathed his saber, and raised it high, the din of gunshot too intense to hear a shouted command. And spurring his bay, he charged the Austrian gun emplacements. His cavalry thundered behind him, three hundred riders galloping up the narrow avenue into the heavily defended gap. Duras soared over the barricades first, his men following closely behind, jumping the gunnery emplacements like steeplechasers, flowing over and through the Austrian gunners full charge, slashing and cutting, slaughtering the enemy, the dead and wounded trampled by the next wave of horsemen.

The Austrians began to break as the French cavalry poured into the fort. The charge brought chaos and with chaos came panic; paralyzed by the overwhelming fierceness of the attack, the cannon having left carnage on a grand scale, the will to fight was slipping away. Units were mixed, men lost their officers, there was nowhere to turn. The cavalry was slashing right and left with ghastly cold-bloodedness, the infantry poured over the walls bayonets drawn, and resistance suddenly melted away. Unlike the French who fought for their country and glory, the Austrian soldiers were members of an army where service in the ranks was considered neither honorable nor desirable. The defense ignominiously collapsed and brief minutes later the acting commander emerged waving a white flag. The battalion commander had been killed in the artillery assault and as the colonel in charge handed over his sword, Duras received it with a cursory bow, his mind elsewhere. No Russian troops had been visible in the melee, not a single tsarist uniform amidst the defenders. "Is Korsakov here?" he asked, his voice sharp, his gaze taking in the redoubts behind the officer.

"No." The Austrian officer stood slightly breathless, his pudgy face pink from his unusual physical exertions. Unfamiliar with combat, he'd arrived from headquarters in Vienna only two days ago.

"Has he been here?"

"Yes." But the colonel's mouth pursed in disdain as he took in the simple cavalry tunic Duras wore over his riding breeches. France's republican officers were considered ruffians by the Austrian command.

"When did he leave?" Duras quietly inquired, his impatience showing in the crispness of his words.

"Yesterday." A cool haughtiness infused his tone.

"*When* yesterday?"

"In the afternoon."

"What was his destination?"

"I'm not at liberty to say."

Fucking martinet, Duras fumed. The Austrian officer corps, aristocratic, unimaginative, and devoted to routine, still operated under the outdated 1769 manual of regulations.[2] The man still thought the quarterings on his family crest mattered. Incompetent old fool.

Motioning for the colonel to be taken away, Duras turned to Bonnay. "Send the prisoners and wounded back with a guard company," he instructed. "And I want a cavalry detachment ready for pursuit in ten minutes, the best horses and riders we have."

"The Russian's twenty hours ahead of you."

"He could be moving slowly if he's with his corps."

"Or moving fast if he's with his Cossacks."

"We'll find out soon enough," Duras replied, undeterred. "Continue the advance upstream to Chur. We'll meet you somewhere in between. And tell Sacerre I'm disappointed in his information. He should have had someone here yesterday."

"With the attack imminent, all the spies were pulled in."

"In future that will be remedied," Duras softly said. "I should have had information on Korsakov's march."

"Why not wait? We're sure to meet him soon."

"I'd rather not." Cool, precise words, his eyes utterly chill.

Bonnay had seen him like this only once before—when personal issues had engaged him on the battlefield. Years ago at Guardolia they'd been badly outnumbered, a ragtag army thrown together to hold back the First Coalition forces in the Ligurian Apennines, and the royalist general with aristocratic arrogance had sent a message, promising to have Duras's head on a pike by nightfall.

"We'll annihilate you," Duras had scrawled in reply.

They had. And Duras had never been underestimated again.

"At least take more than a detachment," Bonnay pressed. "You're not well enough protected riding in enemy territory."

"I'm interested in speed," Duras calmly replied, "and a modicum of stealth. For that I want a limited number of men."

"You're risking too much on a bloody whim," Bonnay declared.

"Indulge me, my dear Henri," Duras murmured. "We can't possibly be reassembled and ready to march in less than two hours. Riding fast, I can be halfway to Chur and back by then."

"Perhaps Korsakov traveled north to Feldkirch. Rumor has it another Russian corps has entered Galicia."

Duras shook his head. "Sacerre wouldn't have missed him at Trubbach had he gone north. Korsakov's on his way to Chur."

"Or the Tyrol."

"You're wasting my time, Henri," Duras said with a flash of a smile. "Get me my detachment."

"Yes, sir," his aide diplomatically replied, realizing Duras wasn't to be deterred. "Would you like to send a message back with the prisoners and wounded?"

"The usual dispatch to headquarters informing them of the victory, Bonnay. You know that."

"I meant to the countess."

"No," Duras smoothly replied, "but thank you for inquiring. You needn't look so relieved, Bonnay. I haven't forgotten my command or our mission. This is a calculated reconnaissance," he went on, smiling faintly, "and while we're scouting enemy territory for the advance toward Chur, we may possibly run across General Korsakov."

Bonnay needn't have worried. Regardless of his personal feelings, Duras was always first a commander. As for Korsakov, should he be found and killed, that meritorious act would serve the French cause well.

6

The spring forenoon in Paris was pleasantly warm, unlike the weather at St. Luzisteig, and the sunshine streaming through Claudine Duras's boudoir windows additionally warmed the twined bodies on the rumpled bed. Their pursuit of pleasure was more leisurely this morning, their senses not yet fully awake, and the rhythm of their bodies bespoke a languid, drowsy ardor—much different from their heated passions of the previous night.

"Your mood always matches mine," the middle-aged man murmured.

"We understand each other," Claudine answered with a small sigh of pleasure.

"Life is sweet."

"*Amour* is sweet, dear uncle, which makes life sweet."

The ex-Bishop of Autun, Charles Maurice de Talleyrand, smiled and then he kissed the soft lips raised to his.

They breakfasted late that morning in the secluded privacy of a small balcony adjacent to the boudoir. Protected
from the spring breezes by a topiary arrangement of ju-
nipers lining the railing, they conversed on a topic dear to
their hearts.

"Pierre Collot made another very nice contribution to my
bank account yesterday," Claudine said. "I was able to supply
him with letters of introduction to Andre's quartermaster."

"How generous of him. But then Pierre understands the
rules perfectly. Or he wouldn't be the richest army contractor in France." Talleyrand minutely adjusted the position of
his coffee spoon. "Which brings Rapinat to mind—another
man of financial acumen." His gaze came up, the spoon disposed to his satisfaction. "He writes me he's having problems with Andre. I don't suppose you could put a good
word in—"

"You have a droll sense of humor, Charles," Claudine
interjected, one brow prettily arched. "If I endorsed Rapinat
to Andre he'd probably have him shot." Her small shrug
was in the way of a dismissal. "*You* put pressure on my headstrong husband and make him listen to the commissioner
sent out from Paris. You're the foreign minister."

Talleyrand smiled faintly over the rim of his coffee cup.
"Perhaps later. At the moment I wouldn't care to reproach
Andre. Your husband is the only general we have who is
likely to gain victories in the coming campaign."

"No one's inclined to recall Bonaparte?"

Talleyrand shook his head. "The Directory prefers a
man of his ambition to be safely in Egypt fighting the
infidel."

"Catherine tells me he sent her a gold necklace said to
belong to Cleopatra." Madame Grand was Talleyrand's current mistress.

"The young Corsican is a consummate politician. Catherine isn't the only recipient of his gifts. Half the assembly—the influential half—" Talleyrand sardonically noted, "have been sent mementos from the land of pyramids . . . along with exaggerated reports of his victories."

"How long will the Directory last once he's back?" Claudine asked, attuned to the finite details of power politics.[3]

"You've been talking to Sieyès, I see," the ex-bishop said of the former Jesuit who now held the imagination of those political factions ready to move beyond the Revolution to a constitutional assembly. "He's looking for a 'sword' for his *coup d' état*."

"But General Hoche is dead and Bernadotte is disinclined to take chances. That leaves Joubert, Macdonald, and Moreau."

"None of whom are interested, I'm told. Perhaps Andre could be persuaded," Talleyrand slyly added.

"How pleasant that would be," Claudine said with a sigh of longing, the thought of ruling France in the role of consort gratifying. Her second sigh was one of regret. "But he detests politics."

"And he's perversely honest," Talleyrand sadly noted. "I'm not sure he'd suit with an agent provocateur like Sieyès even if he were cajoled into the position. In fact, I'm surprised he's still married to you, *ma chère*."

"Don't compare me to a hypocrite like Sieyès," she lazily protested, a whipped-cream confection halfway to her mouth.

"Of course not, darling," he instantly apologized, his gift for diplomacy honed in the hotbed of clerical politics. "You've always lived with a charmingly frank indiscretion."

"Have I not been taught by a master, dear Bishop?" she flirtatiously inquired, remnants of whipped cream on her full-lipped mouth incarnately sensual.

"Ex-bishop, thankfully," he softly said.

She gazed at him for a thoughtful moment, intrinsically shrewd beneath the façade of her glorious blond beauty. "How much do you hate my father for having taken your birthright?" she quietly asked, mildly startled by Talleyrand's undertone of malice, not having heard that inflection before.[4]

"Your father was a babe at the time. My enmity falls on the family trustees. And I exacted my revenge too long ago to dwell on that segment of my life," he casually retorted, his brief revealing malice overcome.

Lounging back in her chair, she cast him a teasing glance. "Revenge? How un-Christian of you."

"You must be restless, darling, to provoke such unpleasant memories," he affably declared. "Do you miss your bold and courageous husband?"

She laughed lightly. "Really, *mon cher,* how provocative of *you*. Andre and I both have very busy lives," she blandly said, "as you well know. But he makes me very rich, for which I thank him. The bankers and army contractors court me assiduously."

"Not only for your wifely access to the great man."

"How flattering you are," she softly said. "Fortunately," she gently added with a nuance of dramatic modesty, "there are those on his staff who still *do* appreciate me."

"Does the puppy Furet continue to write every day?"

"Of course, darling. He was quite dazzled by the holiday we spent together at Saint-Cloud."

"You're an unreserved vixen, my dear."

"Which you like very much," she merrily retorted.

"Very much, indeed," the minister of external relations replied with an answering smile.

Duras's cavalry troop met his army moving swiftly upstream toward Chur late that afternoon. Unsuccessful in overtaking Korsakov, Duras was in a black mood. They'd ridden south to the very outskirts of Chur without seeing a sign of the Russians.

"He must be inside the city," Duras said, frustrated by his reconnaissance, "or farther south on his way to the Tyrol. But the city stands well defended. Are the men ready?"

"They are, sir," Bonnay replied. The swift victory at St. Luzisteig had spurred the army's advance, the passage to Chur accomplished in record time. "They're primed for glory and gold, sir. They haven't been paid for two months."

"Paris thinks we can live on glory alone," Duras acerbically retorted, the pressure for funds from headquarters a constant source of friction. "Have you heard any more about the rations?" The men had marched with only five days' supply of food.

Bonnay shook his head.

"Rapinat should be strung up."[5]

"And if he weren't the brother of the minister of finance it might be possible," Bonnay sardonically replied.

"Think how easy it would be, Henri, if we only had to fight the enemy and not the scum behind the lines as well."

"We could retire to the south of France in much shorter order, sir."

"A pleasant thought." Duras smiled, his native Nice dear to his heart, his visits too infrequent. "Bring up the artillery to that line of hills and we'll see if we can speed this war along."

And with the same savage force that had taken St. Luzisteig, in two days of fighting Duras drove the Austrians out of Chur. The capital of the Grisons canton had been garrisoned by an Austrian brigade, but their retreat up the narrow Plessur Valley was cut off by Duras's advance and they were forced to surrender on March 9. A total of 2,980 prisoners, three colors, and sixteen guns fell into the hands of the French. Duras next began his drive into the Tyrol and four days later the French captured Martinsbruck, the key to the province.

Owing to the corrupt commissariat arrangements, the French troops were now without rations or other supplies and an orgy of looting took place. Duras was so exasperated that he wrote a strongly worded protest to the Directory from the battlefield.[6]

"Damned army contractors!" he swore, exasperated, pacing on the knoll overlooking the city of Martinsbruck and its burning buildings. "How the hell can I continue the invasion if my army doesn't have rations?" he angrily challenged, the question rhetorical, his staff knowing better than to respond in his present mood. He'd worn a path across the grassy hillside the past hour. "Lecourbe tells me my right wing hasn't had food for eight days. It's impossible to live off a country devoid of resources. Dammit, the inhabitants expect us to feed them! The transport was supposed to have delivered the supplies two weeks ago! I *want* Rapinat's head!"

His staff was silent before his tirade, the impossibility of further advance apparent to all. The chance to follow up their victories, to overtake Korsakov's regiment, was now out of the question.

"And I'm supposed to discipline my men for taking food they need to survive? I'm sure the Citizen Directors on their fat asses in Paris have some moral homilies to that effect. Damn their useless hides! Bonnay, what do we have left in the treasury at Sargans?"

"Five hundred and sixty thousand francs, sir."

It wasn't enough, of course—nowhere near enough. Abruptly stopping at the crest of the knoll, Duras surveyed the plundered city before him, his sense of frustration overwhelming. "Delegate squads to go in and drag out the looters," he said with a sigh. "I don't want anyone shot. See that the population has compensation in scrip for their losses. Tell them," he slowly went on, his voice gruff with disgust, "that the scrip will be exchanged for coin next week. And now, gentlemen," he softly said, "I'm on my way to Sargans to squeeze the money out of Rapinat's slimy carcass. Expect me back in three days."

"I'll have an escort readied, sir," Bonnay quickly said as Duras strode toward his mount tied to a munitions wagon.

"You mother me too much, Henri," Duras said, smiling. "I'll forget how to take care of myself."

"There may be Austrian troops in the vicinity, stragglers, deserters. Gontaut, bring up your troop," he ordered, and a young captain jumped to follow his command.

But Duras was already a half mile ahead before the full troop was in the saddle and only Gontaut and his sergeant were able to keep pace with the general.

He rode at a steady pace, saving his charger's strength, for the small villages between Martinsbruck and Sargans were without posting stations. His fury at Rapinat fueled his temper for the first few hours. Their clashes had been ongoing since he'd taken command of the army in January. None of the money assigned to Rapinat for the commissary and supplies was adequately documented, and the degree of corruption was so outrageous Duras's entire army could have dined on truffles and pâté since Christmas. He had incessantly complained of Rapinat to the Military Board in Paris to no avail.

The need for money and supplies was a continuous battle separate from those he fought against the Austrians and as usual it was up to him personally to see that his army was fed and paid. He'd had to take out a personal loan last year to pay his troops arrears. Damn the bureaucracy.

But as Sargans drew near, more potent images of Teo insinuated themselves into his mind. And he felt a growing exhilaration, an irresistible longing, both sensations so pleasing he smiled into the gathering shadows of twilight.

They should reach Sargans by eight or nine and on that happy thought, Duras took pity on his troopers and turned into a tavern yard. His men and the horses needed food.

Scribbling a swift note while their supper was being

prepared, he sent it ahead with one of the tavern grooms with instructions to deliver it to the countess. And when the food came, he enjoyed a hot meal for the first time in days.

Three hours later Duras and his troop rode into Sargans, weary, filthy, cold. Snow was threatening again. "Come in with me," he said to the young captain as they dismounted before the large residence Rapinat had taken over. "I need a witness. And dismiss the others; they could use some sleep."

Striding to the front door, he turned briefly to thank his men and then, pushing the door open, he stepped blood-stained, muddied, and intent into Rapinat's luxurious abode. Two servants came running at the sound of the door slamming shut, and at his curt inquiry, both pointed toward the candlelit dining room.

"Who dares disturb my meal!" Rapinat barked, the harsh repudiation carrying through the corridor into the foyer. "I gave distinct orders—"

"I'll announce myself," Duras said, ignoring the recriminations resonating down the hall, his icy tone arresting the two servants where they stood, his cold gaze more daunting than their employer's threats. "Come, Gontaut," Duras quietly said. "Let's see if we can disturb him."

The room was ablaze with lights, no expense spared on candles or the fire in the fireplace warming the room to summer temperatures. The only diner at the ladened table was the well-fed, heavyset man about to drink from his wineglass.

An expensive bordeaux slopped over the rim of the goblet as Rapinat hastily set his glass down, the widening stain crimson on the white linen. Duras in bloodied uniform and four days' growth of beard loomed in the doorway, his dark brows drawn together in a murderous scowl, his mouth set in a grim line. A shudder ran through Rapinat; a wrathful specter from hell stood on his threshold. His mouth opened and shut before he managed to find breath to speak. "General . . . what—a pleasure—"

Then he went white. Duras's pistol—held with disturbing steadiness in a gloved hand stained dark with Austrian blood—was aimed at his head.

"My men don't have food."

No matter the softness of Duras's voice, Rapinat shivered and his face blanched a shade paler. Duras's reputation as the best shot in the army was legendary. "I'm sure . . . there's some mistake. If you'll consider—"

"Don't bother," Duras growled. "I've heard all your lies before and I don't care to hear any more." He was beyond concern over political repercussions or the influential power of Rapinat's relatives; the sight of the army contractor stuffing his face while his men went without food overrode any feelings of expediency. "I'd like your head on a platter, you bastard, but I'll settle for the numbers of all your bank accounts." Only enormous self-control restrained his impulse to pull the trigger. "Every account," he brusquely clarified. "Even those in your wife's family's name. I want those funds transferred by bank drafts to the Army of Switzerland, the necessary paperwork on my desk in ten minutes." His finger shifted minutely on the trigger and Rapinat squeaked, the muffled sound of terror loud in the quiet of the room. "You'll be under arrest until the money arrives," Duras went on in a voice so cold Gontaut said afterward he thought Rapinat would expire of fear right before his eyes. "And if you ever do this to my men again, I'll skin you alive before I kill you. Do you understand?"

The large man seemed to shrink before Duras's gaze. Unable to speak, he mutely nodded his head.

"Bastard," Duras muttered through clenched teeth and he squeezed the trigger.

Rapinat screamed. The pistol ball parted the army contractor's shiny black hair precisely down the center of his head and he fainted away into his veal cutlet.

"Superb shooting, sir," Gontaut said in admiration.

"A pity I couldn't kill him but I need those bank drafts. And perhaps tomorrow," Duras said with a small smile, "I may reconsider my reckless disregard for his brother's position."

"The Directory needs you, sir." Every soldier knew only Duras could hold off the Coalition.

"Let's hope the politicians remember that when Rapinat regains his nerve and starts screaming for my dismissal. Now see that the cur empties his accounts. Lauzun will help, he understands the status of every sou this side of the Channel. Then take a guard detachment to Zurich, cash the bank drafts, and bring the money back posthaste. Although you haven't had much sleep the last few days. Should I find someone else?"

"No, sir, it would be an honor, sir," Gontaut promptly replied, beaming.

"It's time he stopped fucking with me," Duras softly said, sliding his pistol into the holster at his hip. Helping himself to a veal cutlet from the platter on the table, he suggested Gontaut eat as well. "The servants can get his face out of his supper," he said, taking a large bite of the tender meat. Selecting a second cutlet from the plate, he added with a smile, "I'll send them in as I leave. Good night, Captain. I wish you a lucrative journey."

He stopped next at headquarters, issued orders for Gontaut's escort into Zurich and asked for the newest dispatches.

The stack of messages and mail was formidable considering everything of import had been relayed south to the army at Chur.

"The latest ones, sir," the young aide, Cholet, offered, sorting through the pile. "This one just came in from Mainz." And as Duras's brows rose in surprise at the sight, Cholet handed him an official-looking document engraved with the double eagle of the Russian army. Mainz was a very long way from the Tyrol, Duras mused.

The message was brief, written in diplomatic terms, referring to Teo obliquely as the general's wife. Citing precedent and gentlemanly honor. Asking for her immediate return.

No, Duras thought, as if he alone determined the response, as though precedent and conventions of war didn't exist. Not yet, not now . . . perhaps never. Lifting his gaze to his aide, he said, "Send a tactful reply to this. Allude to the difficulties of an exchange at this time—in the midst of the campaign, etcetera. After being on Bernadotte's staff, Cholet, you know how to extrapolate on nothingness." He smiled. "Assure them of the countess's good health. Sign my name. Send it to Vienna."

"Not to Mainz, sir?"

"To Vienna," Duras softly ordered.

And then for an hour more, he scrutinized the latest reports from Bernadotte's and Jourdan's armies. Archduke Charles was moving closer each day, with Jourdan likely to bear the brunt of the attack. The tone of Jourdan's dispatches was remarkably optimistic, as if he didn't realize the extent of his danger. General Jourdan's Army of the Danube, 41,000 strong, had crossed the Rhine at Kehl on March 1 and was advancing eastward through the Black Forest, meeting no opposition.

Duras's espionage system knew Prince Schwarzenberg's corps, which formed the advance guard of the archduke's army, was approaching Stockach, only miles from the Army of the Danube's last bivouac. He dictated a hasty note to Jourdan apprising him of Schwarzenberg's position although it was unthinkable he didn't already know.

Duras issued orders for a commissary train to be victualed and sent south by morning. And then he called in his spies and questioned them on their most recent reports from the north. Two of his informants hadn't appeared at their prearranged rendezvous yesterday, a worrying circumstance although it wasn't always possible to arrive at the meeting posts as scheduled. Still . . . a warning. He left orders to have any messages coming in before morning to be delivered to him at the burgomaster's house.

7

The note Duras had sent to Teo wasn't a love note. With a stub of a pencil on a sheet of paper torn from his campaign notepad, he'd written "Have a bath ready at nine." And realizing it sounded too much like a command, added "if you don't mind." His name at least was personal. He'd signed "Andre."

But he didn't arrive at nine and Teo had finally sent Tamyr out at ten to see if he'd returned. Relieved to hear that Duras was safely back, she busied herself with seeing that food was prepared for him and his bath arranged. And she felt so gloriously happy that he was alive, she pitied the entire world for their lesser joy. She changed her gown three times and then a fourth, and when she had Tamyr take yet another gown from her wardrobe, her nursemaid dryly said, "He won't notice."

"But I want to look perfect. I want everything perfect," Teo laughingly declared, twirling about the room in giddiness. "I want him to be as happy as I, as utterly blissful. I want him to wonder how he ever lived without me," she grandly went on. "And once he's here, he'll stay and stay and stay . . ."

Wary of so recklessly tempting fate, Tamyr said, "Hush, child, or the gods will take notice of such wild rejoicing."

"*My* gods aren't so oppressive," Teo playfully declared, laughing in sheer delight, allowing herself the self-indulgent pleasure of illusion. "They love *him* too, Tam."

Her old nursemaid had experienced too much in her sixty years to trust the durability of such elation. But how could she begrudge Teo her first true taste of happiness? "I'm pleased, child, that they love you both," she graciously declared. And she wished with all her heart that the young girl she'd helped raise would indeed find a deep and lasting love.

Duras's bath turned cold as did the food but Teo waited as patiently as possible, understanding the demands of leadership, knowing Duras couldn't simply abandon all his responsibilities to come to her. She tried to read, then paced the sitting-room floor, stopping frequently at the window facing the street, hoping she'd catch a glimpse of him in the headquarters building.

She took note of the bustling activity even at the late hour, the various men, uniformed and not, arriving at the guarded door, the small cavalry troop that set out down the street, and she wondered if Duras was missing her half as much as she missed him, whether he anticipated their meeting as eagerly. And then she suddenly laughed out loud in sheer elation because he was actually here, short yards away—not fighting the Austrians or her husband, not in perilous danger, not in some cold, wet bivouac leagues distant— and sometime tonight, she'd hold him in her arms.

For the first time she truly understood the power of love

because her world was utterly transformed and the undistinguished village of Sargans with its narrow streets and modest residences was the paradise, nirvana, and Elysian fields of her dreams. She wouldn't change one puddle in the muddy road or one garish red velvet flounce in the burgomaster's parlor or a single stone of the castle looming over the town.

And he was actually *here*. Restless, impatient, she turned from the window. "Have cook make something fresh, Tamyr, and have the dishes taken from the table. How can he eat cold food? Don't frown at me like that. Cook doesn't care, she told me. Do you think Andre would like quail or fish or beef first?" she went on, her words uttered in a rush. "Men always like meat, don't they? I wish I knew his favorite foods, but I've only seen him eat a few spoonfuls of ragout, and I don't know what wines he likes or whether he likes scented or unscented soap. And his clothes. Should I lay out his clothes? Oh, Tam, help me!" she wailed. "You know *everything*."

So a fresh meal was being prepared in the burgomaster's kitchen under Tamyr's watchful eyes when Duras finally left headquarters. Standing at the window, Teo screamed with delight at the sight of him and raced from the room. She was out the front door in seconds and dashing down the steps in reckless leaps. Immune to the chill night air, unaware of the water seeping through the soles of her slippers, she ran toward him, calling his name.

At the sound of her voice he looked up and saw her, her pale gown flowing out behind her, her smile dazzling even from that distance, her arms opened wide in welcome. A jolt of pleasure struck him with such force, he stopped in the center of the street and held his breath for a moment. And then he smiled. "My darling Teo," he whispered.

Seconds later she was in his arms and he in hers and for a moment civilizations could crumble and continents be washed away and they wouldn't have noticed.

I'm home, he thought, an unprecedented sensation to a

man who'd spent most of his life in transit. "I'm home," he said into the silk of her hair.

"Yes, yes," Teo murmured, holding him tight. "Tell me you can stay."

"For a day . . . maybe two."

"Oh, blissful heaven," she exclaimed, standing on tiptoe to kiss him. "Can I have you for myself alone?"

"Between dispatches," he replied, stroking her arms. "They're being sent to your house."

"I'll help you read them or sit in a corner if you have to work. I'll be quiet."

"Don't be quiet. I like to hear your voice. Oh, Lord," he muttered, noticing the smudges he was leaving on her sleeves. "I'm ruining your gown."

"I don't care, ruin them all, as long as you're safely in my arms. Lie to me, tell me you don't have to go off to battle again."

"Never," he graciously replied, wishing for the first time in his life that there were no more wars to fight.

"We'll sit by the fire and watch our children play."

"I'd like that. I'll smoke my pipe and you'll sew," he teased.

"If I could." Her smile was delicious.

"We'll have someone else sew, then."

"Tamyr is very good."

"There, taken care of. Have you missed me?"

"Every second, every breath and heartbeat. Did you think of me?"

"Even when I shouldn't." Even when it had been dangerous to daydream. "Bonnay was my conscience."

"I must thank him for keeping you safe."

"I had every reason in the world for coming back." And he suddenly recalled Korsakov's letter. "Are you happy here?"

"Now I am."

"No misgivings?"

"Only about the name of our child," Teo facetiously replied. "Tamyr tells me I can't name it Sargans."

"You must be getting cold," he said in a different tone. He didn't wish to think of the reality of children, of names and of places they might never be. Of battles lost perhaps and lives vanished, of a future too uncertain to contemplate. "And I should get out of this uniform."

"Of course," she politely answered, frightened by the distance in his voice.

"Did you get my note?" he asked, beginning to walk toward the burgomaster's house, his intonation one of politesse, as if they were meeting over cards.

"Yes, thank you for letting me know you were safe," she answered, bewildered by his sudden volte-face.

"My apologies for its brevity. I thought afterward that it may have offended you."

"No, of course not. Did I *say* something?" she asked, her gaze perplexed.

"I'm tired, that's all," he lied. "We haven't slept since we left."

"You needn't entertain me. Bathe and eat and go to sleep."

"Not likely," he softly said, turning to smile at her, the warmth back in his eyes.

She felt as though the sun shone again on her world.

Teo helped him undress, startled by the gruesome vestiges of war, the bloodstains starkly evident on his uniform. His tunic was beyond saving, saber cuts slicing the sleeves at several points, a tear below his ribs obviously a sword thrust barely eluded.

"Martinsbruck took longer than we thought," he casually replied to her query regarding the rent garment. "The Austrians had a brigade in the city. Throw the jacket away, toss it out into the hall. Here, I'll take all these," he added, scooping up the rest of his clothes and walking to the door.

She'd apologized for the cool bathwater and offered to have more heated. "I don't care if it's warm or not," he said, stepping into the copper tub before the fire, sitting down, immediately submerging his head, coming up a moment later sleek and dripping. He bathed and shaved swiftly, grateful to wash away the taint of battle, grateful to have the beautiful woman he didn't know a week ago waiting for him on the bed.

He'd refused her offer to help him bathe, not inclined to make love in the cold water, and short minutes later, he rose from the tub. Wiping his hair briefly with a towel, he dripped water on the carpet as he moved toward the bed.

"You have too many clothes on," he softly said, his dark eyes lush with promise.

"You're absolutely beautiful," Teo murmured, her gaze on his skin gleaming wet, the symmetry and grace of his form, his powerful musculature gloriously defined in the candlelight. He had the look of one of Tamyr's northern gods, tall, virile, broad-shouldered, scarred like a warrior— healed saber cuts crisscrossing his chest, old slashes on both shoulders, remnants of wounds on his thighs and forearms, a new one seeping blood down his wrist.

Her small distraught cry drew his notice to it, and stopping before a chest of drawers in this bedroom that had recently been his, he extracted a handkerchief and looped it around his wrist. "It barely cut the skin," he said, tying a simple knot, tightening it with his teeth. He almost said, "Doesn't your husband ever get wounded?"

But he knew better than to ruin perhaps their only night together for a very long time or possibly forever, so he told himself he didn't care that she had a husband, or that the man was a beast, or that she might be carrying his child.

Although the possibility had settled firmly in his mind since her playful comments on the street—unnerving thought, disturbing, fraught with a high degree of anxiety he'd not been able to ease.

Taking note of his frown, she said, "Don't be unhappy when I'm so pleased to be with you."

He stopped just short of the bed where she sat like a young child, her legs dangling over the side, her bare feet visible beneath the soiled hem of her gown. "I'm not unhappy. How could I be with you?" he said honestly.

Her smile did much to lighten his mood; her smile, he thought, could melt the snows of winter.

"*He's* definitely not unhappy," she observed, glancing at his beautifully formed erection.

"He's been thinking about you all the way home," Duras softly said. "And you still have too many clothes on."

"Should *I* take them off or would you like to?"

"Would you mind?" His half-lidded gaze bespoke his fatigue. "I'm very near falling asleep."

"How near?" Her voice was teasing.

"Not that near," he answered with a grin, leaning over to kiss her before falling on the bed. "But I'm viewing the world through an increasing haze as though the sun were setting."

"I should hurry, then."

"Please." He was too tired to even pull a pillow under his head, four days without sleep beginning to take its toll.

She couldn't reach the buttons at the back of her dress though and when she suggested calling Tamyr, he gruffly said, "No." As she leaned against the bed, he forced his eyes to focus on the tiny covered buttons and managed to undo enough to allow her to slip the dress free. The vision of her in her filmy chemise and petticoat rather precipitously roused him to a new level of wakefulness.

When she climbed onto the bed, he moved over to give her sufficient room to sit beside him. And with her hip nudging his, she untied the ribbons at the neckline of her chemise, a feeling of content inundating her soul. She had found him somehow in all the world and she wanted nothing more than to sit beside him like this and feel his gaze on her. His hand came up a few moments later and slipped one lacy strap down her arm and a sudden answering heat flared through her body, altering the tenor of her contentment.

"While you were gone, I thought about you touching me," she murmured. "Of how you could make me feel . . ."

He'd thought of her voluptuous warmth when he was cold and tired, waiting to attack Chur and Martinsbruck, earlier on his vengeful quest for Korsakov—and always in the dark chill hours before dawn. "I thought of this," he simply said.

"I'll be your talisman," she answered, understanding.

"You are." She had been. A strange and new sensation. Then his right wrist began to throb; the saber cut was deep enough, he knew, to require stitches in the morning. And he wasn't sure he had the energy to stay awake much longer. Using his uninjured hand, he slipped the second strap over her shoulder and the sheer silk hung for a moment on her full breasts before he tugged it down over the lush swell.

She undid the small pearl buttons with trembling fingers, the proximity of his rigid arousal stimulus and incentive, her need for him pulsing between her thighs. Pulling the last button entirely off in her haste, she slipped the garment from around her waist and reached for the ties on her petticoat.

"Stand to take off your petticoat." Low, velvet authority.

"Here?"

"Here so I can see you." He indicated an area on the bed with a brush of his fingers. "Lift it over your head."

His voice was without inflection, but the undercurrent of command set her pulses racing when softly uttered words shouldn't affect her so, when she shouldn't respond to any words that sounded like fiats.

"I may not want to," she said.

"But you do." His eyes held her for a moment and then he smiled.

"Don't be so sure," she whispered, feeling the heat rise in her cheeks.

"Has seven days seemed like a long time?" he murmured, watching the flush move down the pale flesh of her throat, over the flaunting curve of her breasts. "Stand up," he whispered, brushing her taut nipple with the back of his hand. "Let's see if you're ready for me."

"I am," she said on a suffocated breath.

"Show me." His whisper caressed her senses.

He steadied her as she came to her knees, his hand on the curve of her hip. "Hold on to my hand," he offered. He stabilized her balance on the soft mattress with a hand on her ankle. "Can you lift your petticoat?" he gently queried.

She nodded, desire overwhelming all else. She pulled the ribbon loose at her waist, grasped the ruffled silk, lifted it, and he saw the pearly fluid sliding down her inner thighs. Shutting his eyes briefly, he resisted the sudden urge to pull her down and plunge inside her.

And when he looked again, she was dragging the garment over her thrusting breasts. She slipped it over her head and tossed it aside. "And now it's my turn," she said in a heated whisper. "Don't move."

Straddling his hips a moment later, she brushed her fingers across the engorged crest of his arousal, circling the smooth distended head, the pads of her fingers gliding downward after a time, lightly grasping the hard, rigid length, forcing it upright.

He didn't move, his entire nervous system expectant, roused, riveted on the lady. He watched her rise slightly on her knees, watched her delicately adjust the ridged head of his erection between the sleek tissue of her labia, felt her move slightly in a minute teasing friction, experienced a new level of lust as she lowered herself the merest fraction.

And suddenly expectation was swept away.

His hands came up, the pain of the saber cut ignored,

his long, slender fingers curved over her hips, closed so hard they left marks on her pale skin.

A small whimper broke the hush of heated breathing.

He glanced at her. Her eyes were shut, a half smile curved her luscious mouth, and fleeting concern dismissed, he pressed downward on her hips as he arched upward in a savage thrust, driving in with a seething violence.

Her scream filled the room, a high, wild, delirious cry that excited him and made him surge larger and longer, bringing him hard against her womb.

He didn't ask if he'd hurt her; he didn't care. He'd been waiting too long to be here, doing this. Feeling this.

But a second later a modicum of reality intruded, and wondering if he'd been overzealous, he murmured, "Forgive me." But he was already lifting her again, driven by urges beyond chivalry and courtesy, drawing her up for another descent. Her lashes lifted marginally and gazing down at him she uttered a deep, satisfied sound of pleasure.

"Are you all right?"

She nodded and smiled, placing her hands over his, guiding him, drawing him back inside her. "Go to sleep," she softly breathed, a lazy smile lifting her mouth, lowering herself slowly, the deliberate, leisurely friction exquisite. "I'll be quiet now."

"I'm awake."

"I can tell . . ."

Moving his hand, he pressed his thumb to the place between her legs, where her flesh rested on his, exerted a gentle pressure that quivered and curled deep inside her. "I needed this while I was gone . . . I thought of this while I was gone . . ." His voice was hushed, his eyes half shut, his thumb nuzzling her moist, dark curls. He traced a lazy circle in the sleek dampness while she whimpered to the movement of his hand and then he slipped his thumb inside her. A breath-held instant passed as wild, seething tremors collided between and around and inside them.

Fatigued beyond weariness, he felt sensations insinuate themselves into every part of him with a skewed impact, acute and pervasive, and he groaned under his breath at the jolting pleasure.

"I'm keeping you here," she whispered.

His lashes slowly raised and he gazed at her with attention. "For how long?" he murmured, lust tingeing his eyes.

"I haven't decided."

An enigmatic seductress, a slender, dark-haired Venus riding his cock—and offering paradise. "One can but hope . . ." he whispered, his smile flashing.

"Be still; I'll move."

He swelled inside her.

"No." She placed a restraining hand on his stomach.

"No?"

"Behave."

His immediate response forced her wider, stretched her, and breathless at the stunning rapture spiking through her brain, she took a moment to catch her breath. "You're not cooperating."

"I didn't know I had to. Are there rules?"

"I was thinking about some," she said with a faint smile. "Obviously—"

"I don't favor rules," he softly concluded, swiftly reversing their positions, the ease with which he'd accomplished the maneuver the result of well-honed muscles and seamless grace. "Now then," he murmured, a smile in his voice, "concerning the passive role."

Lifting her hips, she thrust upward in a slow rhythm of enticement, then lowered herself again, her sleek tissue enfolding him, releasing him, lascivious flesh on flesh. Pulling his face down, she gently bit his lip, held it between her teeth.

His hand came up. Inserting a slender brown finger between her lips, he eased her teeth open, unclenching them. Sliding his fingertips down her chin, he cupped her jaw in the curve of his hand. "I'm new to this cooperation," he whispered, his eyes heavy-lidded, his lower body moving steadily, matching her rhythm.

"I'll teach you."

"We'll teach each other."

"Perfect," she whispered.

They moved together in another kind of perfection, a silken harmony strange at first to an urbane man familiar only with sybaritic intercourse and lushly novel to a susceptible young woman still marveling at carnal passion. She trembled with longing, ablaze for him, and he felt an indelible thrill as if this were his first tryst. His rough hands stroked her tender white skin, his mouth tasted the richness of hers, bit, nibbled, savored, and she took him into her virgin heart and body, thrusting up to meet his driving rhythm, quivering beneath him. The room took on a new heat, their skin slipped together, damp, flushed, and very soon impatience replaced harmony and the rhythm of their breathing changed.

His strong legs swung forward and they both drew in a sharp intake of breath, sensation like a shock, the powerful flux and flow of his lower body moving with consummate skill, Teo's artless response eager, urgent, unconstrained.

They plunged and rocked, fevered, hot-blooded, filling, taking, devouring. He could never get deep enough, pressing home over and over, his gaze veiled, remote, only half aware of her, lost in carnal urges. She moved against him more and more urgently, letting him go only to draw him back again, each stroke making her desperate for the next. His primal antenna, subconscious, discerning, gauged her cresting arousal, waited for that first incipient orgasmic ripple. And when it came and she frantically raised her pelvis to draw him in deeper, whimpering in wild, physical craving, he stayed firmly inside her, his hands hard on her body, and profoundly submerged, he came with her in a violent, shuddering climax.

"Jesus . . ." Braced on his elbows, sweat sheened, panting, his dark curls damp, he could hardly speak.

Teo opened her eyes at the sound of his voice and then shut them again, the last remnants of ecstasy still radiating outward from her pulsing core.

She didn't notice the blood. Several drops had splashed on her shoulder before she slowly opened her eyes and glimpsed the red stain. Redolent still, she lazily took note of a crimson rivulet oozing over his collarbone. And then recognition struck her senses and she came awake with a start. "You're bleeding!"

Brought to a sluggish attention, he muttered an apology, grabbed a handful of sheet to wipe away the blood, and drawing away, he collapsed into a sprawl beside her.

The wound came into view as he lay facedown on the bed; a portion of scab had ripped away. "Don't move. I'll be right back," Teo commanded, rising from the bed.

Eyes closed, Duras mumbled an unintelligible reply, and when she returned with a washbasin of warm water and a makeshift dressing, he was already asleep.

8

She sat up all night and watched him, like a lioness guarding her last surviving cub, adjusting his pillow if he moved, tucking the blankets around him when he rolled over, protecting him from drafts and the evil of the world. Lying beside him at times, she'd watch him breathe or survey at close range the length of his dark lashes or the perfection of his nose or mouth or graceful jaw, deeply grateful for the finite detail, the collective wonder, the sum and parts and glory of the man.

Her happiness was immeasurable, boundless as the sweep of the universe. He was beside her.

Hours later when the shadows were gone from the room and the candles had all burned down, Tamyr opened the door and mimed a question about breakfast. Teo shook her head and waved her away. But the second time she opened the door, she came into the room, holding several papers in her hand, and Teo sighed.

She didn't wake him though, not until Tamyr had gone with orders to return with breakfast and bathwater. And she said to herself, "It's March fourteenth of my twenty-eighth year," when she turned to kiss him awake, wanting to remember forever their first morning together.

He came awake before her mouth touched his, his senses vigilant, and as his eyes flashed open, his gaze held a cool assessment before he remembered where he lay. Then drawing her head down, he kissed her as if he'd not seen her for a millennium.

"Bonjour," he whispered at last, smiling up at her. "Has the world survived while I slept?"

He knew, she thought. "Some messages just came for you."

He pushed himself up into a sitting position as she reached for the papers Tamyr had placed on the bed. Taking them from her a moment later, he swiftly scanned the pages, his brows coming together in a faint scowl on some, easing back into normalcy with others. Saving two of the messages, he placed them on the bedside table, tossed the others on the floor and said with a boyish grin, "We're safe for the interval."

"You're mine?"

"All yours."

"What would you like to do?"

He laughed and lay back against the pillows. "Guess and it has to do with staying in this bed."

"Just in the bed?" she teased.

His lashes lowered delicately. "In this room, then, if you're in the mood for something more adventuresome." Although adventure wasn't high on his list of priorities after having risked his life continuously the past few days and months and years; soft beds and soft flesh and the novelty of food appealed more.

"Should I lock the door?"

"Are you shy?"

"Are you not?"

He thought of the company of men with whom he'd spent the majority of his life, of the lack of privacy, the brutality and lewd amusements. "Of course I am," he lied.

They spent the morning behind locked doors, opening them only briefly for breakfast and bathwater. And when Teo said with lifted brow, "Food or a bath?", after the servants left, Duras unequivocally replied, "Food."

She fed him like a child in bed, and for the man least likely to need care, he indulged her whims because she took pleasure in it, and he kissed her between servings to indulge himself. When the worst of his hunger was assuaged, he said, "Now *you* eat." He didn't feed her because it didn't occur to him to offer; he'd been too long a general. But he did pour her chocolate and unrestrainedly offered kisses and tempted her beyond reason with his lean, muscled nudity and blatant erection.

He lay like a potentate on the pillows watching her dip her breakfast bread into the chocolate.

"How do you expect me to eat with you lying there like that?"

"I'll wait."

"I don't know if *I* can." Her gaze was drawn to his splendid arousal.

'You should eat."

"That's what I was thinking," she murmured, setting her cup down.

"I like the sound of that."

"And I like what I see." He looked breathtakingly beautiful lying against the rumpled linen, his dark head resting on the embroidered pillows. His hair was tousled on top where he'd run his fingers through it, tendrils

curled on the nape of his neck—the stylish haircut with
its Roman antecedents appropriate for a citizen-soldier
of another era. His sun-bronzed arms were spread wide
across the piled pillows, their corded muscles and the
veins that overlay them a vision of strength like the hard,
ridged power of his lean torso and his strong legs covered
with coarse, dark hair sprawled the length of the burgomaster's bed.

Men had lain like this in ladies' beds after battle, she
mused, since the dawn of time. An unmistakable heat in
their eyes, faintly challenging, distinctly libidinous as if,
duty done, they were now waiting for their reward.

And if the erection drawing her attention wasn't so impressive she might have been able to delay succumbing to
such casual assurance. But a sexual frisson fluttered through
her vagina; she unconsciously licked her bottom lip. Fully
extended, the flesh stretched taut, his erection was a shade
lighter than his brown skin. The rigid length rising from a
cloud of dark hair lay thick and arching against his stomach
to navel height, the pulsing veins in high relief, the broad,
swollen head gleaming like satin.

And all she could think of was having it deep inside her.

"I'm ready whenever you are," he said, smiling faintly.

She felt a quick new tremor and his smile broadened.
He knew, she realized, because every woman responded to
him like she did. "Are we all the same?" A small heat infused her tone.

Sitting up quickly, he said, "No . . . don't even think
it." Reaching out, he grasped her hand, tugged her closer,
the amusement gone from his face. "This is all virgin for
me—this wanting, this obsession . . . this love," he whispered at the last. Lifting her hand to his mouth, he brushed
her knuckles with his lips, his gaze direct. "Show me what
you want."

She stared at him. "Me show *you*?"

"I'm not sure," he murmured in a velvety whisper, placing her hand on his hard thigh, stroking the back of it with a fingertip, "exactly what to do."

She scrutinized him from under her lashes, gauging the equivocation in his words, a flutter of expectation warming her senses.

"I've never been with a woman before," he shyly said.

A dramatic silence vibrated in the air; his dark gaze meeting hers was chaste, angelic. A slow smile formed on Teo's mouth. "Never?"

"Never," he said, husky and low. "Although I've always wanted to."

Her glance flickered from his face to his pulsing erection. "It looks as though you want to now."

"Very much," he murmured.

She marveled at the boyish virtue in his expression, his modest tone, the deference in his pose; he was a superb actor. "Have you ever kissed a woman?" she inquired, watching the subtle play of emotion on his face.

He moved his head slightly in negation, his lashes lowered.

"Have you ever been nude like this with a woman?"

He didn't answer at first and then said, as though reluctant, "Only with my governess."

Teo's brows rose. "How old were you?"

"Fourteen." A declaration without any nuance of drama, without a modicum of hesitation.

Was it possible his answer was grounded in reality? Teo wondered, her curiosity piqued. "How old was your governess?"

He shrugged faintly. "I'm not sure. Twenty or thirty."

His reply had the ring of truth. In the eyes of an adolescent, a decade would be indistinguishable. "Did she touch you?" she asked, already knowing the answer.

He nodded.

A perverse thrill surged through her body. "I thought you said you've never been with a woman."

"I was never actually *with* her," he clarified, his ambiguity simply put.

"What was her name?"

His gaze suddenly went shuttered; she'd asked the wrong question. "I don't remember," he said in a normal tone of voice, lying back against the pillows.

"Are we still playing?" she inquired, questioning his disengagement.

"As long as you want, *ma chère,*" he murmured, his smile wicked this time, not virtuous.

"I was thinking about touching you myself."

"I'd be very grateful," he replied.

"Perhaps I should kiss you first—since you're a tyro in love. How would that be?"

Closing his eyes, he shifted upward in a fluid stirring of muscle and she gazed for a moment at the pure beauty of his face and form and didn't wonder that his governess had been unable to keep her mind on her duties.

His lips were warm and smooth when her mouth touched his and chastely closed. Balancing herself on her knees, she placed her hands on his shoulders to steady herself and felt the tension in his body.

It gave her a strange sense of power.

Exerting a mild pressure on his mouth, she forced his lips open, slid her tongue past his teeth, licked his tongue with a flickering caress. He made a sound—a soft growl in his throat that vibrated with tantalizing pulsations deep inside her.

He tasted of sweet coffee and lust, of promised pleasures, and she thought for a fleeting moment of resisting such assurance. But her libido had more potent urges, outvoting reserve, propelling her forward in a languid swaying dip that brought her plump breasts in direct contact with his chest.

When his hands came up to softly fondle her breasts, she squirmed under the shimmering sensations, and a spontaneous pulsation flowed through her vulva. Her soft moan slipped into his mouth and he recognized the sound, knew his role of tyro was suspended.

Slipping his fingers around her nipples, he lightly squeezed, delicately massaged the crests to a taut hardness, flicked and rubbed them with a deft expertise that spiraled a flurry of heat downward, that opened and moistened her and caused her breathing to become an audible sound in the stillness. Sliding his mouth downward, he nuzzled her throat, told her what he was going to do to her in a husky deep whisper—the words explicit, arousing, having to do with submission and need. He bit the soft flesh behind her ear, marking her, holding her like a male animal about to mount a female—primal, possessive.

"I should say no." She shivered under his touch, knowing he knew why she shivered, wondering if a female had ever resisted him.

"But you can't." He slid a finger delicately over her clitoris and her back arched against the staggering sensation. Offering neither platitudes nor apologies, he stroked her breasts and clitoris, her thighs and bottom, between her thighs and deep inside her sweet, scented passage until she was almost fainting for him.

And then abruptly he did what he'd come here to do. He tumbled her back onto the bed and thrust himself into her hard, hard, terrifyingly intent, his powerful rhythm propelling hers, her panting cries music to his ears, driving him, goading him, his gyrations raw, harsh, different from the finesse he'd perfected in all the boudoirs of his past. But his obsession was different too, without explanation or equivalent. And he pounded into her like a madman, demented, forcing her, taking her.

She began coming, crying out in a frenzy he recognized

because her screams echoed the silent ones inside his head and he responded to her climax with a violent desperation as if she couldn't go on without him. And he met her in a long, long coming that tore the breath from his lungs and jolted his body and left him gasping for air.

The sound of marching was heard from the street outside—an omen, a warning, reality intruding into the replete silence.

He cradled her head and licked the tears from her face with light touches of his tongue and offered his love between rough, raucous breaths, his eyes still wild, heated. Then he whispered, "Don't move," and extricating himself from her embrace and the bed, he walked from window to window pulling the heavy velvet drapes closed, shutting out the tread of marching feet. He lit two candelabra to illuminate the room before returning to the bed, before lying down beside her and drawing her back into his arms. "I don't want to hear that," he muttered. He wanted sanctuary and oblivion; he wanted forgetfulness.

His mouth covered hers and she felt his penis rise between them in a slow surging undulation, standing hard again, wanting her. Helpless against the unspeakable pleasure washing over her, she wondered if she'd ever have enough of him, if the molten heat inside her would eventually melt her away, vaporize her. "Hurry, hurry," she whispered, opening her thighs, clutching at him, "I want to come."

"There," he breathed, his eyes full of dark flame, a thrilling urgency flaring through his body as he entered her. "We're here," he added, feeling her engulf him, plunging deep inside her, his brain beginning to lift away, the spreading brilliance swelling, swelling, his ears attuned to her sweet, defenseless whimpers.

It was a soft, soft coming that time—warm and slow and pure. And he held her on his lap afterward and said, "That was nice."

Teo laughed and happily rubbed her cheek against his. "I think I'll keep you."

"Was I on trial?" he impudently inquired.

"And if you were?" Cheeky, unabashed.

"I would have added to my repertoire."

"Things you learned from your governess?"

He didn't reply.

"Where is she now?"

Again, she didn't think he was going to answer but then he gruffly said, "I'm not sure."

He knew; she could tell by his tone. "I don't believe you."

He pondered a moment, weighing courtesy against his reluctance. "She returned to France," he simply said.

"And?"

"And I don't want to talk about it."

"What if I insist?"

"Why would you?"

"Out of flagrant jealousy."

"There's nothing to be jealous of."

"You cared for her." If he didn't there would be no need to protect her so.

"I don't know what I felt," he lied, remembering how he waited for Camille to come to him each night, how he adored her.

"What did she look like?"

"How can it matter?"

"I want to know because your voice changes when you talk of her," she quietly said.

He lifted her from his lap. "I don't ask you about your past."

"Ask me if you like."

"I don't want to," he said, rising from the bed, crossing the room to an armoire set against the wall. She watched him pull a silk dressing gown from inside and slip it on, reminding herself a sensible woman would let the subject drop.

"Tell me her name."

"Jesus," he muttered, glaring at her, reaching for a bottle. "Do you want some?" he asked, wrenching the cork free.

She shook her head.

Shrugging, he poured a glass full of cognac and drank half of it before sitting down across the room.

"Are we having a fight?"

"No."

"Are you angry?"

"No."

"Do you love me?"

He hesitated the merest fraction. "Yes," he said with a smile.

"That's a relief," Teo murmured, stretching languidly. "I thought I might have to apologize profusely," she said, rolling over into a provocative Fragonard pose.

"I saw the original Mademoiselle O'Brien," Duras noted, a half smile gracing his fine mouth. "You're too slender."

"Was she fat?" Teo sat up, her gaze direct.

"Pleasingly plump."

"Do you know every woman of note?"

"Hardly."

"How many countries have you traveled in?" she asked, rising from the bed.

He laughed at her benign interpretation of his travel itineraries, filled as they were with warfare of one kind or another. "Too many," he declared, watching her approach.

"Did you travel with your governess?"

She was standing before him so he had to look up, a faint frown drawing his brows together. "I traveled with her for two years," he curtly said. "My family traveled with her—my sister, my father and mother, myself, from Gibraltar to Constantinople, from Alexandria to Sicily and every port between. Do you feel better now?"

"And you loved her."

"I suppose I did."

"Where is she?"

He sighed, every adolescent yearning, every impossible dream painfully recalled. "In Antibes. She married a judge."

"She left you to marry a judge?"

She married a judge after he left her. "Yes," he said.

"And you missed her."

"I joined the army."

"And you missed her."

"Yes."

"How romantic," Teo gently murmured.

Lifting his glass to his mouth, he tipped the remaining cognac down his throat, thinking of the bluntly unromantic consequences of his youthful affair. Camille had become pregnant; his father had refused to let him marry her and she'd been set ashore at Marseilles weeping and alone. The fortune his father had settled on her had bought her a husband of note who was willing to look the other way when a child was born months premature. "And now this conversation is over," he brusquely said.

"Thank you for telling me."

He dipped his head in brief acknowledgment and reached for the cognac. But it took several more drinks before the old memories were safely locked away again, before Teo coaxed a smile from him.

She opened the drapes and windows after a time when the troops had all passed by and a golden light flooded the room. The spring air brought with it a clean, clear sense of renewal as if the world were all washed and fresh. And Camille receded from his consciousness; even Jourdan's worrying plight yielded to more pleasant *carpe diem* sensations.

They sat together before the open windows, warmed by

the sun, holding each other, gently kissing, speaking of deliberately noncontentious subjects. And they made love before long because carnal desire, unimpeded by the past or future, burned unsated inside them and neither could forget how desperately impermanent their refuge. How few hours remained to them.

Too soon, the world intervened as they knew it would when Cholet brought an urgent message from Jourdan. Apologizing, the pressure of circumstances already evident in his voice, Duras tossed on a dressing gown and went downstairs to meet with his aide. Teo quickly followed, tying her robe sash as she descended the stairs.

He didn't ask her to leave when she appeared in the doorway of the dining room, but motioned her to a chair. Intent on the map Cholet had brought, its corners already tacked to the table, Duras leaned over one section, marking it heavily with red ink.

He was dictating to Cholet as he drew arrows and crosshatches, tracing the march and dispositions of his columns. "Have Bonnay leave a small garrison in Martinsbruck and bring the army back. We need Lecourbe at Schwyz to guard the passes from Italy. Bonnay should be able to bring up more than half our men in"—he shot a glance at Cholet who was writing as fast as he could—"eighteen hours at rapid speed. Unfortunately, we won't have the artillery for two days. The commissary train has to be recalled too. Send off riders to Bonnay, Lecourbe, the commissary wagons, and Jourdan of course. Damn him! I knew this was going to happen."

Jourdan had encountered Prince Schwarzenberg's corps and suddenly realized they formed the advance guard of the archduke's army. He'd sent a pressing message to Duras asking him to threaten the archduke's flank by attacking Bregenz at the east end of Lake Constance.

"I told him a month ago my reports had the archduke's

army on collision course with him. *Merde,*" Duras growled. "And the army's in the Tyrol. To deal with this potential disaster, I'll need a temporary office set up here," he briskly went on. "Send over the maps, Lauzun, and some clerks. It's fine," Duras added, responding to Cholet's look of surprise when he first noticed Teo in the corner of the room. "It's fine," he softly repeated, the nuance of authority crystal clear.

"Yes, sir," his aide quickly replied, gathering up his papers.

"Have our cook brought over too," Duras instructed. "We'll set up some kind of a field kitchen downstairs to feed the staff. And I'll need a surgeon for this wrist," he casually added, his makeshift bandage soaked with blood. "See that the riders are on their way in ten minutes. That's critical. Understood?"

"Yes, sir," the young subaltern replied, and with a precision salute he left.

"A new graduate of Fontainebleau," Duras said, amusement in his eyes. "I was never that punctilious but then the enlisted men in the Royal Army were never expected to be that fine and corsairs lead a rather undisciplined life."

"Yet you win all the campaigns." His reputation was known throughout Europe, as was the rumor he'd once been a corsair.

"I like to win. My father subscribed to the same credo."

"*My* father thought he could win against the mighty Russian empire."

"And he couldn't."

She shook her head. "He kept a regiment at bay for six months, though."

Duras's gaze sharpened. "Where?"

"On a small peninsula near the river Ob. He and my mother and a handful of warriors."

"At Obdorsk? That was your father? The Russians brought up cannon, didn't they?"

"They dragged cannon over five hundred miles of bog and tundra. It took them six months and the lives of hundreds of convicts but human life doesn't count for much in Russia. When my father wouldn't surrender, they destroyed his stronghold, him and my mother and all of his men. I was eight."

"I'm sorry." Duras had come to sit by her as she'd related her tale and he took her hands in his now and, lifting them to his mouth, kissed them. "I won't let them destroy us," he said, placing her hands in her lap, covering them with his.

"Tamyr tells me my father said as much to my mother."

"I don't know the details of your parents' death but I can protect you . . . us. Don't ever think I can't."

"Even against Korsakov . . . and Russia?"

"My father was a mercenary, a corsair who fought for whoever would pay him best. He died of old age on a small island in the Mediterranean. I intend to do the same. With you."

"Really?" she said, tears filling her eyes.

"Really," he quietly answered, gathering her in his arms. Lifting her onto his lap, he held her close, conscious of the magnitude of what he'd promised, utterly sure nonetheless. It was a revelation of sorts for a man who until now had never promised his life to anyone.

The sound of boots on the porch and male voices signaled the end of their solitude. "May I stay if I don't get in the way?" Teo asked. "Our time is so short."

"You can sit on my lap for all I care, but only if you put on something less revealing than this robe."

"I won't be so daring as to sit on your lap, but thank you."

"You needn't thank me. It's a thoroughly selfish move."
He understood as well how few hours were left.

Within minutes the downstairs rooms were transformed into makeshift offices, and after Duras and Teo had
both changed into more respectable attire, Duras held reign
over the plans for mounting a new offensive.

The surgeon worked as the plans were discussed, Duras's
shirtsleeve rolled up, his wrist balanced on the surgeon's
knee. He seemed not to notice the pain, other than to once
say, "Have a care, Georges, it's my sword arm."

Which caused additional sweat to appear on the young
doctor's brow.

Duras called for a cognac when the stitching was done
though and drank it in one gulp. Then he carefully rolled
down his sleeve and, looking up at the men around the
table, said, "Now how the hell are we going to get the cavalry through that swamp?"

Duras was expected to set up an advance on a fifteen-
mile front from Feldkirch to the mouth of the upper Rhine.
The marshy valley was treacherous, difficult terrain, the
archduke strongly entrenched and waiting for them on the
other side. The earliest he could have his men in place
would be three days. Would Jourdan be able to hold out
that long?

No one slept that night, and while Duras didn't seat
Teo on his lap, he held her hand during the war council
that lasted till dawn. Seated beside him at the dining
table, she listened while the officers argued strategy and
logistics. Duras politely listened to his subordinates, but
the bulk of his general staff were still in the Tyrol and ultimately, with or without his general staff, he made the
final determinations for the campaign. As the sun began
to rise, duties were delegated to the various officers, the
clerks were set to work writing the numerous dispatches
required to coordinate four columns marching north, and
Duras took his leave with a courteous bow to his staff.

"I'm available for any questions or comments at any time," he politely said. "Cholet will come for me."

"Hearts and flowers, not his usual style," Major Vigée remarked with raised eyebrows after Duras and Teo left the room. "The lady must be an original in bed."

A thought shared by most in the room. Duras's extraordinary behavior had astonished all his staff.

"I would have thought it damned hard to outdo Claudine," another man declared with a smirk.

"I resent that," young Furet hotly declared. "Madame Duras is a woman of refinement."

"Definitely that," another officer retorted. "The most refined in carnal artistry."

"I won't hear such slander!" Furet protested. "You revile the wrong lady. Claudine is a beautiful woman ignored by her husband."

"Not, however, by all the other males in Paris," Cholet plainly said. "She toyed with you, Furet, and continues to for her own gain."

"Sorry, lad" Vigée said, offering Furet a consoling pat on the shoulder. "Cholet's right. Ask anyone."

"Then why hasn't he divorced her?" Furet indignantly inquired.

"Perhaps because her uncle is Talleyrand," Cholet replied.

"And she's Barras's protégée."

"Or perhaps he hasn't had time," Vigée said, "considering he's been keeping the English and Austrians from marching down the Champs Élysées the last few years."

"Madame Duras's reputation aside, gentlemen," Cholet interjected, not interested in continuing the debate, "in terms of the Countess Korsakova, may I make a suggestion? Regardless of the state of the general's marriage, he is currently enamored with the countess. So unless any of you have extremely pressing business, I'd suggest we not dis-

turb them until Bonnay returns with the army from Chur.
You all have your orders. I'm sure you can manage."

"But if we *have* a question?"

"Naturally if it's important we'll interrupt him. If it
isn't, either Lauzun or I will help you. Agreed?"

And with the exception of Furet, who only resentfully
nodded, all agreed.

9

Duras knew they had that day and night together at most. And while he didn't say as much to Teo, she understood he would soon have to leave.

"It's bad, isn't it?" she quietly said as he locked the bedroom door behind him.

She stood utterly still a few feet away, her face very pale, her eyes huge with sadness.

He shrugged, said, "Maybe not," and held out his hand. When she touched it and he pulled her into his arms, he felt whole again, and he wondered what twist of fate had brought them together from such distant parts. And how was it that he found himself desperately in love with a woman he'd met not two weeks ago.

"You shouldn't have to go," Teo whispered against his chest. "How can you be savior to everyone?"

"I have to try at least. You know that," he murmured, not sure himself there was much hope. Jourdan had blundered into the full strength of the archduke's army.

"Perhaps the battle will be over by the time you can bring up your army."

"We don't know," he neutrally replied, the extent of the problem moot at this point. The real question was where France should set up its next line of defense. And while he'd not suggested anything so negative in the war council, he was already making contingency plans. "We won't know until we reach Bregenz or until Jourdan sends updates. I'd like to take you to Nice sometime," he said, not wishing to talk of war in the time remaining to them. "I have a villa there."

"Take me now." Moving back a half step, she held him at arm's length. "Say yes," she whispered.

"I wish I could."

"Let Bernadotte go to Jourdan's aid."

"I imagine he will." Although with Bernadotte one never knew. He rarely risked his army unless he could garner political advantage. And trying to save Jourdan had all the earmarks of a disaster.

Tears rose in Teo's eyes. "What will I do when you leave?"

"Write me every day." He laced his fingers through hers.

"Take me with you."

He sighed. "No." And drew her toward the bed.

"May I argue?"

He smiled. "No." Grasping her around the waist, he lifted her onto the bed.

"May I threaten you?"

Pulling off her slippers, he cast her a glance from under his lashes, amusement in his eyes. "You could try."

"May I bribe you?"

His smile was wicked this time. "Gladly." He began unbuttoning his shirt.

"I *could* have been thinking of money."

"You don't have enough." He was a wealthy man after fighting the Republic's wars for years; victorious generals were well rewarded.

"Some other bribe, then," she murmured.

He leaned over to brush a kiss down her nose. "Something more personal," he murmured back, sliding his shirt off.

"Something I made?"

He shook his head, a half smile gracing his mouth, his shirt dropping to the carpet.

"Something carnal?"

He paused in mock drama and cocked his head. "Perhaps I could be tempted."

She threw a pillow at him. "Libertine."

He caught it easily. "Only with you."

"You lie. All the women and all the stories—we hear them in Petersburg too," she lightly teased.

"I've never had the time to be a libertine." While the women had always been there, he'd never pursued them. "Although I don't profess to be a monk," he honestly said.

"Lucky for me."

"While you have a natural talent, *mon ange*," he pleasantly said, sitting beside her. "Would you help me with these boots?" His wrist was throbbing painfully.

"Lie down," Teo suggested, "and I'll gladly play valet. You might wish to consider bringing me with you," she flirtatiously added, "and I could help you with your boots every—" His glance arrested her appeal. "On the other hand," she went on brightly, "we could just make love until you go and not think about the war or the danger or having to leave each other?"

Duras's smile was grateful. "My thought exactly."

"I love making love to you."

"Thankfully," he drawled.

"Is that terribly unrefined?"

"You needn't be refined for me, darling. My days in society are rare."

"How long have you been soldiering?" she asked, tugging off his boot.

"Since I was sixteen. My father was able to place me in a regiment near Nice so I could go to sea with him on my leaves."

She looked up at him. "You sail?"

"I've a yacht moored in Nice."

"Does your wife like to sail?" She couldn't help herself; she had to know. Does she pull your boots off too? she wondered, sliding the other boot free.

"Claudine's never been to Nice. Is that better?" He'd heard the envy in her voice.

"I'm glad," Teo simply said.

"I'm more glad, believe me."

Reassured by his caustic relief, she hiked up her skirt, and sat cross-legged on the bed beside him. "Why did you marry her? Surely you weren't coerced as I was."

"When I was involved in politics for a time, I met Claudine at Barras's home. It seemed as though we were both interested in the future of revolutionary France. She, it turns out, simply saw the advantage of being married to me."

"Yet you haven't divorced."[7]

"I left for the Italian campaign a week after our marriage and didn't come home for almost a year.[8] By then I'd heard all the stories about Claudine's conduct in my absence. She told me I was provincial to expect fidelity and perhaps I was. The style of our marriage isn't so unusual. You've seen the same at court in Russia, I'm sure."

"Oh, yes. Emperor Paul sets the tone and he's beyond anyone's conception of conventional."

"*Depraved,* I think, is the word more commonly used."
He didn't ask about her marriage, although the word *depraved* brought it instantly to mind. He didn't actually care to know. "Are we finished with the litany of my life?" Duras lazily inquired. "The past matters little to me." As a man of war he lived for the moment; there was no certainty beyond that.

"I'd like to know everything about you."

"Why?"

Because I may never have another chance to ask, she thought; because she wished to know more about him than a few brief anecdotes. But she knew better than to press him.

They laughed instead and played teasing games and made love and lay in each other's arms in a bed that wasn't theirs in another man's house on the eve of a terrible battle. And pretended they had a future together.

In the hours before dawn she woke with a start, his warmth missing from her side, and frantic, she called his name.

"I'm here." His voice reassured her, his tone calm. "I couldn't sleep."

And she saw him sprawled in a chair near the fire, the half-light of the dying fire illuminating his nude form.

"Would you like some cognac?" His bandaged wrist rested on the chair arm; he lifted the tumbler of liquor he held in his other hand. "Doctor's orders," he murmured, his smile flashing white.

Pulling the blanket from the bed, she threw it over her shoulders and padded across the room.

"Sit with me," he said, putting his glass aside, offering her his hand. And carefully wrapping the blanket around her, he settled her in his lap, her head on his shoulder.

"Your wrist was hurting?" She gently touched his bandaged arm.

"A little. And Bonnay should be back soon."

"How soon?" She couldn't keep the fear from her voice. His arm tightened around her. "Anytime now. He'll ride ahead with the cavalry units."

"I don't think I can be brave." Her voice trembled. "Forgive me. I don't want you to go."

"I don't have a choice. Jourdan's going to lose his army if I don't arrive in time."

"Please, please, Andre, take me with you. I beg of you." She sat up so she could confront him directly. "I won't get in your way, I promise, and—"

"Yes."

"I'll not speak until spoken to, I'll take care of your charger and see that you have food. I won't be any trouble, no matter what happens, not even— *Yes?* You said *yes?*"

He didn't speak for a moment, the degree of anarchy in his brain requiring mastery. "If you agree to the restrictions," he finally said, his gaze clearly troubled.

"Of course," she instantly agreed, the entire world being offered her. "Anything. Anything at all."

"You won't be allowed in the battle zone," he said, his voice so clipped she feared he'd change his mind. "I'll see that you're safely quartered before we move up. But you can accompany us until then. I hope you can ride astride."

"Yes, yes, of course," she assured him, ready to promise anything.

"And expect ribald comments directed at you. I can't divert them all, I won't always be there."

"I won't take offense."

"And I warn you, I'm not sure how much time I'll have with you even if you're with me."

"I understand." She spoke calmly even though exultation filled her soul.

"I found I couldn't leave you," he said so quietly she had to strain to hear him. "I've been awake for a long time trying to persuade myself that I could."

"I'm very grateful," she whispered, not daring to touch him in his present mood.

"There may be repercussions," he gruffly murmured. "We have orders not to allow women with the army. That's not to say those orders are obeyed. But be prepared for disgruntled comments from those officers who've left their mistresses behind."

"Am I your mistress?" Such an impermanent word.

"No, you're the love of my life," he said very, very softly and then his smile appeared, full of wicked charm. "If you were my mistress, I'd leave you behind."

"I'm glad," she said, returning his smile.

He quirked an inquiring brow.

"You fell in love," she clarified.

"Are you now?" he quietly murmured.

"You shan't get rid of me, I warn you." It was a light-hearted threat.

"No fear of that, darling."

"I'll make you happy," she said, her gaze, like her words, clear and direct.

"You have already."

When the commotion of Bonnay's arrival reverberated upstairs, Duras said, "The restrictions begin now, darling, the campaign's *en train*." And he went down alone to speak to his chief of staff.

After they'd exchanged greetings and briefly shared their apprehensions over Jourdan's ability to meet the archduke's army, Duras said with male brevity, "Teo's upstairs." Bonnay's nod was acknowledgment and understanding, and then they set about organizing the rescue effort: assigning companies and commanders; setting the schedule of march;

trying to foresee the course of events. And at last when all the details had been satisfactorily arranged, Duras said, "Teo will be coming with me."

"You've lost your mind, of course," Bonnay calmly replied.

"Probably."

"Is this open to discussion?"

"No."

"You know the new orders concerning women are more stringent."

"I'm aware of all the arguments, Henri. I tried to talk myself out of this for the better part of the night."

"She could be in enormous danger."

"She'll be well behind the lines."

"Cholet tells me Korsakov asked for her return."

"She doesn't want to go."

"*You* don't want her to go."

"That too."

Bonnay smiled. "Now Amalie will want to come with me on campaign. You're going to make this very difficult for us all."

"I trust you can handle your wife, Bonnay," Duras sportively answered.

"I can't handle her at all, but hopefully our four children will prove a deterrent. You'll need a guard for the countess," he added.

"You heard Korsakov's in Mainz."

"Cholet mentioned that. Will his corps supplement the British in Holland or the archduke's army?"

"I'd say the archduke's. I want Vigée's men for Teo's guard," Duras flatly said. "They have less scruples."

"I'll make it clear any Russians sighted are to be killed."

"I'll speak to Vigée myself, but you brief him as well. I don't want her in danger at any time."

"Understood."

"Now then," Duras murmured, inhaling deeply, "the race to save Jourdan is on. Can the advance troops be ready to march by nightfall?"

"With luck, yes."

10

They marched through the night, a rider from Jourdan intercepting them shortly after midnight with an urgent appeal for aid.

In two days of continuous battle, with all of the French units badly outnumbered, Jourdan had been trying to hold back the Austrian offensive at Ostrach, sending reinforcements up to stem the persistent Austrian advance. When one of the French brigades had been cut off and surrounded, a division had pushed through to their rescue. As they covered the brigade's retreat, the withdrawal in turn exposed the flank of the French troops north of Ostrach. To avoid encirclement the northern units joined the general withdrawal. Jourdan's army was pulling back all along the front.

Although Jourdan's forces had inflicted over twenty-nine hundred casualties on the Austrians, they'd lost twenty-five hundred of their own men. And had bitterly discovered that the archduke's army, far from being scattered in small detachments as thought, was advancing in a single, strong offensive.

Responding immediately to Jourdan's appeal, Duras informed him their march should bring them to Bregenz by dawn. At which point he would immediately attack.

Jourdan was in the process of stabilizing his line west of Pfullendorff with Stockach on the right and Emmingen on the left. On receiving Duras's message, he made plans to attack again and issued orders for his army to move forward. Jourdan would personally direct the left flank.

At the gates of a monastery several miles west of Bregenz, Teo was taking her leave of Duras. Sitting their mounts side by side, they were surrounded by staff and guardsmen, the army passing by on the road beside the gates, a sense of urgency in their forced pace through the night. "You're under Major Vigée's command," Duras quietly said, his tone polite, neutral, privacy impossible. "Please heed his orders."

"Yes, of course." She opened her mouth to speak and then reconsidered with the focus of so many eyes on them.

"If I can't personally return for you, one of my staff will bring orders. Don't stray beyond the confines of the buildings." He reached out and touched her gloved hand briefly. *"Au revoir,"* he murmured, his gaze holding hers for a moment.

"Godspeed," she whispered.

Then turning to Bonnay on his right, he crisply asked, "What word do we have of the artillery?" Lightly touching his spurs to his charger's flanks, he was already cantering off as Bonnay replied.

Approaching her, Major Vigée pleasantly said, "The monastery should be comfortable, Countess." And the most defensible in the village although he refrained from saying so. "One of my men will take your mount." He held out his hand.

Teo was dressed in the guise of a cavalry officer, a common pretense for officers' companions on campaign.[9] Throwing her leg over her saddle pommel, she took his hand and slid from the saddle.

A linden-lined path led from the gate to the main entrance, the tree limbs spidery black against the starry sky, two lanterns on the entrance doors shining in the distance. "Let me show you to your rooms," Vigée suggested, offering her his arm. "The general thought you'd enjoy the library during your stay," he went on, keeping pace with her shorter stride. "The monks pride themselves on their collection of hunting lore. I understand you hunt."

"My tribe hunts for sustenance," Teo replied. "My grandfather taught me how to shoot at a young age. Do you hunt, Major?"

"I was raised in Paris so my hunting has been confined to Austrians," he replied with a grin. "No offense, Countess."

"None taken, Major. My alliances are defined within a very small area of Siberia."

"Will you be staying in Switzerland, then?"

She couldn't decide whether he was impertinent or gauche and while she was hesitating, Vigée quickly added, "The general seems taken with you, ma'am, and we all wish him the best, that's all."

"I do as well," she said. "And I hope very much that I can stay."

"We're here to see that the Cossacks don't come for you, so you needn't fear."

"The Cossacks?" Those escorting her from Petersburg were in detention at Zurich.

"Your husband's men, Countess." And at the sudden horror in her eyes, he realized Duras hadn't told her. "You didn't know," he murmured in self-reproach. "Forgive my blunder, Andre didn't make it clear—"

"Where is my husband?"

He glanced around quickly, as though he hoped to be rescued from his dilemma, but the two monks coming out to greet them were still too distant. "I shouldn't have said anything," he mumbled.

"I'd appreciate knowing what sort of danger I face," Teo said, forcing herself to remain calm.

"We'll take care of you. You needn't worry."

"Is Korsakov with the archduke?"

"I don't honestly know."

"Do you *think* he's with the archduke?" She found her heart beating furiously, the impulse to flee overwhelming.

"I don't know." His gaze held hers for a moment. "I really don't."

"But Duras thinks he is or he wouldn't have told you to guard me from the Cossacks. How far is Bregenz?"

"Don't become alarmed," Vigée soothed, her agitation visible. "The archduke is more likely at Stockach."

"Not at Bregenz." Relief flooded through her and she wondered, now that she was removed from Korsakov's suzerainty, how she'd survived in the past. Like a caged animal set free, she felt terror strike in her soul at the prospect of a return to her prison.

"No one will harm you, Countess, while you're under my guard. My word as an officer."

"Thank you, Major," Teo said, her voice a mere whisper, her face pale. "I find the thought of going back to Petersburg extremely unwelcome."

"Duras wants you safe, ma'am, and his orders will be followed."

"Thank you," Teo gratefully murmured. "Thank you very much."

And once the monks had welcomed her to their order and she was shown to her rooms, a more coolheaded counsel overcame her mindless fear. Vigée's guard was strong—sixty men—the monastery itself had the look of a medieval stronghold, and her rooms were situated in what appeared to be an original keep.

If one could feel safe anywhere with Korsakov alive in the world, it would be in this well-defended sanctuary.

But she didn't sleep well, plagued by nightmares and brutal memories, frightened by shadows on the walls, waking with a start at sounds from the outside, seeing Korsakov's face like a ghoulish phantasm in the moon outside her window.

After several restless hours, she gave up any further attempt to sleep and found a seat by the fire, hoping the warm flames and dancing light would help keep her demons at bay. She needed Tamyr's comfort now but her maidservant had been left behind in Sargans. Even more she needed Duras, but he was beyond even her wishes, his life in the hands of the gods.

During the night, Duras with six thousand men had crossed the marsh protecting Bregenz and now faced the strongly entrenched Austrian positions. His artillery was still thirty miles west, making wretched progress through the wetlands, but most of his cavalry had managed to navigate across narrow tracks through the swamp and they waited in readiness for his order to charge. He had little time to contemplate the possibilities; in any event there were few possibilities beyond a deadly frontal attack. And while Duras silently cursed Jourdan for his incompetence, for not following the first rule of warfare—pick the time and place of battle—he directed the disposition of his columns.

As the pale light grew, the Austrian artillery opened up on their exposed position and Duras gave the order to attack. The assault moved over ground completely without cover, the sound of their drums beating the attack rising into a cloudless morning sky, the way before them a killing field. The advance guard began to falter under the heavy bombardment, then gave way. To stem the tide, Duras rode along the front lines, encouraging his men, and the first wave reached the base of the escarpment. The Austrians ordered up two brigades and gradually, after a protracted struggle, the French were forced back down the slope.

Duras re-formed his infantry and under the thunder of Austrian guns they advanced again, while the Austrian cavalry tried to turn the French flanks on the slope. If they could break through there, they could roll up the whole French line. It was a desperate moment for Duras's men. At first they yielded ground and then the second French infantry column charged the Austrian cavalry, followed by Duras's horse that fought its way through the mud and water to face the Austrian cavalry. Pressed by the fierce charge, the Austrians retired. But Duras's army gained little ground under the intense Austrian fire.

Calling up his third column, Duras again ordered the charge only to be met by fresh Austrian troops pouring down from the fortifications. As the French were forced back yard by yard, the last reserves were called up and those reinforcements pressed the assault. A score of men were sacrificed for every foot of ground gained on either side, but at last the Austrians withdrew behind the entrenchments.

Duras now tried to storm the walls, but a severe raking fire from the bastions and the neighboring heights seriously thinned his ranks. He then tried to gain ground to the left of the entrenchments but found himself in a murderous crossfire. Re-forming his depleted ranks, Duras directed himself even farther to the left, but having struggled at great cost almost to the crest of the entrenchment, Austrian troops rushed out to take them in the flank. They had to fall back again in great disorder.

By eleven that morning, fresh reinforcements poured into the Austrian camp and the renewed French assault was a repetition of what had happened before. The carnage was dreadful. Six times they went forward only to be cut down by a rain of fire; each time they were forced back and each time the depleted ranks re-formed. By noon, after five hours of stiff fighting, the French were repulsed with heavy losses, leaving behind fifteen hundred dead and three hundred prisoners.

Fortunately the Austrians were as exhausted as Duras's men and hadn't the strength to pursue his withdrawal. Gathering up his weary troops, he fell back to Constance where he first heard of Jourdan's rout at Stockach. The archduke had struck hard at Jourdan's army, and after suffering five thousand casualties, Jourdan was driven back behind the Rhine.

"Find Vigée," Duras instantly ordered, fear tightening his belly. With Jourdan's rout, the Austrians would be rapidly pushing west; Teo could be overtaken.

As Bonnay called for troopers to go out and search for the major, Duras stood at the window of the mayor's office surveying the tumult and chaos below him. The square at Constance was crowded with wagons and carts filled with the wounded, bands of soldiers resting where they could, the tangle of bodies and conveyances the remnants of his army.

Now that Jourdan was finished, they'd have to withdraw even farther in order to protect their western front and hold it against the archduke's victorious army. The numerical advantage had always been on the archduke's side; everyone had known that from the beginning. Their lesser strength necessitated caution in picking one's battles, knowing when to advance and when to hold. A pity Jourdan was so stupid.

Duras's face was haggard, his right arm in a bloody sling, his face, hair, and uniform black with gunpowder. Cholet was busy at a small table near the door, transcribing a report to be sent to Paris. "Do you want me to mention the Russians?" he asked. Duras had been uncertain earlier whether he wished to send the information on, since the few

Cossacks sighted at Bregenz could possibly have been some Austrian mounted troop.

"No, don't. Keep the message simple. We're pulling back. We'll let them know our position later. By the time they receive the information it won't matter." His voice was raspy, his good shoulder wearily braced against the window jamb, his exhaustion stark. No one had slept for two days nor would they anytime soon with the archduke's army on their heels.

"We'll stay here only long enough to care for the wounded and see that the men are fed," Duras went on. "I want to be west of Constance by nightfall. Set up a temporary field hospital near the lake for those wounded who won't wait until evening and call a staff meeting immediately. With Jourdan finished, we stand alone against the archduke. We'll fall back behind the Thur River and from there to positions covering Zurich. If anyone disagrees they can express their opinion in fifteen minutes. And dammit, find Vigée. I want to make sure Teo's all right."

He didn't know where to begin to find her in the turmoil of the retreat, the scene below indicative of most of the city and surrounding countryside. Four thousand of his men needed provisions and care and he needed to see that Teo was unharmed. He stood by the window, watching for Bonnay's return, hoping to see a familiar face or figure in the crowd.

He fell asleep for a few minutes leaning against the window, and when Bonnay rushed into the room shortly after, the familiar sound of his voice stirred him awake.

"You found her?" He was instantly alert, facing Bonnay.

"One of the troopers found Vigée."

"What the hell does that mean?" Duras growled, an uneasy feeling gripping his senses.

"She's fine," he explained, "but Vigée misplaced her at the temporary hospital that's been set up in the church. She's helping the wounded and apparently walked off into some other room. I left instructions for Vigée to bring her here."

"Where's the church?"

"Around the corner near—"

"Show me."

It was too dangerous in the milling disorder of the retreat to have Teo alone anywhere, church or not, hospital or not. "What the hell's wrong with Vigée?" Duras demanded, striding from the room so swiftly, Bonnay half ran to keep up.

"She just slipped away, sir. He said one minute she was there and the next . . ."

A muscle along Duras's jaw twitched, his displeasure obvious. But he offered no further recriminations during their rapid passage through the crowded streets. "Is that it?" The church façade rose up before them as they turned a corner.

"Yes, sir."

"Where did he see her last?"

"In the main aisle, sir. That's why he didn't worry about keeping her in sight. She was talking to the priest, and who could be safer, Vigée said."

But neither Vigée nor Teo were in sight when they entered the narthex and beheld a scene of tragedy and confusion. The wounded lay in the aisles; those less seriously injured were propped up against the walls or seated on chairs. The fresh straw strewn on the stone floor was already blood-soaked, and the pitiful din of cries for water and assistance resonated through the huge nave.

"Where are the medical officers?" Duras demanded.

"They're on their way. I ordered supplies and medical staff. Vigée sent his men for water. There's a priest, sir. He may know the countess's whereabouts."

He didn't, and after assuring the cleric that aid was en route, Duras searched the side aisles and apse, stopping to speak to the wounded, assuring them of their passage home, thanking them for their courage at Bregenz. It was a slow circuit through the disarray of soldiers lying on the floor, yet Duras's gaze remained alert for signs of Teo. Each passing minute without sight of her added to his discomfort.

They found her a lengthy time later in a small walled garden behind the church, helping a cleric bandage a wounded trooper. Vigée knelt beside Teo, holding the man's leg while she and the young priest wound the remnants of her petticoat tightly around a bloody gash.

"She wouldn't come, sir," Vigée quickly declared on catching sight of Duras, apology in his tone.

"Don't blame him, Andre," Teo said, smiling up at Duras, her gown stained, her hands smeared with blood. "I refused to leave when so many men need attention here."

"The surgeons and physicians are on their way," Duras declared. "They'll be here shortly. Come now, I'll take you to some lodgings."

"Will we be here long?"

"I hope to move out before evening."

"Send someone for me when you're ready to leave. I'll help until then," she replied, her attention returning to the task, the soldier deathly white as they ministered to him.

"Teo."

She looked up again, the single word a soft repressed command. "Vigée will stay with me, won't you?" she queried, gazing at the major over the soldier's injured leg.

"Yes, ma'am. That is," he added, aware of Duras's scowl, "if you wish me to, sir."

Bonnay smiled faintly at the contretemps; Duras was unfamiliar with having his orders disobeyed.

"You don't wish to leave?" Duras murmured, constraint in his voice.

"Excuse me," Teo quietly said to the priest at her side, and rising in a rustle of heavy faille, she walked over to Duras. Taking his hand, she drew him slightly aside. "I'm so pleased you're safe," she gently said. "Would you like me to care for your wound?"

"A surgeon already looked at it. Come away from here, Teo," he said, his tone insistent. "Is that asking so much?"

"To sit somewhere and wait for you?" she countered, her gaze challenging. "Please, darling, I'll be of much more use here. I know how to bandage a wound. If nothing else I can fetch water for the dying and hold their hand."

"I'd prefer you be safely away from this."

"I'm fine with Vigée."

He gazed at her for a moment, debating his degree of comfort against her wishes. "You weren't hurt in the retreat?"

"No. Vigée had us into the saddle the minute he received your message. He didn't even give me time to change, so I rode in this," she said, smiling. "With the skirts hitched up around my knees."

"I'm concerned with you in the turmoil of the city. I'm not sure it's safe."

"Are *you* safe with Jourdan's army gone?"

"For the moment, but we're continuing to withdraw tonight." He smiled at her. "This isn't a discussion about my safety, darling."

"Nor of mine, my love," she sweetly replied.

The smallest silence ensued and then Duras said with the faintest of sighs, "If you won't come with me, you *must* stay at the church so I know where you are."

"Agreed," she pleasantly said, and then reaching up, she brushed her finger over his cheek. "You need a shave and a bath."

"Maybe we can find hot water somewhere tonight." His voice was low, his gaze intimate, and for a moment the disasters of the past few days vanished.

"A heavenly thought," she softly replied.

"Yes," he said, suddenly aware of his utter fatigue. "Vigée stays with you every moment. No exceptions." Steeling himself against his weariness, he briskly went on,

"There may be enemy agents in all this tumult. I want you to understand the risk."

"I understand Korsakov may be in the vicinity."

"We don't have verification but it's possible. Don't take any chances."

"You'll come for me when it's time to go?"

"If I can't, I'll send one of my aides. I worry about you." His voice was scarcely a whisper. "The retreat could be dangerous if Archduke Charlie decides to pursue us."

"I'll stay with Vigée and wait for your summons."

"You'll need clothes."

She glanced at her soiled skirt; she'd not noticed.

"I'll see what I can do."

"Don't fuss."

He grinned. "I'll try not to." Clothing for Teo was one of his smaller concerns at the moment. Signaling for Bonnay, he murmured to Teo in parting, "Stay with Vigée."

"Yes, General." She playfully winked.

He winked back, a languorous drift of dark lashes and enticement.

And despite the tragedy and uncertainty of the times, both felt a sweet rush of hope.

The men who assembled in Duras's temporary office a short time later were the remnants of his staff. Bastoul and Ruby had been killed in the assault; Gazan was badly wounded, and Loison was at the surgeons' having a shrapnel wound treated. No one in his staff was unscathed.

There were no arguments concerning the need to fall back to Zurich. The small Army of Switzerland was isolated in a salient exposed to encirclement by the archduke in the north and the Austrian army in Italy. Their positions in the Tyrol would have to be abandoned, all the garrisons on the east bank of the upper Rhine withdrawn. A few officers suggested abandoning Switzerland completely and making a stand in the Jura Mountains and the Savoy Alps. But Duras refused.

He spent the remainder of the day with Bonnay organizing the withdrawal. The headquarters at Sargans were ordered to pack up and retreat to the west. The greater part of the army still marching up from the Tyrol had to be redirected. His instructions to the quartermaster were extensive and the quartermaster corps worked overtime requisitioning supplies from the local inhabitants. Of the 4,200 men who'd survived Bregenz, all were in need of rations and medical supplies while additional transport was required for the walking wounded.

Very late that afternoon as the final commands for moving out were being implemented, a devastating message arrived from Paris. The Austrians under Kray had defeated Schérer's Army of Italy near Verona and had driven the French back to the Mincio. With Suvorov due to join the Austrians in Italy soon with additional Russian soldiers, the situation for France in the south was becoming desperate. Their own circumstances took on a graver note.

If the Army of Italy was defeated, the Army of Switzerland would find itself alone and in extreme danger.

11

"Duras has your wife with him," said the slender man who sat across the desk from Korsakov.

"*With* him . . . with *him*! Impossible!" The Russian general leaped to his feet, his towering stature threatening, his rage visible as the color of his face changed from pink to red to violent crimson. "It's one of his whores," he spat, leaning forward pugnaciously.

"She waited for him at the monastery near Bregenz," Herr Mingen said, calm before the Russian's wrath, his years as a double agent imbuing him with a cool self-possession. He'd been sent out to search for the general's wife, and while his loyalties lay with Prussia and its king, there was no harm in disclosing the information to Korsakov. "She appeared well guarded."

"She's his prisoner, then," General Count Ilyich Korsakov flatly declared, someone poaching on his personal property inconceivable.

"I spoke with one of the troopers near the stables. Duras is very solicitous of her."

"Solicitous?" The man referred to as the Butcher pronounced the word with a soft malice.

"Apparently after his successes in the Tyrol, Duras spent two days behind closed doors with the countess."

"You misunderstood!" Korsakov thundered, his beefy hands formed into fists.

"No, Your Excellency," replied the man who spoke ten languages without accent.

"If you're wrong, you sniveling dog," Korsakov whispered, his voice quivering with menace, his close-set eyes virulent, "I'll have your liver."

"I'm very certain, Your Excellency," Herr Mingen blandly said, concealing his disgust. Incompetent, brutal men like Korsakov were an all-too-common product of privilege.

"She will be brought back," Korsakov harshly decreed. "*You'll* bring her back," he ordered.

"A very dangerous expedition, General." Mingen's voice was soft, his pale hair gleaming for a moment in the sunlight pouring through the windows as he glanced at the large map on the wall. "And expensive," he gently added, taking in the contested land through which he would be obliged to journey.

"Speak to my aide about the details," Korsakov curtly responded. Did the man think him some shopkeeper to haggle over money? "My Chechens will accompany you."

"Do you wish the countess brought back alive?" the agent inquired. The Chechen death squads were specialized units; they didn't take prisoners.

"I need the countess *alive*. But Duras will pay dearly for his temerity, damn his lowborn hide!" Korsakov dropped back into his chair with a glowering scowl. "Collect your money and supplies and be out of here by morning. I want her back immediately!"

After handling his business transactions with Korsakov's aide, Herr Mingen had one brief detour before meeting his Chechen traveling companions.

The apothecary opened his door at the sight of Mingen, although the closed sign had been in place at his establishment on a side street of Bregenz since yesterday morning when the defensive artillery opened fire.

"Our superiors might like to know Korsakov's death squad will be stalking Duras as of tonight," Anton Mingen told the man he'd shared quarters with at university. Their employer, King Frederick William III of Prussia, was interested in maintaining his neutrality in this war, although the pressures from England and the Second Coalition to join them had been intense. Frederick didn't trust Thugut, however; the Austrian prime minister's designs on his territory were no secret. He preferred Austria be kept busy fighting the French. "Tell the king," Mingen went on, "he might prefer Duras remain alive. There's no other general capable of defending France against the Coalition forces."

"You heard about Kray at Verona."

Mingen nodded. "Making it even more imperative that Duras survive. France is in desperate straits."

"Could you kill the Chechens?"

"Perhaps. It's . . . possible," the agent observed, reflecting on the chances. "But they're trained assassins. I doubt I could dispatch more than one before I'm killed. And I'd just as soon survive this war. How else can I enjoy my ill-gained profits?" His smile warmed his eyes, giving him the look of a choirboy.

"We should send out our own men, then."

"It would give me a pleasant sense of security. I'll leave my expected travel itinerary with you. Duras will fall back on Constance. After he learns of Jourdan's defeat, I suspect he'll be withdrawing farther—he's badly outnumbered. Fortunately, the Chechens don't know the country; they'll have to rely on me as a guide."

"Nor do they speak the language."

"They barely speak at all. It's quite frightening," Mingen said with a flashing smile. "I shall endeavor to keep them satisfied at all costs," he sardonically finished.

"Would Frederick benefit if Korsakov were dead?" the apothecary inquired, his understanding of political subtleties artful.

"Address that question to our superiors in Potsdam. The world at large would benefit from his death, but that's just my personal opinion," Mingen cheerfully declared.

"Do you need money?"

"Yes, of course. Korsakov's money goes into my account. Someone has to pay for this outrageous journey across no-man's-land. There are times when I think I should have continued in my medical profession," Mingen said with a weary sigh.

"But the king needs you."

The young agent rose heavily to his feet, contemplation of his mission daunting. "Wish me luck, Max. I'm going to need it with this one."

A few minutes later, he was considerably richer, Prussian gold weighing heavily in his purse as he exited the shop. At his lodgings, he packed several weapons in his luggage, two of them small enough to conceal on his person. Traveling with trained killers thoroughly without conscience required additional firepower.

The ill-assorted trio left Bregenz that evening.

12

The withdrawal from Constance began at dusk, evacuating the wounded slow paced, the wagons strung out for miles along the route west. Duras's rear guard reported no activity behind them, offering a degree of relief however temporary; the archduke was not in pursuit. They traveled until nearly midnight before breaking to rest. Soon campfires blazed up in hundreds of points of light throughout the mountain valley.

A small inn at the entrance to the valley had rooms for Duras and his staff, although the accommodations were rustic. "Not a problem," Duras had wearily said when Bonnay came back with the news. "Any bed will do."

The rooms were small and the tiny chamber Teo and Duras were shown into had a feather bed, a fireplace, and little else. But it was clean, the fire was quickly lit, and within

122

minutes the innkeeper's wife appeared in her nightgown, a wrapper hastily thrown over it. Bonnay's generous payment in advance had thoroughly ingratiated the French officers to her despite the late hour. Bowing to Duras, she cordially said, "I understand you'd like bathwater and supper."

"Yes, please." Too filthy to lie on the bed, Duras was sprawled on the floor, his back against the wall. "Bathwater first."

The landlady cast a curious glance at the figure lying on the bed. The slender form in uniform was not easily distinguishable in the candlelight and shadow, although the general's aide had used the pronoun *she*. "Would the, er, your companion like bathwater too?" she inquired.

"Yes, very much," Teo said, smiling at the woman's obvious scrutiny.

"Bathwater for two," Duras explained. "Quickly, if possible."

"Of course, sir. The kitchen maids are heating it now. What would you like for dinner?"

"Anything at all for me." His head lazily turned toward Teo. "Tell her what you'd like, darling."

"Bacon and eggs. I have this craving."

Duras's eyes narrowed slightly, his gaze dwelling for a moment on her flat stomach. But his voice was bland when he said, "I'll have the same. With dispatch, please," he gruffly added, not inclined to converse at length in the middle of the night when he was dead tired and his arm ached like hell.

After the landlady left, Teo murmured, "I don't know if I can stay awake until the food arrives."

"Sleep. I'll wake you."

"You're too far away," she whispered, rolling over, reaching out to him.

"I'm also too squalid to touch you." His eyes were half shut. "Wait until I bathe." But he reached out and brushed her fingertips and smiled.

"Do you have another uniform?"

"Probably. Bonnay's efficient. And you have two new gowns," he went on, his eyes shut, his smile reappearing.

"New gowns?" Her head lifted fractionally from the mattress.

He half raised his lashes and dipped his head toward the saddlebags an aide had carried in and dropped near the door.

"You found me gowns?" Propping herself up on one elbow, she gazed at him, charmed by his apparent concern.

"Cholet did."

"Did you give him orders," she teased. "This size . . . and color . . . this fabric?"

"I should have." Duras chuckled and then groaned; even the slight movement was excruciating. The stitches on his wrist had broken open at Bregenz and when the wound had been resewn at Constance, he'd almost fainted from the pain.

"You need laudanum," Teo murmured, slipping from the bed. "I'll see if the innkeeper's wife has some."

"There's a bottle of cognac in my bags," Duras said, careful not to move, pain drumming down his nerve endings.

Quickly fetching the bags, Teo dropped down beside him and unfastened the buckles. Searching through them, she pulled out a small bottle and, easing out the cork, handed it to him.

"My angel of mercy," he whispered, lifting the bottle to his mouth, pouring a long draught down his throat. His discomfort was obvious.

"Should I look at your arm?"

"Not now. Later. After I've drunk this bottle," he said with a small smile.

"Should a surgeon be called?"

"No. He can't do anything. Look at your gowns," he prompted, wishing to change the subject. "Tell me what you think." And intent on obliterating his pain, he swallowed another generous portion of the cognac.

Teo pulled out one of Duras's clean linen shirts.

"The other side," he directed.

Unhooking the other compartment, Teo pulled out a filmy wisp of black lace. Almost transparent, trimmed with red satin ribbon threaded around the décolletage, it looked decidedly like lingerie. "Where did Cholet find this?"

"God knows. I reprimanded him."

"But you brought them along."

"I thought they'd look exquisite on you; not, however, while riding with the army."

"Such reservations, darling," she teased. "Your reputation is not deserved, I see."

"You're for my eyes only," he softly said, the liquor spreading an assuaging balm through his body, blurring the sharp edges of his pain. "There's another one."

It was purple. Teo's eyes widened as she unfolded the brilliant tissue silk. "Did Cholet raid a brothel?" she inquired, amusement in her gaze. An Athenian hetaera would have been well served in the Grecian-style gown. Its bodice indelicately plunged nearly to the waist, and the skirt was slit up both sides to openly display leg and thigh.

"It appears so, although some Parisian belles have been known to display themselves nearly nude in public."

"Really," Teo said, a distinct coolness in her voice.

"So I've heard," Duras sensibly replied. "I've not been personally involved."

"Thank you."

"Your jealousy charms me," he murmured.

"While you aren't allowed to charm anyone but me."

"Gladly."

A knock on the door curtailed any further conversation and their bathwater was carried in.

Short moments later they sat knee to knee in a

commodious copper tub filled with steaming water, the heat from the fire adding pleasure. It was, they agreed, very close to paradise after the discomforts and disasters of the past few days. They were warm, relaxed, contemplating supper in the very near future, and together.

"I'm miles and oceans beyond happy," Teo blissfully murmured.

"I'm alive," Duras succinctly noted, his eyes shut, his head resting against the rim of the tub, the guilt and regret he always felt over the deaths of his soldiers a burden on his heart. Happiness was always countered by the tragedies of his profession. "And I'm with you." It was enough. Tomorrow he would once again face the daunting odds, but tonight he only wanted to forget.

And seek oblivion in Teo's arms.

But he fell asleep over supper and Teo eased the tray from his lap and set it on the floor. She didn't know how to move him from his reclining position against the pillows without causing him pain, so she gently pulled the coverlet over him and left him as he was.

She watched him sleep for a moment, thankful he'd been spared at Bregenz, offering up her own small prayers of gratitude to those gods she knew from childhood. They lived in the trees and sky, in the rushing waters and vast open spaces of her homeland, but she hoped they heard her that night because she wanted them to care for this man she loved. She stood at the small window under the eaves in the mountain valley thousands of miles from her home and gazed up into the starry sky and asked for their boon.

"Save him from his enemies," she prayed, "and from the indiscriminate slaughter. Keep him safe, tonight and always." She hoped the stars above her shone as brightly on the other side of the Urals; she hoped they carried her prayers to her grandfather she'd not seen for so long. "I want to bring him home to you, Grand-père," she murmured into the silence, "and let him come to know you. I want our child to grow strong in the land of my people. I want to come home. . . ."

It was too quiet; the dangers facing them were immeasurable. She felt afraid even after Duras had appeased her fears over dinner.

France was in jeopardy, she'd apprehensively noted. Everything was in chaos, the retreat monstrous, dreadful.

They'd withdraw and regroup, he'd calmly replied.[10] Archduke Charlie wasn't a formidable opponent anyway; in '97 he'd forced him back almost to the gates of Vienna, he'd said with a smile.

Don't you have confidence in me?

Yes, she'd said. Yes, of course.

But how could he win? she thought now in the darkness of the night, staring out at the hundreds of flickering campfires. His retreating army was no longer strong enough to do battle. How could he possibly win against all the armies, when Austria, England, her ruthless husband and their troops outnumbered his, when their superiority was overwhelming?

Their time together could be dangerously fleeting, she fearfully thought.

Turning from the window, she gazed at him, his skin dark against the linens, his black curls in disarray on the pillow, his face in repose, the tranquillity of his breathing in sharp contrast to her own disquietude. His beauty and strength, his indefatigable charm, his love, all were hers— at least for now.

She didn't dare think of the future.

She woke to the warmth of his body and his kiss, the morning sun brilliant in the room, her demons gone. His smile could do that, she decided, basking in its glow. "I'm afraid I neglected something last night," he murmured.

"I didn't want to wake you."

"Always wake me for that," he said with a grin. "Consider it a standing order."

"You were exhausted. Although you seem completely rested now," she mischievously noted, his arousal nudging her thigh.

"Completely," he agreed. Even the pain in his arm had subsided to a manageable ache.

"I don't suppose you're hungry?" A sudden urge for chocolate and whipped cream overwhelmed her.

"In a manner of speaking."

"How nice," she murmured, damping her dietary urges, reaching up to kiss him. "Do we have much time this morning?"

"If Bonnay doesn't interrupt with a message from our rear guard. He's to notify me immediately if we're pursued."

"So if the archduke chooses not to run you to ground . . ."

"Which isn't likely. The Austrian generals have little autonomy. All their orders come from Vienna."

"A disadvantage."

Duras smiled. "Not for us."

"So we may have . . . plenty of time," she purred.

"It's a distinct possibility," he replied, grinning.

"I was wondering, then . . ." The mouthwatering image of breakfast chocolate reappeared in her mind. "I mean, as long as we don't have to leave immediately, that is, would you mind if I ordered chocolate and whipped cream first? I have this ravenous craving for chocolate and—"

"Whipped cream," he gently finished. "Cravings?" His query was hushed, his expression rapt. "How long have you had cravings?"

"I'm not sure," she said, a tiny flutter vibrating down her spine. "I haven't actually noticed, although, come to think of it, Vigée took me to task for eating all his ham and bread the monks packed for us when we left. Fortunately, he found more food for us both at the next posting station because I was still hungry. I ate like two troopers, he said. Ham and bread sounds ever so good now," she said with a dulcet, sweet smile. "Is it too early to call for the innkeeper?"

Duras chuckled. "Bonnay paid them so well, it's never too early," he replied, indulgently patting her hand. Tossing aside the covers, he rose from the bed, walked to the door, threw it open and shouted for the proprietor. His ruffled curls brushed the door lintel as he stood for a moment in the open doorway, his height startling in the small, low-ceilinged room.

"There," he said, pushing the door shut, his affectionate gaze falling on Teo. "Food for *ma chère.*"

"You've wakened everyone in the house," Teo pleasantly chastised.

"I'm sure they're up." His tone was dismissive.

"You've been a general too long, darling. It's very early."

"Then they'll go back to sleep," he unconcernedly said, rummaging through his saddlebags. Pulling out a pair of breeches, he began sliding them on.

"You're not getting dressed," Teo hastily interposed.

"Only temporarily, darling, although it's not often I'm neglected for a ham sandwich."

"Forgive me," she said with a rueful smile, "but I'm really famished."

Dropping down beside her on the bed, he leaned over and kissed her and then very softly said, "If you like, we'll have a cook travel with us so you're never hungry."

"Aren't you pleased about the baby?" she whispered, a kind of awe and wonder in her voice.

"I don't have your faith and it's too early yet," he said, pragmatic and long ago disabused of wonder. "But I'm pleased if you are."

"He must like whipped cream."

"Or *she* likes ham and bread."

"Or *they* like whipped cream and ham and bread."

His brows quirked. "Are you giving me twins?"

"I was a twin. My brother died in infancy."

"Our children won't die."

"No," she said.

And when the landlord arrived at the door, Duras ordered a breakfast to satisfy even a ravenously famished lover.

"You're so sweet," she said, once the man was gone, sliding her arms out from the covers she'd pulled up to her chin to conceal her nudity from the innkeeper.

"You can thank me later." Taking off his breeches, he climbed back into bed, his grin wicked.

"Or now," she whispered, his splendid erection suddenly creating an equally ravenous craving.

"We don't have much time." His voice was hushed, responding to her need.

"It won't take long," she breathed, already moving toward him, greedy, covetous, his magnificent arousal igniting instant lust, and two seconds later she was straddling his hips, reaching for him.

He helped her because he was as eager as she, sexual excess the normal outlet in the aftermath of battle. But infinitely more practiced, he brushed her hands aside and adjusted himself smoothly between the sleek, pulsing tissue of her labia. With a breathless sigh, she sank down his rigid length, impatient, feverish, wantonly in rut. Blissfully impaled on his enormous length, she lightly touched the very base of his erection where their bodies were joined and whispered, "I adore your cock."

"And we adore you," he softly replied, holding her firmly in place, his hands hard on her hips, resisting her initial upward motion, lustful beyond his memory of the word, forcing himself infinitesimally deeper by slow degrees.

"No," he whispered as she struggled against her captivity. "Not yet. Wait . . ." He drove to the deepest depth of penetration, causing her whimper to end in a gasp at the agonizing pleasure. And then he moved a refined, inciteful distance more. Scarcely able to breathe, dizzy, melting, she emitted a small, suffocated scream.

With her body dissolving around him, he slowly lifted her at last and her sigh of longing drifted over him. And nothing mattered in the world for that stark moment as she trembled on the highest point of his withdrawal—neither duty nor reason, not with her senses overcome with an unbearable longing.

She was more sensational than a thousand victories, he thought, his libido flame-hot, and his fingers tightened on her hips, exerted a gentle downward pressure. On the languorous descent she began climaxing in a tantalizingly slow orgasm that intensified by exalted, tumultuous degrees. Panting, frenzied, she clung to him, moaning deep in her throat, absorbing the shocking ecstasy as he forced his hips upward. "Take it all," he whispered, bracing his feet, driving upward, his climax surging, feverish with haste, irrepressible haste.

Eyes shut, her pale throat arched, she panted at each fierce ejaculatory thrust, ravished by sensation, on fire, her nails leaving half-moons in his arms.

He didn't notice, no more than he noticed his throbbing wound. He only felt the hotspur shock of his orgasm, his feelings, raw, carnal—the intensity more acute this time, more ferocious, as if each violent sensation was a perverse reaffirmation of his life.

When the explosive tumult passed, they lay softly panting in each other's arms. Neither was capable of movement. Birdsong outside the windows trilled loud in the sudden quiet of the room, which was pungent with the scent of passion and heated bodies.

"Lust takes on a new meaning with you," Duras murmured, capable of speech first, although his eyes were still closed.

"I didn't know lust existed." Licking his earlobe, Teo resisted the impulse to say, mine. Languorously rolling across his chest, she smiled at him. "Thank you, *mon cher,* for the introductory lessons."

"I've gained new insight into the ancient religions of priestesses." And a new appreciation for life, he thought as he helped Teo move into a comfortable sprawl atop him.

"If I were a temple priestess," she declared, her arms resting on his chest, "you'd be my only acolyte."

"And I'd daily thank the gods for their favor." His mouth quirked into a grin. "Or with you, hourly."

"This isn't usual, is it?"

"No." There was a nerveless clarity in his gaze.

"Will we survive the chaos?" she softly asked, wanting him forever when a host of enemies besieged them.

He was too honest to glibly answer such a heartfelt question, his mortality too fragile. But after the merest hesitation, he said, "We have a very good chance." Then he smiled to mitigate the seriousness of his response. "I can win over Charlie."

She beamed back at him. "Good, because I need a father for our child."

"That's what I was thinking."

He was saved from having to assuage Teo's apprehensions or deal with the implicit perils in his life by the arrival of their breakfast—for which he was grateful. The full array of their enemies required nerves of steel and an undaunted optimism. Not to mention the additional reserves from Lyon that had been promised him since February.

They ate in bed, or rather Duras ate and Teo tested the capacity of her stomach, which proved equal to her eyes' appetite. When he set his plate aside and said "Are you sure?" to her third helping of a cheese omelet and second cup of chocolate, she only nodded, a spoon of whipped cream poised at her mouth. A delicious sight, he decided, as if she herself were a tantalizingly nude savory.

And sometime later when he politely inquired whether she could actually devour a fourth piece of toasted bread and honey, she said, "You should eat more, darling. You missed most of your supper last night." She went on cutting a piece of ham to accompany another bite of cheese omelet. "They have a very good cook here. Did you taste the oatmeal bread?"

"Should I see if he or she could be lured away to Zurich?" he kindly asked, thinking her the delight of his life.

"Would you?" Her eyes glowed with interest.

"I'd be happy to." He'd have this inn taken apart board by board and transported across the world if she wished.

"You're a darling."

"Thank you," he quietly said, leaning over to kiss the honey from the corners of her mouth.

"Ummm," she purred, opening her mouth, luring his tongue inside, offering herself with an enchanting artlessness. And when his mouth lifted after a time and drifted downward, gliding down the pale column of her throat and lower, she sighed in pleasure. He kissed a path into the valley between her breasts, stirring the bounteous flesh, his tongue warm on her skin. Slipping his palms under her breasts, he lifted them and, sitting upright again, he gazed at their plump beauty pinked with desire, the nipples succulent, peaked, the lush mounds weighty in his hands.

"Which should I kiss first?" He lightly squeezed the pliant flesh and the nipples and aureoles darkened, rose to attention. "Look," he whispered. "They're eager."

"I'm eager," she breathed, her body responding instantly,

her breasts so sensitive she could feel the air on them. "I crave sex like I crave food."

"I can give you sex," he murmured, leaning forward and taking one nipple between his teeth.

The infinitesimal pressure of his teeth flared through her body as if she were a slave to love. Her fingers slid through his dark curls, and firmly lifting his head until their eyes were level, she said, "I want you now."

"Are you sure?" he whispered, sliding his hands over hers, easing them away from his head, placing them with delicate precision on her breasts.

She quivered at the imprint of her nipples on her palms, and she felt her body opening as though he'd tripped a sensual trigger.

"How do your breasts feel?" he queried, slipping a hand between her thighs, stroking the damp, swollen verges of her labia.

She moaned softly and rocked in his hand as a ravenous, throbbing ache spiraled upward from the lascivious contact of his fingers.

"Squeeze your nipples for me," he prompted, slipping two more fingers inside her, forcing his hand higher, stretching her.

Please, Andre, she wanted to say but his exquisite expertise made speech impossible.

"How luscious you are," he whispered, his fingers drenched. "All ready for me . . . But you haven't touched your nipples," he said in the softest of demands.

Instantly obeying, she grasped them.

"That's better," he murmured, sliding his fingers free, watching the peaked crests elongate and harden, brushing them lightly with the pearly fluid on his fingers. The crests of her nipples gleamed like jewels as he bent toward them. "My exotic fertility goddess," he murmured, his tongue gently licking. "You're quivering." He nibbled lightly, teased with his tongue, brought her to a panting urgency. And then he straightened and, framing her face with his hands, gently queried, "Would you like my sex now?"

Her eyes were half-shut.

"Look at me," he whispered.

Shuddering with sexual longing, she opened her eyes.

"Say yes," he commanded.

"Yes." Hot, breathless.

"Then lie down," he quietly said, "and spread your legs."

His words struck some iniquitous chord because her gaze refocused, took on a sudden directness. "No orders."

"It wasn't an order."

"You must ask me."

"Would you lie down for me, darling?" he tenderly said.

She smiled, a seductive, lush sight. "On this?" she asked, surveying the breakfast debris scattered across the bed.

His answering smile was wicked, shameless. "Give me a second." Brushing the food aside with a sweep of his hand, he helped her lie down and then parted her thighs, easing them wider with his palms, stroking the silken curve of her inner thighs, moving upward, touching her pulsing, hot center. Sliding a delicate fingertip up the sleek, engorged flesh, he whispered, "Tell me you want me," needing a degree of capitulation in his current mood, not knowing why nor questioning his motives.

"I want you, Duras." Impersonal, cool.

He looked at her, a flashing authority in his gaze.

"Andre," she amended, her exotic eyes amused, "because I need you so."

Gratified, he moved between her thighs, lowering his body over hers, gliding inside her effortlessly, because her pulsing tissue was slick with sperm, satiny. "Is this what you need?" he asked, driving in up to the hilt.

But she couldn't speak. Her orgasm flared, peaked and

she came instantly, as if she were an unreasoning receptacle for pleasure.

"A shame I have a war to fight," Duras softly said, holding her close as she trembled in his arms. "I could fuck myself mindless instead."

She felt him swell larger as he spoke, felt her own wanton response, her new lascivious appetites astonishing. "I won't be able to live without you," she whispered, clinging to him.

"You won't have to," he said, adjusting her minutely for greater ingress. "I'll find a way to keep you near." She was temptation incarnate, he thought, sliding his hand under her thigh, slowly lifting her leg to gain deeper penetration as he drove in, knowing with deadly certainty that she was a rash and reckless whim.

But he meant to have her now, later . . . always.

He came quickly, once, twice, three times, oblivious to all but sensation, driven, obsessed as he often was with her, detached from everything but his need to possess her. And her orgasms blended one into the other, the intoxicating delirium feverish, agonizing, leaving her breathless, insensate.

And afterward as they lay together, he reminded her of the dresses, his imagination, the capacity of his mind and body, absorbed with sex. "Do you think these delectable breasts will fit in Cholet's black lace gown?" he murmured, brushing a lazy fingertip around one nipple.

"Later," she whispered, skittish at his touch, not sure her senses were capable of further stimulation.

"Now," he whispered back, leaning closer, kissing her, his libidinous urges like a living flame inside him. Maybe it was the time or lack of it, the never knowing when next he'd see her, *if* he'd see her. Like a glutton fearing starvation, he wanted to fill his senses with her, feel her in his hands and under him, around him—now when he could. Rolling over her and off the bed, he landed lightly on his feet and, pulling his saddlebags from under the bed, slid the black wisp of silk lace from one of the compartments.

Sitting on the edge of the bed, he drew the filmy fabric down her body and her eyes slowly opened. "Indulge me," he said with a faint smile. "I'm greedy."

"As long as you don't wake me," she murmured, amusement in her gaze, incapable of movement.

"Go to sleep," he offered, knowing better, knowing her better.

"Mmmmm." Her eyelids were already closing, the feather bed gratifyingly soft.

He dressed her as one would a child, carefully lifting her head to slide the bit of lace over her head, slipping first one limp arm and then the other into the small capped sleeves, raising her gently to delicately guide the gown over her shoulders, past the fullness of her breasts, taking a moment to admire his handiwork before pulling the skirt over her hips and legs.

Cholet had a good eye for size, Duras reflected. The gown fit perfectly, the design à la mode but risqué, meant for seduction. The lace was so transparent the flesh tones warmed the eye through the black gauze, the dark hair between Teo's thighs a shadowy suggestion, a lure, her pale, slender legs outlined beneath the voluminous skirt. But the captivating focus was the décolletage, deep and low, outlined in red silk ribbon, tied with a bow at the base of the sweeping curve. A bow that could be easily opened for access, for touching.

And she wasn't sleeping any longer, he could tell; the rhythm of her breathing had changed.

The gossamer lace was exquisitely sensual on her skin, the lightest of sensations, like feathery wing tips or a summer breeze, lushly heated, warming. The surface of her skin glowed with stimulation, the heat spiraling inward, racing through her blood. Teo wondered if the wearer of this gown might drown in sensation.

"Why don't you sit up?" Duras suggested, sliding his hands under her arms.

"Do I have a choice?" she murmured, her lashes half shielding the deep green of her eyes, a sensual undertone to her words.

"You always have a choice, *chou-chou*." His voice was whisper soft, his dark gaze shone with flagrant excess. "Come, sit up for me."

He lifted her effortlessly, his carnal urges overriding the momentary twinge in his wrist as the stitches pulled. And when he'd placed her with punctilious attention against the red-painted headboard, adjusting pillows on either side of her to rest her arms, he said, "You do the dress justice, *ma chère.*"

"It feels . . . delicious."

"Here, too?" He slipped his hand between her legs, smoothed the lace over her mount of Venus, his fingers drifting lower, massaging the fabric with compelling pressure over her swollen labia.

She moaned at the provocative friction, her senses quickening under his touch.

"How do you feel?"

"Restless," she replied, squirming, "wanton . . ."

"Would you like to climax again?"

She shifted away slightly, her flesh still tender from lovemaking. "I can't."

His fingers were damp through the sheer silk, her body roused, dripping wet. "Maybe you can," he murmured. "Maybe you can come a dozen more times."

Her eyes shut against the licentious surge rippling through her vagina. "I'll die . . ."

Leaning forward, he placed his lips gently on hers, eased his hand under the black lace of the skirt and slid his fingers inside her. "No, you won't," he breathed, stroking the sleek, hot tissue. "I won't let you." His words vibrated against her mouth, soothing, absolving, his fingers buried deep inside her intoxicating, and she shivered in longing.

"Open wider for me," he said and her legs fell apart as though she were his to command. "Wider," he softly ordered a moment later, spreading her thighs himself, arranging her legs comfortably, her knees slightly bent, her ankles crossed so her lower body was delectably nude, on display. Sitting back to admire her salacious pose, he adjusted her skirt to more fully expose her sex. "Would you like some cock in here?" he gently inquired, touching her pulsing cleft.

She moved against his hand with a suffocated cry.

"I can't hear you," he murmured, his fingers moving up and down. "Would you like my cock?"

Eyes closed, she nodded.

"I'm not quite sure you're ready."

Her eyes opened wide.

"Ah, there. I like to see that rapacious need."

"I can't wait . . . please."

"Just a few more minutes . . . I thought I'd kiss your nipples first."

"No . . . please."

Her breathing was rough, her skin a glowing blush, her vulva pulsing visibly. She was so damned arousing Duras wondered how long he himself could wait. But he was more accomplished at the game, his talents more inventive, and he understood delay only enhanced the pleasure.

"This won't take long." He untied the red ribbon holding the gown's décolletage in place, easing the fabric aside, exposing her breasts. "Is that too cold?" he unnecessarily asked, stroking her heated flesh.

"Damn you," she breathed, ravenous, desperate.

"You're too impetuous," he gently chided, sliding the superfluous lace bodice under and around her breasts, retying the red bow beneath the plump, ripe mounds so they were suspended and framed by black lace, levered tautly into jutting, delectable globes.

Leaning forward, he gently licked a path around one nipple, and Teo's soft moan trembled in the stillness. His hands came up to firmly hold one lush, ripe breast, to restrain her before his mouth closed over the hardened peak. She was quivering in his hands, shuddering with need, and when he began sucking with a hard, exquisite pressure, she cried out and came with a wild, gasping sob. Releasing her nipple when the last flurry had subsided in her body, he took her face between his warm palms and whispered, "It's better when I'm inside you."

"Anytime," she breathed, green flame in the depths of her eyes.

He chuckled. "Patience, darling. It only gets better."

"Guaranteed?" she insolently murmured, moody, glowering.

"Guaranteed," he serenely replied.

"Damn your shameless assurance."

His brows quirked. "You should appreciate my assurance."

"It offends me on occasion."

"Even now?" His glance flicked downward to his towering erection.

She smiled. "Maybe later."

"Very sensible, darling. Now lie back and I'll see what I can do to put myself in a more favorable light."

"Something expeditious, pray."

"I shall endeavor to please you," he impudently said. "Now shut your eyes and dream sweet dreams."

She felt the feather bed shift as he reached down and she watched from beneath her lashes as he lifted the bowl of whipped cream from the floor. Dipping his finger into the remains of the cream, he carried a dollop to her mouth. "Your eyes are supposed to be closed."

"I take orders so poorly."

His mouth twitched into a half smile, and undeterred, he said, "Open your mouth."

She didn't of course, nor had he expected her to. But when he dropped the dab of whipped cream on one of her nipples, her mouth opened of its own accord at the cool thrill, at the heat racing downward from her ornamented nipple. And with smooth dispatch, he deposited a fingerful of whipped cream in her mouth.

"Gotcha," he whispered, grinning.

She had to swallow before she could answer and by that time her other nipple was decorated with a small pale mound of cream. "I'm not sure I like this."

"Really," he smoothly retorted, delicately touching one peaked crest through the cream.

"You needn't look so smug." A *jeunesse* pout.

"Jewel hard, darling, what can I say?" He touched her other nipple and she drew in a sharp breath. He smiled faintly, surveying the rosy flush spreading over her mounded breasts and very softly said, "I think I'll paint your sex with cream too. How would that be?"

There was no need for her to answer; he could see the tremor shake her body. "That's what I thought," he said. "And then if you don't mind waiting," he silkily went on, trailing his middle finger down her cleft, "I'll lick it all off."

She writhed, melted, an impossible craving swelling inside her.

"You can't move," he said in her ear, putting a hand on her stomach to hold her still. "There, like that," he murmured, spreading a fingerful of whipped cream in a lustrous drift over her labia. "How does that feel?"

She couldn't speak, unbridled sensation dissolving her bones, the throbbing between her legs overwhelming.

Well-grounded in female response, he didn't require an answer but continued smoothing the glossy cream over her flesh, covering all the external surfaces first until they were slickly glazed in white, forcing little dabs of the sweet confection into every sensitive fold and crevasse. The remaining whipped cream conveniently filled her vagina, first one dollop and then another until she was stuffed to overflowing with frothy cream. "You have to look," he gently directed, drawing her slightly forward so she could glance down between her legs. "It looks as though you're filled with enough come for a regiment. You must be very accommodating."

His voice was like velvet and the sight between her legs so lascivious she was convulsed with shame—and wildly aroused. "Are you accommodating?" he inquired in a rough voice that made her quiver inside.

"I don't know," she murmured, powerless against her lust, dying for him.

"You look like you're accommodating in this revealing gown," he whispered. "Your breasts are exposed for anyone to see. What will people think," he went on in a rusty, thick tone, "with your nipples all smeared with come . . . with your sex dripping with come."

He knew, she thought, that he could have her anywhere, any way, and she felt as though she were submerged in a sea of sexual desire, endless, boundless, terrifying, beautiful. "I just want you," she breathed, beginning to tremble, overwhelmed by naked desire. "Please, Andre . . . please, don't do this to me."

His hands came up to grip her shoulders, steadying her, and he dipped his head so their eyes were level. "I'll stop," he said, wiping the cream from her nipples with the sheet. "You don't have to wait anymore." He gently eased her down on the bed. "Should I wipe the rest away or—"

She shook her head.

"Or lick it away," he finished, smiling faintly.

"That," she whispered, the word barely audible, her meaning crystal clear.

"Your servant, my lady," he smoothly replied, moving down between her legs. He gazed up at her a moment later, his chin resting lightly on her mons, his eyes angelic as a choirboy's. "If there's anything you don't like," he murmured, his mouth quirked in a grin, "let me know."

"Insolent man," she breathed.

"But competent."

"We'll see."

Bending his head, he licked a path to her clitoris that elicited an immediate and flagrantly impassioned response. It took some time before she had recovered sufficiently to open her eyes.

"How was that?" he inquired, cheeky and brazen, his dark gaze raised slightly above her mount of Venus.

"Mmmm." She languorously sighed.

"Competent enough?" An impertinent flicker of his brows.

"I should beat you."

"But perhaps not right now," he perceptively declared, placing a finger on either side of her vulva and gently spreading the pink flesh. He glanced upward at her soft groan. "Is that a yes?" he murmured, his smile knowing. "I have to tell you, madame," he went on as though they were discussing a business matter, "there's a whole lot of cream in here." He gently stroked her clitoris, delicately spreading the cream over and around the distended nub while she uncontrollably shivered beneath his hand. "This could take a while."

She seemed not to hear him, too absorbed in the dizzying sensations, the pulsing, unfulfilled ache in the pit of her belly. Lifting her pelvis, she moved against his hand, reaching for surcease.

"Soon," he quietly said, placing a restraining hand on her hip, holding her stationary before he lowered his head and slid his tongue slowly up her cleft. Her panting cries rippled through the small room as he licked away the cream on the outer verges of her labia, tidying up her pink flesh until it was immaculate, his attentions indulgent, gratifying, giving her what she desperately wanted, so that her first orgasm died away with his tongue deep inside her.

There was much yet to do, he told her when she was quiet again, and she didn't refuse his offer or his talents. He took great care in the continuing process to give regular attention to her clitoris before and after he began the critical task of removing the whipped cream from her vagina. It required finesse of hands and mouth and tongue, a simple achievement for a man who'd learned oral sex from a governess who wouldn't allow him to penetrate her for three months.

His governess had eventually succumbed to his persistence and her carnal urges but he'd become supremely proficient by then. No, more than that—a virtuoso after ninety heated nights. He'd learned to a flawless nicety how to provoke maximum sensation in a lady.

Teo was shaking when he finished, when she'd climaxed an endless number of times, when he decided she'd had enough or he hadn't. He climbed on top of her then and plunged inside her and kissed her and caressed her and felt as though the magic between them were attuned to the rhythm of the universe or to some erotic sorcery beyond understanding—something reckless, powerful, mindless. His orgasm was explosive, shattering, ravaging his brain and body, and he collapsed afterward, rolling away so he wouldn't crush her. Lying sprawled on his back he couldn't remember for a moment where he was. "Jesus," he muttered, his voice rough, breathless. He inhaled deeply, trying to quell the shocking impact.

"No more," Teo weakly breathed.

He reached a hand out to touch her. "I'm sorry," he apologized, his voice still faint. "Sleep," he murmured, brushing her fingers with his, forcing himself up on one elbow a moment later to draw a blanket over her.

She was sleeping already and so beautiful he smiled

looking down at her. He wanted her as he'd never wanted a woman. It was terrifying, but there was nothing he could do about it—he wanted what he wanted. She called it love; he didn't know exactly what that meant. But she was his, that he knew, whether she wished it or not.

13

Anton Mingen melded well into any environment, his appearance deliberately nondescript, his talent for languages so proficient, he spoke regional dialects without flaw. The Chechens' Mongol antecedents, however, set them apart, while their glowering countenances would have brought attention to them even if they were cleverly disguised. So King Frederick's agent thought it best to travel at night and rest during the day.

It wasn't difficult to overtake Duras's retreating army; burdened with wounded, they were moving very slowly. And three days later, Mingen and his execution squad took lodgings in the same inn Duras had stayed in the previous night.

Over dinner that evening, Mingen struck up a conversation with the serving maid, complimenting her on her embroidered apron, then expressing satisfaction with the meal, wondering, he said a few moments later, whether she'd actually seen the illustrious General Duras. "Everyone in the village is talking of him," he added. "His generosity extends to paying for his soldiers' food and lodging," he cordially noted.

At which point, the young girl waxed glorious over the general's charm and courtesy. Why, he'd stayed right upstairs, she went on, describing in great detail the events of the previous day.

"He has a lovely lady traveling with him, I hear," Mingen noted, mitigating any illusion to prying by adding, "The groom told me she was very beautiful."

"They both are," the maid replied with a wistful sigh. "And the general's smile is ever so wonderful. He particularly thanked me for bringing his lady a second serving of pudding late last night." Her voice lowered conspiratorially while her eyes widened in piquant animation. "And he were only wearing his breeches, if you know what I mean."

"Ah . . ." Mingen responded with appropriate understanding. "They're lovers."

"No doubt of that," she said with a wink. "He bought her a fancy pink diamond ring big as a pigeon egg from old Calvin down the street and the lady didn't rise from bed until they dressed to leave this morning."

"He has a reputation for the ladies," Mingen offered, his smile deceptively boyish.

"He coulda had any one of us here with no more than a glance our way," the pretty young maid declared with feeling. "Annie wanted to ask him if he'd take a moment from his lady for a quick roll in the hay with her, but we held her back, seeing how he only had eyes for the countess."

"She's a countess?" Mingen inquired, infusing his voice with added respect, wondering whether Duras was actually referring to Teo by name.

"Well, he don't call her countess. He calls her darling and love and other sweetings, but the troopers who guard his person called her countess. A Russian, they said," she whispered, as if the word were dangerous.

And she was reasonably accurate, for the Chechens' evil gazes suddenly focused on her, their limited vocabulary familiar with the word *Russian*. As if their depravity were a palpable energy, she glanced over at them and, turning pale, quickly excused herself on the pretext of work in the kitchen.

They were like dark werewolves, Mingen thought, regarding the two men seated across from him, their gazes pitiless, without humanity, their swarthy skin and dark clothing investing them with a sinister air. While not prone to nerves after years in his stealthy trade, he was sensibly cognizant of their deadly skills. He never turned his back on them.

"Russian countess," one of them muttered, his powerful hands flexing on his beer stein.

"Here?" the other asked, the word muffled through a mouthful of stewed goat meat.

"They're a day ahead of us," Mingen said in an Asian dialect they understood.

But Duras's well-oiled espionage machine was operating in the rear of the retreat as well, his spies on alert for word of the archduke's movements.

A young agent noticed the Chechens that night in Mülheim and immediately sent word to Duras.

Cholet received the message the following morning and relayed it to Bonnay. "We'll have to double the guard on the general," Bonnay murmured, ever cautious. "I'll give Andre the message when the countess isn't near."

But the Directory had received the latest news of Jourdan's rout, reports on Duras's retreat from Bregenz, accounts of the most recent Austrian triumphs in Italy, and couriers from Paris arrived at headquarters that day with mountains of dispatches.

Heated discussion had taken place in Paris about replacing Duras while Jourdan was being recalled to Paris to justify his disastrous defeat. And after much wrangling and disagreement and political maneuvering—the influences of Barras, Talleyrand, and Milet-Mureau, the new war minister, significant—agreement was finally reached, the conclusion inevitable to all who understood military operations. Duras's new appointment arrived in a letter signed by all five of the Directors. The remnants of Jourdan's and Bernadotte's armies had been merged with the Army of Switzerland and put under Duras's command. This new larger command was renamed the Army of the Danube.

Bernadotte, with his ear to the political winds and ever hostile to Duras, had sent an insolent letter to Duras, saying that he intended to go home for some time to recover from chest trouble, but that, when cured, he would return "to perish gloriously with his comrades."

And of course Claudine had included her predictable instructions in the Directory pouches. "I'll leave these to you," Duras had murmured to Bonnay, handing over the lavender letters. So on a day of such moment, with an avalanche of mail and the new combined army requiring immediate reorganization, one message from one agent was overlooked.

With his new appointment, Duras was now responsible for the defense of the whole of France's eastern frontier, from Koblenz up the Rhine Valley to Basel; thence along the Swiss frontier to the Lake of Constance and then southward to the Splungen Pass, a distance of over four hundred miles. The collapse of the French Army of Italy on his right had exposed the whole of his south flank to attack, adding another hundred miles of front for him to hold.

He'd left Teo at noon when the dispatches had arrived and wasn't able to return to her until dinner. But even then he stayed only briefly to dine and, apologizing before dessert was served, excused himself to return to his temporary headquarters at Frauenfeld. "I'll be back tonight," he said, placing his napkin on the table. "There's an incredible number of tasks to accomplish." His dark brows drew together in a faint frown. "Will you be all right without me?"

She smiled. "No, but go. I'll manage perfectly well." Reaching across the small table, she touched his hand, the pink diamond on her finger twinkling in the candlelight. "Tell me you love me."

"I love you . . . now and always," he said, impossible words for him only brief days ago. "I'll return as soon as I can."

"In six months from the sounds of it," she teased.

"I couldn't last that long without you. Perhaps six hours," he said, smiling as he rose from his chair. "Don't wait up, though."

As Duras was bidding Teo adieu, Mingen and the Chechens were in the stables of the same inn, exchanging gold with the groom for the use of his quarters above the loft. They preferred the anonymity although even had they wished to be conspicuous, lodgings were difficult to secure with the entire army in Frauenfeld. Mingen's first task would be to locate the countess and Duras; he knew they were staying at the same inn because everyone was astir catering to the general and his staff, but he needed to know the disposition of their apartments. So as soon as their saddlebags were carried up, Mingen left the Chechens in their hideaway and went out to reconnoiter. Additionally, he wished to discover whether his backup had arrived. With the news of Duras's appointment all over the city, time became critical.

Rumor had it that Duras was leaving tomorrow for an inspection of his entire front.

However rudimentary their language skills, the two assassins had caught bits of the conversations around them since entering the city and understood they were very close to the general's lodgings. So when Mingen left, one of them followed him. The other set off to find the French army headquarters.

It didn't take Mingen long to discover his Prussian colleagues hadn't yet arrived at their proposed meeting site—which left him on his own. Mildly daunted with the city awash with troops, Mingen debated his options on his return to the inn.

Stopping a buxom young maid in the hall, Mingen found that the general had just left.

"And his lady?" Mingen gently inquired, handing the young woman a coin for her trouble.

"In the room at the head of the stairs, sir," she said with a bob of her head. "Eating fresh berries from Paris, she is. A courier brought them this afternoon with champagne for the general's new honors."

Glancing up the stairway, Mingen caught sight of two guards posted on either side of the door. Not sure whether they were to keep the countess in or others out, he took out another coin, a larger one this time. "Would you bring the countess a note from me if I were to give you this gold piece? I knew her once and I'd like to extend my greetings to her."

"You could knock at her door," the maid said, eyeing Mingen with a modicum of suspicion. He didn't wear a French uniform, nor had he the appearance of a wealthy man. "How would you know a countess?"

"I worked for her father," he said, "as a secretary. She would know me as one of her household."

"In Paris?" she asked.

For an indecisive moment, Mingen debated his answer. Did the woman know Teo's history or did she assume Duras's lady was French? "Yes, in Paris," he answered.

"I'd like to see Paris someday."

Mingen's pulse rate returned to normal. "If you deliver a note for me, I'd be happy to give you enough to take a trip to Paris."

She put out her hand and Mingen smiled in satisfaction.

In the current state of war readiness, Mingen knew it was impossible to gain access to Duras directly. Under any circumstances it was difficult to secure a hearing with a general, protected as one always was by a phalanx of subordinates and staff.

Nor could he reveal himself publicly as King Frederick's agent or Korsakov's. Both would put him at risk. Some young aide with dreams of glory might shoot him first and ask questions later, or he could spend the remainder of the war in a French prison camp.

If, however, he could convince Teo of the danger to the general, she could most likely gain him an audience with Duras. And once the general learned of Korsakov's plan, his staff should be able to deal with the two Chechens.

Mingen hadn't reckoned with the Chechens' single-minded purpose. Adept at their trade, they'd already located both Duras and Teo. And while Mingen was in the hotel parlor penning his note to Teo, briefly explaining the danger to Duras, the Chechens were already climbing onto the second-floor porch behind the inn.

The two men balanced on the porch rail, carefully scrutinizing the dressing room revealed through the sliver of space where the edges of the drapes didn't completely meet. The room was only dimly lit and empty; they nodded at each other and went to work.

With the help of a stiletto knifeblade, the window was silently eased open just enough to allow the men to slip inside. As quickly, the window was shut again. The smaller of the two men moved behind the partially opened door and gazed out into the bedroom through the narrow slit between the door and frame. A faint smile creased his swarthy cheek and he nodded once to his partner.

A second later they sprinted through the doorway, dashing toward the bed where Teo lay reading, their approach so swift and sudden, they were almost upon her before she saw them.

She opened her mouth to scream, the sight of the Chechens chilling her to the bone, but a dark hand clamped hard against her mouth. Although she struggled against their hold, kicking and scratching, they easily overpowered her and in a few seconds she was tightly trussed, gagged, and blindfolded.

Stunned by the suddenness of the assault, terrified, an overwhelming sense of doom inundating her senses, she felt herself being carried away. The Chechens' function as assassins was well-known. Would they torture her before killing her? she wondered, the harrowing reflection inciting a paralyzing surge of panic. Then she felt a cool breeze on her cheek, heard a short muttered sound from below, and her pulse rate soared. She was before an open window.

She screamed as she felt herself being thrown, her cry of terror only a muffled murmur through the enveloping gag. In free fall, she instinctively braced herself for impact and then blessed oblivion engulfed her and she fainted, her limp body dropping into the arms of the Chechen below.

The smell of hay and horses invaded her nostrils when she gained consciousness, and lying utterly still, she waited for the tumult in her brain to subside somewhat. Don't move, she cautioned herself; her captors could be watching. And then she thanked all the benevolent spirits for keeping her alive, although she wondered in the next flashing moment whether she had any hope of long-term survival. Where was she, she wondered next, and how long had she been lying on the floor? She had no notion of time or place. No immediate sounds struck her senses. Was she alone?

She tentatively moved her feet, her tied ankles allowing only minimal movement. And waited for a reaction.

The silence went undisturbed.

She wondered if she was going to be left to die like this. It depended, she decided, forcing herself to a modicum of calm, on whether Korsakov needed her alive . . . or how much he needed her alive. Examining the most pressing reasons he might prefer her alive, she turned her attention to possible means of extricating herself from her perilous situation.

Standing at the bottom of the stairway, Mingen watched the maid approach the troopers guarding Teo's door. He'd given her gold coins for the guards as well, hoping the men would be more amenable to delivering his message.

When his note passed into a guard's hand, Mingen released the breath he'd been holding. The first hurdle had been cleared.

The maid winked at him as she descended the stairs, proud of her accomplishment, pleased with her new wealth.

After the guard disappeared through the doorway, Mingen waited, his nerves on edge. But the man reappeared short moments later, dashing out into the hall, obviously discomposed, and pulled his companion back into the apartment with him.

When they both came running out a few seconds later and plunged down the stairs, Mingen experienced an ominous sense of doom.

"Is she gone?" Mingen demanded, putting himself directly in their path. There wasn't time for finesse or discussion; every minute counted. "I know she is," he bluntly said as one soldier began to brush him aside. "You need me because I can find her. Take me to Duras."

Roughly grabbed, he was pushed ahead of them down the stairs and through the corridor to the entrance, a musket at his back.

A highly visible target, Duras was standing before a map mounted on the wall, his staff seated around a table before him.

Concealed behind the church pillars across the narrow street, the Chechens had already agreed on who would shoot whom. The taller man had Duras, while his colleague was to kill the two guards posted outside. Each rifle had two shots. Duras would be shot twice as insurance. The guards once each in the head.

An escape route had been planned through the church and down the narrow alleyway, back to the stables where their horses were already saddled. If Mingen interfered they'd kill him.

They had only to wait for Duras to circle round the table so he'd be well within range. For optimum success they needed him a few feet closer. They were patient men and it was still early. Should Mingen return to their lodgings, he would find nothing amiss; they'd left their saddlebags in the groom's quarters. Teo was secreted away elsewhere—in a small storage room at the back of the stables.

Mingen was talking in a precipitous rush as he walked, desperate to convince the skeptical, silent troopers of Duras's danger. He told them of Korsakov's orders, of his own contradictory mission—revealing more than he wished, but required by circumstances to convey the full magnitude of Duras's vulnerability.

Neither man responded to him; they only forced him

along with the jabbing butt of their rifles. "Not the front door," Mingen protested as they approached the intersection leading to the street running by headquarters. Stopping abruptly, risking a bullet in the back, he explained in rapid phrases that the Chechens would see them or *possibly* see them. They couldn't take the chance.

With seconds crucial, he almost screamed with frustration as he waited for the soldiers to make a decision, their contemplation measured, deliberate. Then motioning him forward, they turned down the mews behind the building and Mingen broke into a run, oblivious to the danger of being shot. If Duras died, the consequences would be disastrous to Prussia.

Cholet had asked for clarification of a phrase he was transcribing from Duras's recitation, and moving around the table to see what Cholet had written, Duras finally came within target range. "Now," one of the Chechens murmured, bringing his rifle up to his shoulder. His colleague followed suit with well-drilled teamwork. The men sighted in, adjusted their stance minutely, carefully took aim . . .

Duras looked up as a commotion erupted in the corridor outside and he'd already turned toward the door when it burst open.

"Down!" Mingen screamed, diving for Duras.

A rifle shot smashed through the window, followed by a second. Glass exploded into the room, spraying the two men in a tangle on the floor.

"Korsakov," Mingen rasped, rolling away from Duras.

The single word was enough to bring Duras instantly to his feet, uncaring about the rifle fire blasting away outside. "Get the gunmen!" Duras shouted. "Find them and bring them back!" Turning to Mingen, who was scrambling to his feet, he brusquely said, "Tell me everything."

"They've taken the countess."

It was possible for Moorish skin to blanch. "When?" Duras said, his voice whisper soft. He didn't ask to whom he spoke.

"A few minutes ago."

"Who took her?" Duras was already striding toward the door, his own safety not at issue.

"Korsakov's Chechens."

"He's a dead man," Duras murmured, motioning for his personal guards to follow him, pulling a rifle from the stand near the door. "Where are they taking her?" he curtly queried, picking up a handful of ammunition, sliding the charges and balls into his pocket.

"They'll go to Bregenz if they manage to get away."

"They won't get far." Duras strode toward the open door. "Where are their mounts?"

"At the Grafenhausen inn."

Duras ran full-out, leaving Mingen behind, leaving his men behind, panic-stricken, not allowing himself to consider the grim possibility Teo might be already dead, thinking instead of finding her—and of revenge.

He must protect her more closely once she was with him again, he thought. Keep her near, take more precautions. Condemning himself for carelessness, he realized he should have known better. Korsakov wasn't a man to underestimate.

And once Duras had Teo back, he'd kill him.

When Mingen and his guards caught up with him, Duras was threatening the ostlers and grooms, interrogating them in a clipped, crisp staccato. Where were the Chechens' mounts? Had they seen the men? Had Teo been sighted? And when Mingen reported the Chechens' horses were missing, Duras barked, "I want a cavalry brigade here in five minutes," his order sending several of his men racing away. "Search the stables," he brusquely commanded the remaining men, before he raced after Mingen, who was taking the stairs to the loft at a run.

The groom's quarters were empty.

"Whom do you work for?" Duras asked only then.

Mingen didn't risk lying; he told the general in brief, breathless phrases, the motive and reasons for his journey. Duras asked him to repeat several details of his conversation with Korsakov, but questioned nothing else. "You needn't accompany us," he briskly said when his queries were satisfied, already turning to leave the room, his mind on possible escape routes for the Chechens. He knew the country much better than they; he knew every road and byway between the Rhine and Vienna.

"If you . . . don't mind . . . I'll follow along," Mingen said, trying to keep pace with Duras who was descending the stairs in leaps.

"Suit yourself, but don't get in the way." An implicit threat underlay the statement.

"No, sir." Winded after running to headquarters and back, Mingen panted in his wake. "But I'd like . . . to report the conclusion . . . of the . . . episode . . . to the king."

"This isn't a fucking *episode*," Duras snarled, turning briefly to cast Mingen a withering glance.

"No . . . of course . . . sir, my apologies . . . sir." His lungs were wheezing for air. "I could show . . . you the route . . . we took from Bregenz. They . . . may not . . . know another way . . . back."

"They apparently know more than you think." Duras strode out into the stable yard where several of his cavalry troops were already waiting. "Explain the route." Gruff, impatient to be off, he began pacing.

As Mingen relayed the information, Duras's charger was brought forward by a trooper. Duras nodded at the mention of each village and posting station, mounted swiftly during Mingen's recital, and slid his rifle into its saddle holster.

Gesturing for a horse to be brought forward for Mingen, Duras put spurs to his charger's flanks and galloped from the yard.

Teo's feet had been untied so she could ride astride, and she was seated before one of her captors, his chest pressed against her back, his arm holding her firmly in place. Still blindfolded and gagged, her bearings tentative, she knew only that the cobblestones of the city had given way after a time to a country road. It still appeared to be night or else her blindfold was especially dense for no light penetrated the fabric.

With her husband a minimum two days' journey away with the state of the war, her only hope lay in her captors' need to stop and sleep or eat eventually. Each minute of delay allowed Duras time to find her. She didn't doubt his pursuit.

If he still lived, she mournfully thought.

But Andre had protection, she reminded herself; he was always surrounded by officers and staff. Praying that he'd survived the Chechens' deadly skills, she implored all the gods of her childhood.

But hours later her spirits were less heartened, and as her body grew weary, her mind dwelled on the more depressing possibilities. Terrible images of Korsakov filled her mind, and in her melancholy, she didn't know whether she'd outlast this abduction. Her husband was a beast without conscience, and despite her annual tribute of gold for his coffers, this time he might not be able to control his rage. He had to know she was with Duras, and if she was truly with child, she wasn't sure in the full tide of Korsakov's wrath whether she could convince him the child was his.

The bonds on her wrists were drawing blood; she could feel the coolness on her skin and the brutal pace they were maintaining was causing her stomach to knot into cramps. And when she first felt the slippery wetness on the saddle after what seemed hours of hard riding, despair over-whelmed her.

Either her courses had begun, days late when they never were late, or she was losing Duras's child. Tears welled in her eyes behind the tightly knotted blindfold; her hopes of happiness were dashed. And if Duras *had* been killed, she thought, wretched and despondent, she no longer cared to live.

At the first village they passed, Duras and Bonnay questioned a number of people, seeking information on the Chechens and Teo.

But no one had seen them.

"We'll go on to the next posting station," Duras said. "If they haven't arrived there, we'll backtrack." His voice was grim; they'd lose valuable time if they were forced to retrace their route.

"Hired assassins aren't likely to be conspicuous," Bonnay said, wanting to offer comfort.

"Let's hope that's the reason," Duras said, his expression closed. His whip came down on his horse's flanks and his charger bolted forward.

At the next posting station two men matching Mingen's description of the Chechens had changed horses. And although they'd seen no woman, one man wore a woman's ring on his small finger. A pink diamond. And the scent of violets clung to one of the men.

"It's them," Duras softly said, marginally relieved. Teo's scent would have been washed away by the wind by now if she wasn't with them. "One must be riding double. How far to the next posting station?"

"Ten miles," the ostler replied.

"Good," Duras murmured, calculating time and distance. "Did everyone hear that?" he said, half turning in the saddle to address his men. "We have them."

Duras was silent as they raced through the night, confident now of overtaking the Chechens, his only concern Teo's safety. How frightened she must be, what a terrible ordeal for her to undergo. "I don't want the Chechens killed," he shouted across to Bonnay as their mounts galloped side by side.

Bonnay nodded.

And then Duras lashed his charger to more speed.

They caught sight of their prey as they exited a long stretch of forest road, the countryside opening up to them, falling away in rolling hills down to a silvery lake. Two riders, far off in the distance, were cresting a rise, the quarter-moon dimly outlining their shapes.

Not daring to openly pursue them, afraid the Chechens might harm Teo to extremity, Duras gestured to Bonnay, then wheeled his horse off the road. Riding cross-country, they could intercept the Chechens short of the next posting station.

After hours of hard riding, Teo was reeling in the saddle, only the Chechen's strong grip holding her upright. It seemed an eternity since she'd begun bleeding; her thighs were slippery on the saddle, her stomach spasms agonizing. Light-headed, she couldn't concentrate, logical thought always sliding away, her mind obsessed with the loss of her child. Even contemplation of her personal danger lapsed before her greater bereavement.

Half faint from her pain, she didn't notice at first that the horses had come to a stop. But when she was lifted from the saddle and deposited on the damp grass, the chill ground revived her. With the sound of hoofbeats receding in the distance, she knew she'd be alone for a time but she also knew better than to hope: the Chechens would return for her as they had done before. She shivered in her light gown, the March temperatures cool, the dampness between her legs chilling.

She was losing all hope for her child, for the cruel pains were unrelenting. Her faith in being rescued was waning as well; they'd been on the road too long. And most devastating, the possibility that Duras had been killed gained more credence with each passing hour. Had he lived he would have overtaken her by now. Yielding to despair, she hiccuped and gulped, an ache filling her throat, but even her tears had run dry after so many hours of crying, as though her body had given up.

Attempting to bolster her flagging spirits, she told herself there had to be a way out. Reminding herself she'd always overcome adversity before, invoking those maxims of courage and resolution that had always given her hope in the past, she tried to remain stalwart. But the weight of her oppression was too much this time, the thought of losing the baby and Duras too tragic.

How cold she felt, how alone.

Concealed behind a privet hedge bordering the road, Duras and Bonnay waited outside the village, only moments ahead of the Chechens, their rifles trained on the curve in the road fifty yards out.

"Do we shoot the horses or them?" Bonnay whispered.

"Wound the men."

Bonnay understood. Beyond interrogating Korsakov's agents, Duras had his own personal agenda.

But when Korsakov's men rode into sight a moment later, Teo wasn't with them and Duras swore under his breath, an unreasoning fear flooding his mind. Astonished, Bonnay saw him move his mount into the center of the road, exposing himself as he aimed his rifle, as if he wanted them to see their assailant. And for a black despairing second before he pulled the trigger, Duras intended to kill them.

But logic prevailed; he needed their information to find Teo. A rifle shot exploded in the quiet of the night, quickly followed by Bonnay's almost simultaneous shot, and both Chechens struggled to hold themselves in the saddle. Looking for a means of escape, they forced their horses left and drove them through the hedge bordering the road.

Duras charged after them, his warhorse plunging through the hedgerow. Korsakov's men were racing for the tree line on the far side of the field, whipping their horses, trying to gain the protection of the shadowed forest.

Digging in his spurs, Duras drew his pistol and, leaning forward over his charger's neck, took aim. But the distance was too great for accuracy, and murmuring low, he coaxed more speed from his mount. Responding to Duras's voice, with gutsy courage, his horse lengthened its stride.

The dark tree line loomed nearer; the possibility of losing the Chechens suddenly seemed ominous. Detesting what he must do, the twin barrels of Duras's pistol flashed twice and both horses broke stride, stumbled a few yards and collapsed. Thrown from the saddle, the Chechens landed hard, their bodies bouncing several times before coming to rest on the stubble of last year's crop.

Duras came to a halt beside the still bodies, his second pistol trained on the men, and when Bonnay arrived seconds later, he said, "Find the Prussian agent to interpret."

When the cavalry troop arrived shortly after, the Chechens were induced to speak. Upon hearing Teo was alive and nearby, Duras left Bonnay to finish the interrogation and ran off to search for her.

But he couldn't find her. The night was almost moonless, dark shadows covered the verges of the road, and the grasses rose knee-high, the hedge adding further gloom to the landscape. He ordered his troopers to fan out on foot, warning them to watch where they walked, wondering if the Chechens' information could be trusted when Teo wasn't found after a lengthy search, fearful she was already far away, taken by someone else beyond his reach.

Night gave way to morning as they covered the adjacent fields and forest and ditches, the horizon rimmed with the softest of grays, the moon low in the sky. "We'll have to move farther down the road," Duras ordered, fear a knot in his stomach.

One of Vigée's troopers found Teo, his shout echoing from far down the road. But frightened by the sight of her motionless form, he didn't dare touch her. The road around him filled up with other troopers, none willing to take responsibility for moving her without Duras's orders. Teo's breathing was too faint, her skin deathly pale, the blood on her gown lurid.

A half-mile away when he heard the cry, Duras sprinted back, the sight of his troopers milling on the road alarming. At his approach, the men parted to make way for him, unspoken sympathy in their eyes. And for an awful moment, Duras thought she was dead. A thousand battle memories flooded his mind when he first saw the blood, tragic, appalling images. Quickly dropping to his knees beside her, he tried to find the pulse in her wrist, touched her cheek to see if it was as cold as her hand, found himself breathing again when he first discovered the faint rhythm of her heart in the vein behind her ear. Thank God, he thought, his most anguished fear alleviated. But she was alarmingly still, he reflected, his fingers swiftly untying the bonds on her wrists, lifting the gag from her mouth. Gently turning her head, he untied the blindfold and willed her to open her eyes and gaze at him with recognition.

But she lay still as death.

"We need a doctor! Find a damned doctor!" Duras shouted, shrugging out of his tunic, quickly covering her. "And get blankets!"

"I'm a doctor," Mingen said, stepping forward.

"How do I know that?" Duras said, eyeing Mingen with suspicion.

"You could wait for one to arrive or take my word for it."

"I want you to understand," Duras said, warning and gravity in his tone, "how important she is to me."

"Yes, sir." Mingen was already well aware of that. The commanding general of the last functioning French army in the field had abandoned everything to find this woman. "If we could have some blankets. And some privacy," he delicately added.

The blankets arrived moments later and the troopers drifted off a respectable distance, leaving Duras and Mingen alone.

"She believed she was pregnant," Duras quietly said, adjusting a folded blanket under Teo's head for a pillow.

"She may have aborted. Do I have your permission to examine her?"

Duras nodded. "And I want the truth . . . whatever her condition."

"Yes, sir." Mingen realized he was in a very sensitive position. While Duras wanted the truth, in reality he only wanted a palatable truth.

He cautiously checked Teo for broken bones, not wishing to move her if she were suffering from a serious fracture. Her unconsciousness suggested a concussion, but on examination her eyes seemed to discount that diagnosis. "There are no broken bones as far as I can tell," Mingen declared. "I'd like to have her carried inside where it's warm."

A cart with a feather bed was immediately procured and a brief time later, Teo was ensconced in the local barrister's bed. A maidservant at Mingen's request brought warm milk and hot water. Instructing Duras to build up the fire, Mingen carefully cut away Teo's skirt. And under Duras's watchful eye, he washed away the blood.

"Can you tell if she was with child?" Duras's voice was hesitant, low.

"It would appear very early in a pregnancy," Mingen equivocated.

"Could this be her menses?"

"If it is I can't stop it. If she's in the early stages of pregnancy, however," he asserted, "I may be able to stop the bleeding. Would you like me to try?"

"There's a choice?"

"I know of a drug that may work. I can't guarantee it." Although he understood there were men who would prefer their mistress not carry her pregnancy to full term.

"She wants this child."

"Regardless, we can simply let nature take its course," Mingen delicately said, taking note of Duras's noninvolvement in the last sentence.

"The bleeding would eventually stop?"

"If she's miscarrying, generally yes."

Mingen's small reservation brought Duras's gaze back from contemplating Teo's silent form. "Why is she still unconscious?"

"Her body temperature dropped quite low. I don't know if you noticed, but most of the blood on her legs was dried. As her temperature lowered, the bleeding diminished. She's been cold for some time."

"She wasn't dressed for the frigid temperatures," Duras murmured, tucking the blanket around her more closely. "Will this unconscious state persist?"

"I can't find any obvious concussion. Once her temperature's restored, she should wake."

"After that, when could the countess be moved? Unfortunately, I need to be in Zurich with all haste." Duras's voice had taken on a crispness; his commitments were urgent.

"It depends on whether you wish me to stop her bleeding. If I give her the potion, I'd recommend not moving her for perhaps a week."

"A week." Duras's voice was scarcely audible.

Mingen waited, understanding how critical was the timetable of events driving Duras, personally impacted by the general's decision, the fate of his king and Prussia in the balance, as well.

"She's convinced of this baby," Duras said with a sigh.

"Some women recognize these changes very soon."

"I can't imagine how she could know after such a brief interval."

"May I ask how brief a time?"

Duras swiftly calculated. "A little over two weeks."

"I see," Mingen said, concealing his astonishment.

"Jesus," Duras whispered, his gaze on Teo, the pressure of affairs intense, the archduke perhaps already on the march. He touched her cheek with the back of his fingers, drew them gently down the graceful curve of her jaw, stood in reflection for a moment. "Stop the bleeding," he finally said, his voice soft, and then turning to Mingen, he repeated in a normal tone, "Stop the bleeding. We'll stay here until she's well."

He was risking much for love of this woman, Mingen thought, genuinely shocked at Duras's decision. But one didn't question a general, certainly not one of Duras's stature.

"I'd appreciate your staying on with us," Duras went on. "Does that require some communiqué through diplomatic channels?"

"It depends on the length of time, sir."

"Until the countess has a baby."

"This baby?"

"*A* baby," Duras plainly said, willing to give her whatever she wanted in gratitude for her life.

"That length of time would require approval, sir."

"Very well. I'll see to it." He nodded his head in acknowledgment. "Now make my Teo well."

The potion of balm, burnet and yarrow infused in hot milk was slowly spooned into Teo's mouth, the two men taking turns with the laborious process, the room heated to torrid levels to warm Teo. Both men had dispensed with their shirts and even then were visibly sweating. The role of nursemaid was so unusual for a man of Duras's rank that Mingen expressed his astonishment in an unguarded moment.

They'd both been up all day and half the night, working side by side to succor Teo, and a comfortable rapport had developed between the two men of such diverse origins. "She'd do the same for me," Duras said, setting down the empty cup.

"An egalitarian viewpoint for a man of your consequence."

"I consider myself fortunate to have found her."

"Today, you mean."

"Yes . . . and two weeks ago." Duras gazed for a moment at the woman who'd abruptly entered his life and introduced him to the wonder of love. "I know how to fight battles and save France from its enemies," he said, half to himself. "That's all I've ever done." Dropping into a chair beside the bed, he shifted into an exhausted sprawl. "Now I'm not sure I'd know how to live without Teo."

"I've never been in love." Mingen stood at the foot of the bed, leaning wearily against the bedpost.

"Nor had I." Duras smiled, recalling Teo's words. "She told me I was. I didn't believe her." A faint smile graced his mouth. "We both thank you for saving her child. She'll be pleased."

"The countess must lie very still for a few days."

"I'll see that she does."

"And your superiors. How will they regard your delay in Neuwilen?"

"I don't have superiors, Herr Mingen," Duras softly replied, regarding the Prussian from under half-lowered lashes.

"Forgive me, sir." Mingen had overlooked Duras's distinctive reputation. His talents allowed him wide latitude; even the Directory was never sure he would obey their orders.

"We'll stay here until Teo is well," Duras affirmed. "Or until the military situation demands"—he smiled faintly—"a change of scenery."

"The archduke may march."

Duras's gaze took on a bland neutrality. "Not if Thugut and his cronies have their say."

"A fortunate rivalry for you."

"Dealing with the Austrian high command is always advantageous to us—they're mired in bureaucracy. Nor do they have resolute generals."

"You have your Jourdans, as well."

Duras sighed. "At least he's finished now."

"May I ask you about Korsakov?"

"No." Blunt and curt.

"He doesn't deserve to lead a corps," Mingen offered, conscious he'd overstepped his bounds.

"Nor do most of the Russian staff," Duras said, his voice neutral once again.

"True. Will you win?"

Duras smiled. "Of course. Do you doubt it?"

"I wouldn't be here if I did."

"Exactly."

"So you knew I'd stay to help you."

"You didn't have a choice." Duras understood the art of war and the underlying national agendas. "But thank you nonetheless. You could have been less honorable and found an excuse to go back."

"The king needs you alive."

"And I need Teo alive."

"Then we can help each other."

"A devil's pact," Duras said with a faint smile.

"I like to think of it as a humanitarian gesture," Mingen replied, his smile equally sardonic.

"Call it whatever you like as long as Teo regains her health."

The bottom line was clearly set.

14

Duras was sleeping in his chair beside the bed, Mingen resting on a chaise near the window, when the small rustle of bedclothes brought them both awake. Duras came to his feet in a bound, his gaze alert, sweeping over Teo with a swift scrutiny. And then his expression relaxed and he smiled. A flush of color brightened her cheeks.

"You look better," he softly said.

"You came," she whispered.

"I wish I'd found you sooner." Sitting down beside her, he brushed her cheek with his fingertips.

Her eyes filled with tears; she knew.

"Don't cry, darling," he murmured, afraid to touch her, softly patting her hand under the blankets. "You'll feel better in a few days. We're going to stay here until you're well."

But her tears only increased, pouring down her cheeks, and leaning close, careful not to jar her, Duras tenderly kissed her.

"I lost the baby." Anguish vibrated in her quiet words.

He shook his head, a small, unequivocal movement. "Not yet." The sudden hope in her eyes tore at his heart. "Herr Mingen is optimistic," he said, standing upright, and as her gaze shifted behind him, he motioned the doctor forward. "Tell her," he said.

"I've given you a drug that's stopped the bleeding."

A small worry line appeared between her dark brows. "Has the baby been harmed?"

"One can't be completely certain, but I don't believe it was. And if you're very careful for the next few days—"

"Yes, yes. Andre," she softly cried, turning to Duras, flushed with exultation, "did you hear? I shall be ever so good and not move a muscle." Her sudden smile warmed his heart and he wondered how he'd ever lived without her.

"It's the best of news, darling. And Herr Mingen has agreed to stay on as your physician."

Her gaze swiveled back to Mingen. "How wonderful," she gaily said. "I shall be your most obedient patient."

"The pleasure is mine, Your Excellency."

"Teo, please. I'd prefer that."

"Yes, of course."

"Would you like something to eat?" Duras interposed, references to her husband generally distressful. "We've a cook of sorts downstairs."

"Food sounds wonderful."

"Now I'm sure you're on the mend," Duras teased. "Although I warn you the menu is limited."

"Where are we?"

"A half day east of Felben." He saw the flicker of anguish in her eyes and knew the harrowing memories of her abduction were afflicting her. "Would you like me to send for Tamyr?" he asked, wanting to offer her comfort.

"Would you?" Pleasure flooded her glance.

"She could be here in a few days."

"You're the most adorable man," she murmured, a husky undertone in her voice.

"Am I?" he said with amusement.

"But only for me," she said, lush and low.

"Only for you," he softly agreed.

"Can you stay with me?" Her gaze flicked to Mingen, who had retreated at their murmurings.

"I'm here for the duration. Let's ask the doctor if you may sit up for dinner."

Herr Mingen agreed she could, but warned against any additional exertions. "I must stress that," he emphasized, directing an earnest glance at Duras.

"I'm warned, Herr Doctor," Duras pleasantly replied. "Rest assured I understand the consequences."

"I'll move my things into the room next door," Mingen said, "now that your ladyship is in more vigorous health."

"Stay near," Duras quietly ordered.

"Yes, sir. I'll direct the cook to make some nourishing dishes for the lady, if you agree."

"Yes, certainly. Now, you must follow his regimen, darling," Duras went on, casting an admonishing glance at Teo.

"I shall be very pleased to nourish myself and the baby, Andre. You needn't become authoritarian on that account," she sweetly said.

"No authority intended, darling."

This from the man who held power over France's armies, over the future of the Republic. Mingen gave the countess considerable points for spirit.

* * *

Duras called for Bonnay before supper to go over the most pressing of their duties. And after Bonnay had offered Teo his salutations and good wishes, the men retired to a small table set near the fireplace to prioritize their agenda.

"How long will we be here?" Bonnay asked, his voice kept low.

"Perhaps a week."

His shock showed.

"Teo can't be moved until then." Duras spoke in an undertone, as well.

"What if the Austrians attack?"

"Our intelligence reports indicate no movement anywhere on the front."

"But if they do?"

"Then we move," Duras quietly said.

"How ill is the countess?"

"She's not ill. She may be pregnant."

"Still?" Bonnay had seen all the blood last night.

"Teo's hopeful."

"And the doctor?"

There was the minutest pause. "With reservations, hopeful as well."

"So we're waiting—"

"Until she's better," Duras confirmed. "Bring Cholet out here and those of the staff we'll need to expedite the retreat to Zurich."

"We'll be operating the rear guard?" Bonnay noted with faintly raised eyebrows.

"Neither of us has done that for a while," Duras drolly replied.

His chief of staff chuckled. "Not since the retreat from Caldiero. We harassed the Austrians with a vengeance that time."

"We'll take them again, but hopefully from Zurich."

"The regiments from Chur are almost there."

"And the Sargans headquarters staff?"

"En route."

"Good. I need a small company to bring Teo's maid-servant out."

"Done. What are we going to do with Turreau's regiments at Schwyz?"

"It's an indefensible position with so few men. They'll have to come in."

"What of the Chechens?"

"They're still alive?" Duras murmured.

"Considering their wounds, they probably won't last the night," Bonnay obligingly replied.

"I'm surprised they haven't bled to death yet." Duras's voice was without pity.

"It's just a matter of time, I'm sure."

"See that it is."

They spoke then of less emotional issues, the organization of the necessary defenses at Zurich of primary importance. They discussed the first line of defense and the second and third, as well, since the archduke's large army presented a formidable foe. His attack was inevitable, with his troops poised to invade. It was just a question of time.

While they talked, Bonnay jotted down notes for the dispatches that would have to be relayed to their commanders. There was a certain amount of initial coordination they could accomplish from a distance, but the quintessential defense would require Duras there in person. Bonnay hoped like hell Archduke Charlie was having another one of his spells.[11] Then with luck this week in Neuwilen wouldn't have disastrous consequences.

Dinner that night was in the way of a celebration for the prospective family unit. The table had been moved closer to the fire, and bundled in blankets, Teo was allowed to sit up for a short time. She was beaming with happiness as was Duras and when she proposed a toast to their child, Duras felt a miraculous awe that surprised him. He thought himself a thoroughly pragmatic man.

"I feel absolutely wonderful," Teo exclaimed, enjoying the champagne bubbles in her nose. "Herr Mingen is a wizard."

"He's a very clever man," Duras agreed, smiling at Teo over the rim of his glass.

"Have you rewarded him?"

"Not yet."

"What do you mean, not yet?" she anxiously inquired, a flicker of fear in her eyes.

"I just meant I've been too busy. But I shall, darling. I'm grateful beyond words for his skill."

"That's better," she said, the relief in her voice audible.

"You're supposed to relax and not worry. Remember what Anton said just before dinner. Have you thought of any new names?" he inquired, wishing to divert her thoughts to less fearful ones.

"Do you have any family names?"

"None I'd use," he said, grinning.

"Were your father's and mother's names so odd?"

"Yes."

"Are you going to tell me?"

His smile was roguish. "I don't think so."

"Then how did you acquire such a normal name?"

"A priest suggested it as a compromise. I was three months old and my parents couldn't agree on a name. My father was raiding on the Ionian Sea at the time. My real name is Andreas."

"Perhaps you'd like an Andreas to follow you?"

"Not particularly," he said with a small shake of his head. "I have no dynastic impulses."

"Do you have any preferences?"

"None at all," he pleasantly replied. "You name the child."

"Would you mind a Russian name?"

His gaze narrowed briefly and then he said, "Not if you wish it."

"My mother's family was Russian."

His brows quirked in inquiry. "Siberia is a long way from Russia proper."

"My grandfather, Prince Samarin, had been exiled."

"He couldn't have approved of his daughter's marriage to a native."

"Society meant nothing to him. His concern was only with my father's political views. He knew how dangerous it was to oppose the state and he wished more security for his daughter." Teo paused, her mind flooded with memory. "He died by his own hand," she slowly went on, "when he learned of my mother's death. Mama was his last surviving child."

"A Russian name would be fine," Duras softly said, thinking Teo had been very alone in the world.

"Thank you." Her eyes glistened with unshed tears. "I didn't think it would matter after all these years." She offered a tentative smile.

"You never forget," Duras said, reaching across the table to touch her hand. His own parents had been dead for years and he thought of them often. "But we can begin our own family. We *are* beginning our family," he added with a smile.

"You have to win this war." Her voice was earnest.

"I intend to."

"And then you'll take me home to Nice?"

He smiled. "First thing."

"I've never been on a yacht."

"You'll like it," he simply said, not mentioning she'd be the first woman to step foot on the *Marguerite*.

"As long as you're there, I will."

"I'll always be there."

Her gaze held his in quiet appeal. "I'm frightened sometimes . . . with all the—"

"I'll keep you safe," Duras promised. "This won't happen again." He had bodyguards in place against any eventuality.

She took a small shaky breath, trying to suppress the awful memories. "Thank you for finding me."

"I would have found you anywhere in the world."

"I'm so weepy again," she apologized, wiping her eyes with the napkin.

"You went through too much." He inhaled to steady himself, vengeance gripping his senses. "You shouldn't have suffered so," he soothed, repressing the violence of his feelings. The Chechens had died slowly that afternoon; he'd had their veins opened, but he wished to kill them again for what they'd done to Teo. "Do you like Mingen's menu?" he abruptly queried as if he were a guest at a dinner party making conversation.

"I do," she said, sniffing.

Leaning over, he took the wet napkin from her hand and wiped away her tears. "Then you should eat more," he coaxed. "My baby needs some food."

"I love when you say that," she whispered. "I love having your baby."

"I'd like to lock the world away and sail off in my yacht with you. And never come back."

"Someday we will."

"I'll see that it happens."

He was a man of great strength and resources, and in the following days, he set to work realizing his goals. Goals that would have daunted a lesser man. He had a war to win. Bonnay and Cholet were permanent residents in the small bedroom on the second floor, and dispatches were sent off in a continuous cavalcade of couriers. Teo was cosseted and fed and superintended with fond and chary prudence by Duras, Mingen, and a great number of servants. She protested once she felt like the goose being fattened for Christmas. "Just fattened for me, *ma chère*," Duras had murmured. "And I'll adore every blossoming curve."

When Mingen pronounced her ready to travel two days short of a week, a coach was readied with a bed so soft, none of the bumps and potholes in the road would jar its precious cargo. Duras rode with Teo occasionally, but he and Bonnay were more often riding alongside, working, Cholet between them scribbling as fast as he could.

Tamyr met them at Bassersdorf and Teo was pampered and ordered about like a child for the remainder of the journey to Zurich. But she was grateful for Tamyr's common-sense advice and company. The baby was still safe, Mingen and Tamyr had confirmed. Duras was at her side; the Austrians weren't on the march yet.

It was a blessed respite.

The quarters found for them in Zurich were per Duras's instructions—the first consideration that of security. And when he lifted Teo from the carriage in the curved drive and walked with her to the doorway, he said with a smile, "Welcome to our first home."

Teo glanced up at the imposing façade of the villa dramatically situated on the heights of the Zurichberg, and then at his smiling face. "You're going to spoil me."

I'm going to keep you safe, he thought. "With the greatest of pleasure," he said instead. "Make a wish when I carry you over the threshold."

The door opened then as though by unspoken command and a stately butler stood at attention in a vast, vaulted hall.

Ignoring him, Duras dropped a light kiss on Teo's nose. "Ready?"

She shut her eyes briefly and then, opening them, nodded.

And as he moved in a long-legged stride across the porch and over the threshold, he felt a level of happiness formerly unknown. He always wished for the same thing—long life. Confident, assured, he could ensure the rest himself.

Keep him safe, Teo wished as he swung her over the threshold. After that, she thought, everything was possible.

With Tamyr to care for Teo and a heavy guard placed around her, Duras left shortly after to make an inspection of his entire front. He recommended to the Directory that the advanced fortress of Mannheim, on the right bank of the Rhine, should be evacuated, as it involved a useless waste of troops in an indefensible position. As for the rest, he saw to the defenses of a lengthy frontier. And as Duras had expected, orders from Vienna were laggard, with the political factions fighting over policy.[12]

The Austrian Chancellor Thugut wanted to retain the archduke's army in Bavaria so this force could watch both Prussia and the unreliable German princes. Therefore Charles was restrained from moving into Switzerland. Troubled and despondent, the archduke had one of his nervous spells, which always appeared in times of stress and frustration, and asked for a leave of absence.

While he recuperated on his estates, Feldzeugmeister Count Olivier Wallis took over command and Thugut busied himself with schemes to replace the emperor's brother Charles.

Duras knew that in Austria political considerations always overrode military plans. Moreover, when he heard Wallis had taken over command, he surmised no major operations were to be undertaken immediately. Grateful the Austrians didn't follow up their victory at Stockach, Duras was given a breathing space to redistribute his forces.

The last week in April, Duras returned to Zurich from his inspection tour. His intelligence services reported that Charles had recovered and the emperor had decided to keep him on as army commander.

"I don't wish to be disturbed tonight," Duras told his staff as they parted after weeks in the saddle, "unless Charlie is within a league of Zurich." His smiling gaze took in the full array of officers assembled in his offices. "Enjoy yourselves, gentlemen, and if you can tear yourselves away from the Zurich coquettes by ten tomorrow morning, I'll see you in my office." Flinging his saddlebags over his shoulder, he walked toward the door.

"The demireps will miss you, sir," Vigée merrily countered, a full cognac glass already in his hand.

"I'm sure you can keep them busy," Duras murmured, exiting the room.

Raising his glass toward the door, Vigée said with a grin, "Any bets whether he gets here by ten?"

"He'll be here before you," Bonnay replied, smiling. "I hear Mademoiselle Georgette has been pining away since you were gone." Vigée's current mistress wasn't known for her faithfulness.

"Georgie doesn't pine, as you well know, Henri," Vigée retorted, his bright smile undeterred by nuances of infidelity. "I only ask for her undivided attention when I'm here. Beyond that I lay no claim."

"How *can* you with a wife of independent wealth?" Cholet lightly interposed.

"An intelligent man," Vigée replied, a roguish lift to his brows. "Luckily Cecile prefers paved streets and the opera nearby."

"Zurich has paved streets and an opera," one of the officers said.

Vigée cast him a sportive scowl. "For God's sake, don't tell her. Now if any of you gentlemen would care to retire to Georgie's with me," he went on with a grin, "she and her pretty friends will try to convince us we were sorely missed."

15

As Duras walked through the entrance gate to the villa, he stopped to talk to the troopers standing guard, thanking them for their vigilance.

"Are the Austrians ever going to move, sir?" one soldier asked. "It's been damned dull."

"We've heard rumors Charlie's finally coming up to scratch," another said.

"We might see the Austrians by the end of the week. Von Hotze seems to be moving," Duras replied. "And then we'll have some excitement."

"It's about time, sir."

Duras smiled. "Guard duty too tame, is it?"

"Well—no offense, sir, and the countess is right nice and all, but it ain't fightin', sir."

"She hasn't kept you busy enough?"

"She's teachin' us how to read with the others, so it's busy enough what with carting the children back and forth and their mothers and such from the camps, but I'm lookin' forward to puttin' Archduke Charlie in his place."

"Children?" Duras inquired. His daily letters from Teo had been without mention of children or reading or anything beyond the bed rest he expected of her.

"The countess's school, sir. What with those of us in the guard who can't read or write much, and the troopers' children who follow the drum and a good number of their mothers—I'd say a couple hundred, give or take."

"Here?" Duras said, repressing an urge to gasp.

"Here and at the camp down by the river. Didn't you know, sir?" the soldier hesitantly asked. "She told Major Lindet that you'd authorized it."

"I may have forgotten," he murmured.

"Well, she's doin' a right fine job, sir. Greer here and me can write our names almost perfect."

"Congratulations. What time does the, er, school begin?" Duras queried, wondering how much time he had in the morning to cancel the scheduled activities.

"Eight sharp, sir. The countess says she expects everyone there bright and early."

"I see. Thank you . . ."

"Hebert, sir. I been with you since Rivoli, sir."

"We've seen a lot of Europe since then," Duras pleasantly declared.

"We'll take them once and for all now, sir."

"We'd better, hadn't we?" Duras said with a faint smile.

"No problem, sir, with you in command."

"I'll see you men in the morning."

"At the school, sir?"

"Perhaps," Duras neutrally replied.

* * *

"A school?" Duras admonished the majordomo he'd left in charge when he walked through the door. He was scowling as he stripped off his gloves.

"The countess assured me of your approval, General." A former employee of the Duc d'Orléans, Ollivier wasn't easily discomfited.

"She did, did she?"

"Very emphatically. I recall her saying you'd given your wholehearted blessing."

One dark brow lifted in reproof. "Quite a few of them come here, I'm told."

"Three days a week, sir."

"Where, for God's sake?"

"The furniture has been moved out of the reception rooms."

"Good Lord. How many?"

"Two hundred, sir."

"Two hundred camp followers. What were you thinking?" Duras brusquely queried. "My lady could catch some disease."

"The countess sees that baths are available, sir. The children and their mothers are quite clean."

"I'm flabbergasted, Ollivier."

"I can see, sir. Dare I assume, the countess failed to mention this to you?"

"The countess had me believe she lay abed every day."

The majordomo couldn't repress his smile. A man of great dignity, he apologized for his lapse of manners.

"Never mind, Ollivier. I won't sack you for showing some human emotion," Duras said, his mouth twitching into an answering smile. "I may, however, dock your salary for letting the countess bamboozle you so easily. Where is the new schoolmistress?" Duras sardonically inquired. "I can but hope school is out for the day?"

"Oh, yes. She feeds them at four and sends them all home with their lessons to memorize for the next class."

"The countess appears extremely well organized."

"She is, sir. Very competent. You'll find her in her sitting room, sir."

Duras mounted the polished marble stairs at a run, restless, mildly perturbed, impatient to see Teo. And when he opened the door and stepped into the room, Teo greeted him from a chaise longue near the windows.

She opened her arms and smiled. "I heard you'd returned."

"You're resting," he said, moving toward her, his boots sinking into the plush Aubusson rug. "You look marvelous."

"I feel marvelous. Kiss me, darling, I've missed you so."

Sitting down beside her, he gazed at her for a moment as though assessing her appearance.

"Is a ribbon askew?"

He shook his head.

"You've forgotten in three weeks what I look like."

Another small negation.

"You're angry with me?"

"Should I be?" he murmured, taking in the sudden flush on her cheeks.

"I'm in perfect health, if that's what you're worried about."

"Good. Do you have something to tell me?"

Her lashes lowered for a moment and when she looked up at him, the green of her eyes showed through the lacy fringe of her lashes. "You heard."

"From several people. I'm surprised I didn't get wind of it while I was gone." He paused. "What if something had happened to the baby?"

"Mingen gave me a clean bill of health. It was that brutal ride, that's all. I've been perfectly fine ever since. Not a twinge or ache or anything. I'm very strong, darling, I always have been. Ask Tamyr."

"She also allowed this?"

"She knows better than to try to stop me. She's been feeding me herbs and potions to make me strong. She wants a boy."

"Good God." He smiled then, helpless against the overwhelming conspiracy that included Tamyr's Siberian magic.

"I knew you'd understand."

"I don't understand at all but you'll explain everything, I'm sure."

"You'll love them, darling. The children are so sweet, so eager to learn, and their mothers are so grateful to you."

"To me."

"You funded the school."

"How did I do that?"

"Ask Lauzun. I'm not quite sure. He even found me enough books for everyone. Did you know he was a Jesuit priest before the Revolution?"

"Half the politicians were priests. The clerical hierarchies were their training grounds. My only concern is you. The conditions in the camps could be dangerous to your health. Are you sure you should do this?"

"I have to do *something*. I'd go stark raving mad if I had to languish in bed all day. And the children are so needy. You mustn't stop me."

"How could I anyway?" Duras affectionately countered. "Or at least I haven't been able to so far."

"You won't be sorry."

"I want a full report from Mingen in the morning on the sanitary conditions. I've seen fevers race through those camps with calamitous results."

"We've handed out soap to all the families. And Tamyr is helping with some of the simple medications. Her knowledge of herbs is extensive. I helped deliver two babies last week too. It's truly magical."

"Jesus, Teo, you shouldn't do that. It terrifies me. Do

you realize how dangerous the camp conditions are? Something could happen to you. How can I protect you?" The memory of her bleeding still haunted him. He'd felt so powerless.

"I'm careful, darling. Tamyr has us wash our hands a thousand times a day. And we don't drink the water in the camps. She's even more cautious than you. I'll be fine."

"We need some guidelines here," he gruffly said.

"Guidelines or orders?"

He softly swore.

"I want this child so much," she appeased. "I'd never do anything to harm it. Don't be angry, darling. Just love me."

His mouth quirked in a rueful smile. "That's the easy part." All the rest—her husband, his wife, the archduke's army, the thousands of miles that separated their countries, the peril facing France—didn't bear thinking of.

"I've missed you terribly and you haven't even kissed me yet, only chastised me."

"Can we talk about the school in the morning?"

"If we do before eight when it opens."

"Could we compromise?"

"On what?" she warily asked.

"Have the school here and not in the camps."

"We'll have to clear out more rooms."

"I don't care if you clear out every room. Except this one," he added with a grin.

"You're so adorable."

"I've heard that before."

"Only from me," she said in a teasing murmur.

"Of course," he said with grace and charm.

"Now you must hold me," she whispered, "and kiss me and make love to me," she finished in a lush purr.

Brief inches from her mouth, he went still, arrested by her last words. Moving upright again, he quietly said, "I'm not making love to you."

Her eyes widened in surprise. "Of course you are."

He shifted away marginally on the narrow chaise. "No, I'm not."

Stirring from her lounging pose, Teo sat up, bewildered. "You can't mean it."

"I might hurt you." His voice was restrained.

"Andre," Teo exasperatedly cried. "I'm absolutely healthy. You won't hurt me."

He shook his head.

"Ask Mingen," she insisted, her voice rising. "He'll tell you I'm fine."

"I don't have to talk to Mingen," he retorted, an unnatural constraint in his posture, his expression a mirror of tightly curbed emotion. "I'm not going to take any chances."

"I'll die of desire," Teo lamented, her gaze imploring. "I wake at night wet from dreaming about you. Do you know how many days you've been gone?" Her voice was a husky whisper, and irresistible need shone in the green depths of her eyes. Touching the buttons of his tunic, she began to unfasten one.

His hand closed hard over hers. "No."

Leaning forward, she pressed closer, her soft breasts enveloping his hand. "You could go very slowly and I'd hardly move. I just want to feel you inside me . . ."

His eyes shut briefly against his lust. He'd never before practiced restraint, yet the past weeks he'd been entirely celibate. He'd not wanted other women when his men had entertained themselves at night. Not out of principle—he didn't believe much in ethics after fighting France's wars for twenty years—but other women held no appeal. His staff had teased him unmercifully. "No," he harshly said, lifting her hand away, abruptly coming to his feet, not sure he could stay in the same room and resist.

"Andre, please," Teo pleaded. "Please . . . for me . . ."

He should walk away, he thought, but that would have required more will than he had at the moment with the warmth of her body only inches away, tempting him, with his own desires sharp-set, agonizing.

"Talk to Mingen," Teo urged. "Please, darling. He'll tell you."

Immobile, driven by carnal urges so flagrant he was near orgasmic, Duras deliberated. And when Teo rose from the chaise, walked across the short distance separating them, wrapped her arms around his waist and clung to him, he said, raspy and low, "I'll see what he says."

Torn between humiliation and need, Duras found his way to Mingen's small office at the back of the villa. Opening the door, he stood in the doorway, silent, irresolute.

Mingen looked up from his desk and smiled. "You're back."

"A few minutes ago," Duras tersely said.

"I suppose you're angry with Teo's school." Mingen assumed that that was the cause of Duras's mindful regard and brevity.

"Yes. You should have known better."

"Will you stop her?"

Duras's flashing smile was more of a grimace. "No more than you could. Which brings me here with a"—he drew in a breath—"damnable dilemma. *Merde,*" he softly swore, bracing himself with outstretched hands against the doorjambs, rocking for a second on the heels of his boots. "I just spoke to Teo," he began, hesitating briefly before adding, "and we're in disagreement on a point."

"About the school?"

Duras ran his fingers through his cropped curls. "It's not about the school."

"But something I could help you with."

"Well . . . that's where we disagree—although Teo thinks you can. Oh, hell," Duras exploded. "Good God, this is awkward."

"This is a sexual dilemma," Mingen said, surmising the topic from his discomfort.

"I've never asked permission before," Duras gruffly said, "not even when I was a youngster." He stood arrow straight, filling the doorway with his height and power. "I'm afraid to touch her."

"You needn't be," Mingen gently said. "She seems to have recovered completely."

"Really." A discernible calm indicated his relief. "You can recover from that much blood loss?"

"Teo wasn't permanently damaged, nor was the child. They're perfectly fine."

"You're sure now about a child?"

"Reasonably sure. Nothing's certain with a pregnancy."

"Which is the point. I don't want to risk anything with Teo."

"She's very healthy, General. Rest assured, you won't injure her. And now since you lost the argument," he said with a smile, "you must apologize to the countess."

"Gladly, Mingen. I don't consider it a loss. And thank you . . . thank you very much for taking care of Teo," Duras added with genuine appreciation.

"Thank you," Mingen responded, "for helping to maintain Prussia's neutrality."

"My pleasure, Herr Mingen." Duras sketched a brief bow. "Have a pleasant evening."

"You as well, sir," Mingen quietly said to Duras's back. He'd already disappeared down the corridor.

"He assured you, didn't he?" Teo maintained when Duras reentered the room, her nervous pacing abruptly coming to a halt.

Duras's voice was temperate. "You're right. He said you're healthy."

She walked toward him with a beaming smile. "I told

you I was. I feel wonderful, not a day of sickness, not a second of indisposition." Taking his hand in hers, she twined her fingers through his. "With the exception of missing you terribly," she said, her voice suddenly hushed.

Lifting her hand, he gently kissed it. "Give me a little time though," he soberly said, dropping her hand, "to get used to all of this." Moving away, he crossed to the windows overlooking the lake.

"Don't you want the baby?" She stood very still, watching his rigid back, her heart pounding.

"Of course I do," he neutrally said, gazing out on the glistening lake, the stern reality of a child having struck him on his walk back from Mingen's office.

"Such enthusiasm."

"What if problems develop? Even Mingen said there's no certainty." He'd never forget the bloody sight of her in the ditch.

"They won't develop, and if they do, Mingen's here. You said you wanted this baby."

"The reality is more sobering."

"What does that mean?"

"I don't know." He'd been gone for three weeks and before he'd left, talk of a child had been more wishful than actual. Turning from the window, he said, "I love you, Teo. There wasn't a minute I didn't miss you the past weeks. I almost sent for you a dozen times."

"You should have."

"I thought you were in bed."

"I didn't *have* to be in bed, but you were so insistent in your notes, I didn't care to discuss it long distance."

"Consider, darling," he said with a sigh, "it may take me some time to become accustomed to—"

"The baby?" She watched him, apprehension in her eyes.

"The baby and your health," he more explicitly defined. "I've never been a father before."

"Do I need a signed note from Mingen?" she said with a relieved smile, better understanding his anxieties. "I've never been a mother before, but I *know* I'm feeling fine. How could I convince you? Should I show you how healthy I am?" she murmured, beginning to unclasp the brooch at her throat.

"Don't," he said, taut and brusque. "I've seen coquettes enough these last weeks."

"Have you now?" Her green eyes flashed with temper.

"I didn't say I touched them," he gruffly replied, dropping into an upholstered chair, leaning back, closing his eyes. "Why are we fighting over this? Both of us will live if we don't make love for a while."

"I won't."

His eyes opened and his dark gaze drilled into her. "I'm not good at sharing."

"I didn't mean that. Will you hold me at least?" she implored. "I've counted the minutes until your return."

He smiled ruefully and opened his arms.

"Tell me what you've seen in your travels," she said, coming to sit on his lap, resting in his arms.

"Four hundred miles of undefended border," he murmured, stroking the dark silk of her hair, contentment inundating his senses.

"Is that worrisome?"

He laughed, her word infinitely too benign. "Yes, but not at the moment. I was thinking more about breakfast in bed with you."

"Or supper in bed?"

He chuckled. "Your appetite continues apace."

"I wish yours did," she purred.

"Hush, I'm trying to be abstemious."

"Maybe we could have Mingen in attendance in case anything were to go amiss," she teased.

He lifted her chin with a crooked finger and his stern gaze held hers. "Shameless hussy."

"Vigée says all men are voyeurs." Her eyes gleamed with amusement.

"*When* exactly did Vigée say that?"

"I overheard him at the monastery. He and a trooper were admiring a very realistic depiction of Saint Sebastian."

"Is that all?" Duras said with relief, his history of shared amusements with Vigée bordering on the sensational.

"He said something about a brothel in Venice and some choirboys with regard to the painting."

It took Duras a moment to catch his breath. "Vigée talks too much. I hope he said it was a staged performance and we were spectators."

"Of course, darling. He also said your mistress was with you. Was her name Dorothea?"

"Cheeky tonight, aren't you?"

"Did she like the young boys?"

"I don't know. I don't remember; I don't remember her."

"I hope your memory of me will be more long-standing."

"Until the oceans run dry, darling. Is that long enough?"

"Yes," she said, reaching up to kiss him. And when he tried pulling away, she held his face hard between her hands and leisurely tasted and nibbled and purred against his mouth.

He could have disengaged himself; he thought about it a dozen times. But celibacy undermined his resolve and his hands came up, stroking her arms, her back, the warmth of her body and the feel of her making his heart beat faster.

She felt a small tremor shake his body, and encouraged, she began to unbutton his tunic, first one button, then another, sliding her hands under his jacket, running them across his chest. She began slipping his neckcloth open.

"No." He caught her hands, but his voice was thick, shaky.

She was making him tremble, the way he did with her, and leaning forward against their hands, she kissed him, a light, undemanding kiss. "Let me kiss you at least," she whispered, dropping another soft kiss on his temple. He didn't answer, his grip only tightening on her hands, but she kissed him because he hadn't said no, and the decorous contact deepened after a time to something less discretionary.

His erection was hard against her bottom, his breathing discomposed, his grip on her hands painful.

"You're hurting me."

"Sorry," he said on a suffocated breath, releasing her. Leaning back in the chair, he shifted his hips so his erection slid away from direct contact with her. He took a deep breath. "I don't want to do this."

"You're being selfish."

His eyes widened and then a small smile warmed his mouth. "That's a first."

"Unfortunately for me," she murmured, a repressed heat in her voice. "Am I supposed to be celibate for the next seven months?"

He stared at her for a moment, looked away to repress his hot-tempered response. When they returned to her, his eyes were cool, flinty hard. "I don't fucking know," he said in a low, poisonous voice. Grabbing her around her waist, he swung her off his lap and surged out of the chair. "I may never fucking know." He was breathing hard when he set her on her feet. "What do you think of that." It was a rhetorical question; he stalked away before she could think of an answer.

Furious, he crossed the large room and, arms braced against the window frame, stared unseeing at the panoramic view. She was asking too much, he fumed, seething with fury. Did she think he *wanted* to refuse her? Christ, he was ready to fuck anything that— He sighed. No point in going there; he was way past ready. And while he believed what Mingen said on a rational level, the memory of Teo's blood-soaked gown still shocked his psyche.

The reality of impending fatherhood also brought with it a complex host of memories, suppressed, silenced, all painful. He'd had a son once years ago, a tortured time for him when he couldn't see Camille, couldn't even write her. He'd only heard months after the birth, after it was too late, that his son had died. And he'd never even had a chance to see him.

When Teo came up beside him he didn't move. She ran her fingertip over the back of his hand pressed against the window frame and watched the black hairs rise at her touch. He turned his head.

"I'm sorry," she said.

He shrugged, blew out an exasperated breath. "What a fucking mess."

"Take your time. I can wait."

The absurdity—that she could wait, that he'd want her to—made him smile. "I'm not sure this is humanly possible."

"We can try," she replied, heartened by his smile. Slipping under his arm, she slid her hands around his waist. "I think I can wait." But her voice was teasing this time, her eyes mischievous, and he received the distinct impression that her concept of waiting had to do with milliseconds. "Dare I bring up Herr Mingen's credentials and expertise?"

He put a hand over her mouth.

She licked a warm path up his palm.

He jerked his hand back.

"I'm finding you extremely difficult to seduce," she murmured, her tone sultry, lush.

"This is hell," he muttered, restlessly raking his fingers through his hair. His lower body shifted as he straightened and raised his arms, his erection making sudden contact with Teo's body. He immediately stepped back but they both had felt it and the tenuous hold he'd maintained on his libido disintegrated.

No longer thinking, only feeling, he took her hand and rubbed her palm against the front of his breeches so she could feel his erection. "Touch me," he said in a husky voice, pushing against her hand. "You can do that for me."

She understood and fumbled to unfasten his breeches, an irrepressible lust gripping her senses. Breath held for a moment, she drew out his hard, jutting penis, fondly touched the silky tip—the magnet, the lodestone of her desire, the instrument of her pleasure. And it moved and swelled under her hand, stretched higher, the crest flaring, as if tempting her, showing off its splendor. She slid a fingertip down its magnificent length and his whole body tensed, anticipation, expectation, rutting need in every taut muscle. Lightly stroking him with both hands, she felt him respond and then her fingers closed around him and he moved against her fingers, forcing his own rhythm, taking charge of the steady flux and flow.

His eyes were closed, his back arched against the building rapture, when she bent her head, touched the satiny tip with her tongue because she selfishly wanted more. Sliding her tongue around the ridged flange, she drew the swollen head into her mouth, sucked it like a lollipop. He groaned, tangled his hands in her hair, and held her head firmly as she slowly drew him into her mouth, eased the length of him out, drew him in again.

"Jesus," he thickly said, pushing her down on her knees, forcing himself deeper into her mouth, his grip so harsh she couldn't move. She tried to pull back but he drove in so far she choked, gagged.

He immediately let her go, swearing as he dropped down beside her, and a second later he was kneeling on the floor holding her, stroking her. "Christ, I shouldn't have done that."

"It's been too long. I'm dying too."

He pushed her hair away from her face, wiped her

mouth with his sleeve, his smile sweet, warm. "I can help you there."

"Maybe I don't want that. Maybe I want the real thing."

His smile broadened at her choice of words but his voice when he spoke was unyielding. "I can't do that."

"That or nothing," she flatly said, famished for him. "You decide."

He looked at her for a very long time, his expression unreadable, his gaze so empty of feeling she wondered if she'd just denied herself sex for the foreseeable future. "All right," he said at last. "You win."

He picked her up and carried her to the bed and when she started to say something he kissed her hard to stop the words because he didn't want to deliberate anymore. And he didn't care if she finished her sentence because he already knew she loved him.

A few short moments later, they were lying nude because he was very good at taking clothes off—one of his areas of expertise. She remarked on it with mild pique but he said, "I'm not going to fight at this stage," poised as he was with the tip of his penis nuzzling her vulva. "Ask me later."

But he was supremely cautious in his penetration, constraint the operative word, his libido tautly curbed, and the first few minutes she pleaded, "More—more—more—more," because he was moving inside her as though she were made of glass. "Look . . . look . . . Will you look? Everything's fine," she hotly insisted, rolling away so he could see for himself.

"See," she cried.

That tantalizing view, all pink and dewy wet and hotly eager, did more to reverse his perceptions than a thousand medical arguments.

He saw indeed.

And nothing more was required in terms of encourage-

ment. He reverted to his more natural self—a highly libidinous male with a gifted imagination and enduring stamina.

The lady was pleased, more than pleased.

Ecstatic.

Several times.

And he was delighted too and ravished on occasion. He
had his lover back.

16

They had a few short days together in Zurich, a blissful, sweet interval in a time of great turmoil. Duras worked at breakneck speed during the days so he could be with Teo at night. And Teo filled her days with the children and her school.

The Austrians had forced the French troops guarding the Valtelline, a major line of communication between Switzerland and Italy, to abandon their positions and Duras countered by burning the Rhine bridge at Schaffhausen. The supplies promised from Paris weren't arriving and the six demibrigades he'd expected from the Republic of Helvetia hadn't appeared.

In the Grisons, some ten thousand peasants led by priests and encouraged by the Austrians seriously hampered communication and supply lines. With Austrian numerical superiority already a source of concern, the Directory aggravated the situation by ordering Duras to send fifteen thousand men to the hard-pressed Army of Italy. Two days later Duras felt it necessary to evacuate all of the Grisons.

Although Duras hadn't explicitly told her, Teo understood one of the corps under the archduke was already on the march. The news was everywhere in camp and the wives of the soldiers were preparing to follow their men; several battalions had moved east already.

The first week in May, von Hotze made a strong attack on Menard's division at Feldkirch, driving it back across the upper Rhine and recapturing Chur. But the Austrians suffered heavy casualties and their progress was slow. Their next attack was delivered a week later when Nauendorff crossed the Rhine at several points between Waldshut and the Lake of Constance, establishing himself along the river Thur between Grossandelfingen and Pfyn, north of Winterthur.

This was a serious threat to Duras's line of communications. He at once made plans to move his command post from Zurich to Winterthur.

"I'm going with you," Teo simply said, as he entered their apartments the night before he was scheduled to leave. "And there's no point in discussing it. If the soldiers' wives can follow their husbands, so can I. I can help them, Andre. You know how difficult it can be for them to survive on the fringes of battle."[13]

The conversation had been ongoing since his return. And he'd not discovered a relevant argument now that worries about her health had been substantially negated. She worked long hours every day without apparent distress, her energy undiminished. "You know the rules, then," he said, unbuttoning his jacket, then tossing it on the settee. "And when I order you back, you must go without argument. I won't tell you until it's absolutely necessary. I don't want the Austrians to capture you," he finished, deliberately not mentioning Austria's Russian allies.

"I understand." She didn't demur, in full accord on that point.

"Lauzun will fit up commissary supplies for your protégés. I'll give you ten wagons, but you're obliged to ration out the foodstuffs on your own." He sat down to pull off his boots. "I can't spare the men."

"Gladly. Thank you, darling. There are several women who can drive the wagons. You met Jeanne-Marie," she said. "She's organized the women into small companies."

"*You* will have a guard at all times."

His fatigue suddenly showed, she thought; his schedule had been strenuous the last few days. "I know. I shan't argue about that," she offered. "Are you hungry? Ollivier tells me dinner is ready whenever you like."

"I'm not hungry."

"When did you last eat?"

He shrugged, a myriad of last-minute details racing through his mind. "I don't know. This morning with you probably." His gaze was unfocused, his reply detached.

"Where are you?"

His gaze came round to her. "I'm sorry, darling. I know where I am and where I'd like to stay. Tell me what Ollivier has for dinner."

"Trout and new spring peas and wild strawberries."

"And pudding for dessert," he said with a smile.

"Of course. How could I survive without pudding?"

"The food may be more rustic in Winterthur."

"I'll make my own pudding, then."

"A resourceful woman."

"I managed to find you, didn't I?"

"Did you now?" he replied, reaching out for her and pulling her between his legs. "And in order to keep you happy I may have to make love to you tonight," he murmured, sliding his arms around her waist.

"Would we have time before dinner?" she whispered.

"I'd much prefer eating you to trout," he breathed. "An appetizer," he whispered, feeling for and swiftly unfastening the hooks at the back of her dress. "Where's your chemise?" he murmured a moment later, casting a playful glance upward.

"I thought I'd save time," she said with an arch glance. "I've been waiting for you for almost two hours."

"Ummm, a luscious prize at the end of a hard day."

"Or a hard prize at the end of my day."

He laughed. "You sound ready."

"Oh, yes," she murmured, slipping her bodice free. "An appetizer for you," she whispered, leaning over and placing her nipple in his mouth.

His breeches were unbuttoned in a flash, and mouth full, he eased her down on his lap, his erection sliding deep inside her, her blissful sigh ending in a contented moan. She wrapped her legs around his hips and he put his hands under her bottom and raised and lowered her in a leisurely, slow undulation, capturing her nipple in his mouth on the ascent, biting it, not hard, just tasting it, as if they had all the time in the world. As if they were just passing time while they waited for dinner to be served on an ordinary night in their ordinary lives.

He played with her breasts and kissed the hollow at the base of her throat and nibbled her ears. But she could never wait, always wanting him as soon as he entered a room, even before he touched her, and always in the most physical way.

She felt the first small convulsion begin and clutched at him to hold him deep inside her. He whispered affectionately, "You're so easy," and tightened his hold on her bottom to meet the rhythm of her strokes, joining her in their own personal heaven.

He was the sexiest, most beautiful man on earth, she blissfully thought, and he loved her and she loved him.

How simple it seemed on a warm spring night with his body against hers.

How appealing.

Duras's command post was established in Winterthur by the following afternoon and the next morning he counterattacked with Oudinot's and Soult's divisions, driving the Austrians back with the loss of 740 killed, 1,400 wounded, and 3,000 taken prisoner. The total French loss was under 800. Nauendorff's troops retired to the line of the Rhine.

But the continuing threat to his communications and the enemy's superior numbers convinced Duras that he could no longer maintain his forward troops in the exposed salient east of Zurich. Before the Austrians could attack again, he withdrew his center sector to the entrenched camp which he'd organized to cover the town. At the same time he withdrew his left behind the river Limmat. This gave him a very strong defensive position with the Glatt marshes a continuous water line in front of it.

For the moment, Duras had managed to stabilize his front, but the archduke was already bringing in reinforcements from Germany.

Two days later the Austrian advance was renewed when they closed up to the new French line. In the center Jellachich's corps was opposite Zurich while farther south von Hotze advanced to the northern shores of the Zurich and Walen lakes. On June 3, the archduke struck at the French positions around the city. After a day of bitter fighting the Austrians finally abandoned the battlefield. But on the morning of June 4, they renewed their advance, the archduke's three corps converging on the Zurichberg, the key to the battle, the two-thousand-foot height dominating the roads around Zurich as well as the bridges over the Limmat River.

Exceptionally heavy fighting raged around this mountain as the Austrians tried again and again to capture and hold the summit only to be driven back each time by reckless French bayonet attacks. Duras took charge personally at each threatened point, forcing the Austrian offensive back, bringing up fresh reinforcements, shifting battle units, riding three horses into the ground in the course of the day.

From the villa windows, Teo watched the assault, never before witness to a battle, anxious, horrified, trembling whenever she'd catch sight of Duras riding out in front of his men, seemingly oblivious to the gunfire, never faltering or retreating. White-knuckled, she'd grip the window ledge and pray until he'd disappear from sight again.

How could he do what he did—day after day, year after year? she wondered. She was appalled by and simultaneously in awe of his unflinching courage. It was nothing less than incredible, inspiring.

And when the light began to diminish, she watched the Austrians withdraw and felt such relief she collapsed where she stood.

Having failed to break the French lines or to secure a foothold on the Zurichberg, and having lost over 3,000 men, the archduke called off the battle. The French casualties were half those of their opponents, amounting to 502 killed, 729 wounded, and 500 prisoners. General Oudinot, always in the thick of the fighting, was severely wounded and General Cherin, one of Duras's staff, died of his wounds. Duras only had time to send a note to Teo that evening; he and his staff were up all night assessing their positions.

On the following day torrential rain fell and the Austrians remained inactive. The French were also worn out, their method of constant local attacks contributing to troop fatigue. Fearing the Austrians would renew their assault the next morning, not sure he could withstand another day of heavy fighting, Duras decided to abandon his entrenched camp and the Zurichberg and withdraw his center to a stronger position on the Utliberg, two miles southwest of the town. This dominating peak, 2,850 feet high, commanded all the country north and west of Zurich. The withdrawal was carried out unmolested during the night of June 5 and on into the early morning hours of the sixth. Duras's position was now stronger than before, the disadvantages of fighting with the town of Zurich and its eleven thousand inhabitants actually in the front line overcome. And although the Austrians could claim to have captured the important town of Zurich, they could not advance a yard beyond it.

Duras's evacuation of Zurich and his withdrawal to the Utliberg caused grave dissatisfaction in Paris. This feeling became still more acute after the minor *coup d'état* of June 18 when three of the Directors were replaced.

Letters came daily from the Directory complaining of Duras's inaction and insisting he go on the offensive. The political factions opposed to him were publishing scurrilous reports of the disasters at the front, blaming Duras. Bernadotte, the new war minister and Duras's enemy, was doing his best to remove him from his command, going so far as to sign an order for his dismissal. Additionally, the problems of local supply were becoming so serious that Duras finally fired all the army contractors and set up army units to do the foraging.

Disgusted by all the political ineptitude and acrimony, he finally wrote to the Directors:

> Since I am informed that my detractors are trying to criticize my military operations and what they call my inaction, I must point out to you that during the past two months I have repeatedly called attention to the terrible lack of supplies provided for this army . . . For more than a month now some divisions have been reduced to one-third or even one-quarter of their proper ration . . . If I had fertile country ahead of me, there might be some point in advancing. But the farther I move forward, the farther

*I should be removed from my sources of supply. The means
of transport are nonexistent. The war minister, whom I
have asked for 600 pack mules, knows very well that I
have not been given a single one. The army which I command is 60,000 strong, but it has to cover a vast extent
of territory with its right at Vevey and its left at Hunin-
gen. Any forward movement of its center would be highly
dangerous. I would only undertake it if I had the means
to guarantee some sort of success . . .*

*If some experience and some successes in the profession
of arms lead me to insist too strongly that the Army of the
Danube cannot yet assume the offensive, and if I am too
firmly convinced that the movement which you order me to
make is premature and would lead to disaster, then, Citizen Directors, you need only approve my request that you
will appoint a successor to relieve me in command of the
army.[14]*

"Screw them and their ridiculous orders," Duras raged.
"I'm supposed to put my men in jeopardy for incompetents
like them? Let Moreau take over." Bernadotte had suppos-
edly handed over the command to his friend Moreau. "The
Austrians will overrun the borders in a week."

"Barras and Roger-Ducos can cancel Bernadotte's orders," Bonnay said, seated beside Cholet, who was transcribing the letter. The men were outside the small cottage
Duras had taken over as living quarters, a rough table and
chairs substituting for an office. Tall pines surrounded
them, the summer sun filtered through the branches, and
the view of the plains below was spectacular.

"Bernadotte would like to be king," Duras fumed, bad-
tempered and testy. "A shame he can't win any battles. He'd
have a better chance."

"Paris hasn't ordered your replacement yet," Bonnay
pointed out.

"I'm surprised Moreau would even consider taking the command. The bastard is afraid of rifle fire."

"But then he doesn't appear in the front lines, *mon ami,*" Bonnay calmly said, sympathizing with Duras's wrath but more cool-headed.

Duras spun around on the dried pine needles covering the ground. "Don't you ever raise your voice?" he said, breaking into a smile.

Bonnay shrugged. "Damned sure not for Bernadotte. He'll be gone in a month; his list of enemies is lengthy."

"So I shouldn't ready myself for retirement?"

"There's men enough in power who know better than to lose you."

"But until then . . ." Duras sighed. "I'm tired of these carping letters and of the fools demanding I attack."

"You've been ignoring them for a month now."

"We need the reinforcements they've been promising me since spring. And," he sardonically murmured, "it would help if we had food and fodder too."

But cooler judgments prevailed in Paris and a successor wasn't named. Reinforcements finally began to reach his army and by July over eighteen thousand men had arrived in Switzerland. Throughout the month, the lines around Zurich remained quiet, and while it was impossible to forget the war camped on the heights of the Utliberg, the summer days and nights were balmy, the breeze refreshing, and the Austrians neither strong enough nor well organized enough to launch a major attack.

Duras and Teo had time together those weeks before the offensive began and their small cottage under the pines became an oasis from the world. Tamyr didn't intrude on their solitude unless Teo asked for her help, understanding how fleeting was their time together. It was a constant in everyone's mind; no day passed without news of the Austrian movements. Additional Russian troops were expected as well—any day.

"It almost reminds me of home," Teo said one evening as they watched the sky change from the glow of sunset into dusk. "The pines and the immense sky, the cool air. Do you think you could come home with me sometime?"

"When this is over I'll go anywhere at all with you." Duras's hand lay over hers as they sat side by side. "The farther away from this the better." The pressures were becoming more intense, his counterattacks gaining good terrain every day. His positions were well sited and strong, his reinforcements slowly arriving, bringing his army up to strength. Very soon he'd be ready to attack.

But before that he'd have to send Teo away.

He'd talked to Bonnay already and Mingen had agreed to accompany Teo and Tamyr to Paris and stay with them until the child was born. The necessary papers had arrived. They were in Bonnay's quarters: authorizations for passage to Paris; passports; letters of credit on his bank; instructions to his lawyers—everything Teo would need to live with their child should he not survive.

The baby was just beginning to show, making it more imperative she be safely away while she could still travel. Tomorrow he'd bring up the subject, he told himself. But he didn't, nor the next day.

Bonnay finally spoke to him about it and Duras snapped back, "I know. I know." Reluctant to let her go, he'd become thin-skinned about the matter.

"She's too much on your mind. You have someone check on her five times a day when we're in the field and we won't be within riding distance once the offensive begins."

"I don't need your advice." Duras walked away and stood in the doorway of the shed Bonnay had requisitioned for quarters.

"If she's safely away, you won't have to worry or wonder if she's adequately protected or—"

"Jeopardize my men by my actions," Duras said with

a sigh. "Thank you, Henri," he quietly added, turning around, "for reminding me."

"Her presence is making the campaign more difficult for you," Bonnay graciously said.

"At a time when all my attentions should be focused on the campaign. I'll send her back—tomorrow," Duras finished with a small smile.

"She and the baby will be less vulnerable, sir."

"Yes, much safer," Duras murmured as if he needed to say the words to convince himself. "How many children do you have, Henri?" Duras had never paid more than the most superficial attention to his subordinates' families.

"Four, sir."

"All healthy?"

"Thankfully, yes." It was a time when childhood diseases seriously threatened young lives.

"Jesus," Duras softly exclaimed. "I worry endlessly about Teo, about the delivery—how she'll contend with it alone, how I should be with her. And then I worry about the child after it's born. Will it be healthy? Will I live to see it? I never worried before about anything."

"As long as all the campaign details were to your liking," Bonnay said, smiling faintly.

"Don't remind me of the present incompetencies. Those aside, Henri," he went on with a moody grimace, "Teo has drastically changed my priorities."

"Unfortunately Suvorov keeps winning in Italy." The French were defeated at Cassano on April 28, again at Trebbia on June 17.

"If Joubert can't hold him in Liguria, soon we'll be facing the generalissimo."

"But first the archduke."

Duras smiled grimly. "It's time she left."

But when he told Teo the next day, she shouted "No!" and slapped him viciously. He stood motionless as she pummeled him, shouting, "No, no . . . no," screaming and crying, maddened, distraught, until she finally collapsed sobbing in his arms.

His eyes were wet for a brief moment as desolation swept over him. But he swallowed hard and holding her close said, "I'll come for you in a few weeks."

"You lie." Her voice was muffled against his chest.

Sadly he was; Suvorov wouldn't reach Switzerland before late September at the very earliest. "It won't be for long," he soothed, lifting her in his arms and carrying her to the single chair Cholet had scavenged for their rough parlor. Sitting down, he held her tightly, not sure himself how he'd face the coming weeks without her. "I thought you could go to Paris and wait for me. Mingen will escort you."

"I won't go."

"Our offensive begins in two days," he quietly said. "You have to think of the baby and I have to know you're not in danger."

"I'll stay with the women and children behind the lines. Mingen can stay with me, Tamyr—"

"No," he harshly said, lifting her away so she had to look at him, so she could see the determination in his eyes. "How the hell can I run this campaign if I'm wondering if some Austrian corps has overrun the women's camp? How can I even think straight if I know you and my child are hungry and cold and God knows where in this bloodbath? No," he said in a rough whisper, "you cannot stay."

"Tell me how long I have to be away?" she fearfully whispered, her life, her happiness linked to him.

"God, Teo, I don't know," he raggedly said, drawing her back into his arms. "Two months, three—Christ, I've been here since January and the Austrians keep building up their armies. Mingen will take you to a small house I have in the country near Paris. You and the baby will be safe."

"I might never see you again."

"*Yes* . . . you will."

"Let me stay a few more days. I could move to Bremgarten; that would be secure. Or why not Basel?" she said, looking up at him. "It's completely safe there and not as far as Paris."

He shook his head. "If we can't hold against the archduke, his army could be in Basel in a day." If they couldn't hold, all of France would be threatened. "Paris offers the most security."

"Tell me when I'll see you again. Lie to me."

"Certainly by Christmas. The armies will be in winter quarters."

"I'll have the baby by then."

"You must do everything Mingen says," he anxiously said, tracing the downy curve of her brow. "I worry."

"Between Tamyr and Mingen," Teo replied, her gaze mischievous for a moment, "I'm not sure I'm needed."

He smiled. "Have Mingen telegraph me with the news."[15]

"You must stay safe for us," she whispered.

His eyes were grave. "Tell my child about me."

"Don't say that." Fear trembled in her voice.

"This may be the last time I see you," he murmured, "and I don't want to leave you without telling you how much I love you. And how much happiness you've brought me." He lightly touched her chin, cupped it in the curve of his fingers. "Tell our child I wanted very much to be there," he said, "and I'll always be watching over you."

"I'll die without you," she breathed, heart-stricken.

"No," he whispered. "If I don't come back, live for us both instead."

"You'll be home for Christmas, I know it, and then we'll be together again." How could she say good-bye to him as if they'd never meet again when she couldn't even survive the thought?

"And we'll grow old together," he said, wanting the dream as much as she.

"You said something about a dozen children once," she whispered.

"I remember," he quietly said. "I'd never felt that way before."

"Nor had I. My happiness began that night."

"With luck," he said, "I'll make you happy again."

They made love that night with all their senses opened wide, their consciousness acute, exceptional. They could feel each other breathe, their hearts beat in time, their skin, their flesh meld into one flesh. And they loved each other wildly, desperately . . . sorrowfully, both feeling the same long, sad pain.

Their life together would be broken now.

When at last they fell asleep, he held her close to him, his arms locked around her in a viselike grip, not wanting to let her go.

But her carriage was ready very early as ordered. Mingen and Tamyr waited beside it; Bonnay and Cholet, Vigée and his troopers, were there as well to say adieu. There was no more time for private good-byes. Her mind gripped with a single thought—she was losing Duras forever—she walked with Duras into the small yard outside the cottage. Bonnay and Cholet wished her Godspeed and sent messages with her to their families. Vigée handed her a small bouquet of field flowers and said with a grin, "If you see Madame Vigée tell her I'll need my quarterly payment early."

She smiled; it took all her strength.

The troopers who'd attended her school had written her a note expressing their good wishes, each signing his name.

She shook each one's hand, wondering if she would die of pain.

"The men love her as much as Duras," Cholet murmured to Bonnay.

"They all volunteered to escort her to the border," Bonnay said in an undertone, "even knowing they'll go sleepless. They must be back by tomorrow night for the attack."

Duras was handing Teo into the carriage and when she was seated he quietly said, "I'll love you always, no matter where I am." Setting a booted foot on the step, he leaned in and kissed her one last time.

"Come back to me," Teo whispered, tears streaming down her cheeks.

He nodded, not wishing to lie, the truth unpalatable. He touched her fingers, then touched his heart and softly said, "Take care of our child."

Moving into the carriage, Tamyr took Teo into her arms and held her close, talking to her in her native tongue, soothing her.

"She's more precious than life to me," Duras quietly said to Mingen before he entered the carriage. "Make sure you have the best assistance for the delivery. Telegraph me if you have questions about anything at all to do with Teo's comfort. If I'm not within reach you have the letters to my lawyers and bankers. I've sent them instructions as well. And thank you," he said. "You need only name your price and my bankers will comply."

"You in turn must try to survive," Mingen said. "I'm quite determined you do."

"Not as determined as I," Duras murmured.

"Charlie has no bottom, you know that. He lives in fear of his brother, the emperor."

"Bottom or not, he outnumbers us substantially. So we'll just have to be more clever."

"Not too difficult with a Habsburg."

Duras made an attempt to smile. "I keep telling my staff that. Go now. It breaks my heart to see her cry. And take care of my child."

"It's been a pleasure knowing you, Duras."

"You might consider a less dangerous line of work once this war is over."

"Are you offering me a permanent position?"

"If my life happens to allow permanence, I am indeed."

"I'll see you at Christmas, then."

"With luck," Duras said.

17

While Duras was consolidating his position by undertaking an offensive to recapture the St. Gotthard Pass, rendering his right flank more secure, Austria decided to violate the Coalition's strategic plan for the invasion of France. That gave Duras his long-sought opportunity to launch an effective counterblow.

In mid-August the entire Russian corps, thirty thousand strong under Korsakov, had arrived at Zurich to reinforce the archduke. The original plan was for Suvorov, after defeating the French in Italy, to lead his Russian corps into Switzerland. His troops would join Korsakov near Zurich to form a single Russian army. This force plus Condé's émigrés, a total of some sixty thousand men, would move west, turn the Rhine barrier and then drive across the unfortified Franco-Swiss frontier. At the same time, the

Austrian troops in Switzerland were to move into southern Germany and from there cover Korsakov's right flank.

The presence of the Austrian army on Korsakov's right flank was essential to the success of the Allied strategy. It was especially vital that the archduke protect Korsakov while Suvorov was in transit between Italy and Switzerland, because during this period the French would outnumber the Russians at Zurich and only the presence of the Austrian army in close support of Korsakov could prevent Duras from attacking.

The Austrian chancellor, Thugut, however, was devising a diplomatic scheme that would expand the Habsburg domains, a coup that would betray both his English and Russian allies. Determined to gain control of the Low Countries and northern Italy without having to agree to any limitation of Austrian authority in either area, he was planning on sending the archduke's army through Germany into Holland.

On August 14 the French pushed the Austrians out of Grimsel, one of the key towns guarding the St. Gotthard Pass. By August 18, despite the heavy resistance of eight Austrian battalions commanded by General von Hotze, the French had retaken the whole of the St. Gotthard Pass while other units moved on Glaris.

To counter the French successes in the south, the archduke decided to attack their positions along the Aar River. The Austrian engineers, however, failed to examine the ground carefully, and when they tried to throw a bridge across the Aar on the night of August 16, they discovered that their bridging material was insufficient. Duras rushed two companies of Zurich riflemen to the scene and the snipers rapidly picked off the Austrian sappers who were still trying to complete the bridge on the morning of August 17. At mid-morning French light artillery batteries arrived and opened fire, making the

Austrians' task completely hopeless, and soon after Duras agreed to a cease-fire to allow the Austrians to withdraw their pontoons.

The next day the archduke, despite weeks of protest, was ordered to take the imperial army into Germany. He left two Austrian corps, those of von Hotze and Jellachich, totaling about forty thousand men, to support Korsakov.

Duras's position was vastly improved.

Which was fortunate because on the other fronts the situation was disastrous, the defeats in Italy causing ever-increasing alarm in Paris.

That alarm was evidenced in the immediate excursions made by several politicians of note to the small country house Teo occupied. Her first caller appeared the morning after she'd arrived. Tamyr was still unpacking in the bedroom, Mingen had ridden into the city to present Duras's letters to his bankers and lawyers, and Teo was strolling in the lush summer garden that bordered the Seine.

A tall, dark, imposing man was walking toward her down the slope of green lawn, a servant following him in some haste from the house.

"Forgive my intrusion, Countess," he politely said, bowing gracefully. "I'm Paul Barras and I'd like to welcome you to Paris." The servant had reached them as Barras finished speaking and began stammering an explanation. "I'm sure the countess won't blame you," he said with a smile, waving him away. Turning back to Teo, who decided the ex-Vicomte de Barras was as bold as Andre had warned, he went on, his smile meant to charm. "I also wanted to offer my assistance as you settle into your new home."

"Thank you, Citizen Barras," Teo politely said, "but I'm intent on a quiet, secluded life while I'm here."

"I understand completely." His gaze took in her slender figure. Her pregnancy was not obvious under the high-waisted gown, although he was aware of it. His intelligence service was excellent. "But if you should like to socialize occasionally in some of the quieter circles of society, please don't hesitate to call on me. In fact we're having a small dinner party tomorrow night if you'd care to join us."

Teo noted his raking glance and realized her coming child was no secret. "The journey has left me fatigued, but thank you for asking."

Duras's newest concubine had a cool composure, Barras noted, and no yearning to storm society. Unlike the last Russian countess Duras had shed, who was now enjoying the favors of the wealthy navy contractor Simon, and participating in all the soirées of note. "Perhaps later, then. You may know some of our acquaintances already. Madame de Staël spent some time in Petersburg and you must know the Countess Gonchanka," he softly said, his gaze speculative.

"I only know *of* her," Teo replied. "We never met in Petersburg."

Her poise was remarkable, Barras thought. Natalie's stories of finding her in Duras's bedroom, which had become common currency in Paris salons, were true after all. "She knew the general too, I understand," he smoothly said, as though they were discussing mutual acquaintances.

"He never mentioned her." Teo's green eyes were direct, open.

And very beautiful. Barras wondered if Duras was discarding this woman like Natalie and all the rest. If so, there might be reasons beyond Duras's consequence to court her favor. Barras collected women, the list of his mistresses lengthy. Thérèse Tallien, currently his official hostess at the Luxembourg, was pregnant like the countess. "Will Duras be joining you in the near future?" A new element of charm infused his voice. It was the question everyone wished to know.

"He didn't think it likely with the Austrians intent on invading France."

"France is most fortunate to have his talents," Barras unctuously declared. "He's our most stalwart defender."

"The only one at the moment," Teo dryly remarked. "Italy is lost, I understand."

"A terrible disaster; young Joubert dead, his wife inconsolable . . . I presume Duras sent you back to safety. Will the commander be taking the offensive soon?"

"I'm sorry, Citizen Director, the general never confided in me on military matters."

"Of course," he smoothly said, his smile ingratiating. He had a distinct feeling she knew very much what went on at headquarters. "Duras is most fortunate in your companionship. His marriage was never amiable." He paused for a moment as if in deliberation and then feigning concern said, "A word of warning, my dear, about Andre's wife. She's likely to upbraid you should you meet. Claudine's a ruthless woman, completely without scruple." He smiled faintly. "Like her uncle, I'm afraid. You should be aware of her capacity for treachery."

"We're not likely to meet. I prefer the country."

"And you won't be entertaining?"

"Not at all."

"A shame, my dear, with so many people eager to meet you, but then you must consider your health."

"My health is excellent."

"I only meant," Barras suavely countered, "how much more salubrious the country air. The city can be fatiguing. If the responsibilities of office weren't so demanding I should choose to live in blissful isolation like this myself. Duras has a pleasant home here."

"Unfortunately he can seldom enjoy it."

"Perhaps very soon he may."

"You're very optimistic, Citizen. The imperial army he faces is sizable, had you not heard?"

"Duras is less optimistic, then?" he inquired, prying.

"He's realistic—a factor in his successes despite his detractors who carp at him from the safety of Paris."

"You defend the general with spirit, madame."

"Anyone acquainted with his talent and experience does, sir."

How beautiful she was championing her lover, Barras thought, her cheeks slightly pinked, her breathing faintly agitated so her plump breasts rose and fell beneath the white muslin of her gown, her exotic Tatar eyes bright with earnestness. "You should beard his detractors with such conviction, madame. They would all be converted. I understand your husband opposes Duras at Zurich," he blandly added, watching her closely.

"I see my maid signaling me from the window. Good afternoon, Citizen," Teo blandly said. "I'm sure you can find your way out."

Glancing at the windows facing the garden, Barras saw no sign of activity. "May I escort you to the house?"

"No, thank you." Her smile was polite. "You have a long drive back to the city. If you'll excuse me." And leaving him in a flurry of white muslin and scent, she walked away.

Barras watched her ascend the slight incline and disappear through a garden door. Did she indeed have Duras's ear? he wondered, contemplating the usefulness of Duras's latest mistress. Was she cognizant of the general's plans? Did she know if Duras knew of the conspiracy to topple the Directory? Was she dangerous or merely pretty? He'd have to send Thérèse to visit her; perhaps his mistress could insinuate herself into the countess's confidence.

That summer with the military reverses in Italy, the neo-Jacobins were thundering against the "traitors in government responsible for our defeats." Disgust with the present regime and with the eight-year-old war was strong enough that most of the French people were ripe for counterrevolutionaries. In the opinion of many, France was ripe for a dictatorship.

Sieyès, Barras, Talleyrand, and Fouché had been plotting in the small house Talleyrand shared with his current mistress, Madame Grand. By August, the final touches for the *coup d'état* were in place. Everything was settled except for the choice of general. The matter was vital for the army would be the arbiter of the coup's success. Thus they needed a general who could control the army, and who better than Duras with his reputation for victory. It was essential to know whether Duras was interested in joining their cause.

When Mingen returned from the city, Teo told him of Barras's visit. "He just appeared in the garden," she said, setting her pen aside, the letter she was writing to Duras on the desk before her.

"Barras isn't the type of man to be put off by a servant," Mingen replied, dropping several small parcels on the settee. "He's without fear—which accounts for his surviving the Revolution despite his noble birth. He probably wanted to be the first to see you. Society thrives on gossip."

"I'm not interested in society. I told him as much."

"That may curtail further visits." But Mingen's contacts in the city had informed him of the conspiracy about to blossom into fruition and he rather doubted Barras had driven an hour from Paris simply to look at Duras's mistress. There was no point in alarming her with rumors, however. "Andre wanted me to give you these," he went on, sorting through the parcels until he found the two he wished. Setting them on the desk, he added, "I had to fetch them in the city."

"You know what these are?"

He nodded. "Would you like privacy?"

"No, stay. I need company to allay my fears. Barras has a sinister air; he unnerved me." She began untying the red ribbon holding the leather packet together.

"No one will dare touch you," Mingen said, sitting down across from her. "Duras's reputation is adequate protection."

"What is this?" Teo said, unfolding the sheaf of papers.

"The deed to this property, and barring another reign of terror, it should remain legal. It's in your name."

"Is Andre leaving me?" Lavish gifts were often a means to dispose of a mistress.

Mingen shook his head. "It's for you and the child if he . . . doesn't return," he softly finished.

"You shouldn't have given it to me now," she whispered, her eyes bright with tears. "I don't want to think about that."

"He wanted you to feel secure regardless of what the future holds. It's only a precaution," he quietly went on. "The other papers are the bank accounts in your name."

Teo refolded the sheets and slipped them back into the leather envelope, sniffing, wiping her tears away with the back of her hand.

Scrupulous in his friendship to Duras, Mingen offered only his handkerchief, not the comfort she needed. But it tugged at his heart to see her pain. "Open the other one," he said, pushing the small parcel toward her. "This won't make you cry."

"Actually I cry all the time these days," Teo said with a tentative smile, pulling the silver bow open. "Tamyr tells me it's natural with pregnancy." A small box of celadon leather lay inside the silver tissue and when she opened the lid a glittering diamond ring sparkled in the sunlight.

"There's an inscription," Mingen prompted.

Lifting the ring out, she turned the wide band of diamonds in her fingers until the engraved words were visible.

"Together always" it read beneath their entwined initials. "See, I'm crying again," Teo whispered, touching the delicate script, feeling as though she were touching Duras across the miles.

"I'm to tell you it's a wedding ring."

Her gaze came up.

"His lawyers are beginning the preliminaries for his divorce. I carried instructions to them this morning."

She slipped the ring on her fourth finger. "It's perfect," she murmured.

"He measured your finger one night while you slept and shipped the knotted string to Paris."

She smiled. "I'd only be happier if he were here beside me."

"There, I knew you'd smile."

"Does he have a chance?" she softly asked.

"I spoke to some friends of mine this morning and news from Vienna is heartening. Thugut has won this round—the archduke has been ordered into Germany. The emperor is furious with him for defying his orders in June. This is all petty court bickering but extremely helpful to Duras."[16]

"*All* of the archduke's army is moving into Germany?"

"No one knows yet, but any withdrawal of troops will be advantageous to the French."

"So Andre might be home for Christmas."

"There's a chance." There was also a chance he would be offered a post in the new Directory being plotted at Talleyrand's house, a post that might preclude a bigamous new wife. Who could forget that Korsakov was still very much alive? But Mingen didn't mention that; no point in dashing her good spirits when the position was still moot.

"I'm going to pray very hard for that eventuality," Teo said. "And thank you, Anton, for such pleasant news. If I finish this letter to Andre now, will it still go out tonight?"

"I'll have it brought into the city and sent out with the military courier."

"He's wonderful, isn't he?" Teo blissfully said, her melancholy vanished.

"He is indeed," Mingen agreed.

18

Talleyrand, notorious for his corrupt financial transactions, was having lunch with Jérôme Gothier, one of his bankers, in a busy café of the Palais Royal. The exchange of information on army contracts and government bills had been satisfactorily concluded and the men were enjoying the view from the windows. The Rue de Rivoli, a fashionable promenade for demireps and actresses, was awash with a continual parade of beautiful young women. At the sight of a splendid blonde with a spectacular bosom, Talleyrand said, "She has a remarkable resemblance to Claudine."

Mention of Claudine jogged Gothier's memory for a very new bit of gossip. "Did you hear Duras has given instructions to begin divorce preliminaries?"

Talleyrand sat up straighter, his gaze no longer on the ladies walking by. "Are you sure?"

"Genlis, Duras's lawyer, was apparently given written orders this morning."

"Duras's latest paramour is at his country retreat, Barras tells me. He was on his way out there when I saw him."

"She's Korsakov's wife, I hear. A cozy, incestuous attachment," Gothier ironically remarked.

"Duras has a penchant for excitement," Talleyrand blandly noted. "But divorce? I can't believe he's serious about the woman."

Gothier shrugged. "Perhaps or perhaps he doesn't care to share his wife with you." The portly man's brows rose in amused speculation.

"Claudine's amorous activities have never concerned him in the past. They have a civilized marriage—or had," Talleyrand added, his eyes narrowed in contemplation. "Perhaps Claudine and I should look into this." As one of the conspirators, Talleyrand was aware of Duras's possible role in the coup. "Although I find it startling he'd take such a drastic step after all these years."

"Perhaps he's in love," Gothier said with a smirk.

"Duras may make love but he doesn't *fall* in love."

"It happens," Gothier noted, a nuance of smugness in his tone. "Look at Meudon. At seventy he has two young children and dotes on his wife."

"Meudon's senile," Talleyrand rebuked. "Duras is far from that." But it was worrisome at this late stage of the coup. He needed Claudine's husband; he needed the family relationship intact. There was no one else trustworthy.

"Did I mention Duras deeded the house to the Russian woman?" Gothier added with a smile.

Talleyrand's mouth formed into a grim line for a moment and then he casually leaned back in his chair and smiled across the table at his colleague in corruption. "If you don't have better news for me soon, Gothier, I'll have to withdraw my government contracts."

"I thought you'd like to know, Charles—useful information, as it were," Gothier serenely replied. "And no one else will give you a twenty-percent commission for those contracts and we both know it," he added, unintimidated.

"It's damnable news at this particular moment, that's all," Talleyrand grumbled.

"Because of the Austrian advance?" Gothier smoothly inquired.

Did he know something? Talleyrand wondered, suspicious of Gothier's almost palpable smugness. "Yes, of course, because of the advance. Now, if you'll excuse me," Talleyrand cordially said, rising, "I've an appointment of some importance."

Gothier watched Talleyrand limp away, surmising his important appointment might be with Duras's sumptuous wife. He wouldn't mind having such a voluptuous *and* amenable niece. Did she call him uncle or Charles, he wondered, when she fucked him?

Claudine didn't believe Talleyrand at first.

"I made inquiries and it's true," Talleyrand bluntly said, sitting down to rest his crippled foot. "The question is what are we going to do about it?"

"Kill the bitch," Claudine snapped, standing stock-still in the middle of her drawing room, her eyes blazing.

"Something less incriminating, my dear," Talleyrand sardonically said. "Perhaps we could have her imprisoned as an enemy in wartime. God knows, the Austrians have had Lafayette languishing in prison in Austria for years."

"Perfect." Her sudden smile held a high degree of malice.

"Except Duras would kill us," he murmured.

"Have her disappear, then," Claudine callously said. "Anyone could have taken her."

"Rumor has it an attempt was already made. Duras left

his army waiting and went to find her. I wouldn't care to have him on my trail."

"Maybe Andre will die in battle," she ungenerously suggested.

"Let us dearly hope not, my stupid goose. We need him to hold the army in check for us." Sighing, Talleyrand held out his arms. "Come here, my pretty bonbon, and fuck me. I always think more clearly after an orgasm."

After speaking to Barras that evening, Talleyrand discovered that Duras's mistress was not only living in seclusion but was receiving no visitors. So when he and Claudine left for their social call the following forenoon, their entourage included a half-dozen postilions and three flunkies, enough support staff to see that they gained entrance to the countess's drawing room.

"What a long, tedious journey this is," Claudine complained before they'd even left the outskirts of Paris. "I never understood what Andre saw in this *distant* place, this hinterland. It's impossible to get an ice or a decent coffee and certainly there's not a soul worth talking to." Glancing from left to right as the open barouche bowled down the road, she disregarded completely the sublime summer landscape, the fresh morning sun, the scent of flowers in the air.

"Perhaps he communed with nature like our mad Rousseau."

"God knows what he did out there," she sullenly declared, a frown marring the porcelain perfection of her features. "I refused to set foot in the house."

"Maybe he kept it for his doxies, my dear, and preferred you not inhabit it."

She gave him a scornful glance. "Really, Charles, have you been hibernating since your return?"[17] Women don't interest Andre long enough for him to bring them to his house."

"Does he fish?" Talleyrand incidentally inquired.

"He might. Manton sends him rods."

"Then he may spend his time in completely innocuous pursuits."

"A touch of the cleric still clings to you, dear uncle. How moralizing that sounds," she noted with an arch glance. "Why should I be concerned how he spends his time?"

"You needn't, of course," Talleyrand drawled, "unless he chooses to spend it in court eliminating you from his life."

"That would be the only exception," she silkily agreed. "We must see that this strumpet is sent away."

"Her dismissal may not curtail Andre's plans for a divorce."

"Of course it will," Claudine replied. "What other reason would he have if not that?"

"Female intuition?" Talleyrand mocked.

"Call it what you will, Charles, it's true," Claudine retorted, confident of her assessment. "Will you threaten her?"

"I'd prefer discussing this all with a degree of courtesy, Claudine. So be warned, your temper isn't allowed this afternoon." A skilled diplomat, Talleyrand never raised his voice or insisted when persuasion better served his purposes.

"Yes, yes . . . you needn't take that tone with me," she huffily replied, casting him a sulky glance.

"Don't pout, darling. You're too old for that jejune pose."

"At least I'm not as old as Madame Grand," she tartly retorted.

Talleyrand smiled, too experienced to be drawn into a juvenile row. "Are we a bit out of sorts this afternoon, my dear? Let your dear uncle take care of this unfortunate situation, and once we have Duras back under the conjugal roof, we'll both be in better spirits." Barras had been as concerned as Talleyrand at news of Duras's divorce plans. With timing so critical, their plans couldn't afford sudden changes. And players like Duras were essential. "Why don't we see what the Countess Korsakova would like in exchange for leaving Paris and returning to the remote country of her origins."

Mingen tried to turn them away at the door, explaining the countess was sleeping, but Talleyrand said, "We won't take more than a few minutes of her time. The future of the country's at stake." He gently added, "I must insist." And the two bulky retainers standing a short distance away glared at Mingen with distinct hostility.

The man was intent on shoving his way in if necessary, Mingen realized, and their establishment was staffed by only a few old retainers. Duras had misconstrued the amount of interest his lover would invoke. "I'll see if I can wake the countess."

"We'd appreciate your effort," Talleyrand pleasantly replied.

When Mingen returned to tell them Teo would soon be down, he found them already installed in the drawing room.

"I can't stand for long on my poor leg," Talleyrand unctuously said from the comfort of a down-cushioned fauteuil. "I hope you don't mind."

On the way back downstairs, Mingen had taken a small pistol from his room, and the feel of it in his coat pocket gave him a certain sense of security. "The countess will see you soon," he said, ignoring the obvious hypocrisy.

"Send coffee in," Claudine ordered, lounging on a chaise like a voluptuous, blond Cleopatra. "Iced if you please," she demanded.

"The countess gives instructions to the servants," Mingen retorted, unmoving.

"Who exactly are you?" He dressed like a clerk or secretary, Talleyrand thought, but he had predator's eyes.

"I'm the countess's physician."

"Is she ill?"

"No," Teo replied from the doorway, "I'm in very good health." And walking past Mingen, who stood slightly inside the entrance to the room, she added, "I understand this visit has to do with the future of France. I can't imagine how I could be involved." She didn't sit but remained standing, her summer gown of primrose muslin one of a score Duras had had delivered to the house before her arrival.

"That's a Madame Teillard gown," Claudine petulantly said, recognizing the premier dressmaker's touch. She dressed only the highest circles of society.

"Is it really. And you are?" Teo coolly inquired.

"I'm Madame Duras," Claudine snapped. "Does *your* husband know you're sleeping with *my* husband?"

Teo turned and began walking from the room.

"Hold your tongue, Claudine," Talleyrand said, swiftly coming to his feet, his voice chill as ice. "Please, Countess, I beg your forgiveness," he implored, moving after her as rapidly as his crippled foot allowed.

Mingen had drawn his pistol from his pocket and aimed it at Talleyrand. "The conversation is over," he said.

"Don't be dramatic, Doctor," Talleyrand smoothly replied. "You're outnumbered and my men are better armed." He gazed past Mingen and Teo to his two powerful servants in the foyer who stood with their pistols drawn. "Come, Countess, sit down. We have some mutual concerns. I'll see that Claudine behaves."

"The bitch is pregnant, Charles. Look at her," Claudine exclaimed, as Teo moved back into the room, the light muslin of her gown clinging for a moment to her form. "If I knew Andre wanted a brat so much I would have given him one."

"One more word from you, Claudine, and my men will carry you from the house."

"I should think this concerns me more than it does you, Charles," she tartly responded, uncowed, "so kindly reserve your authority for the others." No longer lounging, she was sitting stiffly upright, the pressure of her grip on her parasol handle turning her fingers white.

"There are matters considerably more important than your jealousies, madame," Talleyrand crossly retorted. "I won't put up with your tantrums. Say no more."

"I won't allow him to divorce me," Claudine said, her gaze on Teo malevolent, ignoring Talleyrand as though he hadn't spoken. "And if you think you're going to take him from me, you slut, I'll see that you rot in prison like the spy you probably are."

Talleyrand was already limping toward the door, waving for his men, as Claudine rose from the chaise and began walking toward Teo. "Don't you touch her," he barked at Claudine. "Control yourself!"

Teo backed away from the vengeful woman moving toward her with her parasol extended like a pointed weapon. "Andre always has sluts like you," Claudine spat. "You're not the first—you're the hundredth or thousandth. And don't think getting a brat by him will help you. He has those too, all over Europe. He pays them off, just like he'll pay you off. He fucks *everyone*," she rapped out, pugnacious and glowering. "Do you understand, you little hussy? *Everyone.*"

Mingen wrenched the parasol from Claudine's grasp only inches from Teo's stomach. Undeterred, she lunged at Teo, reaching for her throat, but Talleyrand caught his niece's shoulder enough to spin her around and a second later he had her securely in his grasp. Deceptively strong beneath the languid guise he displayed to the world, he dragged her away.

"Andre won't get a divorce from me, you bitch," Claudine raged. "Not unless he gives me every sou he has! Every sou and franc and piece of silver plate, every scrap of furniture and property!" she screamed as Talleyrand's two liveried servants, taking over from him, hauled her kicking and shrieking from the room.

"See that she stays in the carriage," Talleyrand ordered, his voice raised enough to be heard by his servants over Claudine's clamor. Carefully adjusting his coat cuffs as he turned back to Teo and Mingen, he reached out and closed the double door behind him, muffling Claudine's outcries. "I shouldn't have allowed her to come with me," he apologized. "Now if we could begin again on a more cordial note," he went on. "Please be seated. I intend you no harm, Countess. Please," he repeated with a bow, waving her into a chair. "You're quite welcome to stay, Doctor. I understand your concern for the countess's health."

He seated himself with a slight awkwardness, his deformed foot making him less graceful. "Claudine has personalized this issue when the reason I drove out here today has in truth to do with the future of France. Let me explain." In a brief excerpt he outlined the impoverished state of the economy, the unfortunate reverses in the war, the debilitating restrictions in governing the country with the two houses of the assembly in constant disagreement. "I can't divulge details, of course," he went on, "but several members of the Directory are inclined to offer General Duras an important role in changing the political direction of France. He would become one of two members of the new Directory with virtually unlimited powers to govern. Do you understand how important it is at the moment for his private life to appear at least on the surface harmonious and conformable?" he said with delicate significance. "I'm afraid a liaison with the wife of a Russian general—currently at war with us—would seriously compromise his image," he gently added. "You have to agree, Countess, that he's eminently capable of ruling this country."

Teo could scarcely breathe as each word fell from Talleyrand's lips in measured, reasonable tones. The opportunity for Andre seemed immeasurable. And as the silence lengthened and her world began falling apart, Talleyrand waited for her reply. "Yes," she said, finding her voice at last. "He's extremely capable."

"What do you want?" Mingen brusquely said, not sure Teo could maintain her composure much longer. Her face was drained of color.

"If the countess could persuade the general to withdraw his divorce proceedings temporarily, or perhaps if she could return to Russia for a short interval while all the necessary events unfold, France would be grateful. She could renew her friendship with the general at a later date—with our blessing—once his position as head of state is secure."

"When do you have to know?" Teo asked, her voice stronger than she expected with her life collapsing.

"In the next two weeks if possible." Talleyrand's voice was cordial, as if they were discussing some idle bit of gossip.

"What of the war in Switzerland?"

"MacDonald or Bernadotte could replace Duras."

"And gain a victory?" Did the man not realize how critical the balance of power was there?

"Perhaps we could delay the, ah, events until Austria is crushed," Talleyrand acknowledged. "I expect you and the doctor are more cognizant of the state of affairs in Switzerland than I."

"Crushing Austria isn't a military exercise to be lightly undertaken on a summer afternoon."

"I didn't mean to minimize the task, Countess. We on the political sidelines overlook at times the demands on our generals."

"The Austrian army is vastly superior in numbers."

"But surely our soldiers are more capable." A politician's bland assurance.

"If I return to Russia and the general still decides on a divorce, what then?"

"I can only speak from an observer's position and I wouldn't wish to denigrate the general's steadfast regard for you, but in the past General Duras has demonstrated a—shall we say—distressing impermanence in his relationships."

"I see. You regard this as simply another of his transient liaisons."

"Regrettably, madame, he's not yet shown much respect for fidelity."

The baby chose that moment to kick for the first time and Teo gasped at the astonishing sensation. Was it some prophetic response? she wondered, her mind in tumult, awe and wonder, sheer happiness and opposing gloom all running riot.

"Are you in pain, madame?" Talleyrand solicitously inquired, leaning forward in his chair.

"No," she quickly replied, feeling another tiny flutter. "Herr Mingen, would you fetch Tamyr for me?"

"Dare I leave you, Countess?" Her breathing was slightly agitated.

"I'm fine. And Citizen Talleyrand has made his position abundantly clear. Is that sufficient discourse on the matter, Citizen?" she inquired, feeling strangely energized by the positive affirmation of her child. "Rest assured, I'll consider all you've said."

"The nation would be grateful, Countess. And my apologies for my niece," he added. "I deeply regret exposing you to the embarrassment of her incivility."

"I regret it as well," Teo replied, regretting more the thought of Andre having Claudine for a wife. How could she possibly make him happy?

Mingen stood, signaling the end of the conversation, and content with the tenor of their conversation, Talleyrand accepted his dismissal with good grace. He stood, bowed, and took his leave with all the courtly charm of his noble heritage.

"If you would convey your decision to me in some fashion, Countess, I'd deeply appreciate your kindness."

"I'll only promise to consider what you told me," Teo replied.

"Thank you, kind lady," Talleyrand said, and with a final bow, he walked from the room.

Mingen immediately went to fetch Tamyr and the baby seemed to realize it now had an audience for a flurry of kicking ensued. Teo held her hands over her stomach and felt a quiet contentment that despite the political machinations, Duras's despicable wife, and the wrenching decision that faced her, she would have Andre's baby.

"That's a healthy kick," Tamyr declared, delicately touching Teo's stomach. "A boy kicks like that, wouldn't you say, Herr Mingen?"

"I wouldn't hazard a guess," Mingen diplomatically replied.

"I don't care whether it's a boy or girl," Teo happily asserted. "I feel so much pleasure, I feel connected to the universe," she expansively exclaimed. "And in this benign mood, tell me, Anton, what of Talleyrand's conversation is to be believed?"

"Let me question some of my sources for a kind of consensus. Although," he went on with a negligent shrug, "the plotting and conspiracies are endless."

"First Barras and now Talleyrand. They're nervous at least," Teo said. "And if the possibility of Andre becoming a Director is genuine, I could never stand in his way."

The pressures had begun; the coup must be very near, Mingen thought. "Let me ride into the city this evening," he neutrally said, "and see what's in the air. The cafés are a hotbed of factional debate."

"Talleyrand has resigned as foreign minister. Is he aligning himself with this new régime? Do you think they've contacted Andre yet?"

That was the pertinent question, Mingen thought. Or were they sounding out a dozen other generals as well?

Would Duras accept if a directorship were offered him was an added question. "I'll see what I can find out this evening," he replied, faintly alarmed for Teo's safety if the conspirators feared her presence. None of them was above the most vicious acts. And Claudine's threat of prison wasn't to be taken lightly.

That evening with his authorizations from Duras, Mingen sent a telegram to the general enlightening him on Barras's and Talleyrand's visits. It was a brief message in code, ending with the suggestion he remove Teo to a more secure location. Advise, he closed.

News from the Prussian agents he contacted that evening suggested an authenticity to Talleyrand's conversation. Lucien and Joseph Bonaparte were keeping a close surveillance on their brother-in-law Bernadotte. Apparently, they feared he was being offered the position of "sword" in Sieyès's plot while their brother Napoleon was exiled in Egypt. Lucien had been sending frantic messages for weeks to Napoleon imploring him to come home before it was too late. But they'd received no reply and assumed their messages hadn't escaped the British blockade.

Before Mingen and Teo could discuss what he'd learned the previous night, their morning breakfast was interrupted by another caller. Emmanuel Sieyès was at the door.

Interested in what had brought him out so soon after Talleyrand's visit, Teo agreed to meet with him.

Once described by Robespierre as "the mole of the Revolution," the plump former Jesuit priest, in his element in the atmosphere of plot and counterplot, greeted Teo with effusive compliments. But once the courtesies had been exchanged, the weather had been disposed of, the state of the garden and grounds praised, he said with an oily charm, "I understand Citizen Talleyrand was out to see you yesterday."

"He came with General Duras's wife," Teo said. "Naturally I was surprised."

"He inquired, I presume, into the general's activities?"

"What activities precisely?" Apparently Claudine was dismissed as irrelevant.

"The state of the war, madame."

This was the man who had betrayed first Danton and then Robespierre in the days of the Terror, so Teo spoke with caution. "As I mentioned to Citizen Talleyrand, the general never confided in me. Our friendship was separate from his military activities."

"You rode with him to Bregenz, followed him in the retreat to Zurich, were in daily contact with him for months. Fouché led me to believe the general was very close to you."

Teo took notice of his deliberate mention of the minister of police and carefully selected her words. "I understand a full-scale battle is imminent. It was a question of the archduke's advance."

"The archduke's no longer in Switzerland."

"Where is he?" Teo innocently inquired.

"I thought you might know, madame."

"He was in Switzerland when I left for Paris."

"Ah," Sieyès murmured, his pale eyes chill. "And you have no contact with your husband?"

"None."

"Your physician, Herr Mingen, was in Paris last night."

A small shiver went down her spine; they were being watched. "He's vastly interested in politics," she lightly replied. "He tells me the Parisian cafés are alive with debate."

"Are you interested in politics, madame?"

"Not in the least, Citizen Sieyès. I leave such concerns to men."

"Will you be staying here long?"

"The general gave me leave to stay as long as I wished."

"Does he plan on joining you soon?"

"I'm afraid the state of the war makes his plans uncertain."

"I understand you're with child."

"Forgive me, Citizen, if I find that too personal a comment." She kept her voice cordial although his grilling interrogation made her extremely nervous. He wasn't a man to be trusted.

"Duras has a reputation for the ladies, you know."

"His wife mentioned that. I find him devoted to his career. He's been of great service to France, I understand."

"He could perhaps be of greater service to his country. How would you respond to that, madame?"

"I would be pleased for him."

"You'd be in the way."

Certainly a blunt, misogynist delivery, Teo thought. "I see," she said, not feeling any more explanation was required to such rudeness.

"If he's recalled to serve his government, you could have no public role in his life."

"You've made yourself perfectly clear, Citizen. Is there more on your agenda?"

"I think that will suffice for the moment," he crisply said, rising. "Pray stay out of Paris. Fouché has orders."

"As you wish," she politely said.

Mingen walked into the drawing room shortly after Sieyès left and, walking to the window, watched his carriage disappear down the drive.

"You heard," Teo said.

"He doesn't have Talleyrand's charm."

"He has no charm at all. Do we leave or stay?" she inquired, alarmed by Sieyès's ruthlessness.

"We leave tonight. He and Fouché are far too dangerous."

"They saw you in Paris last night."

"They saw me only when I wished them to. We'll leave by the river after dark."

"And they'll cast us as spies for our flight."

"Better than rotting in the Château d'If. Tell Tamyr to pack only a small portmanteau and it might be prudent to stay inside the house today. One can't be certain with Fouché; he sometimes exceeds his orders. Will you manage without me today? I don't wish to leave you in fear."

"I'll help Tamyr pack and take a last stroll about Andre's home. I don't expect Fouché to strike so quickly since they might need Andre on their side."

"That necessity, I hope, will give us sufficient time to find more amenable surroundings. Would you consider Prussia as a temporary home?" He needed to obtain passports today and travel authorizations through the German principalities.

"Would you take me home to Siberia instead?" she quietly said, somehow in the past seconds understanding what she must do for herself and Duras.

"Could Korsakov find you there?"

"Not far back in the forests. I find the solitude appeals to me suddenly. And how would Korsakov know what happened to me in the chaos of war? I could have been killed."

"What name would you like on your Russian passport?" Mingen asked with an understanding smile. "I could see to a fictitious death certificate as well."

No trumpets sounded but Teo knew she'd made the right decision because a calm enveloped her as if a great struggle were over. "You're the dearest friend, Anton," she softly said. "Can a death certificate really be issued?" And when he nodded, it seemed for a moment as though she were invested with all the power on earth. "In that case," she said with a warm, encompassing smile, "give me a southern name on my passport—something from Georgia. So when I cross the border no one will think of Siberia." And then ruthless reality erased the smile from her face and a flicker of anguish showed in her eyes. "Do you think I might see Andre before I go away?"

"Perhaps," Mingen carefully replied, considering the possibility remote. "I'll telegraph our plans to him, although there's no way of knowing if he can reply."

"I understand," Teo said, steeling herself against the ache in her heart.

"He never thought your presence here would cause such controversy; he won't be expecting us to return. He wasn't aware of the newest conspiracy to gain power. With the failure of Bonaparte's Egyptian campaign, those who wish a change of government have renewed hopes."

"While I only hoped to wait for the birth of my child and Andre's homecoming."

"The course of events have overtaken us. It was a short holiday," he said with a rueful smile.

"I don't envy Andre working with the men who came to call. They would betray their own families."

"Duras knows them. He knows their limitations."

"They need him, don't they?"

"As you saw. Each man in his own way is counting on Duras to bring him to power."

Her expression was wistful. "Perhaps I can have Andre later when they no longer need him."

"Take heart," Mingen said. "He may not be interested in their proposal and you may have Duras beside you as soon as the war ends."

"But how could Andre refuse them? He's a man of duty and honor; his country needs such a man." And she wondered too in the small recesses of her mind whether her callers had been correct in their assessment of Andre's capacity for permanence in his relationships. Was she deceiving herself in thinking his love for her was more lasting than his liaisons in the past?

"We'll see," Mingen gently said, his own perceptions of

Duras's political aspirations quite different. But Teo needed
to be taken to safety, of that he was certain.

"Am I selfish in wishing myself away from this scrambling for power?" Teo quietly asked. "Am I deserting him?"

"It's a matter of danger, pure and simple. Duras will
understand."

"A log home in the depths of the forest takes on a comfortable, peaceful charm."

"Then we must see that you find it."

They left that night, moving quietly down to the jetty
on the riverbank, where Mingen helped them into a small
dinghy and rowed them across to the opposite shore. A carriage was waiting at an inn nearby and by morning they
were well away from Paris.

Twice they changed carriages and once they stopped
overnight at an out-of-the-way village while Mingen rode
to a military depot several miles away, looking for a reply to
his telegram.

None had arrived.

"He's on campaign," Mingen said on his return. "It may
not be possible to reach him."

Five days later they were nearing Basel where they
would strike out on a northern course through the principalities of Germany and Teo was suddenly overcome with a
sense of panic. In her reasonable moods, she could deal with
her separation from Duras, telling herself it was an honorable course—her personal feelings sacrificed to a greater
good. And there were several alternate possibilities to the
political cabal in Paris, she reminded herself, that would restore Duras to her. He could decline their offer; they might
find another general more expedient for their plans; Duras
might insist she stay with him—felicitous thought—or the
war could be over soon and she could return to him. But
there was no reply to Mingen's telegram at any of the

telegram relay points on their journey east and in a day at most she would be outside French territories.

It was no longer possible to view their separation in altruistic terms when her window of opportunity was fast narrowing and she might never see him again. It was no longer possible to think benignly of leaving Duras. She wanted to ride to him wherever he was and plead with him to let her stay.

But Mingen wouldn't agree, nor would Tamyr, nor would, ultimately, Andre. And in the portion of her brain that functioned despite her pain at losing him, she realized how unlikely it was for her to find him in the battleground of Switzerland.

Duras had been on the offensive all across Switzerland since she'd left, Mingen had told her. The French were taking back lost territory. St. Gotthard had been recaptured; Glaris and Lucerne were theirs again, and the Austrian pickets at Zurich had been withdrawn nearer the city. Duras was never in one location for long.

And when Basel came into view that afternoon, she almost broke into tears. They'd stay the night and in the morning begin their journey north.

The hotel stood on the banks of the Rhine, the room Mingen arranged for her beautiful and large with a balcony overlooking the river. The setting sun gleamed off the buildings across the river, the medieval town looking as if it were cast in gold. A peaceful beauty infused the scene. The war hadn't intruded yet on this border town.

How close she was to him on the frontier of Switzerland and yet how impossibly far with no imaginable way to reach him.

Where could he be? she wondered. At least he was alive, she comforted herself; news of his death would have been abroad in the town. There was solace in knowing he lived, there was hope.

She sat at the window until the sunset gave way to evening and the first stars appeared in the sky. And when Tamyr came in to coax her to bed, she complied like a docile child, but she didn't sleep. She lay awake counting the church bells on the quarter hour, repeating the litany of strokes in a singsong silent chant of lament—never . . . never . . . never again—on each vibration, thinking she would die of her pain.

She'd considered herself beyond sorrow and desolation—accepting, surrendering to the circumstances; she'd believed self-denial and honor would sustain her.

But she was wrong.

19

The sound of horsemen riding fast came faintly to her ears at first, the reverberation intensifying as she listened, horseshoes on cobblestone a distinctive rhythm. The increasing uproar brought the hotel staff to wakefulness as it rolled through the town on the hill and swept down to the river. Teo heard doors slamming shut and footsteps running up and down the stairs. The torches were lit suddenly on the façade, their flickering shadows reflected on the river.

The thunderous barrage swept into the square facing the hotel and eddied to a halt, the bass resonance of men's voices replacing the frenzied drum of hoofs. The clamor poured into the hotel, shouts and cries, a din that rose up the stairs and filled the corridors.

Booted feet and the jingle of spurs rolled up the stairs in a riot of sound as the men moved into the dining rooms that had been hastily thrown open. Then the ringing echo of a single pair of spurred heels running down her corridor struck Teo's senses. Her heart stopped.

When the sprinting footsteps came to a halt at her door, she bolted upright in bed.

A key was jammed into the lock, turned quickly in a metallic scraping of metal on metal, and she ripped the covers away and leaped to her feet.

She was halfway to the door when it flew open and he stood there, a huge dim shadow in the dark, his loosely slung sword swinging, catching the light.

"I was afraid I'd miss you," he gasped, his breathing labored.

"Andre," she whispered, afraid to move, afraid this was a quixotic vision.

Stepping over the threshold, he shoved the door shut, stripped off his sodden gloves in a blur of movement. "I'm all wet," he apologized on a suffocated breath, covering the distance between them in three great strides.

Then his arms closed around her and hope filled her heart.

"I've been riding since morning," he murmured, holding her close, crushing her. "I sent a message," he whispered into her hair, grateful, thankful, believing in some benevolent spirit. "But the telegraph lines don't work when it rains. I thought you'd be gone."

She clung to him as though she were drowning and he was her lifeline. "How long can you stay?" she asked.

There was never enough time.

Never a future.

Only snatched bits of happiness.

"Just a short time." He shouldn't have left Glaris; they'd ridden through two Austrian pickets to get away. "The men are downstairs eating before we ride back, but I wanted to see you before you left Switzerland."

"Do I have to go?" She was without pride.

He didn't answer and she thought for a moment he might tell her no. "You'll be safer at home," he finally said. "I wish you could stay but we're launching attacks on Zurich soon."

"What of Talleyrand and his cohorts?" She had to know.

"I have to win this war first; screw the rest. Could we have some light?" he murmured, releasing her. "I want to see you; I don't care about the politics." Taking her hand, he led her to the bed. "Don't let me fall asleep," he said, reaching for the flint, his voice heavy with weariness. "Cholet's coming for me in two hours."

"Sit . . . lie down," she offered, pushing him down on the bed. "I'll light the candles." It was enough to have him with her, she thought, chastising herself for being ungrateful. She'd prayed for days for such an eventuality, for another chance, and now that he'd ridden all day and half the night to be with her, she was badgering him, making demands.

The flint sparked and then the candlewick caught and flared in the darkness.

"You look beautiful," he whispered, gazing up at her as the candle glowed. "I've thought of you every minute since you left."

"I know there's a God because he answered my prayers," she murmured, sitting down beside him, touching his damp hair.

"I'm soaking the blankets," he apologized, beginning to unbutton his jacket. "It rained almost all the way to Basel. How are you and the baby?" he asked.

"Better now that you're here."

"Me too. To hell with the war," he said with a grin, looking very young with his disheveled hair and flashing smile. "Perhaps at thirty-seven it's time to retire," he added, tossing his jacket on the floor.

"Come live in the woods with me," Teo said, picking up his jacket and laying it over the footboard to dry.

"Just the three of us." He slid off a boot and tossed it.

"No one else."

"Until the next baby." His smile was glorious.

"You'll have to hunt and fish to feed us."

"Gladly. Did you bring my fishing rods?" The second boot dropped to the floor.

"Fouché might have noticed; we packed lightly."

"Bastards," he muttered, pulling his shirt over his head. "They had no right to harass you."

She put out her hand to take his shirt. "I'd rather be here with you anyway," she said, draping it over the end of the bed, feeling a quiet happiness in helping him, wishing it were possible to have a life together.

And when she turned back to him he was unbuttoning his breeches. "Let me help you," she softly said.

"I can't believe it's you, that I'm here." He'd been constantly on the move the past weeks, fighting the Austrians on a dozen fronts, and when he'd arrived at headquarters again and found Mingen's telegram, Basel had seemed impossible to reach in time. "Pinch me or something. Umm, that's nice," he murmured, cupping Teo's hand, following its slow descent. "You must be a fey sprite and I must be dreaming to feel this good." And then he touched the buttoned collar of her sleeping gown. "Take this off so I can see you and the baby. I could feel him . . . or her when I held you. Are you feeling like a mommy?" he murmured, brushing his hand over the rounding curve of her belly.

"I'm feeling fat but healthy." She slid the top button open.

"You *look* healthy," he whispered, helping her unbutton the gown. "You look adorable too in this high-collared white linen," he added, brushing a fingertip down the lace-edged neckline. "All modest and innocent—as though you've never let a man into your bed."

"Only you," she quietly murmured.

"And I did this to you." His voice was velvet soft as he slipped his hand inside her gown, ran his palm over the ripe fullness of her breast. "Baby's making these . . . very big," he murmured, sliding the pale linen off her shoulders, baring her lavish breasts. He lifted their heaviness, bouncing them lightly on his palms so they quivered, so a shimmering heat glowed deep and hot inside her. "They look full to the top." His hands slid up the voluptuous plumpness, his fingers closed on her nipples. Lightly at first, the merest pressure of forefinger and thumb, and then he tugged, gently stretching the swollen nipples.

She sucked in her breath at the shocking pleasure.

"You need me, don't you?" he whispered.

"Desperately." A single word of breathless longing.

"I'm so glad I found you tonight," he murmured, reaching out to push her gown over her hips, astonished at the incredible thrill he felt at seeing evidence of his child. He gently stroked the small rise of her stomach, his sense of pride profound, as if it were a personal triumph. "Will it be all right to make love?" His voice held a delicate courtesy. "Do you feel—"

"An overwhelming lust."

His smile flashed up at her. "Just checking."

"If we only have two hours . . ." she suggestively murmured, a licentious glow in her eyes.

His brows languidly rose. "You want me only for sex?"

"At the moment, yes." Desire throbbed in a steady, feverish rhythm through her body.

"Ah . . ." he breathed with a gratified smile, "the darling I remember."

"While *he* looks very much as I remember," Teo purred, taking his erection between her hands and drawing its rigid length upright, stroking it like a cherished treasure. "Has he missed me?"

"More than you can imagine."

"Should I kiss him hello?" As she leaned forward, his arched penis stirred in her hands.

"He remembers you fondly."

"The feeling's mutual," she murmured, touching the satiny tip with her tongue.

His entire body tensed.

"I should put a lock on him," she whispered, her breath warm on his skin.

"He has one on—or did until now."

Her gaze swung up from the little ridge she was caressing with her tongue. "I'm honored."

"I'm in love. It changes the rules of the game." He touched her chin with his fingertips, lifted it away. "Come here," he said, his voice husky and low.

He drew her down beside him and then just held her for a long, quiet time, hungry for the feel of her. The warmth of her body seeped into his, the wonder of the child between them touched his soul. "I've thought of this . . . of holding you like this—"

"Stay with me," she said against his shoulder.

"Someday I will." If the Austrians didn't kill him, he thought. Rising on one elbow, he gazed at her, wanting to preserve her image in his memory—every exquisite detail, every blooming curve and graceful charm. "You look sumptuous," he tenderly said, tracing the veins faintly visible on her extravagant breasts. "Like a fertility goddess, all ripe and fruitful." His hand glided over her disappearing waistline, the roundness of her belly. "You're mine forever," he said with a remote intensity, his hand coming to rest on the silken curls between her legs. He lifted his dark gaze, wanting affirmation, as if he couldn't tell from the frantic rhythm of her breathing, from the blatant desire in her eyes. "Tell me," he said, the heel of his hand gently massaging.

"I'm yours," she said, moving against his hand, vulnerable, glowing with desire.

Bending his dark head, he brushed her ear with his mouth. "You're my world. . . ." He slipped a finger inside her and then another, stroking her moist, pulsing flesh.

She raised her hips with a great urgency, stirring against his bewitching rhythm. "I want more." A soft, heated demand.

"I'll give you everything I have," he whispered, shifting his weight, moving over her, easing between her legs.

"Now, please . . ." Her voice was quivering. *"Now."* The word caught in her throat as he pressed forward, forced himself through the tensile, sleek tissue of her vulva. Advancing with exquisite slowness, he glided deeper, feeling her luxurious warmth closing around him, wanting to slow down every sensation, to prolong the agonizing rapture.

She touched his chest, his shoulders, his face, her hands moving in distracted, helpless flutters, her senses on fire. "Andre," she whimpered, the turbulent delirium overwhelming.

"I'm here," he whispered, raw feeling in his words.

Her hair was loose, wild on the pillow, her face and throat flushed. Reaching up, she clutched his face between her hands. "Stay always," she pleaded, a mild terror gripping her when the noise downstairs rose faintly into the corridor outside.

"I'll never leave you," he murmured, knowing she wanted the words however dissembling, knowing even as he spoke that tonight might be all they would ever have.

Her eyes filled with tears.

He loved her then gently, gently, kissing away her tears, telling her of his love, his words sweet as springtime, lyrical, rosy-cheeked words that made her forget the men downstairs and the preciousness of their time together. He moved slowly as he spoke, gliding in and out, holding himself deep inside her for brief, exquisite moments while she gasped, stimulated to a delirious degree, and then he'd withdraw again as she clung to him. And before long impassioned need inundated thought completely and her fear dissolved in an opulent haze, her sadness burned away in the fiery flames of lust.

"Touch me, touch me," she cried. And he touched her everywhere while she melted, dissolved. He touched her to the deepest depth, touched her senses, her mind, her body, her sweet, wanton sex until she was spent at last, until he collapsed . . . until they lay replete.

They were half asleep in each other's arms when Cholet knocked on the door. Duras softly groaned, made some rapid calculations in his mind, and shouted, "Twenty minutes more."

His eyelids fell shut again, but only for a moment, and then glancing down at Teo, he whispered, "Are you sleeping?"

"Yes, I can't move. You'll have to stay."

"I'll tell Cholet to fight the war without me."

"That's what I was thinking."

"Now returning to the real world once again," he murmured, sliding up against the pillows, lifting Teo into his lap. "I was thinking—"

"That I could go with you," she said with a smile.

Placing a restraining finger on her mouth, he said, smiling back, "I was thinking the war could be over by the first snows. Barring some manifestation of bravery we've not yet seen while recapturing most of our lost territory, we might finish the Austrians off soon. I could come for you by December or January."

"You may be offered a Directorship. Mingen must have wired you."

"I have no interest. That clutch of scoundrels need my command of the army, not me. They'll find someone else."

She debated for the briefest moment the degree of her unselfishness and then said, "France needs you *because* of those scoundrels."

"I can serve France by winning their battles. Mingen will tell me where to find you. Expect me."

"You'll be stopped at the border. My husband will see to that."

He smiled. "You have no faith, *ma chère*. This winter I'll be there."

"I'll have a light in the window," she softly replied.

He kissed her then, a lingering, bittersweet kiss of love and farewell, the sweetest, saddest kiss in the world. For he had to drive the Austrians from Zurich now, and then from Switzerland, and there were no guarantees anyone would survive the bloodbath. And if after that he and her husband were still alive, he had to find Korsakov and kill him.

"Write me when the baby is born," he said. "I want to know on the instant—or in your case," he added, smiling faintly, "a much longer instant."

"The post goes by a hundred miles south."

"Tell me if you can," he amended, "and wait for me. I'll come for you and our child."

"I'll wait forever," she whispered, and throwing her arms around his neck, she clung to him, her tears cool on his chest, the scent of her filling his senses. And then he slowly untwined her arms from his neck and kissed her eyes and cheeks and nose and lastly her mouth with an aching tenderness.

"Cholet will be back soon. And Zurich is still standing," he said with a sigh. "Wish me luck."

"I wish you," she said, tracing the beauty of his mouth, "only victory and good fortune."

He briefly held her fingers to his mouth and then lifted her from his lap. Rising from the bed, he stood utterly still for a moment trying to shake off his fatigue, and then drawing in a breath, he reached for his breeches.

She watched him in silence as he dressed, not knowing if this was her last sight of him: his muscled, scarred body flexing, moving with grace and power, the sepia tones of his

skin gilded by the glow of the candlelight. He'd smile at
her occasionally. The warmth and affection in his gaze were
her bulwark, she thought, against the coming chill of her
solitude. And she'd smile back and think how lucky she'd
been to have known him.

His uniform was still damp so he grimaced and grumbled in discomfort as he slipped into it, and when he muttered in expletives as he sat on the edge of the bed struggling
to pull on his wet boots, she came to her knees behind him,
leaned against his back, and said, "Let me help."

"With that kind of help, darling," he said, flashing a
grin over his shoulder, "I won't ever get out of here. Put
something on or I'll never leave."

Kissing his ear, she moved away, understanding the
time pressures driving him, and rummaging for her nightgown in the shambles of the bed, she found it and slipped
it on.

Standing once again, he was swiftly buckling on his
sword belt, the gold-chased scabbard beautifully engraved,
the words those of gratitude from the Republic for his victories in Italy in '97. *"Merde,"* he muttered a second later,
tossing his wet leather gloves aside. "I can't wear these."

Then the expected knock sounded on the door and his
head came up like a wolf on the scent. "I'll be right down,"
he said, his voice raised enough to be heard in the corridor
outside. He quickly glanced around the room, a habit after
sleeping in strange places so often, and then he walked over
to the bed.

Teo didn't want to cry during their last minutes together so she dwelled instead on the joy he'd brought to her
as she stood to meet him.

He was already remote in his dark uniform—his cavalry
boots and black leather breeches, the navy wool of his unor-
namented jacket, his black silk neckcloth—a grim, forbid-
ding image of war. The jingle of his spurs and scabbard

were the only sounds in the silence, the hush of parting a suffocating presence in the room.

"Think of me," he softly said, drawing her into his arms, his damp clothes cool through her linen nightgown.

"Every second," she murmured, lifting her face to his. "And you must live."

"I'll see you in a few months." His head dipped and his mouth brushed hers, a gentle kiss without emotion, for his consciousness was straying, listening for the noises outside the door.

"I'll wait for you," she said, standing on tiptoe to touch his lips one last time, clinging to his hand for a second more.

He smiled as he slipped his hand free. "I love you."

She nodded, her mouth trembling. "Always," she breathed as he turned to go.

He paused at the door, and swiveling around, he gazed at her, his dark eyes darker in the shadows, his expression softening for a moment. "I'm very glad you wanted my child," he whispered.

And then he was gone.

She cried until she couldn't cry any more, until her tears were depleted and the misery of the world had closed around her, and then she fell asleep exhausted. Tamyr wouldn't wake her in the morning, refusing despite Mingen's harangues, and it was well into the middle of the afternoon before they left on the next leg of their journey.

In the following days as they made their way through all the petty German principalities, occasionally running across units from the archduke's army, their Prussian papers offered them security. Mingen was by turn charmingly cultivated and ruthlessly autocratic, adopting whichever guise was necessary, seeing them through the various bureaucracies with aplomb.

Teo couldn't have done it alone and she thanked him often for his solicitous care. "Duras and I are on a mission from God," he'd facetiously reply. "Two reprobates with a common goal."

"Is Andre winning?" she'd ask whenever he'd conversed with some official at a posting stop or border crossing.

"Korsakov is losing the war," he would always say. With the archduke's army withdrawn into Germany, Korsakov was in charge of the imperial army until Suvorov marched up from Italy, and Teo found it both strange and blissful that he no longer seemed a threatening shadow in her life. Her fear was gone as if it were absolved by some benevolent spirit; she'd found new depths of strength within her and new reserves of acceptance, and she wondered if the child she bore contributed to her sense of wholeness. It was love too, she knew, that had changed her so. She'd been given a great happiness no one could take away.

And Mingen's understanding had helped as well. They'd spoken of other marriages like hers that were so prevalent in the aristocracy, of the barbarous inhumanity of bartering young women for financial and political gain. Teo was only one of thousands of women coerced into brutal marriages, women taken as hostages was all too common.

But she'd found her way out and blissfully found love as well. Each day small epiphanies reminded her of all she had and she was perhaps more grateful for having known such pain. She had reached a new understanding by the time they arrived at the Russian border; she was reconciled to her parting from Duras.

It was the middle of September.

Archduke Charles's army was attacking the French Army of the Rhine around the fortress of Philippsburg and driving it back to the left bank of the river.

In Italy, Suvorov had received instructions from Vienna to go to Switzerland, and while he'd protested, he discovered the archduke had already moved out of Switzerland. He had no choice then but to go to Korsakov's aid.

The British at this point continued their attempts to stave off disaster by offering Vienna new compensations, but these efforts all failed. On September 10, Prime Minister Pitt suggested to Grenville, his foreign secretary, that England offer to compensate Austria for Italy in return for allowing Holland to take the Austrian Netherlands after the war. Three days later Pitt stated his willingness to back Austria's claim to Piedmont against the objections of the tsar, but Thugut remained unmoved. Since Austria was in actual occupation of northern Italy, Thugut felt no need of British diplomatic support in retaining these conquests. Pitt had no other leverage. By the middle of September, Pitt came to the conclusion that he couldn't trust Austria and that England would have to consider carrying on the war with only Russia as an ally.

Moving the archduke's army north wasn't necessarily a bad strategic move because it would force the French to divert troops to the Rhine instead of reinforcing Duras's army. The blunder was rather the Austrian decision to attack Mainz instead of Basel and Belfort. By moving on Mainz, the archduke's army marched too far north to support Korsakov should the French attack in Switzerland, and even if the French remained on the defensive and the two Russian corps joined forces safely, they wouldn't be strong enough to attack Duras with more than a fair chance of success.

To make matters worse, the Austrians didn't wait for Suvorov's arrival in Switzerland before moving toward Mainz. So while the Austrians were moving on Mainz and Suvorov was marching up from Italy, Korsakov's army had to face a French force near Zurich that was almost equal in numbers.

As a result of Thugut's desire to regain control of the Low Countries, the Austrians presented Duras with a unique opportunity to attack one of the Allied armies on very favorable terms and rescue a seemingly desperate situation.

Duras's plans were *en train*.

20

Since the first Battle of Zurich in June, Duras had reorganized the army into eight combat divisions, a reserve division, and a division of the interior. He had also revised his command system, appointing several new and energetic commanders. Away from Zurich, Turreau commanded the 9,100 men of the First Division in the Valais, and Lecourbe's Second Division of 13,500 men held the area round the St. Gotthard Pass. In the vicinity of Zurich: Soult's 9,950-man Third Division was on the Linth River; the 9,100 men of Mortier's Fourth Division faced Zurich; Lorge's Fifth Division of 9,000 troops and Menard's Sixth Division with 10,600 men held the line of the Limmat River; and Klein commanded the 5,460 men of the Seventh Division, which Duras had placed behind Lorge and Menard. Elsewhere, the 7,950 men of Chabran's Eighth

Division held the line of the Rhine as it flowed in an east-west direction through Switzerland. The Division of the Interior had 3,400 men and devoted its efforts mainly to guarding the army's communications line with France and hunting down royalist partisan bands. The Reserve Division was 4,680 men strong and the artillery comprised 1,050 troops.

Facing this force was Korsakov's 27,350-man Russian corps. It held a line stretching from Zurich to the Limmat River and from there to the Rhine. An Austrian force of 21,800 men under von Hotze manned positions along a line stretching from Lake Zurich along the Linth River to Dissentis in the Grisons. To the south, Suvorov with 30,400 men was moving toward Switzerland.

The minister of war told Duras that "the result of this campaign and perhaps the destiny of the Republic rests on your force and on your courage."

Duras was well aware that his army was the only corps fit to resume the offensive and a successful attack would not only relieve the pressure on the Italian front but also force the Anglo-Russian army out of Holland. He was busily preparing for his offensive. Replacements, rations, and ammunition flowed steadily to the front until by the third week in September his army was ready to strike.

His objective was not just to force Korsakov to retreat but to annihilate his corps as a fighting force. His tactical plan was to convince the Russians that he was going to strike north across the Rhine, while in fact he prepared a series of strokes in the vicinity of Zurich.

Duras ordered Chabran and Menard to make diversionary attacks along the Rhine while the main assault force, fourteen thousand men drawn from Menard's, Lorge's, Klein's, and Mortier's divisions, struck across the Limmat at Dietikon, seven miles from Zurich. The main force was to seize the Fahr plateau, thereby splitting the Russian front, and then send brigades to the left and right. Units moving left were to contain Russian units along the Rhine, while the troops advancing to the right were to threaten the northwest approaches of Zurich. While the main attack moved out, another division was to move against the western face of Zurich and still another unit was to strike at the city from the south. As the pincers snapped shut around Zurich, Soult was to break out on the central front. His objective was twofold: to defeat von Hotze's Austrians and to prevent them from reinforcing Korsakov.

The operation planned for September 23 required simultaneous execution to ensure its success, but on the twenty-second, Soult informed Duras he wouldn't be able to complete construction of the bridge he needed to cross the Linth until the morning of the twenty-fifth.

Headquarters at Bremgarten was a hive of activity, the mobilization of the offensive requiring round-the-clock activity. The weather had been humid for weeks, the pace frantic; everyone's nerves were on edge. Duras swore on reading Soult's message, tossed the folded sheet aside and stalked into his office, slamming his door with such violence the young ADCs jumped.

No one in the operations room spoke, the hum of conversation abruptly curtailed.

"I'll see when he wants to reschedule," Bonnay calmly said into the silence. A faint smile twitched the corners of his mouth. "Soult's lucky he's sixty kilometers away."

"Don't let him out of his office for a while," Vigée drawled with his customary insouciance.

"Just make sure your regiment is ready," Bonnay cautioned, his hand on the doorknob to Duras's office.

"We're always ready, *mon ami,*" Vigée replied, his flashing grin lighting up his eyes. "My pets are chafing to kill some Russkis."

"They'll have their wish in short order." Bonnay liked Vigée despite his occasional chiding; the man was good at his job. "Cholet, have the couriers ready to ride in ten minutes. Every squadron has to be informed of the new schedule." And turning the knob, he pushed the door to Duras's office open and entered.

"We can't afford this delay," Duras muttered, scowling at Bonnay. "Fucking Suvorov is in Bellinzona already—past there by now," he grumbled. That morning they'd received news of Suvorov's progress; he was south of the Saint Gotthard Pass, poised to invade Switzerland. "This offensive has to be over before he reaches Altdorf."

"Soult's had problems getting materials for his bridge."

"We all have problems," Duras growled, his dark brows meeting in a straight line. Shifting lower in his chair, he gazed up at Bonnay, challenge and discontent in his gaze.

"What's the earliest we can reschedule? Cholet has the couriers outside." Bonnay knew better than to argue with Duras in his current mood.

"Soult says the morning of the twenty-fifth." Taking a deep breath, Duras expelled it in vexation and then said, clipped and curt, "The assault begins at daybreak on the twenty-fifth. No changes for any reason. We cross the Limmat at first light." Sitting up, he placed his palms gently on his desktop, aligned his fingertips as if in an exercise of restraint, and said in a more moderate tone, "Send in Dedon. I want the transport boats moved to Dietikon tonight."

"We'll take Zurich before Suvorov reaches Altdorf," Bonnay maintained with assurance, his confidence in his commander complete.

Duras smiled faintly. "Damn right we will."

At five in the morning of the twenty-third, the troop transports—sixteen large boats and thirty-seven lighter ones—were all at Dietikon, hidden from the Russian sentries across the Limmat.

Menard, commanding the Sixth division, openly prepared for a crossing at Brugg on the twenty-fourth. He assembled all his officers, consulting with them, preparing a pontoon bridge and his boats for launching—all in order to give the Russian troops opposite him at Vogelsang the impression that the main attack would come at Brugg.

Before midnight of the twenty-fourth—with Duras personally directing the operations—the boats, hidden a thousand feet from the riverbank, were hand-carried down to the water. The fastest and lightest boats would cross the ninety meters of river with the first troops; a second group of larger boats would cross next and a third group would land troops on a small island in the river defended by Russian sentry posts.

Pontoon men, spread out along the left bank in three divisions, waited for the signal to launch the boats. Foy, in command of the artillery, had all his artillery pieces, their wheels muffled in rags, silently rolled into place by 2 A.M. Charged with protecting the assault troops, his gunners were at the ready.

The advance guard, grenadiers and skirmishers from the Tenth Light Brigade and the Thirty-seventh Demibrigade, commanded by Gazan—thirty-three and recently appointed general of brigade—were deployed in battle positions fifty feet from the river's edge.

The brigades of Bontemp and Quetard were at Nieder-Urdorf and Dietikon; the reserve under Klein was in the valley of Schlieren, facing Zurich, ready to help Mortier's left if the Russians attempted to leave the city.

By 3 A.M., everyone was deployed, all the units precisely in position, waiting for the signal to attack. The cavalry order "Roll cloaks!" came at 4:30, the practice synonymous in the French army with a sign that combat was imminent. The rolled cloak worn bandolier fashion protected against a cut to the left shoulder, the principal stroke of an enemy cavalryman.

Everyone checked their weapons for the last time.

At 4:45—first light—Duras gave the command to attack and the engineers raced forward to launch their assault boats. In seconds, two of the overloaded skiffs were aground on some willow roots, the noise bringing the Russian sentries awake. Gunfire immediately erupted from the woods where the sentry posts were located. Foy's artillery responded, blasting away at the enemy, and the Russians quickly withdrew.

Cries of *En avant!*, Forward!, Let's go!, resounded from every direction and within three minutes six hundred men of the advance guard had crossed the Limmat.

Once the drumbeat of the charge sounded, Foy's artillery moved to their new positions in support of the troops racing toward the plateau of Fahr. The Russians threw a brigade against Duras's bridgehead, but French sharpshooters cut it to pieces and the Russians recoiled.

The boats continued transporting troops rapidly across to the other side and when Duras saw that there were sufficient troops to maintain their new position, he gave orders to have the pontoon equipment brought up.

At 5:00, work began on the bridge while sappers who'd gone across with the first wave were cutting a road through the woods for the use of the cavalry and artillery.

By 6:00, Gazan's assault troops had taken the Russian positions on the heights and were in possession of Kloster-Fahr. By 7:30, eight thousand men were on the opposite bank and by 9:00 the entire division had crossed the Limmat.

In the meantime, Menard's feint at Brugg had completely taken in the Russian general Dourasov, who immediately sent for help to meet what he considered the main French assault. Mares, one of Duras's ADCs, sent to Brugg that morning to report on the feint, wrote back: "It seems to me, my dear general, that the enemy makes it very easy for you; it seems that they do not want to abandon their position and your decision to cut the Russian army in two is accomplished."[18]

Duras turned his attention on Zurich.

With hardly a pause, Duras sent two demibrigades to his left, while two others led by Oudinot moved toward Zurich. The immediate objective was the Zurichberg, the large hill that dominated the city's northern approaches. As Oudinot's men closed in on the Zurichberg, Mortier threw his entire division against the western approaches of the city. Shaken by the suddenness of the attack, the Russians abandoned their forward positions and retired hastily behind the city walls. Korsakov, however, recovered his nerve, sent up two fresh battalions and ordered a counterattack. Storming out of Zurich, the Russians blunted the French drive and pushed them back at the point of the bayonet.[19]

Immediately ordering Klein's reserves up from Schlieren, Duras rallied his men to stave off the onslaught. Recklessly brave, calmly indifferent to the showers of grapeshot and bullets, he was everywhere in the front lines, outdistancing his ADCs, who struggled to keep up to him, urging his men forward, riding in the midst of the attack columns, slashing right and left, sabering Russians with a wild ferocity, his presence inspirational to all who surrounded him.

Colonel Humbert, having been exchanged after his capture in Ireland, led his battalion of grenadiers and plunged headlong after Duras into the advancing Russians. For a few moments the foes remained locked in mortal combat, but it was the Russians who finally broke and went reeling back toward Zurich. In desperation Korsakov threw his cavalry reserve into action. Duras ordered up French field artillery batteries that galloped up, unlimbered, and firing canister at near point-blank range, shattered the Russian horsemen into a welter of screaming men and animals. The gunners then manhandled their cannon into positions from which they could support Oudinot's attack.

As the fighting raged in front of Zurich, Oudinot led the men from the Tenth Light Brigade, the Thirty-seventh, Fifty-seventh, Second, and 102nd Halfbrigades, a Swiss unit, and a cavalry regiment toward the suburbs of Zurich and the Zurichberg. Realizing the full extent of the French threat, Korsakov launched a violent counterattack in a desperate effort to keep open his only escape route. As the Russians poured out of Zurich the French field guns opened fire. Tearing huge gaps in the Russian lines, the gunners succeeded in bringing the enemy to a virtual standstill. Duras's men then closed in. They engaged the shaken Russians in vicious no-quarter combat and drove them back to the very foot of the Zurichberg.

At noon a silence fell over the carnage. Neither the French nor the Russians, both stunned by their losses and the bitterness of the fighting, had the strength to resume combat. The generals, however, soon rallied their men. In front of Zurich, Mortier's sharpshooters began to enter the western suburbs. To the north, French infantry moved up the Zurichberg. Russian bayonet charges rolled them off the slopes. Duras then sent men around the Russian right. Having committed his last reserves, Korsakov was unable to check this new threat and had to abandon control of the mountain. He pulled his troops back into the northern suburbs and ordered them to fortify the houses for a last-ditch stand. The French pursued. The Russians poured a withering fire into the French assault columns, which recoiled, leaving the streets carpeted with their dead. Renewed attacks made no headway, but shortly after dark, Oudinot pushed combat patrols to the top of the Zurichberg. During the night he strengthened his hold on the mountain, a move that spelled doom for the Russian army.

As fighting raged before Zurich, Soult's division was also on the move. Prior to the general assault, Soult had created a special commando unit to seize a foothold on the Austrian side of the Linth River. On the night of September 24 the commandos plunged into the icy Linth and reached the Austrian bank undetected. Moving with murderous silence, the commandos sabered the Austrian sentries, captured several artillery emplacements, and slipped a cable back to their own side of the river. Soult then rushed fresh troops to the Austrian bank and by 5 A.M. on September 25, twelve hundred infantrymen were probing into the Austrian lines. Von Hotze, the Austrian commander, received word of the French attack and dashed off into the foggy morning to rally his troops. Racing through the mist, he inadvertently blundered into Soult's leading elements. French fusiliers cut him down. Von Hotze's death made effective resistance impossible. As Soult's engineers threw a pontoon bridge across the Linth, Austrian officers mounted a series of ill-coordinated company and battalion-strength counterattacks. These the French easily repulsed and then plunged deep into the Austrian positions. By early evening Soult's brigades had penetrated the Austrian main line of resistance, unhinged the center of the Allied front, and made it impossible for the Austrians to detach units to assist Korsakov's embattled regiments at Zurich.

During the night Korsakov rejected Duras's offer to arrange a peaceful evacuation of the city, keeping Duras's peace envoy prisoner in defiance of the rules of war. Korsakov then called a war council that resolved to break out of the French trap and escape northward into Germany. Korsakov detailed five battalions and a cavalry regiment to hold the French in the western suburbs. Four battalions were to retake the Zurichberg and six more were to hold the city itself while the rest of the corps with its supply and artillery elements dashed north.

In the early morning hours of September 26—before daybreak—Russian infantry stormed out of Zurich, raced up the mountain slopes, and bayoneted the surprised Frenchmen off the peak. Swarming into the suburbs, Russian troopers in bitter hand-to-hand fighting cleared the narrow streets and houses of French sharpshooters. The main column then moved out, but Duras quickly recovered his balance and initiative and threw in a series of violent and effective attacks. His horse artillery galloped forward and pounded the city. Packed into the narrow streets, hundreds of Russians perished helplessly under the hail of shot and shell. Meanwhile on the Zurichberg, Oudinot reorganized his command and lunged back up the slopes. Snipers decimated the Russians and storming columns smashed through the weakened lines. Oudinot's battalions regained the peak and then raced for the city gates where Korsakov's grenadiers prepared for a last desperate stand. Under a withering blast of musketry the Russians held their ground and died where they stood.

Clambering over the bodies of their slaughtered foes, the French burst into the northern section of Zurich. There they found the rear-guard battalions and most of the main column, delayed by Duras's artillery barrage, still bottled up in the streets. Unable to deploy, the Russians could do nothing to prevent the French from pouring volley after volley into their helpless lines at point-blank range. The French mowed down rank after rank of green-clad Russian infantry, while bolting horses dragged guns and wagons into the mass of dead and dying men, adding further horror to the slaughter. Additional French units broke through the south-central gates and their muskets added to the growing carnage. When the smoke finally drifted off at the end of the day, over three thousand Russian corpses littered Zurich's streets. Over five thousand men including 142 officers remained as Duras's prisoners, as well as all the Russian artillery and baggage, while the remnants of Korsakov's column, no longer a coherent fighting force, fled painfully along the roads to Germany.[20]

Having shattered the Allied front in Switzerland, Duras immediately prepared to pursue Korsakov's remnants and crush them. He made plans to head two infantry divisions and his cavalry reserve in their pursuit northward.

At a hastily called staff meeting, he said to his weary officers, "I'm asking for volunteers—a small company of cavalry to accompany me on a personal mission to overtake and kill Korsakov." He surveyed the men seated around the table, his gaze neutral. "There's no need to tell anyone he's well protected with his Cossacks. I'd prefer men without family obligations."

"Count me in," Vigée said, "and my troopers to a man will go. They'd consider it an honor to lend assistance to the countess."

No one questioned Duras's reasons for putting himself at risk, and one after another, his officers offered themselves and their men.

"Thank you," Duras said with a faint smile, "but thirty will suffice. I'll let you gentlemen decide who will go. We leave at daybreak. Your best horses, no added baggage, but a ration of oats for your horses. We'll be traveling fast to overtake him." As he stood, Bonnay rose with him. A myriad of details had yet to be arranged for the French forces moving toward Constance to drive Condé's émigré forces from the town and those moving south with orders to destroy Suvorov.

"Make sure your sabers are newly sharpened," Duras added as he turned to go. "The Cossacks handle their blades well."

"You're not to go with me," Duras said to Bonnay as they walked into an adjacent room. "That's an order. Someone has to stay behind and coordinate the army movements."

"Will Lecourbe be able to hold Suvorov?" On September 24, Suvorov's advance guard had reached the St. Gotthard Pass and slashed its way through the French defenders at a cost of two thousand men. The French had then retreated to the Devil's Bridge, an immensely strong position on the Reuss River. A tunnel-like path, five feet wide, flanked by solid rock on one side and a seventy-five-foot drop on the other, led to the bridge.

"Lecourbe has his cannon on the path. That should delay Suvorov for a time even with the Russian propensity for using soldiers as human cannon fodder. All I need is two days, and if everyone weren't so tired, I'd leave tonight. With the bulk of our army swinging south in forced marches to reinforce Lecourbe and Soult, I expect our lines to hold until I return."

"You're putting your life at risk when victory is almost ours."

"I need to do this for Teo."

"And for yourself."

"Is that so strange?" Duras countered. "How else will she be safe from him?"

Bonnay grimaced. "It's just that time's so critical now. What if Suvorov breaks through? He walked right through our armies in Italy."

"He walked through Moreau, which is a simple task. Moreau lost the battle of Trebbia as well when he sat back and did nothing for MacDonald. And Joubert was too young and inexperienced to have been given a command. There. Do you feel better now?" Duras drolly inquired.

"Tell me Lecourbe and Soult can hold and I'll feel better."

"They can." An unequivocal response typical of Duras's style of command. He had confidence in the men he'd invited to serve under him. "Now what final orders have to be sent out before I leave in the morning?"

The discussion was over.

21

It was still dark when Duras woke and dressed, his quest for vengeance compelling. He didn't wake his orderly, but quietly slipped out of his quarters and walked down the shell-scarred street to headquarters. He hadn't slept much, debating the routes in his mind most likely taken by Korsakov; he couldn't afford to be wrong. The fate of the Republic was still under threat.

In the hour before his men appeared, he scrutinized the maps on the wall, trying to calculate Korsakov's immediate destination. The remnants of the Russian corps would most likely flee east, he decided, toward Bohemia. He boldly marked the route on the map.

Bonnay appeared first with his orderly and the latest messages from Lecourbe's couriers. "He's holding," Bonnay said. "The Russians haven't managed to break through."

"Send every reinforcement we have to him. Move head-quarters down to Altdorf so we'll be nearer the engagement. I'll be back in two days."

"With the Butcher's head in a sack," Vigée cheerfully said, hearing the last part of the conversation as he strolled into the room. "I don't suppose there's any coffee for my brandy."

Bonnay pointed to a steaming kettle his orderly had carried in with him.

"You should be someone's wife, Henri," Vigée pleasantly said, striding to the table in the corner. "Such an eye for detail."

"And you should be someone's child," Bonnay countered with a smile.

"Preferably someone young and beautiful with a soft lap and big tits." Vigée winked wolfishly.

"I don't suppose you're sober," Duras said, casting a tolerant eye on his best cavalry officer.

"Not precisely," Vigée pleasantly replied, accepting a cup of steaming coffee from Bonnay's orderly. "But almost, enough to see me through this exhilarating manhunt. Good sport on a fine fall day," he cheerfully finished, pouring brandy into the cup from his flask. "My troopers are looking forward to some souvenirs."

"No ears, Vigée," Duras warned. "I trust we understand each other since that last episode."

"Chmiel was made to understand, sir," Vigée said with appropriate deference to his commander, who'd raised holy hell after the last scouting trip into enemy territory.

"Good. Glad to have you and your men along," Duras said, knowing that the killer instincts of Vigée's troop were ideal for the pursuit. "I'm favoring the road to St. Gall," Duras went on. "Although Korsakov may be riding for the Prussian border."

"St. Gall, sir," Vigée unhesitantly said. "His Cossacks

particularly like the women there." A brothel of some repute was situated in the town. "Korsakov and his guard need women every night, I hear."

Duras had heard the stories as well; Korsakov's handpicked Cossacks had a reputation for rape and brutality. "They stayed somewhere last night, then."

"And their heads are aching this morning."

"Is everyone ready?" Impatient, Duras thought only of killing the man who'd abused Teo.

"They're bringing the horses around," Vigée replied, quickly draining his coffee cup.

"Two days' rations are packed for each trooper. Don't eat all yours this morning," Bonnay sportively warned Vigée as he moved toward the door.

"I'll be eating *Russian* rations by tonight," Vigée cheerfully replied, waving as he exited the room.

"*You* eat," Bonnay said, handing Duras a flask of coffee.

"Later." Taking the flask, Duras smiled at the man who'd served him so well. "When this is over, we need to see to your next promotion."

"Just come back. We can't face Suvorov without you."

"Relax, Henri. I'll be back in two days."

"You should let someone else cut his throat," Bonnay grumbled, anxious that the risk to Duras was too great.

"I want the satisfaction," Duras said, his voice flat.

They traveled fast, resting their mounts only twice, stopping often at villages to question the inhabitants about a Cossack troop. Since early morning they'd been on Korsakov's trail; the distinctive bodyguards were easily recognized.

When dark came they stayed on the trail, though the moonless sky made tracking more difficult. Stars appeared only in patches in the gray-blue sky, clouds hovered low, and an inhospitable coolness chilled the autumn air. But the turf was soft, covered with occasional clumps of tall dry grass, and Korsakov's large troop left tracks evident even in the dim light.

The soft, damp earth absorbed the sound of horses' hoofs and Duras's men moved silently through the night, their tack muffled, conversation limited to hand signals. Willow trees lined the track alongside the river, their long branches swaying in the night wind. And then the trees began disappearing and an open field, scarcely visible, unrolled before them.

They smelled the smoke first and then saw it rising over the edge of a ravine, saw the red glow of fire as a blush on the horizon. Leaving the horses behind with two men, they crept cautiously through the underbrush lining the riverbank. On all fours they crawled to the edge of the ravine and gazed over the precipice.

Below them in the bottom of the dark bowl of the earth, gathered around bonfires, Korsakov and his Cossacks, inclined to plunder, accustomed to violence, were engaged in an evening of brutal entertainment. The scene was inhuman, a vision from hell.

Knapsacks and coats were scattered all around. There were four small tents and a larger one in striped silk before which Korsakov, robed in red brocade, seated in a campaign chair, surveyed his camp. Two naked women were chained to stakes at his feet. All around the fires were the Cossacks, and each man had a woman or two with him. Some were bound and thrown onto the ground; others were gagged, their clothing torn, the whiteness of their skin gleaming in the light of the flames.

Some women were struggling in their captor's hold, their high-pitched screams and cries animal-like in the night, counterpointed by the laughter of the men.

A young girl was running wildly among the men, trying to avoid them, but each time a man let the girl go, he tore away part of her dress. When she was naked and nearing the bushes bordering the camp, three men overtook her, pushed her back toward the light and dragged her down and swarmed over her.

At the farthest edge of the illuminated area two girls stood back to back, one armed with a stick, the other with a saber, fighting off the pack of men who were trying to get them. Finally the girls ran toward the steep slope of the ravine and desperately started to climb straight toward where Duras's men lay. "Let us go! Let us go!" they pitifully cried and Duras aimed his rifle. Each trooper made ready to shoot, waiting for Duras's order.

"Not Korsakov," he softly said. "He's mine." He waited until the command passed down the ranks in a rippling murmur, wanting to make sure everyone understood, and then he fired.

The gunshot was deafening in the hollow below them, echoing from wall to wall, blending with the shouts from the Cossacks as they scrambled for their rifles, the shrieks of the wounded, the yells of horror and fear from the women.

Duras's men emptied their rifles, methodically reloaded and fired once, twice, three times, picking off the Cossacks like targets in a fishbowl, until Duras caught sight of Korsakov running toward the picketed horses, carrying a naked girl under one arm, as though she were no more weighty than a parcel.

"Hold your fire," Duras shouted, already sliding down the steep slope of the ravine, estimating the distance between himself and Korsakov, between Korsakov and the horses. Leaping and sliding, he plunged recklessly downward, keeping his prey in sight. Oblivious to the Cossacks' gunfire exploding around him, he reached the ground in a flying bound and raced through the camp, jumping over campfires and dead Cossacks, over weeping women and saddlebags.

The horses were agitated in their roped-off paddock and Korsakov was having difficulty steadying his mount. Holding tightly to the horse's halter, he was trying to pull the animal around and heave the woman onto its back, but the animal reared and backed away, the herd around it eddying like a restless tide.

Drawing his saber, Duras ran full-out, praying Korsakov wouldn't get the horse under control before he covered the distance between them.

Wresting the animal's head down with a brutal wrench of his arm, Korsakov flung the woman up and, leaping up behind her, positioned her as a shield. Grabbing at the reins, he caught them in his fingertips, adjusted his grip, and digging in his heels, spurred the horse forward.

Sprinting full-out, Duras focused on his prey. Nothing else mattered, not the scene he'd just witnessed, not the war, not Suvorov's threat from the south. Only the man he'd come to kill.

"Korsakov!" Duras's cry rang out above the crackling gunfire and high-pitched screams, echoed in undulating waves into the night.

On catching sight of Duras, Korsakov bellowed with a cry of rage that shook the heavens. "Die!" he thundered, charging straight at Duras like a maddened bull.

Coming to a halt, Duras stood his ground and raised his saber. Unflinching as the horse bore down on him, he watched Korsakov close the distance. At the last possible second, in a blur of movement, he swung his saber in a vicious arc and leaped aside.

Its front legs slashed, the horse went down, throwing Korsakov and the woman off with such force, the woman lay stunned on the ground. Korsakov rolled to his feet with amazing agility, considering his bulk, his teeth bared like an animal, his eyes dark with hate.

He still wore his crimson robe like a boyar or hetman from some earlier time, the long skirts swirling about his ankles. With an oath, he ripped it off and tossed it aside, revealing his huge body in loose Cossack breeches, low boots, and nothing more. A long-bladed Cossack knife—kinjal—hung from his waist; the saber he wielded was oversized as well.

"Come and get me," he roared, drawing his kinjal out, his face apoplectic, his straw-colored hair disheveled, bristly, like an albino boar, his huge chest gleaming in the firelight.

Although Duras was tall, Korsakov was a giant of a man and Duras's whipcord-lean body would be at a disadvantage against such brute strength. With a tactical eye Duras surveyed his adversary as he quickly unbuttoned his tunic and shrugged out of it.

Korsakov's reach exceeded his, Duras assessed. He carried too much weight though, and his dissipation showed. An advantage perhaps, but regardless of the odds, tonight he intended to be Korsakov's angel of death.

In a portion of his brain Duras had taken note of the subsiding gunfire, of the lessening cries and shouts, but not until Vigée hove into view, running fast into the periphery of his vision, did the world intrude.

Vigée's rifle was raised.

"He's mine!" Duras cried in warning, swinging quickly to the left and right, taking in the scene of carnage and the position of his men. "Don't anyone touch him!"

A marginal hush descended on the firelit scene. And then Duras turned back to the man who had drawn him so far from his duty and said to him, "I'm taking your wife from you."

"Not when you're dead, you won't," Korsakov defiantly proclaimed.

"Just give me the word and I'll finish him off," Vigée offered, his rifle at the ready.

"No." Duras was already advancing.

"Take this, then," Vigée said, lobbing a kinjal in the soft dirt beside Duras's feet.

Retrieving it, Duras balanced it for a moment in his palm. The handle was smooth from wear, like his saber. And for a moment he wondered if he were any less barbarous than Korsakov, the number of men he'd killed too numerous to recall, his need for personal vengeance against this man a primitive ferocity.

And then Korsakov said, "I'll kill my whoring wife after I kill you."

And Duras remembered why he'd come so far.

A savage light shone in his eyes and he moved forward, intent on eliminating Korsakov from Teo's life. The men stalked each other in diminishing circles, watching, wary, unsure of their opponent's strengths and weaknesses, waiting for the right opportunity to strike. More impulsive, Korsakov lunged first, his saber flashing.

Sidestepping the deadly blade, Duras whirled away, nicking Korsakov's arm with his kinjal as he spun around.

Swearing in a stream of expletives, Korsakov clutched at the thin line of red on his upper arm.

"Kill him!" a woman screamed. Her cry was instantly muffled by one of Duras's troopers. A gathering audience began to mill on the verge of the dueling ground, and a shrill tone vibrated in the air, repressed, controlled by Duras's men. The besieging girdle of sound, like a muffled, angry shriek, seethed from the raped females hungry for Korsakov's blood.

"Maybe I should just turn you over to them," Duras said.

"If you do, I'll take some of the bitches with me," Korsakov snarled, lunging at Duras while he was distracted by the sight of bloodied, naked women breathing vengeance.

Duras managed to spin away before Korsakov's saber blow cut the bone, but the wracking agony in his shoulder almost brought him to his knees. Trained as he was to the inch, his reflexes took over and he swung out of range. Furiously marshaling his senses against the brutal pain, he quickly assessed the extent of the damage. His left hand still gripped the kinjal, but any movement was torture.

Shifting his stance, he set his teeth to meet Korsakov's next rush, in which the oxlike body swooped toward him with incredible speed. With sheer grit Duras parried Korsakov's powerful downstroke, the jarring crack of blade to blade sending shock waves through his wounded shoulder.

He wasn't able to slip away quickly enough that time, his reflexes blunted by the corrosive agony, and Korsakov slipped under his guard, catching Duras's sword arm with the kinjal.

Sucking in his breath, Duras recoiled, putting distance between them.

"It doesn't look as though . . . you're going to have my wife," Korsakov said with a triumphant smile, his breathing rough, his chest heaving, his face red from his exertions. "She'll be my property again . . . to do with as I please."

Duras stood utterly still, conserving his energy. "I'm going to kill you," he quietly said, as if he weren't savagely wounded, as if his indefatigable spirit was means enough to accomplish the task. And then his father's voice came to him, vivid as life, reminding him with shrewd expediency that honor was wasted on dishonorable men.

How many times had he fought with knife and sword at his father's side, against the Barbary pirates encroaching on his father's territory. They had been as depraved and ruthless as Korsakov. "Kill them quickly," his father would always say, disciplined, eminently qualified to deal with his foes. "This isn't a gentleman's game."

Korsakov saw that the front of Duras's shirt was soaked with blood and smiled. "If you were another second slower, I would have taken your arm off," he crowed, standing legs spread wide, confident in his victory.

"If you were smarter," Duras calmly said, failure inconsistent with his principles, "you wouldn't have stopped until you reached Russia."

"I could just wait and watch you bleed to death. Gentlemen like you," the Russian sarcastically intoned, "believe in fighting their own battles."

"Did I mention your wife is pregnant with my child?" Duras softly murmured.

Korsakov's mouth twitched in a monstrous grimace. Then his teeth clenched shut and with a roar of fury he attacked, his saber raised high. Two hurtling, maniac leaps and his blade swept downward, aimed at Duras's skull.

Duras spun away to the left to protect his useless arm, and drawing on all his remaining strength, he moved to the attack. Ignoring the white flashes of light exploding in his eyes, he focused on his target, ducking under Korsakov's blade in a lightning crouch, aiming directly at his belly, putting the entire weight of his body behind his sword arm as he swung.

The sword sliced through to Korsakov's spine, dropping the huge body like a rock. Eyes wide with shock, Korsakov would have died in agony. But, a man of honor, Duras dropped his saber, shifted his kinjal to his right hand, and administered a swift *coup de grâce* to Korsakov's heart.

And the spirit died in his enemy's eyes.

The women openly screamed for Korsakov's body, wanting to slice him into pieces and feed him to the dogs. But Duras, swaying on his feet, wearily said, "Keep them away. Get everyone dressed. We move out in ten minutes." And then he sank to his knees and, falling in a languid motion, crumpled to the ground.

"Someone sew up this shoulder," he rasped, gazing up at the crowd of troopers who'd rushed to his side, "while I rest for five minutes."

He was awake while his shirt was cut away and Vigée's most adept trooper rinsed his wounds with brandy, then took even stitches in Duras's brown flesh. He felt better after two hearty measures of brandy dulled the prick of the needle, and when the wound was bandaged he came to his feet unsteadily but without help.

Vigée personally eased a new shirt up Duras's arms and over his head and said with a smile as he buttoned the collar like a doting mama, "I would have killed him, sir, no offense, if you were in danger."

"I know, Vigée," Duras said, a faint smile lifting the corners of his mouth. "That's why I brought you along."

They left Korsakov and his Cossacks lying dead in their hellish amphitheater, allowing the abducted women first plunder of the booty for their vicious ravishment.

An unseemly pleasure warmed Duras's spirits as they began their return journey, a shameful joy he realized even as he relished it. In an earlier time, he could have cold-bloodedly killed his rival, but civilization required more subtle reasons now. If he had a conscience—not a surety after twenty years of making war—it was a balm perhaps to know that Korsakov deserved to die for a thousand reasons more than his.

He smiled at his rationalization, having considered himself immune to such niceties. Perhaps love had changed him. It had, of course—he knew that as well as he knew the number of weeks it would take to mop up the last Austrians and Russians from Switzerland. And on his swift journey back to Zurich, his pleasure tended to focus on the fact that there was now a finite limit to his separation from Teo.

Lecourbe held on at the Devil's Bridge for four days, but Suvorov kept flinging his grenadiers straight into the murderous cannonfire. The path was soon choked with the bodies of the dead and dying. The rocks below were also strewn with corpses, but the Russian soldiers continued to clamber over their comrades' bodies and advance.[21]

Finally running low on ammunition, the French cannoneers pulled back across the bridge. Again Suvorov threw his men forward and again hundreds perished in a vain attempt to force the French position. Suvorov then sent a picked force of grenadiers and Cossacks down the slopes into the Reuss Valley. This attack group managed to make its

way through the snow and threaten the French flank.
Lecourbe realized that he could no longer delay the Rus-
sians. Satisfied that he had inflicted severe punishment on
Suvorov, he withdrew north to await reinforcements from
Duras.

Two days later leading elements of Soult's division after
several days of forced marches joined Lecourbe's force near
the southern end of the Lake of the Four Cantons. Arriving
just in time, Soult's men helped Lecourbe's tired and bat-
tered units beat back Suvorov's advance guard and scotched
all further Russian efforts to march toward Zurich.

At this juncture Suvorov learned of Korsakov's defeat
and he realized Duras would soon turn on him. He decided
to lead his command in a desperate march to the northeast
in order to reach Germany before the French could trap him
in the snow-filled Alpine passes and cut him to ribbons.

It was too late though; he was caught in a trap.
Lecourbe's right flank had closed in on his rear in the Reuss
Valley, cutting off his supply column. Duras then brought
Mortier's division south from Zurich through Schwyz to
Altdorf and the bulk of Soult's division to Weesen, blocking
both ends of the Linthtal. Leaving Zurich on the evening of
the twenty-eighth, Duras hurried by Zug and the Lake of
Lucerne to meet Lecourbe near Altdorf late on the twenty-
ninth and pushed northeast, hot on Suvorov's trail.

On September 29, Suvorov posted a rear guard at the
mouth of the Klonthal Pass and, mounted on a small sturdy
Cossack pony, led the rest of his corps toward Glaris. The
French in turn closed in on both ends of the column.

Unable to escape to the northeast, Suvorov decided to
march due east into the Grisons. He recalled his rear guard,
abandoned his artillery and wounded, and led his tired
corps forward. For a week the Russians staggered eastward
over incredibly rugged terrain. Plodding knee-deep through
snowdrifts, exhausted men dropped out of line never to rise

again. Blizzards obliterated trails, horses and soldiers disappeared into crevices, and the thinning lines, stretching for miles, finally reached Germany.[22]

The Russian corps was almost totally destroyed.

With France's military and political fortunes at their lowest ebb, Duras had saved the nation.

It was his greatest triumph.

But soon after, fate intervened to change Duras's hopeful plans and the course of history. On October 9, after having eluded Nelson's frigates in the Mediterranean, a small ship landed at St. Raphael.

Bonaparte was back in France.

And exactly one month later, the *coup d'état* of 18 Brumaire dissolved the two legislative bodies of the Republic by armed force and concentrated supreme authority in the hands of three Consuls—Bonaparte, Roger-Ducos, and Sieyès. The second and third Consuls didn't survive long. Within the month, Bonaparte ruled alone.

And Duras was summoned to Paris to be given command of the Army of Italy.

He refused at first; he had personal plans, he needed time to recuperate after ten months of campaigning. But Bonaparte wouldn't allow him to refuse. All the territory won by the French in Italy had been lost, he said. The army was in a shocking condition, discipline no longer existed, he said. Duras was the only one to whom he could entrust the rehabilitation of the shattered army. "It's your duty," he said. "France needs you."

Conscientious, accountable, Duras knew there was no one else.

With an aching sadness he wrote to Teo, explaining why he couldn't come to her, why she couldn't join him yet. He was leaving for Italy in a few days; he'd been given extraordinary disciplinary powers to restore order to the army. Even his old enemy Berthier, now war minister, showed him friendship—an indication of the army's desperate straits, he

added. He'd write to her soon—although he knew his letters would be months delayed before they reached her. He
hadn't heard yet of their child, he wrote. Please let him
know how they were. He spoke of his great love, of missing
her a thousand times a day, but even as he penned the
words, he wondered if they'd ever meet again.

It was the first time he'd consciously considered their
separation as permanent. And he found himself unable to
breathe for a moment. He'd always thought soon—next
month or certainly the month after, when the armies were
quiet in Switzerland. Even when Bonaparte had called him
to Paris he'd arranged a dozen excuses for what he'd heard
was going to be his new command. He could refuse. He
knew that and he'd intended to. But when the full extent of
the danger was made known to him, he understood that
nothing stood between the Austrians in Italy and the south
of France except the army he could pull together by March
when the Austrian offensive would begin.

So tomorrow he would leave for his new command. His
carriage was packed, his aides en route south, Bonnay already at their temporary headquarters in Nice.

He wished with all his heart he could see her, he went
on; he hoped all was well with their child. But beyond those
hopeful dreams lay a devastated army that hadn't been paid
in six months, with units that had mutinied and others who
were begging for bread from house to house. There were no
supply depots, no repair shops, no hospitals, no arms,
equipment, or clothing. And to add to his difficulties a typhus epidemic was raging at Nice and fourteen thousand of
his men were ill. His predecessor, General Championnet,
had died of it.

He sent his love, this man who short months before
hadn't recognized the word. She was in his heart and soul, he
wrote; she *was* his heart and soul. Remember me, he said,
feeling comfortless and stricken. And at the end, he added,

in case you haven't heard, Korsakov is dead. He'd done that for her at least, when he'd done so little else.

Desolate and moody, he sat alone in his carriage on the journey south, drinking more than he should, short-tempered and sullen, without conversation for his aides. Even the sight of Nice didn't cheer him when the carriage rolled over the crest of the hill and the azure bay sparkled in the sunshine.

But Bonnay, aware of the reasons for his ill humor, treated him gently. And by the second day, inundated with work, he had little time to dwell on the past.

It took Duras a month to clear up the worst of the difficulties and on February 10 he moved his headquarters to Genoa.

There was no time in those spring months to think of himself, to look beyond the huge enemy army they faced. They were attacked on three fronts in overwhelming numbers the first of April and by April 24 Genoa was under siege—completely cut off from the world.

22

Duras's letter was delivered to Teo four months after it had been written, carried the last stage on foot through the thick forests that surrounded her home.

And when she first held it in her hand, she realized she wasn't prepared for the impact. To see it on this warm spring day was like going back to that sad, sad night in Basel with his men below waiting for him, with their time so brief.

She felt all the hurt and sadness again.

The wash of memories.

She stared at the letter, at each word on the outside sheet, her name and location, the slant of his letters, the graceful curves and bold slashes, knowing he'd formed each flowing line. She gently ran her fingers over the writing on the smudged, worn paper and the memory of him came back so strongly, it seemed as though his hand reached out to touch her fingers.

She showed the letter to their young son lying in his cradle beside her chair and he smiled at the happy sound of her voice as she told him of his father and he reached for the scrap of paper with his pudgy pink fingers. "It's from your papa," she repeated, remembering Duras standing at the door, turning back to her before he left that night, thanking her for his child. She was deeply grateful he was alive; rumors of Russia's defeat had never been substantiated by the government. He'd been victorious for France, she'd thought when the first bits of gossip were carried down the trails into her country. And she was pleased for him.

But the smile vanished from her face as she read the letter and her eyes welled with tears. She hadn't thought it could hurt so horribly, but she was wrong. The pain made her gasp when she thought she'd long ago talked herself into a sensible wisdom about Duras. She'd always told herself he might die and she'd never see him again. She'd prepared herself for that. She'd not prepared herself sufficiently for his desertion.

When she'd read the letter through, she set it on the table and picked up her cooing son and held him so tightly he squirmed and struggled and protested with a loud wail. At the baby's cry, Tamyr came running in from the kitchen where she'd been giving the messenger tea and bread.

"He made you sad," she said, irate that Duras had made her darling cry, the letter's sender common gossip at every post stop from Paris east. And walking across the polished floor strewn with fur carpets, she held her two babies in her arms.

"He's off fighting again," Teo whispered, tears streaming down her face.

"He'll come when he can," Tamyr soothed.

"I thought he really meant it." Teo's voice was filled with hurt.

He did, Tamyr thought, when he said it. But she'd never thought Andre Duras would actually give up his life and travel to the ends of the earth for Teo. "He'll come, little bird," she lied. "When the wars are over."

"They'll never be over." He'd left her seven months ago—seven months to forget.

At that moment the baby decided he'd been still too long, and arching his back, he waved his little arms, kicked his legs, and screamed at the top of his lungs.

"Let me take Pasha outside and show him the new calf. He likes the barn," Tamyr offered. "And you sit down and write to the general. Tumen will take your letter when he leaves."

Teo reread Duras's letter, desperately wanting to believe his words of love, but the sad reality of his duty and obligation to France was closer to the truth. His sentiments were probably no more than suave, meaningless phrases, testament that his reputation as a transient lover had been well earned. And she'd been unbearably naïve about him.

But she wrote to him because he was in her heart, was a part of her, and she couldn't bring herself to completely sever her life from his. She told him of her love as he had written of his, giving him news of his son, explaining how Mingen had stayed with her until after the birth. I named our child Andreas Pavel, she went on; Pavel was my grandfather's name. We call him Pasha. The Russian diminutive suits him; he already commands the household. He looks like you, she wrote, her son's startling resemblance to his father a source of great joy to her. She went on then to describe their country life and the small events that filled her days. It's very peaceful here, she said, unlike the tumult of your life. I wish you peace and happiness, she said at the end, a kind of sad acceptance pervading her mind.

There it is, she thought—the wistful hoping was over. He was halfway across the world from her, engaged in battle again; there was little possibility he'd ever see his son. I

think of you when I hold him, she'd offered, and now that
she was staring at the page, she wondered if she should have
omitted the sentiment, whether he'd be embarrassed with
her continuing affection, at the connection between them
when a new woman must be warming his bed by now. She
knew how unnatural celibacy was for him.

I offer you sincere thanks for my freedom, she added in
a postscript, her tone more formal. The trustees sent me
word of Korsakov's death. I am deeply grateful.

And in a post-postscript, she wrote quickly before she'd
change her mind and succumb to prudence: Our love to you
always.

She signed it simply Teo and Pasha and added the
baby's little thumbprint and a lock of his hair before she
sealed the letter.

And then she got on with her life because Andre Duras
would always be planning the next battle or the next campaign or the needed strategy to support and maintain the
French Republic. His life didn't allow for a remote home in
a forest so far from the sound of cannon—for a wife and a
son . . . for a family.

At the moment a home in the forest would have been
exceedingly welcome to Duras. Genoa had been without
food for almost a month and all rations were reduced to the
minimum. The soldier's daily ration was now: 5 1/4 ounces
of ersatz bread, 8 1/2 ounces of horseflesh, and 1 3/4 pints of
wine. Civilians received only half this ration, prisoners of
war still less. The only available meat was horseflesh and
even that had become so scarce that it had to be supple-
mented with dogs, cats, and rats.

Several attempts had been made to break through the
siege but the Austrian forces were too powerful and Duras's
troops too few and eventually too physically exhausted to
fight.

On May 28 Duras ordered Miollis to make a last sortie

to the northeast, but it met with no success. As soon as Duras heard of Miollis's reverse, he put himself at the head of two battalions and covered the retreat of his troops. This was the last offensive attempted.

But the thirtieth was a day of some emotional excitement as this was the day when Bonaparte's arrival was expected to raise the siege. A message had been smuggled the week previous with news of Bonaparte's crossing of the Alps and Duras was determined to hold out until then.

But the thirtieth came and went, and then the thirty-first. Duras's troops began deserting, the civilian population was getting out of control. Hundreds were dying daily of typhus and starvation.

On June 1, Duras sent Colonel Andrieux, his acting chief of staff, to Austrian headquarters to arrange terms of capitulation. He had two days' rations left in the food depots. But the negotiations took three days more, with Duras unyielding on several items. He refused to sign any document that contained the word *capitulation*. Some French vessels must remain in his hands for transport of his wounded to Antibes. And his troops were to march out of the garrison with their arms and baggage.

On June 4 the terms were finally signed and Duras and his staff, with fifteen hundred men and twenty field guns, embarked in the five French privateers lying in the harbor and sailed for Antibes.

That same evening Admiral Keith, the chief principal for Britain at the negotiations, wrote to his sister: "I have signed a capitulation with the most brutal fellow I ever met."

Duras's dogged resistance at Genoa had contributed materially to the success of Bonaparte's Reserve Army. With the bulk of the Austrian troops investing Genoa, Bonaparte entered the northern Italian plains unopposed by any Austrian army of note. And by the time Ott marched from

Genoa to the aid of the Austrian army under Mélas it was too late.

Bonaparte had just won the Battle of Marengo.

But the political situation in Paris was disturbing; Fouché, Sieyès, and Talleyrand were still conspiring and Bonaparte through his brother Lucien, who was minister of the interior, was made aware of the danger to his position.

A few brief days after Marengo, Bonaparte summoned Duras to Milan and handed over to him command of the Army of Italy together with the Reserve Army and left for Paris to defend his position as First Consul.

There was no other senior officer with the ability or experience of Duras so once again he was put in the position of reorganizing and reequipping an army that hadn't been paid for months. It was the most onerous and exasperating of his problems, and before long he was at odds with the War Ministry. He wrote repeatedly to the ministry explaining the difficulties of supporting an army without funds and received only complaints in return. After two months of discord and strained relations, Duras received notice from Carnot, the war minister, telling him a new commissioner was being sent down to purge his administrative services of all excess officers.

"It's time," Duras said to Bonnay one morning, tossing the Carnot letter aside, "to consider my life of retirement. Someone else can deal with these politicians in Paris. Sorry, Bonnay, but I'm going to desert you."

It was late July, the negotiations over the line of demarcation in the treaty with Vienna were as tiresome and acrimonious as usual, procurement of cash to pay the troops was an ongoing problem, and now some commissioner was arriving to tell him how to administer his army.

"I feel a need for a leave as well," Bonnay said with a faint smile. "Amalie tells me I'm about to become a father again. She's going to require my personal attention."

"You needn't go because of me, Henri. Your diplomacy

will hold you in good stead even with the latest cretin sent down from Paris."

"No, it's time, I think," Bonnay murmured. Both men had suffered during the siege. There was no glory in starving to death and Bonaparte's ruthlessness in sacrificing the army in Genoa when he could have come to their aid had left both men with a kind of permanent disenchantment. "Will you go to Nice?" Bonnay inquired.

"I'm not sure," Duras slowly replied, his life without purpose or joy. He'd drifted into his old libertine habits of late, disturbed with not hearing from Teo, brooding over the possibility she'd found someone else, guilty too for his desertion of her. And with no lack of women clamoring for his attention, it had been easy to revert to the casual immorality of his past. Although his cool detachment was so discernible, Bonnay wondered if he actually spoke to the women in his bed.

"You're welcome to join me at Rueil." Bonnay's château in the country west of Paris served as his summer home.

"Too tame, I think," Duras said with a smile. "But thank you. I may go to Istanbul. My mother had relatives there."

Taking a risk at offending, Bonnay said, "You could take a summer trip to Siberia."

Duras looked out the window for a moment and when his gaze swung back his eyes were shuttered. "I'm not sure I'd be welcome. It's been almost a year."

"The child must be—"

"Eight months old."

"You should go."

Duras smiled. "I recall you saying that to me the first night Teo arrived in Sargans."

"And I was right."

"You're too much of a romantic, Henri. By now she's forgotten those days in Switzerland."

"I could have travel permits for you in a few days. We're

no longer at war with Russia." He grinned. "At least for the moment. Hell, you could travel up the St. Gotthard Pass without getting your head blown off."

"A pleasant thought." Duras was silent for a moment, his fingers tapping lightly on the polished surface of his desk, his mind discomposed by a host of uncertainties. She could be married by now for all he knew. He swore at such unwelcome thoughts. Then he looked up and softly said, "Get me a map."

Bonnay had travel documents in three days and very early one morning, Duras left Milan in a carriage sturdy enough to withstand the long journey. Three post stops later a courier overtook them with an important dispatch from Bonnay. When Duras opened the envelope sealed with Bonnay's stamp, he found a letter from Teo enclosed and a scrawled note from Bonnay, saying, "I hope it's good news."

It was.

It was all he'd wished for. She loved him still, he perceived between the careful, cautionary phrases; he was hopeful and comforted. And he had a son she'd named for him. He found himself smiling at that. And when he touched the tiny fingerprint with his callused finger, tears filled his eyes. He placed the silky lock of hair in the pocket over his heart and sent the carriage back to Milan with the courier. Purchasing a fleet thoroughbred, his baggage limited to what would fit in his saddlebags, he was back on the road twenty minutes later, his mount settled into a steady canter.

Impatient, he rode twenty hours a day, resting just long enough to snatch a few hours of sleep each night, buying new horses as needed, eating on the run. He crossed into Russia a week later and reached Moscow six days after that. He stayed half a day in the city to procure maps, for the wilds of Siberia were well off the beaten path.

The road from Moscow to Nishney Novgorod through Kazan, Perm, Ekaterineberg, and Tobolsk was well-maintained with post stations every five or six miles. He passed through thick forests of fir and pine, birch and larch; the days were beautiful and sunny as though the weather were cooperating with his swift journey north. His passports were checked occasionally but Bonnay had seen to all the necessary documents from the ministers, governor-generals, and his imperial highness, and the only points of delay were the occasional brief hours of sleep.

At Tobolsk, he rented a hotel room for a few hours, bathed, shaved, had his clothing cleaned and pressed, had his hair cut, checked and rechecked his maps. He forced himself to eat because the image in the mirror after he'd shaved off his rough beard showed his cheekbones with too stark clarity and he didn't want to frighten Teo.

It would take two days more to reach Samarov, the last village on the edge of the wilderness. He'd find himself a guide at that point. Teo's address was a spare notation of two lines with neither locality on the maps.

He reached Samarov late at night, having traveled almost three thousand miles in twenty-four days. And he slept through the night for the first time since he'd left Milan.

He dressed with special care the next morning and then chastised himself for acting like a young buck on his first assignation. But he recombed his hair for the third time, his unruly curls refusing to conform, and decided to change his waistcoat after all, substituting a plain cream linen for the white silk he'd first put on. His riding coat was black, his chamois breeches and top boots comfortable country wear. Dressed in mufti since leaving Milan, he was no longer a general but a simple man returning to his family.

He found he suddenly needed a drink, not sure of his welcome, not certain Teo hadn't found someone else to comfort her in the months of their separation. Her letter was dated four months ago.

Two drinks later, the man who fearlessly led his troops

into the mouths of firing cannon had stabilized his nerves
sufficiently to begin the last leg of his journey.

The track through the forest passed through heavy
stands of birch and poplar, mountain ash and pine. The
summer day was idyllic, the temperature pleasantly warm,
the birds singing in the trees. His guide, riding a sturdy
long-haired pony, turned occasionally and smiled at him as
if to encourage him. They had no common language since
Duras spoke neither the native dialect nor Russian. But the
hotel clerk had given the guide instructions, and when Teo's
name had been mentioned, the guide had nodded his head
vigorously and smiled.

They rode five hours into the forest across small streams,
through steep ravines, up granite outcroppings or around
them if the incline was too steep for their mounts. Until at
last his guide stopped at the border of a small pasture and
waited for Duras to ride up. Pointing across the meadow,
he spoke three brief words, indicating a log home and out-
buildings bordering a silvery lake.

Although set deep in the wilderness, the house was
palatial, two stories high with several stone chimneys and
windows that opened in panels so one could walk outside. A
number of summer porches adjoined the house, their roofs
and railings flamboyantly detailed in carvings and sinuous
fretwork, the whole framed by elaborate, colorful flower
gardens and crushed-rock paths. It was a noble's dacha.

He'd pictured something quite different as a wilderness
retreat and for a moment he was taken aback until he remembered Teo's Russian grandfather was a prince despite his
exile and her native grandfather had sent tribute in gold each
year to Korsakov. His republican sensibilities were mildly
shocked, now that he'd come face to face with her dynastic
background.

But his guide was already riding toward the house, so
he followed, anticipation overwhelming all else in his mind.
Tamyr came to the door when they dismounted, shooing a

young boy before her to take the men's horses. And speaking quickly to the native man, she bowed slightly to Duras, her expression neutral, and ushered the men into the house. Directing the guide down a hallway, she waved Duras into a parlor. "Tea?" she said, the universal word understandable in any language.

Duras's brows came together. "No." He hadn't ridden three thousand miles with only marginal sleep to be offered tea. "I want to see Teo," he said. "Is she here?"

Tamyr answered him in a flurry of indecipherable words, motioning for him to sit down.

Shaking his head, he brushed past her, strode out into the entrance hall, and surveying the wide staircase rising in three levels to the second floor, stood in the center of the hall and shouted Teo's name.

A scurry of running feet responded to his raised voice and within moments the front hall was awash with curious servants gazing at him.

Swearing, he swept past them and, pulling the door open, strode outside, stood on the filigreed porch and yelled "Teo!" so loudly the birds stopped their singing.

A response so faint he questioned his hearing echoed through the trees.

He shouted again.

And the answer this time was the voice he'd ridden a month to hear. Running in the direction of the lake, he called her name once more, his heart beating like thunder in his breast.

He was halfway around the small lake when she appeared from a grove of birch at a run, waving, calling his name as she caught sight of him.

Seconds later she was in his arms and he was swinging her around and kissing her and laughing in sheer joy.

"You came," she whispered, thinking Tamyr's gods were superb creatures to have brought him here to her, when she'd given up completely.

"Did you doubt it?" he said, the way a man would, already forgetting his gloomy indecision in Milan, setting her down, smiling at her.

"Oh, yes—very much," she replied, thinking of his letter and how she'd locked away her love and memories. "But I'm pleased to be wrong," she gently noted, gazing up at him with a fine discernment. "Tell me how you decided to come, how you found me, how long you've been on the road, how you still love me madly," she finished with a warm smile.

"I love you madly, you know that. How could you not know that?"

"Ten months," she softly said, "temper one's optimism." She didn't mention the women.

"I couldn't come at first—I wrote." He too didn't mention the women.

"Are the wars over, then?" Her voice was bland. And while she shouldn't ask so soon, in these first warm, breathless moments when he'd told her he loved her, she had to know.

"They are for me. I'll tell you everything later—all the politics and cynical diplomacy. I don't want to think about it now. Tell me about our son."

It wasn't a complete answer, but it was sufficient for a man who'd ridden across half of Europe and Russia to see her. She was consoled. "Come see him," she said, taking his hand. "We were having tea down by the lake." Talking with pride of their son, trying to come to terms with the reality of Duras's presence, she led him through the rustling grove of birch to a green trimmed lawn shaded by towering willows. A sumptuous Isfahan carpet was spread on the grass, a silver samovar set on a nearby table, a tea service arranged on fine linen spread over the carpet. And reclining on the silken rug in a casual sprawl, a handsome man played with a plump baby. The man's cropped chestnut hair gleamed in the sunlight, his lean, muscular body stretched indolently across the crimson pile, and he was barefoot like Teo, Duras jealously noted. The baby was playing with the silver buttons on his shirt as the man smiled and talked to him.

With force of habit, Duras reached for his nonexistent saber. "Who's that?" he growled.

"Pasha's doctor."

"He lives here?" His voice was whisper soft.

"Of course. What good would it do to have a doctor five hours away if Pasha becomes ill."

"You could have an old doctor."

Her eyes widened momentarily; the intrusion of an authoritarian male in her remote hermitage could alter the pattern of her life. "Are you jealous?"

"Damned right I am."

"You needn't be," she mildly said. "We're only friends. Come, let me introduce you to our son and Konstantin."

She was incredibly naïve, he thought, restraining his temper with difficulty. There wasn't a man alive who would aspire to be only friends with Teo.

His voice was gruff when he acknowledged the introduction.

The sound of Duras's voice startled Pasha, who was at an age when any stranger entering his world was viewed with suspicion, and while observing Duras, he clung to Konstantin, his dark eyes wary.

When Duras made a move to touch him, he screamed, clutching the doctor so tightly, the man winced. "Should I take Pasha to the house?" the young man inquired.

"No," Duras curtly said, his tone that of a general in command.

"Why don't I hold him," Teo suggested, dropping down on the carpet. Lifting her hands to her son, she took him from the doctor. "That's your papa," she softly murmured to her son, kissing his soft cheek, but after a quick peek at Duras, the baby buried his face in his mother's shoulder.

"I'd like to be alone with my family," Duras said, beyond manners and banal conversation after a twenty-five-day marathon journey, furious to find a man with Teo.

"Don't be rude, Andre," Teo said, her glance instantly censorious. How dare he.

"Forgive me, Doctor," Duras said in a tone so rife with sarcasm, the baby looked up in curiosity.

"Thank you for your company, Konstantin," Teo politely said, dismissing him, not wishing an audience with Duras in his autocratic mood. "Tell Tamyr the cook should set dinner back an hour."

"Or two," Duras murmured; he had plans to make love to Teo in the very near future.

Teo ignored him, and her warm smile for the doctor raised Duras's level of displeasure.

"Will you be all right?" Konstantin quietly inquired as he rose, his glance briefly swinging toward Duras glowering at the border of the carpet.

"Yes, you needn't worry. Andre forgets he doesn't have an army here. If you'd be so kind," she went on, overlooking Duras's grim expression and Konstantin's faint worry lines, "would you tell Tamyr I was thinking of roast duck for dinner? Do you like roast duck?" she coolly asked, turning to Duras.

"Food isn't a high priority for me right now," he brusquely replied.

By now Pasha was fascinated by the unusual undertones passing back and forth, the crisp nuances unfamiliar in his bountiful world. He regarded Duras with an open scrutiny although he was careful to maintain a firm hold on his mother's shoulder.

As Konstantin withdrew, Teo heatedly said, "You're not allowed such rudeness to my staff. It's inexcusable. I hope you can control yourself at dinner."

"Don't count on it," he growled. "I've a real problem with that young doctor living with you."

Her eyes sparked at the insinuation. "He doesn't *live* with me."

"Damn right he does and I'll bet you Napoleon's war chest he'd like to become much better acquainted."

"Every man isn't like you, Andre." She spoke quietly in deference to Pasha, but her voice was acid. "Konstantin is a true friend."

Duras swore softly at the ridiculous female platitude. "Good, then he won't mind if I don't let him fuck you."

"Don't think you're going to walk back into my life and start giving orders," she said, bristling at his words. "I just found release from a marriage like that."

"Don't compare me to Korsakov," Duras snapped. "The man was an animal. By the way, you can thank me for killing him."

She shrank back before the dark violence in his gaze.

"Jesus, Teo," he whispered, instantly expiatory, dropping to his knees on the carpet, his dark gaze rueful. "I've been riding day and night for almost a month to be with you. And I find you with this—this—"

"Doctor."

"No, with this man who watches you with lust in his eyes. Don't tell me you can't see it."

"I haven't . . . I don't. How can you say that? You've always been the only man I've ever wanted."

"Then send him away."

"That's not fair."

"I'm not interested in fairness. I'm interested in his departure. We'll find an old doctor, a very old doctor," he muttered.

"Konstantin stays," she quietly said.

His head came up, his jaw clamped shut, and he stared at her with blazing eyes.

"You're not the commander in chief on my estate. I own a tract of Siberia that takes two months to cross on horseback. I'm my own authority here."

He exhaled in a long, slow release of air. "Why are we fighting?"

"Because you want Konstantin to leave and I won't have it. If you expect me to exist under such rigid constraints, tell me you've been faithful to me all these months and we'll have some basis for debate," she declared, her green eyes challenging.

He didn't answer. He shifted from his knees to a seated position, distancing himself in the process, putting an expanse of crimson lozenges and riotous rose designs between them. "You wouldn't care to hear."

"Well, then," she said, surprised at the degree of her resentment when she'd known all along, "there's no further need to discuss this."

"I'm sorry, if that helps. *Very* sorry," he quietly apologized, wanting to tell her how he'd always wished every woman was her, knowing how indefensible such a statement would be. "There's no excuse."

"Thank you," she coolly replied. "I'd hate excuses."

"Bonnay convinced me to make the journey here."

"I'm not sure I care to hear this."

"I didn't mean it that way," he said, instantly contrite. "I was sure you had married someone else by now."

"I *have* had several offers," she said with a rudiment of a smile, now that Duras's contrition was warming her heart. "Konstantin, for one, asked me to marry him." A small degree of revenge motivated her as well.

"I knew it, dammit," Duras hotly exploded, contrition instantly eclipsed by quick-tempered jealousy. "I saw that."

Teo shook her head. "He was just being nice one day after Pasha was born and I'd been crying for you," she explained. "He offered to take care of us."

"Thoughtful of him," Duras dryly said.

"Mingen told him he had to get in line," she went on, playful and teasing. "Mingen had offered to take your place as father too, as did my neighbor Prince Dyakov and—"

"Good God," he interposed. "Am I safe from no one?"

"You're safe from everyone, darling," she said, no longer teasing. "I only want you."

He absorbed the simplicity of her declaration for a long moment, studying her as though the veracity of her words would be exposed on her face. "Really," he finally said, smiling faintly, appeased.

"Truly. From the first night you walked into the dining room of the burgomaster's house in Sargans," she softly affirmed, "I was lost."

"You did have a notable effect on me as well."

She smiled. "I remember."

"So are you ready to get married?" he asked. "Now that my rivals have been refused."

"Are you proposing," she inquired oversweetly, "with such disarming grace? Don't you know a woman expects a modicum of romance in these matters?"

"I thought riding three thousand miles in twenty-five days might be disarming enough, even romantic."

She laughed and was joined a second later by Pasha's gurgle of joy as he recognized his mother's well-being. "I'm placated," Teo murmured. "Even embarrassed by my thoughtlessness. One question more though—will this be a bigamous relationship?"

"No."

Apparently he wasn't going to elaborate. "Did Claudine take all your money?" Teo went on, vastly curious after meeting his wife. "She was threatening to beggar you as she was pulled screaming from your house."

"Would it matter?" That lack of information again.

"Of course not," Teo replied, amused by his resistance to discussing Claudine. "Remind me to show you my gold mine."

"And sexy too," Duras drawled. "This must be nirvana."

"Hush." She glanced down at her son. "Pasha's listening."

Duras leaned forward. "Will he let me touch him?" he murmured. "I wore his thumbprint off the letter you sent."

"When he gets to know you, he will. Did you notice how brown he is? Like you and just as beautiful."

"I noticed," he said, his smile shameless.

"Insolent man," she said with a grin. "He will be infinitely more modest although he's very clever already. He's almost walking and he loves to splash in the lake and he says *Mama*."

Hearing the familiar word, Pasha repeated it, and when Duras laughed and clapped his approval, he performed for his audience by repeating the word until both his parents were laughing with delight. Sensing Duras was a friend, Pasha pushed away from his mother and dropped to his knees, crawling across the carpet to pull himself up on Duras's knee.

His father put out a hand to steady him, and when the baby clutched his fingers and smiled at him, Duras's throat closed with a poignant ache. How lucky he was, he thought, to have a healthy young son, to be alive on this warm summer day, to have Teo's love. "I suppose the doctor can stay," he said.

"I suppose he can," Teo retorted, "unless you want to sleep alone tonight."

"I wasn't planning on waiting until tonight. Actually this carpet is rather soft."

"*Andre.* Have you no discretion?"

He didn't of course. "Does the baby ever nap out here?" he calmly asked.

Teo smiled, remembering his boundless will. "If you walk him, he'll fall asleep."

"Done," he said, lifting his son into his arms and rising in a swooping ascent that caused a fit of giggles to bubble from Pasha's mouth.

"He's drooling on you."

"I'm used to it; women do it all the time."

She lunged at him and he sidestepped. "Now, now, keep your hands to yourself for a little longer while Pasha and I discuss an afternoon nap." And then he surprised her by singing an array of lullabies with a husky sweetness that tugged at her heart.

This was the same man who led his men into battle, she thought, and defied death a thousand times; the man who defeated the armies of the Coalition when no betting man would have given him a chance. And now he held his son with such tenderness. Pasha's lashes were drifting shut in erratic small bursts of movement, his breathing changing into the soft rhythms of sleep. Duras smiled at her over Pasha's head and blew her a kiss.

When he carefully placed Pasha on the carpet some time later, Teo covered the baby with her shawl.

"I was thinking you might like to gather some rosebuds with me," Duras murmured, indicating the flowering bushes on the verge of the lawn.

"Someone might come."

He grinned. "I was planning on it."

"Libertine. I meant Tamyr or a servant."

"That's why I'm offering you the privacy of my rosebushes."

"I don't suppose you'd like to wait until tonight."

"Would you?"

She smiled. "I think I might come if you simply touch me."

"True," he murmured, recalling her ready passion. "But I thought you might like a trifle more prolonged sensation."

"How prolonged?" She could feel the pulsing between her legs accelerate.

"You decide," he whispered, holding out his hand.

And when she placed her fingers in his, she began to tremble.

"It's been a long time," he softly said, pulling her to her feet. He lifted her into his arms in a swift, heady sweep of powerful, flexing muscle and, kissing her, carried her behind the rose hedge.

Sliding her body down his in a slow, lingering greeting, he set her on her feet. She ran her hand down his breeches at the last, her palm trailing over the soft chamois, feeling the smoothness, the hard swell of his erection. Tantalized, her body opened, recognizing him, and she reached for the buttons on his breeches.

His fingers closed around her wrists, pulling her hands away. "Not so fast, *chou-chou,*" he murmured. "I've been waiting too long for this."

"But Pasha may wake up," she whispered, impatient, needy.

He shook his head.

"You don't know." Her voice held a small heated petulance as it always did when she was dying for him.

Glancing over the flowering hedge, he observed his son in blissful repose. "He just went to sleep." Gently swinging her hands, he smiled. "Plenty of time."

"Andre!"

"Allow me a moment," he said with a grin. "I just rode three thousand miles for this."

"I'll attack you," she turbulently asserted.

"That would be interesting. And then what would you do?" he sportively inquired.

He was right of course; how could she force him? "What if I plead?" she asked in a less vehement tone.

He laughed and, lifting her hands to his mouth, kissed her knuckles. "I thought you wanted prolonged sensation."

"I changed my mind."

"Do we have time to remove our clothing?" he playfully teased.

"Do you know how long it's been?" She'd all but stopped breathing. "Eleven months . . ."

"I'll hurry," he said, understanding she was beyond whimsical play. Releasing her hands, he quickly pulled off his jacket and neckcloth, unbuttoned his shirt just enough to tug it over his head. Frantically struggling to undo the tiny covered buttons at her neckline with trembling fingers, Teo was only partially successful when Duras, after spreading his shirt on the grass, said, "Let me." Nimbly working the buttons free, he eased the gown off her shoulders.

She helped, wrenching the sleeves down her arms, pushing the froth of printed muslin past her hips. Fumbling with the ribbon at the neckline of her chemise, her senses in tumult, she felt like a skittish, untried maid on her wedding night. The yellow ribbon only knotted more tightly in her hands and she swore in exasperation.

"I'll do that," Duras said with a small smile.

"You're too cool," she hotly impugned, gazing up at him as he deftly unraveled the knot in the ribbon.

"And you never are. It's one of your many charms," he whispered, touching the swell of her breast above the lace-edged neckline of her chemise. "These are beautiful," he murmured, sliding the fine batiste away, caressing her breasts, his hands warm, gentle. "Very showy."

"They don't seem to fit in my clothes anymore," she breathed, languid waves of heat drifting downward from his stroking hands. "Since the baby . . ."

He lifted the heavy flesh, let it fall, felt its weight and bounce. "You're not nursing anymore . . ." His voice was silky, low, his fingers moving to her nipples, gliding over them, feeling them grow harder under his touch.

"I stopped"—she groaned softly, the spiraling heat rippling down her vagina—"three weeks ago."

"So I missed having you feed me. How big they must have been full of milk." Their size was still sumptuous, great. "Next time," he whispered and she felt a drop of liquid desire slide down her thigh.

He gazed at her, lush, half undressed, her flesh glowing in the sunlight, her green eyes hot with desire, and he wondered how he'd lived without her so long.

A light breeze floated through the willows, the leaves fluttering in the sunlight, the heavy scent of blooming rose perfuming the air, and Teo, half nude like some glorious, alluring nymph of summer, gazed up at him with unbridled longing. "I feel as though I should recite some Ovid," he whispered, bending to kiss her.

"Or compose a sonata," she murmured against his mouth, a heady kind of dizzying bliss in the air.

"I *have* to thank Bonnay," he said, heartfelt and grateful.

"We'll send him . . . something lavish." She understood now what it had taken for him to venture so far on a hope.

"The world tied up in a bow wouldn't be enough for"— he caught his breath as he slipped her chemise down over her hips, watched it fall to the ground—"for this."

"Welcome to Siberia," Teo whispered.

"I like the view," he murmured.

"Now you must undress," she softly ordered.

He was already pulling off his boots before she finished speaking.

Lying on the makeshift bed, his scent lingering on his shirt, she watched him, watched his attenuated, finely honed muscles moving under his brown skin, rippling across his shoulders, down his arms as his fingers worked the gold buttons through the pliant leather of his breeches. "There," he murmured with a soft finality, slipping the last button free, looking up briefly to meet her gaze, a smoldering heat in his dark eyes. The pale chamois was stripped down his hips and thighs with haste.

His erection was gigantic.

She felt a purple haze begin to color the world. His naked body was so gorgeous it bordered on sinful. Lithe, powerful, capable, she knew, of the most sybaritic pleasures. Following the line of dark hair running down his torso and belly to his genitals, her gaze came to rest, lingered on his erection curving upward, its head large, beautifully formed, graceful like the rest of him.

Rapacious greed flared through her.

"I'd lock the door if I could," he said, moving toward her across the small expanse of green grass. "Although a little terror never hurts."

She was trembling when he lay between her legs.

"You're safe," he murmured, misunderstanding her tremors, his lips brushing her earlobe. "No one can see."

She was liquid, melting, the sensations so familiar with him, so natural—the ache between her legs intense, as if she were coming apart at the seams.

He kissed her softly, lowering himself by degrees, his biceps swelling, guiding himself into her. Easing past the pulsing tissue of her labia, he pressed into her hot wetness. Slowly, slowly, so she could feel the pressure, the folds of her inner flesh absorbing the ridge of his penis, then the entire head, the long, hard length until she gasped, her body shuddering around him, welcoming him home.

Holding him close, her hands glided down the subtle ridges of his backbone to the indentation just above the swell of his buttocks—the hair there soft, fine. And she lifted her pelvis to him and drew him in, heard the hollow echo strumming, vibrating in her ears, felt the first fluttering spasm. Her climax was beginning before he'd completely entered her.

She opened her mouth to scream.

"The baby," he whispered, his hand covering her mouth.

She gripped him fiercely, holding him inside, not letting him go, and his climax began to peak, as if he were young again, out of control. It had been too long for him too and he drove deeper, driving in so she whimpered into his hand and wrapped her legs so tightly around his hips he could barely move. But indulgent when he could have broken away, he stayed where she wanted him and their senses reeled, their bodies gently rocked, their minds grew feverish with lust.

"Please, please, please," she cried, biting his hand, and he poured into her with an explosive rush because she wanted him to, because she spoke to him not only in those fervent pleas.

And he heard her.

It was a shuddering, breath-held, gasping orgasm, hushed, constrained, that lasted for a fine-drawn, emblazoned eternity, that shocked their nerves and cut to the soul that made up for their long, grievous months of deprivation.

The willows above her were dappled in sunlight when Teo opened her eyes, brilliant chartreuse and golden movement. "You're as fine as I remembered," Teo softly breathed.

He smiled but didn't open his eyes, didn't move.

"Are you alive?" Her voice was teasing.

"I'm not sure." His reply barely audible.

"Will you stay?" It was the most persistent of her thoughts with Duras.

His erection came to life inside her, moved, swelled, sent a thrilling message through her sensory pathways to her brain.

"Yes," he said, opening his eyes at last, the long dark lashes lifting, unveiling the beauty of his gaze. "I'm staying."

His arousal grew larger as he spoke, triggering small waves of intoxicating rapture in the heated recesses of Teo's body.

"We need a priest."

"Later."

"Soon." He drove in, rigid again, unsated. "Very soon."

"Yes," she agreed on a blissful sigh.

He made love to her slowly then, his initial, impetuous lust partially assuaged. And the next time she made love to him as he lay sprawled on the cool green grass, gleaming with sweat, still panting. She stroked the dampness of his chest, licked the salt from his neck, moved slowly down his body, kissing him softly with her lips and tongue, his fingers in her hair.

And when she touched his penis, half curled in repose, his breath caught and it came to life. She smiled; she could do that to him.

An orgasmic scent clung to their bodies; she was wet from him, from herself, and when she straddled his hips and moved downward, he slid inside her, glided on a shimmering pearly river, sank in right up to the hilt and sighed, "Oh, God."

Their bodies slithered and slipped on each other, perspiration making it difficult for Duras to retain a firm grip on Teo's hips, a kind of frenzy invading their minds, the world reduced to an undulating rhythm, to unabashed sensation.

It resembled a small piece of heaven that summer afternoon under the willows, a private, sequestered homecoming—feverish and heated, sweetly luxurious, indulgent.

A paradise of deeply requited love.

Much later when the sound of breaking china indicated their son was up, Duras quickly kissed Teo and whispered with a grin, "Put on your clothes, you hussy." Swiftly slipping on his breeches with an expertise acquired in countless boudoirs over the years, he leaped over the rose hedge and scooped up his son before he poured the sugar bowl over his head.

"Come see your mommy," he said to Pasha, strolling over to peer over the flowering hedge. "She's just waking up from a nap too. Did you find your nap refreshing, darling?"

"I adore naps," Teo purred, still half undressed, her gown in disarray, opened at the neckline, swirled high about her thighs.

"I remember that about you," he said, his voice wickedly seductive, thinking he should have her painted like that. A picture for private viewing.

"What would you say," she said in a husky murmur, rolling over on her side so her breasts fell out of the low décolletage like ripe fruit, "if I told you I have this curious sensation?" Her green eyes were still languid, half-lidded. "This unmistakable feeling . . . this irrepressible perception"—she stretched deliciously, luxuriously—"that you just made me pregnant."

His brows flickered upward for a moment, and his smile spread lush and warm. "I'd say I believe you this time, *ma chère*."

EPILOGUE

In the spring their daughter was born in Nice, delivered by their new family physician, Anton Mingen, and Odile Aurore spent her first six months sailing the Mediterranean with her family. But France needed Duras and too soon he had to leave to fight the Coalition again. In the next decade he served his country on several occasions, but as the empire came into being, he no longer felt the same allegiance. All the republican principles he'd fought for were destroyed under Napoleon's dictatorship.

He retired then with his growing family, his five children the delight of his life. The seasons dictated their choice of homes: summers at Teo's dacha; winters at Duras's villa in Nice; spring in Paris; fall at their country house on the Seine. On occasion they'd sail for months at a time.

They ignored as much as possible the political struggles, the cabals and conspiracies, Napoleon's deification, his downfall, the Restoration. The pattern of their lives was designed outside the artful world of the Talleyrands.

Their love endured and deepened, their joy in each other a daily gift of delight and happiness. They often recalled the chance circumstances of their first meeting and considered themselves the very luckiest of people to have found each other.

Until one day an unforeseen occurrence jeopardized their generous good fortune. Their oldest daughter, Odile, having met a man of dubious background at a literary salon in Paris, told her parents she intended to marry him.

"She's much too young and vulnerable and he's forty-eight," Teo anxiously noted, having received their daughter's passionate declaration in a note delivered to their country house that afternoon.

Duras turned back from the winter view of the Seine outside the window, his expression grim. "Worse yet, he cheats at cards."

"I don't know if I should mention Langelier has a mistress tucked away in the Marin," Pasha casually declared, shifting his long legs draped over the arm of the couch into a more comfortable sprawl. His lack of sleep last night was beginning to catch up with him. "Dilly should look beyond his suave charm and his dramatic propensity to quote Goethe."

"You know how important poetry is to her," Teo retorted, worried for her daughter's future. "The man's turned her head."

"Let's hope that's all the blackguard's done," Duras growled, his tall form silhouetted against the gray sky. "Perhaps it's time to make a call on him."

"I'll join you," Pasha cheerfully said, undraping his legs and pulling himself up into a seated position. Running his fingers through his wild black hair, he lazily stretched. "I hear he's good with a rapier," he murmured with a gleam in his eyes. "Why don't I stand you second, Papa, or you could second me," he pleasantly added. "That should put an end to his pursuit of Dilly."

"For heaven's sake," Teo exclaimed. "Nothing so drastic is required. You men could just talk to him, couldn't you? I'm sure Odile is the merest flirtation for him."

Pasha knew better; he knew Philippe Langelier. They gambled at the same clubs and met occasionally at the same demirep entertainments, such as the one last night. And the man needed money. "I'm sure a talk will suffice," he said, not wishing to alarm his mother. "If you want, Papa, I think I know where to find him now."

"Don't wait up," Duras said to Teo, walking over to kiss her good-bye.

"I won't," she said, rising from her chair. "But I'll sleep more peacefully in Paris," she significantly added.

Duras knew better than to argue when he heard that tone of voice, but he was firm on one point. "You can't see Langelier."

"Very well," Teo grumbled. "I suppose men have all that manly talk that might soil my ears."

Duras glanced at his son, who smiled. "We're going to scare him to death, Mama. It won't be a pretty sight."

"As long as you're not violent. Although I daresay," Teo went on, her mouth curved into a smile, "a small scare might just do the trick."

It turned out slightly different.

When father and son walked through the opened door of Langelier's apartment, they discovered he'd been murdered by someone more disgruntled than they. Langelier's beautiful mistress was standing naked on his bed while his still warm body lay in a spreading pool of blood.

"A man with an axe did that—just five minutes ago," she calmly said, brushing aside a honey-colored curl from her forehead. "And I can't move with all that blood," she added, apparently less concerned with her nudity or her lover's demise than wetting her feet. "Would you lift me down?"

Pasha was more than willing; she was utterly gorgeous.

"Thank you," she softly said, her lush violet eyes lifted to his as he set her down in the adjacent room. "I don't know what I'm going to do," she murmured with a small sigh.

No thought was required, no hesitation or reflection. Pasha pleasantly said, "Perhaps I could help. . . ."

NOTES

1. See page 47. Ranges of field guns and howitzers varied according to elevation, loads, wind conditions, and projectiles fired, but the practical outer limit for the eight- and twelve-pounders was 800–900 yards. It was 800 yards for six-pounders and 700 yards for four-pounders. As one would imagine, effectiveness diminished with distance or when the target was protected, although the twelve-pound round shot could penetrate six-foot-thick earth ramparts.

For the individual soldier, long-range bombardment by round shot, against which he had no chance to reply, was terrifying. Coignet describes such a situation at Essling in 1809 when a regiment of the Imperial Guard of France, supported only by some small battalion pieces, came under the fire of a large Austrian artillery concentration. "To the left of Essling," he recounts, "the enemy planted fifty pieces of cannon. The fifty pieces thundered upon us without our being able to advance a step, or fire a gun . . . the balls fell among our ranks and cut down our men three at a time. . . ."

2. See page 51. Established in 1566, the Hofkriegsrat, a mixed military-civilian body, was primarily an agency of routine administration and not a command and control organization, although it did serve as a planning staff and handled replacement and logistics. It elaborated schemes and, with imperial approval, passed them on to field and regional commanders. Nominally it was responsible for officer entry and promotions at the junior levels, though the regimental proprietors had a good deal to say on this point, and the emperor reserved the right to appoint all field, staff, and general officers. It directed the ordnance, engineering, and supply departments, issued all routine orders, and enforced discipline. From 1762–74 various reforms organized the council into three functional departments, publica—military and political affairs; oeconomica—finances and supply; and judicalia—military justice. The first two, geographically subdivided into sections, were headed by military senior generals, while the justice department had a civilian head. To simplify administrative procedures, corresponding divisions were introduced in each of the twelve regional commands, the generalcies or Generalkommanden. This organization, introduced in 1766, remained in force until 1801.

Subject to the Hofkriegsrat, but outside its direct chain of command, were a number of agencies including the Director General of Artillery, the Director General of Engineers, the Feldund Hauszeugamt, dealing with ordnance and arsenals, the Reichswerbungsamt, for recruiting in the Holy Roman Empire, the General Vicar, Chaplain General, the Oberste Feldarzt, the General-Kriegs-Commissariat, the Commissary General, as well as civilian agencies such as the Hauptverpflegungsamt, responsible for provisions, the Oberst-Schiffamt, which looked after river transport, as well as additional agencies concerned with matters of pay, the care of invalids, and contracts.

The result of all this was much confusion and an endless stream of directives, minutes, and returns clogging up the military administration at all levels. For example, in 1772, the Hofkriegsrat sternly directed every company on the military border in Croatia to maintain seventy-two separate files, render two weekly, ten monthly and two quarterly reports, as well as a consolidated return every six months, all in proper form and forwarded with endorsement through proper channels to Vienna. And then there was the story about the enormous file generated by the Lower Austrian Generalkommando's request to keep a cat because mice were nibbling at the papers in the headquarters' attic. Nothing could be done without a proper request and authorization. Needless to say, it was difficult for the Austrian command, mired in organizational structure, to fight a war against the new French army that lived off the land and operated swiftly and decisively as an offensive strike force.

3. See page 56. Sieyès had been with the Directory since May, having returned from his Berlin embassy. The feeling in the air was Jacobin. Since the Fructidor coup of 1797, royalism had been under close surveillance; in spring and summer 1799 the military situation reawoke memories of the threatened homeland. If police reports are to be believed, however, Jacobinism was peculiar to the political and military classes in a somewhat lethargic Paris. In June the councils voted a *levée en masse,* mobilizing five classes of conscripts and in August a compulsory loan was collected from the rich; in July, there was a fearsome law passed on hostages, intended to terrorize internal enemies once more.

The country was in a state of chronic disobedience.

And Sieyès was in a position of power once again, the Revolution back in the grasp of its inventor. The former vicar general of Chartres had made himself master of the Executive, with the complicity of the councils' political left, led by the Corsican deputy Lucien Bonaparte. The deputies had nullified Treilhard's election to the Directory, then forced La Revellière and Merlin de Couai to resign. The chosen replacements were obscure and republican, two qualities necessary for supporters of a constitutional revision: Louis-Jérôme Gohier, former minister of justice under the Convention; Roger-Ducos, ex-Conventionnel regicide; and a general without any glory—but Jacobin—Jean François Moulin.

In the Directory, Sieyès had only one rival, Barras, who had been there from the outset and for that very reason was worn out, a symbol of the discredit into which the regime had fallen. Sieyès's following included post-Thermidor centrist republicans, the ideologists of the Institut, which was the result of the reorganization of schools in 1795, Daunou, Boulay de la Meurthe, Marie-Joseph Chénier, Pierre-Louis Roederer, not to mention Talleyrand, who had just left Foreign Affairs and was sniffing the wind. Sieyès found himself the leader of the postrevolutionary Parisian political milieu, the focus of extraordinary esteem, credited with having a constitutional plan that would at last provide the Republic with institutions. A civil savior, since the military one—Napoleon—was in Cairo.

In the France of that era, a *coup d'état* backed by the army had become sufficiently customary for the plan to come almost naturally into Sieyès's mind. He still had to find "the sword," as he called it. He had spoken about it to Joubert, a young Republican general appointed to the Army of Italy, which was a promise of glory; but Joubert had been beaten and killed at Novi on August 15. Sieyès was thinking of Moreau, when Bonaparte disembarked at Fréjus.

4. See page 57. At the age of four, while in the care of a peasant woman, Talleyrand injured his foot in a fall from a chest of drawers. And because of that accident, which left him a cripple, the young Talleyrand was disinherited, forced to renounce his right of primogeniture in favor of his younger brother. Since he could neither fence nor dance, he could never hope to succeed either at court or in the army, the only two callings proper for the heir of the ancient line of Périgord. The only course possible for Talleyrand was a career in the church, where he might rise in wealth and eminence. Unfortunately he had the deepest aversion to the calling. But he was sent at age seven to the Collège d'Harcourt where he was commanded to obey and believe. He never did; his natural instincts urged him to disobey and question—something he did all his life.

In terms of family, Talleyrand considered himself a virtual orphan "who never enjoyed for a week of his life the joy of living beneath the paternal roof."

5. See page 58. On taking over his new command in Zurich on December 10, 1798, Massena had to immediately deal with the usual problems of finance and administration for the troops

were short of rations and in arrears of pay. He took to task the chief civil commissary, a man named Rapinat, who had diverted away from the army the very heavy contributions he'd exacted from the Swiss authorities. Rapinat was the brother-in-law of one of the Directors and in a strong position to do as he liked. Massena, however, brought him to heel.

The particular manner of financing the French army created vast temptations for the commissioners. Essentially the army lived off the land and Paris sent out commissioners, independent of the military command, to levy contributions from local conquered governments in support of the army. Since the positions were appointed, unfortunately many of the commissioners were connected to the civil ministers in Paris and large amounts of money raised from conquered territories often enriched personal fortunes.

Rapinat's reputation was notorious enough for a contemporary humorist to write the following lines:

La pauvre Suisse, qu'on ruine,	*The poor, ruined Swiss*
Voudrait bien que l'on decidat	*Leave it to us to decide*
Si Rapinat vient de Rapine	*If Rapinat comes from Rapine*
Ou Rapine de Rapinat!	*Or rapine from Rapinat!*

6. See page 59. Chur had been taken by Massena on March 9 but it was impossible to follow through on his successes due to the shortcomings and corruption of the commissariat. His army was without supplies. On March 18, Massena, thoroughly exasperated, wrote this strongly worded letter to the Directory:

Citizen Directors, I do not feel that I can possibly invade the Tyrol with an army which has rations only for two days; I should only sacrifice the army and myself if I did. These difficulties have not prevented me from carrying out your orders to invade the Grisons; in order to do so I have collected and exhausted all available resources. . . . Our rations are finished and transportation now becomes more difficult; my right wing, commanded by General Lecourbe, has been without rations for eight days. Citizen Directors, the Army of Switzerland has to traverse a country devoid of resources; indeed we shall soon be obliged to feed the inhabitants as well.

　　Citizen Directors, I have already drawn your attention to this situation in my letters of 6 January and 5 February. In that last letter I told the War Minister that, if he could not provide my supply and transport, I should prefer to hand in my resignation, rather than face the certainty of dishonour . . . I now feel compelled to resign my command and to ask you to nominate my successor.

　　7. See page 99. Divorce was allowed in France by the decrees of December 28, 1793, and April 23, 1794. Either a husband or wife could seek a divorce and since marriage was simply a civil ceremony after the Revolution, divorce was easy. Incompatibility could be given as sufficient reason. When Napoleon as First Consul signed the Concordat with the Pope in 1801, Roman Catholicism was restored as the official religion of France and a nuptial mass was added to the civil ceremony. Under the 1804 Code Napoléon women lost freedoms and property rights that had been theirs even under the old regime. "A wife must promise obedience and fidelity in marriage" is inscribed in one of the articles of the Code. There was one exception in the Code's attempt to restore family values: divorce laws remained flexible. France noted this and Josephine's barrenness, and believed that the First Consul Napoleon had his own reasons for making this exception.

　　8. See page 99. The relationship between Duras and his wife was partially based on the circumstances surrounding Napoleon and Josephine's marriage. Depending on whose memoirs are cited, the nuances vary, but the story remains essentially the same. Barras, tiring of his newest mistress, Josephine, offered her in marriage to Napoleon, who was madly infatuated with her. As added incentive, he offered Napoleon the command of the Army of Italy—Josephine's dowry as it were. Josephine was reluctant to marry Napoleon, but was convinced by Barras and her friends that the marriage would be advantageous. At the time, Josephine was one of three reigning belles in Parisian society—although at thirty-three, she was past her youthful bloom, concerned for her

future, and had recently broken off her affair with the handsome, dashing General Hoche, who had gone back to his wife.

Napoleon and Josephine were married March 6, 1796, in a brief civil ceremony. She kept her own name and reduced her age by four years; Napoleon added two years to his—he was six years younger. Two days later Napoleon left for his command in Italy. From March 8 until July 13 Napoleon wrote his wife at least once a day, letters exploding with longing, frustration, and explicit sensuality, asking her to come immediately and join him in Italy.

Josephine replied occasionally, but she was busy with her host of friends in Paris and had just begun a new liaison that would become the most passionate love affair of her life.

By the end of June, Napoleon's letters, including those sent to Barras, were so consumed with jealousy, talk of suicide, and threats of leaving his command in Italy and coming back to Paris if Josephine didn't join him, that Barras literally dispatched Josephine across the Alps. After a last supper at the Luxembourg, Josephine was bundled, sobbing, into the first carriage in a convoy of six and sent south.

Massena, my inspiration for Duras, wasn't the same style of man as Napoleon. He wouldn't have sent pleading letters to his errant wife, but Napoleon was sexually inexperienced with women and Massena was not. Josephine was Napoleon's first grand passion and perhaps his only one—a youthful, mad rush of ardent love and intense emotion not previously experienced. Josephine was a sophisticated woman of the world, innately sensual, feminine, comfortable in a society that required a woman to have an expertise in male flattery to survive, and Napoleon fell under her spell.

Keep in mind that at this time, Napoleon was thin, sickly-looking, with lank, greasy hair and a sallow complexion. His head was too big for his body, his legs were thin and spindly, and he had scabies sores all over his face. Hardly a physically appealing sight for a beautiful woman living in the society of the rich and powerful.

9. See page 107. While Napoleon was on campaign in Egypt, he learned of his wife's affair with Hippolyte Charles and in his anger he decided on a divorce—a public and sensational divorce. The letter he wrote to his brother Joseph asking him to begin

making the necessary arrangements was intercepted by British cruisers in the Mediterranean. Josephine's son Eugene, an aide to Napoleon in Egypt, had also written to his mother warning her of the events and his letter was captured as well. Both were published in full in the London newspapers in English and French.

When Napoleon heard of the publication in the British newspapers, he had his staff organize an evening of Egyptian dancers for him. But none of the women appealed to him. He complained they were too fat and he didn't care for their perfume. But as soon as he saw pretty twenty-year-old Pauline Fourès, he knew how to take a very public revenge on Josephine. Pauline, a blond and rosy milliner's apprentice, was still dressed in the uniform—blue coat and tight white breeches—of her husband's regiment, which she had worn in order to embark for Egypt with him. Bonaparte issued orders for Lieutenant Fourès to take urgent dispatches to Paris. Only a day out from Alexandria, Fourès's ship was captured. The English captain, familiar with Cairo gossip, made a point of returning the French lieutenant to Alexandria on parole as rapidly as possible. There Fourès was enraged to find his Pauline installed in the commander in chief's palace and presiding over his dinner parties. He protested, but Napoleon had a rapid divorce pronounced and was said to have promised marriage to Pauline if she could produce a child.

Another instance of paramours in military dress: when Massena went to Spain in May 1810 to assume command of the Army of Portugal, he was accompanied by his seventeen-year-old son, Jacques-Prosper, his secretary, Vacherat, and a small entourage. They were escorted by two hundred horsemen through countryside thick with guerrilla bands.

On the morning of May 11 one of Massena's aides arrived at the palace in Valladolid announcing that the general would arrive later in the day. Eager to impress his new commander, General Junot collected a delegation of some two hundred officers and chasseurs to ride out and welcome Massena and his staff. A league beyond the city they sighted an open carriage, trailed by a convoy of carriages and wagons, racing toward the city. After Junot formally greeted him, Massena's calash was escorted to the palace through the streets of the city, which were lined by troops in brilliant uniforms. Apparently some embarrassment occurred when

Massena alighted from his carriage. His young traveling companion, dressed in the guise of a cavalry officer with the Legion of Honor, was none other than his current mistress, Henriette Leberton. According to the malicious Baron Marbot, "When Junot rushed in accompanied by the Duchesse, he fell into Massena's arms; then before all the staff he kissed the hand of Mme. Leberton . . . and introduced his wife. Imagine the astonishment of the two ladies. They stood petrified and did not speak a single word. Massena had the wit to restrain himself, but he was deeply hurt when the Duchesse d'Abrantes, pleading indisposition, immediately departed." Madame Junot refused to be in the same room with Madame Leberton during Massena's stay in Valladolid. Since her own reputation was far from virtuous, her attitude annoyed Massena and problems arose.

10. See page 127. Although there was little affection between the two men, Napoleon's assessment of Massena's qualities as a commander is generally fair.

"He had a strong constitution and would ride tirelessly, night and day, over rocks and through the mountains; that was the kind of war that he specialized in and understood thoroughly. He was decided, tough, fearless, full of ambition and self-esteem; his outstanding quality was doggedness, he was never discouraged. He was slack about discipline, negligent in administration and he had no conversational powers. But at the first sound of a gun, in the midst of cannon-balls and danger, his thoughts acquired strength and clarity. If he was defeated, he would return to the charge as if he were the victor."

11. See page 175. Archduke Charles (Carl Ludwig 1771–1847), third son of the Emperor Leopold II and younger brother of the Emperor Francis, was the youngest and ablest of the Austrian commanders. He suffered from mild epileptic attacks that would plague him all his life, often aggravated during times of stress and frustration.

12. See page 180. Archduke Charles, realizing the importance of Switzerland, had submitted a war plan early in December of 1798. His plan, however, was changed by the chancellor

Thugut who, with the support of the emperor and assisted by General Bellegarde, was working on his own plans. In this war more than ever before, interference from Vienna restricted the scope of field commanders and Thugut interjected his own ideas into strategy and even grand tactics. Although there was bad blood between Charles and Thugut, the primary cause of their disagreements was that for Thugut political considerations overrode military plans. He perceived Austrian political interests to lie primarily in southern Germany and northern Italy, not in Switzerland. Moreover, Bellegarde, acting as his chief military adviser, feared that the French held a clear tactical advantage in the mountains.

The archduke reacted strongly to Thugut's plan and submitted his objections to his brother, the emperor. The emperor's reply was angry. He accused the archduke of "insubordination" and "an eruption of an exaggerated sensitivity" and hinted at "unpleasant consequences" if Charles persisted. Taken aback, Charles answered in a long, abject letter, assuring the emperor of his complete devotion. Yet he was not reconciled to the situation, and from his headquarters, he complained to his old mentor, General Lindenau. "When I came here," he wrote, "I had hoped to concentrate my main army—some 80–90,000—against the enemy, but I received no support and instead Bellegarde went to Vienna and I was ordered to detach 17 battalions and 8 squadrons to help form a reserve army of 56,000 under Bellegarde." Charles explained that he had protested, only to be sharply reprimanded and that "in this manner I lost 30,000 foot soldiers which are doing nothing in the Tyrol and all this so that Bellegarde can cut a good figure without any risk."

Charles recovered from his illness before Thugut's plans to replace him could be realized, and the archduke requested he be allowed to retain his command. The emperor replied on May 4, "I have decided to keep you on as army commander." But he ordered him to "abandon for reasons that you are aware of, all enterprises which might entangle you in Switzerland." And to make sure the order was obeyed, Charles was to have his chief of staff make an "account of all events, troop movements, etc." to be forwarded to Vienna daily. This bickering between the court and Charles was very useful to the French in Switzerland.

13. See page 201. Throughout history soldiers have seldom been celibate and camp followers represented a serious problem for all armies. The women did indeed suffer in the field, marching with the troops, sharing their privations and dangers. Sometimes they carried the packs for their men, nursed them when wounded or sick, and often a devoted wife would search a battlefield hoping to find her husband alive. During retreats women and children, the weakest, suffered the most. Women became, largely by necessity, expert foragers and looters.

Cantinières, uniformed and attached to a particular regiment, were unique to the French army. The *cantinière* was appointed by the *conseil d'administration,* a body of officers and men presided over by the colonel, which ran the internal affairs of the regiment. Often married to a sergeant, the *cantinière* kept her wagon stocked with small luxuries and comforts—cognac, tobacco, and the like. The trade was profitable but also dangerous. The women often developed a strong attachment to their unit. During the Peninsula War, hearing that the well-liked Brigadier Simon had fallen wounded into British hands, the *cantinière* of the 26th declared that "we shall see if the English will kill a woman." She crossed the lines, nursed Simon, and "though she was young and very pretty," as Marbot records, returned unharmed to her regiment. And then there was Catherine Baland of the 95th, who encouraged men in battle and distributed her goods free in the firing line. She received the coveted *Légion d'honneur* in 1813.

14. See page 207. In answer to the Directory's complaints about his inaction, Massena wrote to them on July 23. The letter proves that Massena had both the wisdom and courage to disobey orders issued by unqualified men.

15. See page 212. The telegraph lines to Zurich ran from Chappe to Huningue to Paris via Strasbourg. A telegraph line was also constructed to the Italian front.

16. See page 224. It was Thugut's plan to avoid a large-scale Austrian involvement in Switzerland and leave operations to the two Russian corps. What Thugut forgot was that the Russians were neither equipped nor trained to operate in the mountains

and that success in Switzerland was vital to the successful prosecution of the war.

In a rare defiance of orders Archduke Charles had crossed the Rhine into Switzerland and fought the first Battle of Zurich on June 4. After having suffered 3,400 casualties against 1,600 French, he hesitated pressing on, having exceeded his orders and fearing that he would be blamed for heavy losses. The British agent Wickham reported that Charles had entered Switzerland "without any authority from Vienna" and that "HRH not only has never been able to obtain the slightest mark of approbation from his court" and "is, or affects to be, extremely uneasy on that account."

In fact the emperor was annoyed and on July 10, Charles finally received a cool letter ordering him to remain passive until relieved by Suvorov's corps from Italy and the Russian auxiliary corps from Germany. Three weeks later, formal instructions confirmed this arrangement. After the Russian arrival, Charles was to command the imperial army between the Neckar and Switzerland. He was to cross the Rhine near Mannheim, though only as a demonstration, while in reality he was to prepare going into winter quarters. Charles's objections that this was the end of any prospect for taking Switzerland, the key position in Europe, were overruled.

17. See page 229. During the September Massacres of 1792, Talleyrand sailed to England ostensibly on a government mission, in reality to escape the massacres. When Louis XVI was guillotined on January 21, 1793, England began to look less kindly on "representatives"—however ambiguous—of the revolutionary government and Talleyrand was expelled in May 1793. He went into exile in America. Through the sheer relentless persuasion of Germaine de Staël, who managed to get Boissy d'Anglas to make a speech in the Legislative Corps insisting that Talleyrand had been unjustly proscribed since he hadn't emigrated in 1792 but had actually been dispatched on an official mission, he was exonerated. Marie-Joseph Chénier had also come to his aid, using what was left of his stagecraft to make an even more impassioned appeal for the wronged patriot. Talleyrand was allowed to return to France. He set sail from Manhattan in June 1796.

18. See page 265. It was essential that the Russian forces be split in two so Massena could concentrate on taking Zurich without worrying about having to face the combined Russian army. Dourasov was not only duped by the feint but remained at Brugg all day without moving or attempting contact with the Russian forces on his left. He made it possible for Massena to advance on Zurich without fighting a rear-guard action.

The Russian officer corps recruited from the gentry were poorly educated, often hardly literate, imprudent, negligent, and generally incapable of a quick decision in an emergency. The nobility entered the army through various cadet schools and later took up appointments in the Guards or in elite mounted regiments. They were cultured, though not well educated, and lacked competence in administration and staff work. Nonetheless, especially if well connected, they found their way into general headquarters where as Colonel Campbell scornfully commented, they "spent their time drinking, gambling or sleeping." Napoleon is supposed to have said that a French private took more interest in the planning and conduct of a battle than senior Russian officers. Before Austerlitz, the young aristocratic officers were overconfident, brash, boastful, underestimating their opponents and blaming all previous setbacks on the alleged cowardice of their Austrian allies.

Tsar Paul also had a damaging effect on the army. Half-mad, he indulged his interest in military matters by molding the Russian army into his image of the Prussian army. In keeping with this picture-book idea, Paul introduced his own manual, a gathering of outworn precepts culled from an inferior textbook from Frederick the Great's time. Officers who were experienced and competent at staff work were transferred to regimental duties and inexperienced men installed in their places. Men with no gift for training soldiers but good managers of parade-ground displays were given command of regiments. During his short reign 333 generals and 2,261 officers lost their commissions. Obedience and observance of regulations were regarded as most important. At parades Paul would sentence men to floggings and reduce officers and noncommissioned officers to the ranks on the spot; one day a whole regiment, having failed to please the tsar, was given this order at the end of the parade:

"Direction: straight ahead! To Siberia—march!"

Officers took to carrying enough money on their persons to cover the cost of a journey to Siberia should they be sent to exile from the parade ground.

This atmosphere of intimidation and fear did little to encourage officer initiative.

19. See page 266. Regardless of the conflicting foreign and native influences in the Russian military establishment, the common soldier changed little; he just fought for a different sovereign. Always noted for his tenacity and ability to suffer hardships, in the attack he was fearless and never intimidated by casualties. It has been claimed that the Russian soldier lacked instruction in how to retreat, and though this is untrue, the Russians always fought best with their backs to the wall. Until late in the Napoleonic Wars the Russians fought much as their grandfathers had done, and although new regulations tried to modernize tactics, most commanders continued to rely on the solid column and the bayonet. The preferred method of warfare (and Suvorov's favorite) was "One must attack!!! Cold arms—bayonets and sabers!" And wave after wave of soldiers were sent forward, bayonets drawn.

20. See page 269. Massena sent three telegrams from Zurich to the Directory informing them of the results of the battle.

On September 25: "I have passed the Limmat at Dietikon, we are at the gates of Zurich."

September 26: "The army entered Zurich in force at two o'clock at night. General Soult's division has reached the Linth between the lakes of Zurich and Wallenstadt. The Russian and Austrian armies are in complete rout. I'm pursuing them."

September 28: "Both the Russian and Austrian armies are totally destroyed, the Russians went through Thur, we are pursuing the Austrian corps and the Bavarians who had just joined them in the number of 8,000. General Hotze was killed on the battle field; the baggage train, six flags, plus 100 pieces of artillery are in our possession. The losses in the two armies in dead, wounded and prisoners, among which are 6,000 wounded that were abandoned, are more than 20,000 men. Three Russian generals are in our pos-

session. General Suvorov in person attacked my right, I'm marching on him."

21. See page 282. Suvorov had made good progress in his
march into Switzerland and he hoped to reach Altdorf by September 14. But Lecourbe and the Devil's Bridge were in the way.

Six miles along the treeless Usern Valley was the Urnerloch,
a tunnel over two hundred yards long with a clearance of less
than five feet across. Four hundred yards beyond it, the Reuss,
falling in a foaming torrent, raged seventy-five feet below the terribly exposed Devil's Bridge, beyond which towered a sheer and
rocky wall.

On the morning of the fourteenth, Suvorov's main force
joined Rosenberg and the advance guard proceeded down the
Usern dale. There they faced one perpendicular stone mountain
standing like a wall, in the middle of which was a narrow opening
made by nature, called the Devil's Hole, leading to the Devil's
Bridge, and continuing for about seven hundred feet into the
mountain. A French gun at the point of exit swept the tunnel.
Soon it was choked with the bodies of dead and dying men. No
one could survive the passage of those few feet between the close
and dripping walls in the face of that gun. But the men tried, and
besides those who fell in the tunnel during the pileup that ensued, there were others who were pushed over the precipice near
the entrance to it. Eventually a flanking party of three hundred
under Colonel Trubnikov somehow traversed the mountain overhead and fell upon the French left. Miloradovich rushed some
men through the tunnel. Lecourbe immediately called back his
men from the right bank of the Reuss. The gun was thrown down
into the river and they withdrew over the Devil's Bridge, breaking it behind them.

Meanwhile two hundred fusiliers had descended the fall to
the left, and when a fordable point had been found, a battalion
was sent down after them to try to get to the French rear. More
Russians groped their way hand in hand through the cavern of the
Urnerloch while the French sharpshooters perched on the heights
above the broken Devil's Bridge took aim as they massed between
the tunnel and the bridge. The Russians tried desperately to rush
the bridge. But it was impossible. Murderous fire sent a constant

succession of men hurtling down into the teeming waters of the Reuss and the steep slope up to the Urnerloch behind them was soon covered with bodies.

22. See page 284. Suvorov's retreat through the mountains was an unbelievable nightmare.

As the Russian soldiers climbed up to a height level with the clouds, the snow changed into mounds of ice embedded in snowdrifts. Each step on the treacherous cliffs could be one's last. The thinning lines stretched for miles. There was no order, no discipline. Each man walked where he would, choosing his path according to his own judgment. The weakest fell down and didn't get up; those wanting to rest sat down on the icy slopes and surrendered themselves to death. The injured were abandoned. The marchers were assailed by a cold and hostile wind and beating rain, which froze on them. Some were so borne down by ice they could hardly move. There was no shelter, nothing with which to light a fire. A blizzard obliterated the track, a footprint disappearing in the snow within seconds. Men crawled on or stumbled forward hand in hand. A mounted officer, trying to find the way, suddenly disappeared, swallowed up together with his horse by a crevasse.

Of the 3,000 men that began the retreat, no more than 1,800 were left after the passage over the Alps.

ABOUT THE AUTHOR

SUSAN JOHNSON, award-winning author of nationally bestselling novels, lives in the country near North Branch, Minnesota. A former art historian, she considers the life of a writer the best of all possible worlds.

Researching her novels takes her to past and distant places, and bringing characters to life allows her imagination full rein, while the creative process offers occasional fascinating glimpses into complicated machinery of the mind.

But perhaps most important . . . writing stories is fun.

Look for Susan Johnson's thrilling
historical romance, available
from Bantam Books

SEDUCTION IN MIND

Turn the page for a preview.

AN IMPOSING BUTLER ushered them into Frederic Leighton's studio, despite the inconvenient hour and the artist's custom of receiving by appointment only, and despite the fact that the artist was working frantically because he was fast losing the sun. Although perhaps a man like Leighton was never actually frantic, his sensibilities opposed to such plebeian feelings. Ever conscious of his wealth and position, particularly now that he'd been knighted, he cultivated friendships in the aristocracy, as his butler well knew.

The room was enormous, with rich cornices, piers, friezes of gold, marble, enamel, and mosaics, all color and movement, opulence and luxury. Elaborate bookshelves lined one wall, two huge Moorish arches soared overhead, stained-glass windows of an oriental design were set into the eastern wall, but the north windows under which the artist worked were tall, iron-framed, utilitarian.

Leighton turned from his easel as they entered and greeted them with a smooth urbanity, casting aside his frenzied air with ease, recognizing George Howard with a personal comment and his two male companions with a cultivated grace.

Lord Ranelagh hardly took notice of their host, for his

gaze was fixed on Leighton's current work—a female nude in a provocative pose, her diaphanous robe lifted over her head. "Very nice, Sir Frederick," he said with a faint nod in the direction of the easel. "The lady's coloring is particularly fine."

"As is the lady. I'm fortunate she dabbles in the arts."

"She lives in London?"

"Some of the time. I could introduce you if you like."

"No, you may not, Frederick. I'm here incognito for this scandalous painting." A lady's amused voice came from the right, and a moment later Alexandra Ionides emerged from behind a tapestry screen. She was dressed in dark blue silk that set off her pale skin to perfection; the front of the gown was partially open, but her silken flesh quickly disappeared from sight as she closed three sparkling gemstone clasps.

"It's you," Ranelagh softly exclaimed.

Her eyes were huge, the deepest purple, and her surprise was genuine. "I beg your pardon?"

"Alex, allow me to introduce Viscount Ranelagh," Leighton said. "My lord, Alexandra Ionides, the Dowager Countess of St. Albans and Mrs. Coutts."

"*Mrs.* Coutts?"

"I'm a widow. Both my husbands died." She always enjoyed saying that—for the reaction it caused, for the pleasure it gave her to watch people's faces.

"May I ask how they died?" the viscount inquired, speaking to her with a quiet intensity, as though they were alone in the cavernous room.

"Not in their beds, if that's what you're thinking." She knew of Ranelagh, of his reputation, and thought his question either flippant or cheeky.

"I meant . . . how difficult it must have been, how distressing. I'm a widower."

"I know." But she doubted he was distressed. The flighty,

promiscuous Lady Ranelagh had died in a riding accident—and very opportunely, it was said; her husband was about to either kill her or divorce her.

"Would you men like to stay for drinks? Alex and I were just about to sit down for a champagne." Leighton gestured toward an alcove decorated with various colorful divans. "I reward myself at the end of a workday," he added with a small deprecating smile.

A bottle of champagne was already on ice atop a Moroccan-style table, and if Alexandra might have wished to refuse, Leighton had made it impossible. Ranelagh was more than willing, Eddie had never turned down a drink in his adult life, and George Howard, like so many men of his class, had considerable leisure time.

Ranelagh seated himself beside Alex, a fact she took note of with mild disdain. She disliked men of his stamp, who only amused themselves in ladies' beds. It seemed a gross self-indulgence when life offered so much outside the conventional world of aristocratic vice.

He said, "Meeting you this afternoon almost makes me believe in fate. I came here to discover the identity of the exquisite model in Leighton's Academy painting, and here you are."

"While I don't believe in fate at all, Lord Ranelagh, for I came here today with privacy in mind, and here you all are."

He smiled. "And you'd rather us all to Hades."

"How astute, my lord."

He'd never been offered his congé by a woman before and rather than take offense, he was intrigued. Willing females he knew by the score. But one such as this . . . "Maybe if you came to know us better. Or me better," he added in a low murmur.

Their conversation was apart from the others, their divan offset slightly from the other bright-hued sofas, and the three men opposite them were deep in a heated discussion of the best routes through the Atlas Mountains.

"Let me make this clear, Lord Ranelagh, and I hope tactful as well. I've been married twice; I'm not a novice in the ways of the world. I take my independence very seriously and I'm averse, to put it in the most temperate terms, to men like you, my lord, who find amusement their raison d'être. So I won't be getting to know you better. But thank you for the offer."

Her hair was the most glorious deep auburn, piled atop her head in heavy, silken waves, and he wished nothing more at the moment than to free the ruby pins holding it in place and watch it tumble onto her shoulders. "Perhaps some other time." He thought he'd never seen such luscious peaches-and-cream skin, nor eyes, like hers.

"There won't be another time, my lord."

"If I were a betting man—"

"But you are." Equal to his reputation as a libertine was his penchant for high-stakes betting. It was the talk of London at the moment, for he'd won fifty thousand on the first race at Ascot yesterday.

He smiled. "It was merely an expression. Do I call you Mrs. Coutts or the Dowager Countess?"

"I prefer my maiden name."

"Then, Miss Ionides, what I was about to say was that if I were a betting man, I'd lay odds we are about to become good friends."

"You're too arrogant, Ranelagh. I'm not eighteen and easily infatuated by a handsome man, even one of your remarkable good looks."

"While I'm not only fascinated by a woman of your dazzling beauty but intrigued with your unconventional attitude toward female nudity."

"Because I pose nude, you think me available?"

"So blunt, Miss Ionides."

"You weren't interested in taking me to tea, I presume."

"We'll do whatever you like," he replied, the suggestion in his voice so subtle, his virtuosity couldn't be faulted. And that, of course, was the problem.

"You've more than enough ladies in your train, Ranelagh. You won't miss me."

"You're sure?"

"Absolutely sure."

"A shame."

"Speak for yourself. I have a full and gratifying life. If you'll excuse me, Frederick," she said, addressing her host as she rose to her feet. "I have an appointment elsewhere."

The viscount had risen to his feet. "May I offer you a ride to your appointment?"

She slowly surveyed him from head to toe, her gaze coming to rest after due deliberation on his amused countenance. "No, you may not."

"I'm crushed," he said, grinning.

"But not for long, I'm sure," she crisply replied, and waving at Leighton and the other men, she walked away.

Everyone followed her progress across the large room and only when she'd disappeared through the high Moorish arch did conversation resume.

"She's astonishingly beautiful," George Howard said. "I can see why you have her pose for you."

"She *deigns* to pose for me," Leighton corrected. "I'm only grateful."

"I'm surprised a woman of her magnificence hasn't married again."

"She prefers her freedom," Leighton offered. "Or so she says."

"From that tone of voice, I'm surmising you've proposi-tioned her," Eddie observed. "And been refused."

Leighton dipped his handsome leonine head in acknowl-edgment. "At least I'm in good company, rumor has it. She's turned down most everyone."

"Most?" Ranelagh regarded the artist from beneath his long lashes, his lazy sprawl the picture of indolence.

"She has an occasional affair, I'm told."

"By whom?" Ranelagh's voice was very soft. "With whom?"

"My butler seems to know. I believe Kemp's acquainted with Alex's lady's maid."

"With whom is she currently entertaining herself then, pray tell?" The viscount moved from his lounging pose, his gaze suddenly intent.

"No one I know. A young art student for a time." He shrugged. "A banker she knew through her husband. A priest, someone said." He shook his head. "Only gossip, you under-stand. Alex keeps her private life private."

"And yet she's willing to pose nude—a blatantly public act."

"She's an artist in her own right. She accepts the nude form as separate from societal attitudes."

"Toward women," the viscount proposed.

Leighton shrugged again. "I wouldn't venture a guess on Alex's cultural politics."

"You're wasting your time, Sammy, my boy," Eddie told Ranelagh, waving his champagne glass toward the door through which Alex had exited. "She's not going to give you a tumble."

The viscount's dark brows rose faintly. "We'll see."

"That tone of voice always makes me nervous. The last time you said *We'll see*, I ended up in a Turkish jail, from which we were freed only because the ambassador was a per-sonal friend of the sultan's minister. And why you thought you could get through the phalanx of guards surrounding that harem, I'll never know."

"We almost made it."

"Nearly cost us our lives."

"You worry too much."

"While you don't worry at all."

"Of course I do. I was worried Lady Duffin's husband was going to break down the door before we were finished last week."

"So that's why Charles won't speak to you anymore."

The viscount shrugged. "He never did anyway."

Alexandra didn't have another appointment, but feeling the need to talk to someone, she had her driver take her to Lady Ormand's. This time of day, she'd have to sit through the tedium of tea, but not for long, since Rosalind's guests would have to leave soon to dress for dinner.

She felt strangely agitated and annoyed that she was agitated and further annoyed that the reason for her troublesome feelings was Viscount Ranelagh.

He was just another man, she firmly told herself, intent on repressing her astonishing reaction to him. She was no longer a missah young girl whose head could be turned by seductive dark eyes and a handsome face. Nor was she some tart who could be bluntly propositioned, as though he had but to nod his perfect head and she would fall into bed with him.

But something remarkable *had* happened when they met, and try as she might to deny his startling sexual magnetism, she was impossibly drawn to him.

Unfortunately, that seductive power was his hallmark; he was known for the carnal eagerness he inspired in females. And she refused to succumb.

Having spent most of her adult life struggling against conformity, trying to find a role outside the societal norms for women of her class, *needing* the independence denied so many females, surely she was strong enough to resist a libertine, no matter how sinfully handsome or celebrated his sexual expertise. Regardless, she'd not slept with anyone since her disastrous affair with Leon.

Reason, perhaps, for her injudicious impulses now.

But after Leon, she'd vowed to be more prudent in her choices.

And Ranelagh would be not only imprudent but—if his conduct at Leighton's was any evidence—impudent as well.

Inexhaustible in bed, however, if rumor was true, a devilish voice in her head reminded her.

She clasped her hands tightly in her lap, as though she might restrain her carnal urges with so slight a gesture. Impossible of course, so she considered spending a few hours with young Harry, who was always so grateful for her company. But gratitude didn't have much appeal when images of Ranelagh's heated gaze filled her brain. Nor did young Harry's sweetness prevail over the shamelessly bold look in Ranelagh's eyes.

"No!" she exclaimed, the sound of her voice shocking in the confined space, as was the flagrant extent of her desire.

She desperately needed to speak with Rosalind.

Her friend was always the voice of reason . . . or at least one of caution to her rash impulses.

But when the last teatime guest had finally departed and the tale of her introduction to Ranelagh was complete, Rosalind said, "You have to admit, he's the most heavenly man in London." She shrugged her dainty shoulders. "Or England or the world, for that matter."

Alex offered her friend a sardonic glance. "Thank you for the discouragement."

"Forgive me, dear, but he *is* lovely."

"And he knows it and I don't wish to become an afternoon of amusement for him."

"Would you like it better if it were more than an afternoon?"

"No. I would prefer not thinking of him at all. He's arrogant and brazenly self-assured and no doubt has never been turned down by a woman in his life."

"So you're the first."

"I meant it facetiously."

"And you've come here to have me bolster your good judgment and caution you to reason."

"Exactly."

"And will that wise counsel suffice?"

Alex softly exhaled. "Maybe if you're with me day and night."

Rosalind's pale brows rose. "He's said to have that effect on women."

"And it annoys me immeasurably that I'm as beguiled as all the mindless women he amuses himself with."

"You wish your intellect to be in control of your desires."

"I insist on it."

"Is it working?"

Alex shoved her teaspoon around on the embroidered linen cloth for a lengthy time before she looked up. "No."

"So the question becomes—what are you going to do?"

"I absolutely refuse to fall into his arms." She glared at her friend. "Do you understand? I won't."

"Fine. Are there matters of degree then?"

"About what?"

"About falling into his arms. Would you, say, after a certain duration, or never in a million years?"

Alex shifted uncomfortably in her chair, tapped her fingers

on the gilded chair arm, inhaled, exhaled, and was silent for several moments more. "I'm not sure about the million years," she finally said.

"You're boring the hell out of me," Eddie grumbled, reaching for the brandy bottle at his elbow.

Sam looked up from his putt. "Go to the Marlborough Club yourself."

"I might." Refilling his glass, Eddie lifted it in salute. "As soon as I finish this bottle."

"After you finish that bottle, you'll be passed out on my couch," Sam murmured, watching the ball roll into the cup on the putting green he'd had installed in his conservatory.

"You don't miss a night out as a rule," Eddie remonstrated. "Did the merry widow's refusal incapacitate you?"

"Au contraire," Sam murmured, positioning another ball with his golf club. "I'm feeling first-rate. And I expect she's in high mettle as well."

"She turned you down, Sam."

"But she didn't want to." He softly swung his club, striking the ball with exquisite restraint.

"And you can tell."

The viscount half smiled. "I could feel it."

"So sure . . ."

"Yes."

"And you're saving yourself for her now?"

"Jesus, Eddie, if you want to go, go. I don't feel like fucking anyone right now and I drank enough last night to last me a week."

"Since when haven't you felt like fucking someone?" his friend asked, his gaze measured.

"What the hell are you insinuating?"

"That you fancy the voluptuous Miss Ionides with more than your usual casual disregard."

"After meeting her for ten minutes?" Sam snorted. "You're drunk."

"And you're putting golf balls at eight o'clock when you're never even home at eight."

Sam tossed his club aside. "Let's go."

"Are you going out like that?"

The viscount offered his friend a narrowed glance. "None of the girls at Hattie's will care."

"True," Eddie muttered, heaving himself up from the leather-covered couch. "But don't do that to me again. It scares the hell out of me."

Sam was shrugging into his jacket. "Do what?"

"Change the pattern of our dissolute lives. If you can be touched by Cupid's arrow, then no man's safe. And that's bloody frightening."

"Rest assured that after Penelope, I'm forever immune to Cupid's arrow," Sam drawled. "Marriage don't suit me. As for love, I haven't a clue."

"I'll drink to that," Eddie murmured, snatching up the brandy bottle as Sam moved toward the door.

But much later, as the first light of day fringed the horizon, Lord Ranelagh walked away from Hattie Martin's luxurious brothel pervaded by a deep sense of dissatisfaction. What had previously passed for pleasure seemed wearisome now; a jaded sense of sameness enervated his soul, and sullen and moody, he found no pleasure even in the glorious sunrise.

Walking home through the quiet city streets, he was plagued by thoughts of the bewitching Miss Ionides, wondering where she'd slept or, like him, not slept. The rankling thought further lowered his spirits. By the time he reached his town house, he'd run through a mental list of any number of men who might be her lovers, the image of her voluptuous body in the arms of another man inexplicably disagreeable.

It shouldn't be. He should be immune to the nature of her liaisons. He had met the damned woman only a day ago and there was no earthly reason why he should care who the hell she slept with.

He snapped at the hall porter when he entered his house, immediately apologized, and after making some banal excuse, pressed ten guineas into the servant's hand. When he walked into his bedroom a few moments later, he waved a restraining hand at his valet, who came awake with a start and jumped to his feet. "Go back to sleep, Rory. I can undress myself. In fact, take the day off. I won't be needing you."

His young manservant immediately evinced concern. The viscount was accustomed to being waited on, his family's fortune having insulated him from the mundane details of living.

Recognizing his valet's hesitation, Sam said, "I'll be fine."

"You're sure?"

"Why not take Molly for a walk in the park," the viscount suggested, knowing Rory's affection for the downstairs maid. "She may have the day off as well."

"Thank you, sir!"

"Go, now." Sam waved him off. "All I want to do is sleep."

In a more perfect world, he might have slept, considering he'd been up for twenty-four hours; but Miss Ionides was putting an end to the perfection of his world *and* to his peace of mind. He tossed and turned for more than an hour before throwing aside the blanket and stalking over to a small table holding two decanters of liquor. Pouring himself a considerable amount of cognac, he dropped into an upholstered chair, and sliding into a sprawl, contemplated the injustice of Miss Ionides's being so damned desirable.

Half a bottle of cognac later, he decided he'd simply have to have her and put an end to his lust and her damnable allure. He further decided his powerful craving was just the result of his not having what he wanted—her. And once he'd made love to the delectable Miss Ionides, that craving would be assuaged. Familiarity breeding contempt, as they say, had been the common pattern of his sexual amusements. In his experience, one woman was very much like another once the game was over.

But this particular game of seduction was just beginning, and glancing out the window, he took note of the position of the sun in the sky. The races would be starting soon at Ascot, the entire week scheduled with prestigious races, the Season bringing all of society to the track.

Including Miss Ionides, if he didn't miss his guess.

Rising from his chair, he walked to the bellpull and rang for a servant. He needed a bath.

Don't miss any of the sensuous historical romances of

Susan Johnson

___29957-3	*Blaze*	$5.99/$7.99 Canada
___57213-X	*Brazen*	$5.99/$7.99
___29125-4	*Forbidden*	$5.99/$7.99
___56328-9	*Love Storm*	$5.99/$7.99
___29955-7	*Outlaw*	$5.99/$7.99
___29956-5	*Pure Sin*	$5.99/$7.99
___56327-0	*Seized by Love*	$5.50/$6.99
___29959-X	*Silver Flame*	$5.99/$7.99
___29312-5	*Sinful*	$5.99/$7.99
___56329-7	*Sweet Love, Survive*	$5.99/$7.99
___57215-6	*Taboo*	$5.99/$7.99
___57214-8	*Wicked*	$5.99/$7.99

Ask for these books at your local bookstore or use this page to order.

Please send me the books I have checked above. I am enclosing $____ (add $2.50 to cover postage and handling). Send check or money order, no cash or C.O.D.'s, please.

Name _____

Address _____

City/State/Zip _____

Send order to: Bantam Books, Dept. FN 69, 2451 S. Wolf Rd., Des Plaines, IL 60018
Allow four to six weeks for delivery.

Prices and availability subject to change without notice.   FN 69 12/97